GWEN & ART ARE NOT IN LOVE

LEX CROUCHER

BLOOMSBURY

LONDON OXFORD NEW YORK NEW DELHI SYDNEY

BLOOMSBURY YA
Bloomsbury Publishing Plc
50 Bedford Square, London WC1B 3DP, UK
29 Earlsfort Terrace, Dublin 2, Ireland

BLOOMSBURY, BLOOMSBURY YA and the Diana logo
are trademarks of Bloomsbury Publishing Plc

First published in Great Britain in 2023 by Bloomsbury Publishing Plc

A catalogue record for this book is available from the British Library

ISBN: PB: 978-1-5266-5179-2; eBook: 978-1-5266-5177-8;
ePDF: 978-1-5266-5178-5

6 8 10 9 7

Typeset by RefineCatch Limited, Bungay, Suffolk
Printed and bound in Great Britain by CPI Group (UK) Ltd,
Croydon CR0 4YY

To find out more about our authors and books visit www.bloomsbury.com
and sign up for our newsletters

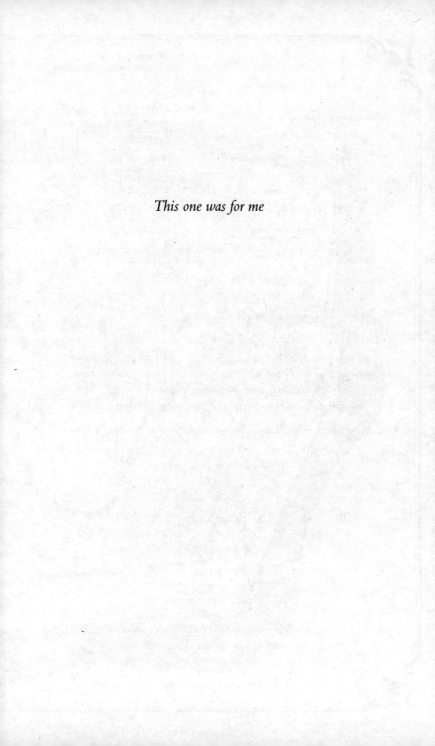

This one was for me

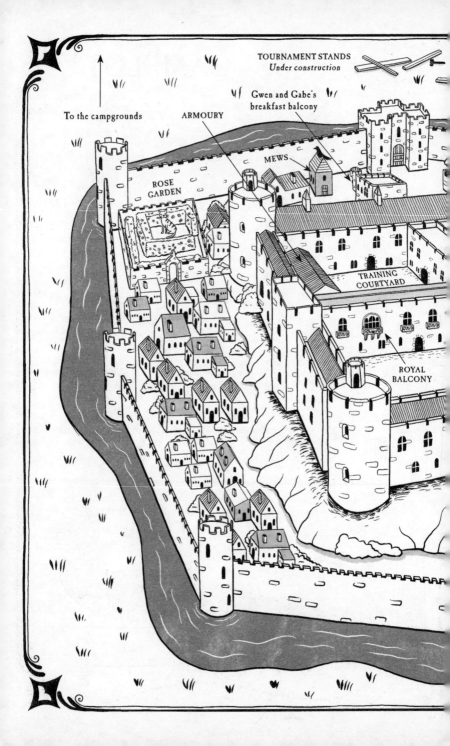

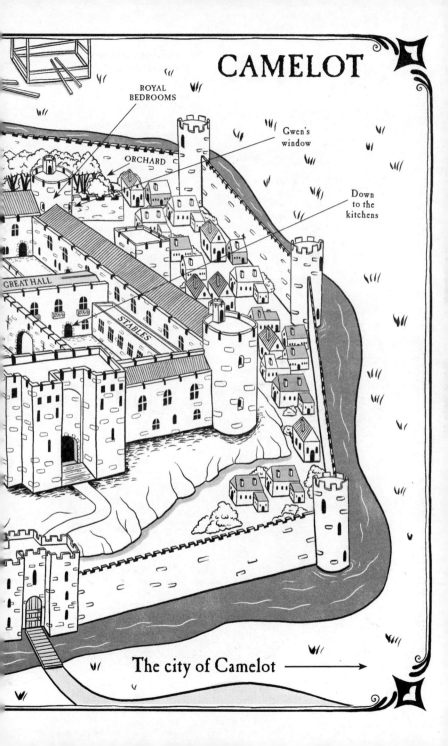

His royal highness King Allmot of England hereby declares that the royal tournament at Camelot will commence on the first day of Whitsuntide.

(Please disregard dates announced in previous declarations. Construction will be completed by Whitsun.)

Knights of daring and valour who embody the chivalric spirit are encouraged to fight for their king in the lists, at archery, in single combat and the melee, until a victor is proclaimed on the nineteenth day of August.

Please bring your own swords, maces and morning-stars, as none will be provided.

When Gwen woke up, she knew she'd had the dream again –
and that she'd been *loud*. She knew she'd had the dream because
she was feeling exhilarated, loose-limbed and a little flushed
in the face; she knew she'd been vocal about it because Agnes,
the dark-haired lady-in-waiting who slept in the adjoining
chamber, kept biting her lip to keep from laughing and
wouldn't look her in the eye.

'Agnes,' Gwen said, sitting up in bed and fixing her with
a well-practised and rather imperious look. 'Don't you have
water to fetch, or something?'

'Yes, your highness,' said Agnes, giving a little curtsy and
then rushing from the room. Gwen sighed as she stared up
at the bed hangings, lush velvet heavy with embroidery.
It was probably a mistake to send her away so soon – she
was young and flighty, and would likely be off gossiping
with anybody she encountered. At least Gwen's nocturnal
exploits wouldn't stay top billing for long. Today was
no ordinary day; tournament season was finally upon
them. Any mortifying morsels Agnes slipped the other
ladies-in-waiting would be forgotten in all the excitement
by noon.

When Agnes came back with a pitcher of water Gwen stepped out of bed, raised her arms above her head so that Agnes could remove the thin tunic she slept in, and then stood yawning and blinking in the early morning light as she was scrubbed and oiled to within an inch of her life. Agnes was just easing a new shift over Gwen's shoulders when the door was nudged open and a tall, pale, copper-haired young man walked in, his head buried in a stack of parchment.

'Have you seen this?' he said, not lifting his eyes from the page.

'Er. Gabriel,' Gwen said, looking at him incredulously. 'I'm not dressed.'

'Aren't you?' Gabriel looked up and frowned at her briefly, as if she had removed her clothes just to inconvenience him. 'Oh. Sorry.'

'The Greeks wrote a lot of plays about this sort of thing,' Gwen said, as Agnes rushed over with a dress to cover her, her fair skin flushing a delicate pink. Her blushes were probably less to do with the impropriety of the situation and more to do with the fact that almost every woman at court harboured a persistent crush on her brother. Many had tried to catch his eye, and so far, all had failed. He wasn't really one for talking at all, unless it was to Gwen. She had always held this as a point of pride.

'The Greeks wrote a lot of plays about putting on dresses?' he asked now, brow still furrowed, as Agnes yanked the dress inelegantly over Gwen's head.

'No,' Gwen said, emerging with quite a lot of her hair

4

stuck to her mouth. 'You're missing the ... Are you even listening to me? You walked into *my* room, you know.' He turned over the piece of parchment he was reading to peruse the other side, not acknowledging that he'd heard a word. 'Gabriel. *Gabe*. Can you hear something? The sound of a spectral voice upon the air? It almost sounds like I'm talking.'

'Hang on, G,' he said, raising a hand to indicate that he needed a moment. Gwen considered this, and decided he hadn't earned it. '*Ow*.'

Gwen had taken one of the brocade slippers Agnes had offered to her and thrown it at him with considerable force.

'Please arrive at the point with haste.'

'Ah – fine,' Gabriel said, still rubbing his head. 'Father is having me look at the accounts with Lord Stafford – costs for the tournament season mostly, but I also saw *this* and I thought ...' He trailed off, handing her the parchment so she could read it for herself.

Agnes started expertly weaving Gwen's long red hair into braids as Gwen's eyes skimmed quickly down the page, taking in an extensive list of assets. Chests full of silks and damask, an ancient jewelled dining set, endless porcelain vases; all marked to be leaving the crown's coffers in the coming months. Comprehension dawned as she reached the end of the page and the entry denoting the enormous Biblical tapestry of Ruth and Naomi that currently hung in her chambers.

'This is my dowry,' she said slowly. 'Gabe. My *dowry*.'

'I suppose it's that time already,' Gabriel said, with a sympathetic grimace.

'Shit,' said Gwen, sitting down heavily on the end of the bed.

'Shit,' Gabriel agreed.

In theory, being betrothed since birth could have been a comfort to Gwen, especially as it was to somebody so close to her own age. It meant there would be no nasty surprises; no new political alliances to forge with elderly, ornery nobility through marriage. Better the devil she knew, et cetera.

Unfortunately, this was encapsulated far too literally in the man she had been sworn to marry. Arthur Delacey, heir to the title Lord of Maidvale, was – in Gwen's opinion – the devil incarnate.

They had met for the first time on the day she was born, barely more than a shrimp and already promised to him; he'd been two years old, shuffled into Camelot along with his parents and hundreds of other families courting favour with the crown. She could just picture Arthur's affronted little face, scowling down at her in her cradle, disappointed already. She had often wondered if her parents had considered committing wholly to the bit and calling her *Guinevere* to match him, but had chickened out just in time and chosen *Gwendoline* instead, the uncomfortable legacy of the former's extramarital affairs with roguish knights staying their hands.

Her first true memory was of Gabriel giving her a piece of warm, fragrant honey cake, sneaking it to her outside the kitchens before dinner to calm a tantrum.

Her second memory was of Arthur taking it from her. It had been sixteen years, and she was still angry about that honey cake.

Among other things.

He had pulled her hair at mass. Mocked her relentlessly at feasts. Tripped her in the courtyard in front of every petty lord and lady of the realm, and then stepped smugly over her as she lay sprawled on the cobblestones with a skinned knee. The first stirrings of summer meant that a visit from Arthur was nigh, and so she learned to dread brighter mornings and hawthorns in bloom. On her ninth birthday, she had tried to get ahead of him by setting a trap outside his chamber, enlisting Gabriel's help to stretch a thin length of twine across the doorway; he had stumbled spectacularly over it and broken his wrist in two places. The guards had apprehended him a week later trying to push a feral cat through her bedroom window one-handed.

That September, the queen had politely suggested that it might be best if they were separated for the time being. Gwen had been so happy when she heard the news that she had skipped around the castle all day, buoyed by the prospect of Arthur-free summers. Her skipping had ended abruptly that evening when she heard her father refer to Arthur as her 'betrothed'.

'Gabe,' she had said, seeking him out in his favourite corner of the library. 'What's a *betrothed*?'

'It's the person you're going to marry,' Gabriel replied, looking up from his book.

'I was afraid of that,' she said glumly. 'Who's your betrothed?'

'I don't have one.'

'That's not fair.'

'No,' Gabriel had sighed. 'I don't suppose it is.'

★

Family breakfasts, which had once been a constant in Gwen's life, had become rarer in recent years. The carefully curated work–life balance that used to allow the king to linger to discuss economics with his son or to play a rapid-fire game of chess with his daughter had disintegrated as tensions grew throughout his kingdom; he and the queen now had daily schedules packed from dawn until dinner with council meetings, public audiences and conferences with diplomatic envoys that lasted long into the evening. Gwen and Gabriel had adapted; they usually breakfasted alone on the covered balcony, an oasis of calm in the busy castle.

The rest of Gwen's day followed a strict schedule of her own making. After breakfast she went for her morning walk, with Agnes plodding silently at her heels; lunch was usually taken in her chambers, followed by reading and harp practice. The late afternoon was always dedicated to her embroidery. Gwen had been meticulously stitching sprays of white roses and blue forget-me-nots on an enormous blanket for the past three years, at the behest of her mother, who had said something about 'marriage beds' and 'wedding nights' that Gwen had immediately chosen to forget. She liked embroidery – liked the certainty of it, the soothing repetition and symmetry – and with a needle in her hand it was easy to still her mind and wilfully disregard the issue of the blanket's intended destination.

Supper was sometimes a family affair taken in their own private dining rooms, but more often than not her father would insist that Gwen trudge down to the Great Hall with him and eat with a hundred eyes on her, the room packed to the rafters with courtiers and squires and various other shades of hangers-on.

She treasured these mornings, when it was just her and Gabriel on the balcony under a thick canopy of clematis and honeysuckle, and she could push aside the remnants of her breakfast and while away half an hour thrashing him at chess before she fell back into the familiar weave of her day.

Gabriel was in particularly bad form this morning; even still reeling from the shock of her dowry, she had him cornered in ten short minutes.

'Are you playing poorly on purpose because you feel bad for me?' she said, as he frowned down at the pieces.

Gwen loved chess. It flexed some hidden muscle, some part of her mind that usually lay dormant; as a result, she was calculated and ruthless, and left little room for her opponent to enjoy himself for even a moment.

'Not everybody lives for the triumphs and defeats, the epic highs and lows of the little black and white squares,' Gabriel said, ineffectively pushing a rook right back to where it had been two turns ago. 'Sorry. I'm actually just *this* bad at chess.'

'Your *cat* isn't this bad at chess,' Gwen scoffed. 'And also, checkmate.'

'Well. Very good. You've thoroughly obliterated my tenuous sense of self-worth.'

'Don't try to make me feel sorry for you just when I'm warming up to a nice gloat, it's not sportsmanlike.'

Gabriel just sighed, sat back in his chair and squinted out over the battlements. Gwen followed his gaze. The view from the north side of the castle, which housed the royal quarters, wasn't cluttered with the chaos of the city; from here Gwen could see the orchard and the mews, and, in the fields beyond the outer wall, the top of a large wooden structure that had been slowly growing in size for the past few months. Workmen scurried around it like ants, making everything ready for the tournament season ahead. The sky was a hazy blue, the weather already hot for late spring, blossom falling in drifts from the trees and gathering in the moat. Under different circumstances, this would have been a thoroughly delightful day.

'He might be better,' Gabriel said eventually, knowing precisely what she was thinking about without needing to ask. 'You haven't seen him for years.'

'I saw him last year,' Gwen countered. 'From a distance. At the Feast of St Michael, when that horrible earl hosted us and you were home with the grippe.'

'And?'

'*And* he sneered at me from across the room and whispered something in a page's ear and they both laughed so hard they almost fell over.'

'You don't know he was laughing at you.'

'He pointed. He smirked. He did . . . an impression.'

'Of what?'

'My dancing.'

'Oh,' said Gabriel. 'Well . . .'

'Be helpful or be quiet,' Gwen said, slumping forward on to the table.

'Sorry,' said Gabriel, reaching over to pat awkwardly at her hair. 'I really am. You know I'd help if I could.'

Gwen did know. He was far too soft-hearted; *he* wouldn't

ever force her into a marriage for political gain, no matter how much he needed it. Some day he would be king, and those decisions would be his to make. Gwen knew he dreaded it more than anything. There had been rather loud whispers over the years that he was too weak – too gentle – too *quiet* to rule, and their father was trying without success to encourage him to conduct himself with more mettle and conviction; Gabriel dealt with all of this by retreating into books and ledgers whenever possible, seeming to hope that if he disappeared into the furthest and dustiest reaches of the castle, then everybody might forget about him and crown somebody else instead.

Gwen thought this relatively unlikely.

'What did he look like?' Gabriel said, and Gwen was confused for a moment before remembering that they were discussing her least favourite subject.

'Like the squire to Satan,' she said. Gabriel raised an eyebrow. 'Oh, I don't know. Smug? Conceited? Abrasive? He's grown his hair very long, kept flicking it about to try to make all the ladies blush.'

'And did they?'

'You know they did,' Gwen said crossly. 'Agnes let slip that he's been leaving a trail of devastation across the countryside.'

'I heard that too, actually. Maidens deflowered. Inns drunk dry. Trees uprooted.'

'Do you think Father's heard?' Gwen said hopefully.

'Maybe mutterings,' Gabriel said, leaning back in his chair. 'But nothing substantial. Not enough to make him renege on a decades-old agreement.'

11

Gwen sighed. 'Gabriel. How much gold would I have to slip you to murder me?'

He gave her a sad sort of smile. 'Gwendoline. It's nothing personal, but I just don't have it in me. It'd kill two birds with one stone though, wouldn't it?'

Gwen laughed darkly. 'I wouldn't go so far as to presume that they'd let you off your royal duties for a little thing like sororicide.'

'No,' Gabriel agreed. 'But they might think twice before putting a sword in my hand – so that'd be something, wouldn't it?'

The door to the balcony opened so suddenly that they both jumped; Lord Stafford, their father's very pompous steward, was standing there looking exceedingly harried. He was wearing stockings in such an aggressive shade of chartreuse that Gwen had to blink a few times to regain full range of vision.

'Your royal highness,' he said to Gabriel, sounding desperate. 'The ceremony.'

'Oh, Christ,' said Gabriel, getting up abruptly and knocking the chessboard to the floor. 'Sorry! I forgot. I'm coming, I'm coming.'

Stafford stepped aside to let Gabriel pass, and then glared down at Gwen, who had knelt to pick up the chess pieces.

'You're expected too.'

'Well, when you say it like *that*,' Gwen said, making a point of getting very slowly to her feet, 'how could I possibly refuse?'

Tournament season didn't actually start for another week, but the opening ceremony brought all the knights and noble families together early so that they could size each other up, plan courtships and start betting their money, livestock and wives on the outcomes of the events. The huge stands to the north of the castle, set around one large arena that could be configured to host the joust, melee, single combat and archery contests, were built anew every year; they had once again experienced construction setbacks, and wouldn't be complete until right before the first event, so the opening ceremony was to take place in the castle's largest and most southerly courtyard. Gwen would be expected on the royal balcony that overlooked it, used for speeches and appearances and inexplicably popular group family waves.

She had never been particularly interested in tournament season as a child; she was happy with her routine, loved plans repeated to satisfaction every day, and the tournament disrupted her so thoroughly that she sulked about it every summer, often attempting to read a book in her lap while knights grappled for her father's favour just a few feet away. Over the past few years, however, she'd found certain aspects of the tournament to be worth the change of pace.

When she reached the balcony, her mother and father were already seated on the wooden thrones that had been dragged out for the occasion. Gabriel was straight-backed and attempting to smile in the chair next to her father. She crossed to her mother's side and sat down, giving a half-hearted and informal sort of wave at the crowds gathered below as she did so.

'Whatever you are doing with your hand,' her mother said out of the corner of her mouth, 'cease immediately.'

The courtyard was large, cobblestoned and rectangular, with the entrance to the Great Hall at one end and an archway that led to the smaller yard containing the stables at the other. Courtiers were packed around the edge, dressed in their finery, and knights were being announced one by one as they trooped in under the arch with their households and sponsors, to cheers and occasional boos.

It seemed to stretch on for hours. Gwen felt her interest waning, her posture wilting in the hard-backed chair.

'An unusually high cultist turnout among the competitors,' said the queen in a low voice, as somebody entered to less than enthusiastic applause.

'Unusual but welcome,' replied the king, his gaze following this latest knight as he rode briskly across the courtyard. 'I asked Stafford to ensure we were making an effort to bridge the divide, and it seems his hard work has paid off.'

'Well, your cousin is not here,' said the queen. The next competitor was introduced, and she narrowed her eyes as she watched him. 'Ah – but I see he sends his dog.'

Gwen watched as the pallid, translucent-looking Sir Marlin entered the courtyard, unsmiling. He was more commonly referred to in whispered gossip as 'the Knife', due to the fact that he was short, thin and uncommonly bloodthirsty. Relations between the king and the Knife's sponsor and liege, Lord Willard, were somewhat strained, to say the least; when the last king had died leaving no direct heir, there had been a brief skirmish for power that had seen Willard throw his hat into the ring despite the fact that the throne had already been promised to Gwen's father. Willard had been bolstered by the backing of many

Arthurian cultists – those who believed wholeheartedly in the magic of King Arthur and his enchanted sidekicks, the stories that good Christians had long decided were simply fables and legends – and had been working his way up to being quite the legitimate threat. The potential for a real battle had been quelled by the timely invasion of the King of Norway, who had fancied a stab at England himself but had been chased away when most of the nobility united behind Gwen's father to keep him at bay.

It did not make for happy family reunions. In fact, Gwen had only met Lord Willard once before, and had not liked the look of him one bit; he was very tall, grim-faced and brusque, and the enormous dark cloak he wore, sewn all over with various cultist symbols, had made him look like an ill-tempered bat.

Sir Marlin crossed the courtyard to only scattered applause and more than a few low hisses. A set of stout and jovial-looking twins was announced next, Sirs Beldish and Beldish, and then there was a pause before the next burst of fanfare; Gwen heard a ripple of interest move through the crowd, and her ears pricked up.

'For God's sake, not this charade *again*,' her mother sighed. Gwen leaned forward, straining to see past the crowd obscuring the archway into the courtyard. This charade was the highlight of her summer – no, her *life* – and frankly the only thing that made the tournament worth attending.

'Lady Bridget Leclair,' shouted the Grand Marshal, a bearded man called Sir Blackwood, a little reluctantly. 'Of House Leclair.' The crowd erupted into jeers and laughter, jostling each other to get a better look. Lady Leclair ignored them all, face impassive as her enormous horse carried her into the yard under a banner sewn with what looked like a golden wheel on a background of deep maroon. Her straight, black hair was cut bluntly across her forehead and above her broad shoulders; she should have looked ridiculous, like an overgrown pageboy, but somehow it suited her perfectly. Even from a height Gwen could see her steady gaze, her lashes dark against the golden brown of her skin. Thanks to meticulous eavesdropping, Gwen had learned that Lady Leclair was one year her senior and that she was Tai, her line hailing from the Sukhothai Kingdom. Gwen had tried to ask Gabriel about the place as nonchalantly as possible; he had reached for a book and responded with a detailed and entirely useless speech about trading ports.

As Gwen watched, somebody threw a coin at Lady Leclair's head. The knight didn't even flinch, her hands sure at the reins as she leaned forward and steadied her horse, her lips moving ever so slightly as she murmured something in his ear. The only female knight in the country – probably in the whole world – and she bore all the shouting, excitement and ridicule as casually as if she were going for a countryside hack.

'I don't know why we have to put up with this ridiculous spectacle—' the queen started, but the king cut her off with a raised hand.

'She has the right to be here, Margaret. Weather it another year, and perhaps she'll give up.'

Gwen barely heard them. Last night's dream was suddenly coming back to her in vivid colour.

It had been the first day of the joust, and Gwen had been

sitting in the royal stands; her parents weren't there, but Gabriel was, wearing a hat with an enormous feather in it and reciting Chaucer incessantly in her ear. It was customary for knights to show deference to the king before their event began, approaching the royal stands to bow and receive royal assent, and in the dream Lady Leclair had come riding right up to Gwen on a unicorn to present her with a single, soft pink rose. When Gwen had reached for it, Bridget had instead given her a roguish smile, reached over with one gauntleted hand to tilt Gwen's chin towards her, and then kissed her so hard that Gabriel had stopped reciting poetry and muttered 'Crikey!' as he tumbled off his chair.

'Your highness,' Lady Leclair had said, her voice dipping dangerously low as her fingers tangled in Gwen's hair.

'My fair knight,' Gwen had whispered huskily in reply.

She knew that she often spoke aloud in her sleep; knew upon waking that she had certainly done so again this time, and that Agnes had heard her say it. Perhaps repeatedly. She could only hope that it was all she had said.

Gwen didn't even realise she had risen up out of her chair, her hands gripping the edge of the balcony as she drank in the sight of Lady Leclair's approach, until her mother cleared her throat pointedly; she looked over to see her entire family staring at her. She loosened her grip and glanced back down at the courtyard at the exact moment that Lady Leclair looked up; their eyes locked, and the knight gave an almost imperceptible nod of greeting before urging her horse on.

Christ, Gwen thought as she sat back down, blushing furiously. *Not all this again.*

17

2

The man in the very large boots was going to kick Arthur's skull in if he didn't move in the next few seconds. The thought floated in his mind for a moment before the implications really set in, and he rolled out of the way just in time.

'Get *out*,' the man roared.

'I'm already out,' Arthur said, squinting up at him from the ground. 'You helped me get here. Very obliging of you.'

'You insolent little—' Arthur saw the boot coming with more warning this time, and scrambled to his feet. There was mud all down the front of his tunic, and he registered distantly that he'd lost his hat.

'Pleasure to make your acquaintance,' he said, with a little half-bow. 'A very fine establishment indeed, top-rate and truly above expectations.' He turned to leave, but paused as something occurred to him. 'Oh – have you seen Sidney?'

'Who the *hell* is Sidney?'

There was a loud scream from somewhere inside the inn; a ground-floor window was flung open, and a second later a short, well-built young man fell out of it, clutching what looked like half his coat.

'Ah,' Arthur said brightly. 'Never mind.'

'I'm here,' Sidney shouted, somewhat redundantly. 'Don't worry. Just – can't find my bloody – knife.'

'Who's that then?' the red-faced innkeeper spat. 'Your *bodyguard*, come to fight your battles for you?'

'I mean, you're saying it in a very disparaging tone, but in essence – yes.'

The innkeeper advanced on him, fists raised; Arthur almost fell over backwards in his haste to get away.

'Horses 'round back,' Sidney shouted in his direction, waving his half-coat over his head for emphasis.

'Right you are,' Arthur said, legging it as fast as he could around the side of the building. He could hear Sidney grunting with effort behind him, struggling to keep up.

'Weren't you meant to be the distraction?' Sidney panted.

'Er. Yes. But I got – distracted.'

The horses looked at them disapprovingly as they rounded the corner. Arthur tried to mount his in one leap, but miscalculated and almost fell off the other side.

''S'all right,' Sidney said, squinting back over his shoulder once he'd scrambled up into the saddle. 'He's not coming.'

'Good,' Arthur said, turning his horse in a slow circle.

'Wait,' said Sidney. 'He's coming now. He's definitely coming. And he's got a big stick, Art. A *really* big stick.'

'Lucky bastard,' Arthur said, before digging his heels in and setting off at a clumsy canter down the road, Sidney close behind him.

When they reached the large courtyard in front of the main house two hours later, the sundial told Arthur that it was mid-afternoon. This was mildly unsettling. Hadn't it just recently been the middle of the night? And come to think of it – did that mean it was Wednesday?

'Is it Wednesday?' he asked Sidney aloud as they dismounted, handing their horses off to the stable boy. There was a large barrel of rainwater sitting by the servants' entrance; they crossed to it and started disrobing to deal with the worst of the mud.

'How would I know?' Sidney grunted as he pulled his tunic over his head.

'Isn't it your job to know things?'

'No. It's my job to keep you alive. And you are alive, aren't you?'

'Probably,' Arthur said, checking himself for evidence of mortal wounds. There was a large bruise forming on his shoulder, where the innkeeper had punched him.

'What's my face like?'

Sidney grimaced. 'God. *Rubbish*. Really awful.'

'No, I mean – is it all roughed up?'

'Oh. No, then. It's fine. Cut on your eyebrow.' Arthur bent over the barrel and stared at his reflection. It was actually quite a large gash on his eyebrow, and it was still bleeding.

'Arthur,' came a stern voice from behind him; he turned around to see Mrs Ashworth, the grey-haired woman who had once been his nursery maid, glaring at him from the servants' entrance. '*Why* are you half-naked in the yard?'

'Afternoon, Ashworth. Is it Wednesday?'

'Why are you half-naked *and* bleeding?'

'I don't understand,' Arthur said, turning to Sidney, 'why nobody on my staff can give me a straight answer about the Wednesday thing.'

'It's Thursday,' the laundress called wearily as she walked past, ignoring the fact that they were both half-dressed.

'Finally!' Arthur cried, raising his hands in celebration. 'Give that woman a raise.'

'Don't say things like that,' Mrs Ashworth said sharply. 'You know I can't.'

In any normal household, a former nursemaid wouldn't have been occupied with matters of salary and raises – in fact, in any normal household, one might expect the nurse-maid to have moved on once her charge reached the ripe old age of nineteen, with no future spawn incoming. Instead, when Arthur's mother died, Mrs Ashworth had fallen unofficially into the role of running the house. There had been a brief power struggle when Lord Delacey had remarried, but when his second wife had sadly also perished, Mrs Ashworth had picked up where she'd left off; Arthur's father would say that it all seemed to run itself, but when tradesmen or tone-deaf bards or out-of-work pages came to the entrance and asked for the person in charge, Ashworth was always the one they called for.

'Looking lovely as ever, Joyce,' Sidney said, grinning at her.

'I can't give raises but I can carry out sackings,' Mrs Ashworth said, eyeing him suspiciously. 'Put that away, Sidney – you're going to have someone's eye out.'

'You flatter me,' Sidney said, but he gamely trudged into the house to get dressed, and Arthur followed him.

'Is he home?' he said to Ashworth as he passed, trying to keep his tone neutral.

'He's in his study,' she replied, with a sympathetic tilt of her head that Arthur hated deeply. 'He's on the warpath about something, Art. Were you supposed to be somewhere today?'

Arthur racked his brains. 'No, I don't think so. But then – maybe? If it's Thursday.'

'It is Thursday.'

'All right. Well. I'll go and see what he wants.'

When Arthur entered, washed and dressed, the Lord of Maidvale was sitting at his desk, writing a letter. There was a half-empty decanter of wine next to the ink bottle. Arthur lived in hope of the day he would mistake one for the other.

The walls of the study were cluttered with portraits, coats of arms, old papers of provenance and an enormous family tree in self-important gold walnut ink. There had once been a map in pride of place on the south wall; Arthur's mother had sat with him here, a pile of rosewater and saffron sweets between them, as she introduced him to the expanding world. She had shown him the vast seas, the distant continents stretching out towards the east; Iran, a place that existed to him only in stories, where his grandparents had started their long journey to England. He had traced the lines with his chubby finger, not really understanding; by the time he was old enough to have questions about any of it, his mother was long dead.

Arthur had crept in a year after her funeral, looking for traces of her, and found the map gone.

Lord Delacey looked up now as Arthur walked in; he was very red in the face.

'Where the hell have you been?' he said. 'No, don't

answer that, I don't want to know. Do you want to guess what I'm writing this very minute?'

'A poem?' Arthur ventured sullenly, leaning his back against the closed door.

'Oh, *very* funny,' said his father. 'I'm writing to the *king*. I'm writing to the king *grovelling* with every word I know for "sorry" in every possible language. Why do you think that might be?'

'Because you're fair at languages, but terrible at poetry?' Arthur said, knowing it was a mistake before it had even left his lips. He ducked just as the ink bottle smashed against the door next to his head; ink poured down the wood and pooled on the floor, soaking into his boots. He knew his face was flecked with it, but he stared defiantly at his father anyway, refusing to lift a hand to wipe it away.

'You were supposed to be at the opening ceremony today, Arthur,' his father hissed dangerously. 'I told you a thousand times. The *tournament*.'

Arthur took a steadying breath. His father hadn't told him anything of the sort. He knew the tournament must have been coming up, and that he was expected to attend this year, but they had never discussed specifics; he'd presumed that at some point he'd be dragged into this room and told that it was time to go, but the day simply hadn't come. Except – apparently it had, and his father had neglected to tell him, and of course that was somehow *his* fault. Arthur opened his mouth to argue, but then a piece of shattered glass crunched underfoot and he changed his mind.

'Sorry,' he said through gritted teeth. 'I forgot.'

23

'When I *named* you, Arthur, I expected better of you . . .'

Arthur knew that it was now safe to stop listening for at least a few minutes. There were only so many times you could listen to the exact same monologue about 'lineage' and 'dynasty'; about the traitor Mordred, who begat Melehan, who begat a long line of perpetual disappointments, and chiefly about all the ways in which Arthur had failed to live up to the legacy of the once-great king. Arthur Pendragon, purportedly Arthur's relative many times removed, was such a fixture of his father's lectures that if he'd fallen through time and encountered the man, Arthur's primary inclination would have been to kick him right in his damned round table. If they had ever really been royalty, over the past few centuries the Delacey family had done an extremely good job of squandering their connections; their only real legacy was Arthur's father's frankly unhinged obsession with the Pendragon name and these bloody speeches.

'You will go *now*,' Lord Delacey said finally, getting unsteadily to his feet. 'Have Ashworth pack your things. You're going for the summer.'

'What?' Arthur said, straightening up. 'The *summer*? *All* summer?'

'You are to begin your formal courtship with the Princess Gwendoline,' he said, while Arthur gaped at him. 'Close your mouth, Arthur. It's long past time for you to grow up, stop being so bloody selfish and do something of worth with your life. You are to be pleasant to her, to earn her trust – to be the very picture of a devoted fiancé. I expect you to write to me – *look at me when I'm talking to you* – write,

Arthur, to inform me of any developments at Camelot. Leave nothing out.'

Arthur could have said something then about his father's embarrassing desire to collect gossip like a bored, empty-headed courtier, but the decanter of wine looked heavy enough to inflict serious damage, so instead he just nodded and turned to leave.

'*Worthless,*' he heard his father mutter as the door slammed behind him.

He found Sidney in the gardens, throwing bits of bread for a squirrel.

'We're going to Camelot,' he said dully. Sidney glanced up, grinning. 'Don't look so bloody happy about it.'

'Can't help it,' said Sidney. 'I love a good city. Women. Booze. Banquets. And I've never been to Camelot.'

'You have such a beautiful way with words.'

'Besides,' Sidney continued, as if Arthur hadn't spoken. 'Might be good to have a change of scenery. Might help you feel less . . . mopey, since you-know-who.'

'I don't mope,' said Arthur, reaching for the bread Sidney had been throwing and taking a bite. '*Ugh*, this is stale.'

'Why do you think I was throwing it away? Dog had it in her mouth for a bit, too.' He laughed as Arthur immediately spat it out on to the flagstones. 'Manners, Art. Can't be doing that in front of your blushing bride-to-be.'

Arthur pulled a face. 'Go and tell Ashworth to pack my things. We're there until September.'

'What am I?' Sidney said as he got to his feet. 'Your bloody servant?'

'I hate that joke *so* much,' Arthur said despondently.

'Bring as much wine as you can carry. It's going to be a very long summer.'

Their things were sent on ahead of them, and once they had negotiated the country lanes surrounding the Maidvale estate it was essentially a straight shot down one very long road to reach Camelot, which meant they could just point their horses in the right direction and relax.

'When did you last see her?' Sidney asked as they ambled along side by side, leaning across the gap to pass Arthur the bottle of wine.

'I don't know. Years ago, probably,' he said, taking a large sip for courage.

'She's not bad-looking,' Sidney offered. 'As far as I'm told.'

'No. It's her personality that's the problem,' Arthur said darkly. 'You know she broke my wrist?'

'Do I *know*? 'S' probably inked on the inside of my skull. You've told me about a hundred times.'

'It's never been right since,' Arthur said, feeling a phantom ache now as they drew ever closer to the castle. 'It's why I can't hold a sword properly.'

'Yeah,' said Sidney, laughing. 'That's *definitely* why.'

'She's awful, Sid. I've never seen somebody so caught up in their own *majesty*. She was five years old and already stomping about giving me orders, and running off to my father to tell tales on me. When we got older she started writing all these nasty little things in her diary about me, and hiding it under a tree like some sort of deranged squirrel when she thought I wasn't looking.'

'Well,' said Sidney consolingly. 'You're not children any more, are you? Maybe she's different.'

'I doubt it,' said Arthur. 'If anything, she's probably worse.'

'That's the spirit,' said Sidney. 'Now, drink up.'

It was the middle of the night when they crossed the moat; there was a bit of explaining required to get the guards to open the gate, Sidney digging about in his pockets to find the letter bearing Lord Delacey's seal, but eventually the king's men reluctantly stepped aside and let the two tipsy young men from Maidvale ride into the castle courtyard.

'Right,' Arthur said, shaking his head to try to clear it.

'Right, what?'

'Stables . . . to the right. Oh, *shit* – Sid – I'm going over!'

Arthur landed hard on his bruised shoulder and rolled over on to his back, swearing fluently. A stable hand stepped politely over him and took his horse, and he heard two sets of hoofs clopping softly away from him. He knew he needed to get up, but couldn't find the strength or the motivation to do so at present.

'You look like a pillock,' Sidney observed, appearing in his field of vision and offering him an arm.

'Can you go ahead and tell them . . . tell them we've arrived, and that we need rooms?' Arthur said as he was hauled to his feet. 'I'll stay here.'

'In the courtyard?' Sidney said. 'In the dark?'

'I'm putting off going inside for as long as physically possible,' Arthur said, sitting down on a conveniently placed barrel. 'Self-preservation. You understand.'

'Not really,' Sidney said, shrugging and walking confidently off in the direction of the nearest door.

27

It all looked just how it had done the last time Arthur had been there, but smaller somehow, which he supposed made sense; he had been eleven, and skinny, and at least a foot shorter back then. He harboured a long-festering resentment for every crumbling stone in the walls of this place, every banner and hanging and loose door handle. It was less a castle, more a prison.

The one advantage was that his father wasn't there, and was so tied up in apparently vital meetings with people Arthur had never heard of that he probably wouldn't put in an appearance for weeks. That thought alone was enough to cheer him up considerably.

There was bread baking somewhere nearby, and Arthur only realised how hungry he was when he rose instinctively to follow the smell. He crossed the courtyard, stiff from hours of riding, and followed the stairs down to the warren of corridors that led to the kitchens.

When he reached the door, already mentally rehearsing the charming niceties key to the acquisition of snacks, he crashed so violently into somebody coming out of it that he lost his footing and tripped backwards, smacking his head hard against the stone floor. Something strangely soft hit him in the face as he lay there with his ears ringing from the impact; when he opened his eyes, rather dazed, he saw that he was surrounded by what looked like little balls of rolled marzipan.

'On the floor again,' he observed to himself. 'Fantastic.'

'Again?'

Arthur attempted to sit up and winced as searing pain shot through his head. He tried again, more slowly this time, and then opened one eye warily. A tall, gangly, red-headed young man was standing in front of him, holding an empty platter that looked as if it might at one time have held quite a lot of marzipan. Arthur's mind raced to catch up with what he was seeing, and then it clicked; Prince Gabriel. Older, taller, all jawline, eyebrows and elbows now, but unmistakeably him. The last time Arthur had seen him, he and Gwendoline could have been twins.

Not any more. He was a man now. The future king, in fact. Gaping at Arthur. In his nightshirt.

'Evening, Gabriel,' he said, trying to get to his feet with as much dignity as he could muster considering that there was squashed marzipan falling from his hair as he did so.

'Arthur Delacey? Is that you?'

He strongly considered saying no. 'Yes. Hello. I'm here.'

'I can see that,' Gabriel said, frowning at him. 'Lost?'

'Hungry,' Arthur said, brushing down his clothes.

'Drunk,' Gabriel observed flatly. Arthur shrugged.

'Can't a man be both? Why do you have the entire country's supply of marzipan, anyway?'

'I was also hungry,' Gabriel said, looking morosely down at the mess on the floor.

'Oh. Well. I'm going in there,' said Arthur. 'Do you want . . . There might be some more, or—'

'No,' Gabriel said stiffly, handing him the empty plate as if Arthur were a serving boy. 'Goodnight, Arthur.'

'A joy, as always, Gabriel,' Arthur said; he thought he heard a little agitated exhalation of breath as the prince walked away. Arthur was left alone in the hallway, suddenly feeling very stupid. 'Sanctimonious bastard,' he said consolingly to himself, before going in search of bread.

It was dangerous to want things, and Gwen was out of practice.

In fact, the only thing she had truly wanted for years was to be left alone.

Her mother waged a constant war against this tiny, precarious hope, but Gwen had kept it alive, refusing to become more involved with the ladies at court, make friends with the spawn of high-born families like Agnes, or in any way prepare for life as the future Lady of Maidvale. She didn't see the point, because she did not intend to change; she would certainly not stop taking her daily walk, or working on her embroidery in the afternoon, or spending the majority of her day in her own company, even once she was married.

If she thought about it too much, it might have been depressing that her only real wish was for the absence of something – so she didn't think about it at all. She kept to her routines. They made her feel safe. If she wasn't allowed to desire anything for herself, then she thought she should at least get to keep that.

Lady Leclair was a problem. Looking at her felt a lot like wanting something.

On her way down to a family breakfast the morning after the opening ceremony, Gwen decided, for perhaps the five hundredth time since she had first set eyes on the knight of House Leclair, that it was best not to think about that either.

She had far more pressing matters to attend to.

'Father,' she began, watching as the king held up a letter and squinted at it, covering it in quite a lot of soft cheese in the process. 'I've been meaning to talk to you about Arthur Delacey.'

'Actually,' her father said, wiping some of the cheese on a napkin, '*I've* been meaning to talk to *you* about Arthur Delacey.'

'Well. Yes. I just think we should talk this through before we do anything rash. Is it really the best—'

The king sighed and raised his index finger, a signal rarely employed with his family but universally understood to demand instant silence.

'He will be staying for the summer, Gwendoline. It is long past time for you to become reacquainted. You are nearly eighteen, after all – you must have known this was coming.'

'I had hoped,' Gwen said, choosing her words carefully, 'that the circumstances that led to the agreement in the first place might have changed.'

Her father didn't look unsympathetic, but unfortunately he also didn't look like a man about to drastically change his mind. 'You know that the Lord and Lady of Maidvale lent me invaluable support when I took the throne, Gwendoline, despite the fact that Delacey is a cultist through and through and could have easily thrown his lot in . . . elsewhere. You also know that I am a man of my word.'

'So because of an old alliance that doesn't even benefit us any more, I have to suffer?'

'We *do* still benefit from it,' her father said, looking at her evenly. 'Lord Delacey may not hold as much power as he once did, but now is not the time to upset him or any of his faction. And you do not have to *suffer*. You have to marry.'

'Same difference,' Gwen said, feeling her cheeks getting hot.

'Gwendoline,' said the queen. Gwen waited with little hope to see if her mother was about to come to her aid. 'Would you please *stop* picking at your nails.'

Gwen put both hands under the table and curled them into fists instead.

'Father,' Gabriel said quietly. 'I've heard some . . . particularly *unsavoury* rumours about Arthur Delacey's behaviour over the past year, and I had a brief encounter with him last night that all but confirmed them.'

'Yes,' said Gwen, throwing Gabriel a look of gratitude and seizing this opportunity to appeal to her father's sense of propriety. 'I understand that you gave your word, but shouldn't we weigh up the benefits of honouring the match with the possible damage he might do? To the crown? To our reputation?' *To me*, she added silently.

'We will do no such thing,' said her mother, looking exasperated. 'You're not a child any more, Gwendoline. It is high time you accept both him and your responsibilities as the future lady of his house and lands.'

'I'm not going to move to his house and lands!' Gwen said. 'I'm going to stay at court, so frankly I don't see the point.'

'The *point*,' said her mother acidly, 'is that you may not have a choice! And you'll still be expected to help manage his affairs—'

'I know you're not one for change,' the king cut in with a touch more sympathy, breaking the seal of a new letter with his knife, 'but give him a chance. He might surprise you. And – please do *try* not to break any of his bones this time.'

'I can't promise anything,' Gwen muttered, but her father was once again buried in his correspondence, and her mother was eating in perturbed silence.

'You saw him?' she asked Gabriel as soon as they had left the dining room. 'Did you talk to him?'

'Sort of,' Gabriel said, already walking automatically towards the library.

'How can you *sort of* talk to someone?'

'It was the middle of the night and he was trying to steal food from the kitchens. Oh, and he fell over. It was hardly a scintillating exchange.'

'He fell over?' Gwen said. 'God, I wish I'd seen that.'

'Don't worry,' Gabriel said drily. 'I have no doubt that the performance will be repeated.'

Gwen successfully managed to avoid Arthur all day. She walked in endless loops around the grounds with Agnes, making polite but stilted conversation, and then retired for lunch, followed by a solitary afternoon in her chambers mostly spent drumming her fingers against things and sighing.

When she was called to supper in the Great Hall, Gwen knew she couldn't put off seeing her betrothed any longer; she had Agnes pull out her finest spring dress in delicate pink and gold silk damask, braid her hair up out of her face and weave cherry blossoms into it. When she met Gabriel on his way down to dinner, just as late as she was, he raised an eyebrow at her.

'You look nice,' he said pointedly.

'Oh, shut up.'

She noticed that he'd also made an effort; he was wearing an embroidered blue doublet that she didn't recognise, and his hair was actually combed. 'Did Elyan dress you? What's with the jacket?'

He looked down at it as if he'd never seen it before in his life. 'Oh? No. He's gone back to Stafford.'

Lord Stafford managed the running of the royal family's affairs, and it was the bane of his life that Gabriel refused every man of the chamber sent his way; they each lasted roughly a week before Gabriel felt too horrified by the familiarity and proximity and had them quietly sent to work elsewhere. He'd be left by himself for a month or so in glorious peace while Stafford lined up another doomed replacement.

The hall was packed; most of the people who'd come to watch the opening ceremony had also been invited to dine with the king tonight, which meant that the long wooden tables were overflowing with guests messily pouring wine, shouting to each other in greeting and jostling for a better position. Gwen assumed that Arthur would be among them, and felt a little smug about being able to bypass the crowds and walk straight up to the royal table on the dais, but stopped short when she saw who was sitting next to one of the only two empty seats.

'I'll give you everything I own,' she said quietly to Gabriel. 'I'll give you—'

'Sit by me, your highness,' Lord Stafford called, plummy as ever, an upsetting amount of peacock feathers in his hat. 'I had something I wanted to discuss with you.'

Gwen knew he wasn't talking to her. He was never, ever talking to her.

'Of course,' Gabriel said politely, crossing to the seat without daring a backward glance at Gwen, who had no choice but to sit down next to Arthur.

She deigned to give him a quick once-over, and was glad to see that he looked miserable. He had dark shadows under his eyes and quite a nasty-looking cut on his brow. He was staring sullenly into his soup, and although he didn't say anything when she sat down next to him, she saw his shoulders tense.

She was fully prepared to ignore him all evening, but her mother was deep in conversation with her father on her left, and when she tried to lean in to their discussion her father caught her eye and raised a knowing eyebrow. She sank back into her seat, resigned to her fate.

'Arthur,' she said factually.

'Yep,' he replied, just as accurately.

'Rough journey, was it?'

'Nothing compared to the destination,' he replied, with a tight-lipped smile.

'What a thrilling surprise to find you at my table.'

'Believe me, it wasn't my idea,' he said gloomily, picking up his drink. 'Your mother cornered me on my way in. Wouldn't even let Sid come with me.'

'Who's Sid?'

'Sidney Fitzgilbert. My body-man. He's the short, ugly one over there.' He waved a hand towards one of the long tables, and Gwen saw a stocky, dark-haired and perfectly good-looking man raise a hand to wave cheerfully. He was pale but slightly sunburned, and had stew all down his chin. She did not wave back.

'Delightful.'

'He is, actually. A ray of sunshine. Compared to some.'

'Oh *come on*,' Gwen said, finally snapping. 'You're nine-teen now, not eleven. At least attempt civility.'

He turned to look at her with pure disdain in his narrowed eyes, gave her a slow once-over, and then returned his gaze to her face.

'No,' he said. 'I don't think I will.'

'You're going to be here all summer,' Gwen said. 'Arthur. You might be here *forever*.'

'Well. God. I suppose you're right,' he said, sighing and looking around. 'Must find a way to get through it. Face it head-on.' Gwen was just about to nod and say something vaguely approving when he gestured to a serving girl walking past. 'Some wine, please, and keep it coming. All summer.' He turned to Gwen and gave her a sweet, entirely artificial smile. 'Maybe even *forever*.'

'Oh, go to hell, Arthur,' Gwen hissed. He raised his newly filled glass in a mock toast.

'There's the Gwendoline I remember.'

They sat in silence until the queen leaned over to talk to Arthur; he immediately sat up straighter and answered all her questions pleasantly, even charmingly; *yes* he'd kept up with his reading, *no* of course it wasn't an imposition to be called here for the summer, *yes* he still loved to dance. It made Gwen all the more annoyed – he *was* capable of playing nice, just not with her.

After dinner, there was to be music. Gwen was usually able to sneak away at this point in the evening, offering excuses of sprained ankles or miscellaneous 'women's troubles', while everybody grabbed partners and rushed to take their positions for the dancing – but as she tried to move towards the exit her mother's hand closed around her upper arm like a vice.

'Dance with your guest, Gwen,' she said through a terse smile.

'Mother,' Gwen said seriously. 'Call the guards. He threatened me with a knife.'

'I *told* you not to say things like that any more,' her mother said, taking her by the shoulders and steering her towards the dancers. 'Lord Stafford's poor nephew almost soiled himself when they grabbed him.'

'I hope he really does kill me,' Gwen said glumly. 'Then you'll be sorry.'

She could have sworn that as her mother walked away Gwen heard her mutter, '*I wouldn't count on it.*'

Gabriel, of course, did not have to dance. He stayed seated, listening to Lord Stafford and nodding at regular intervals. She thought, not for the first time, that her brother would *love* for his only duty to be marriage. He wasn't betrothed to anyone in particular; he could find someone kind and thoughtful and studious just like him, and retreat to one of the crown's houses in the country to garden and adopt a hundred cats and live out the rest of his days in peace.

But that wasn't his inheritance. Royal sons meant promise – they carried the hope and glory of their lineage, however reluctantly; royal daughters were born to be promised to somebody else.

Gwen's somebody else was already standing in the men's line, waiting for her. She wondered how her mother had found the time to force him into dancing too, when she had been so busy corralling her own daughter. Perhaps she had brought in co-conspirators.

Arthur didn't look particularly pleased, but when the music started he didn't drag his feet; he danced with an easy grace that Gwen couldn't help but envy. She hated him for being good at it, while she was always inches away from endangering someone's toes. She hated the smug smile on his face as they had to grasp hands; the small, mean snort of laughter she heard when she missed a step and almost went careening into the couple next to them.

Most of all, she hated how much dancing required her to look at him. He *was* handsome, it was impossible to deny – although her knowledge of his truly appalling personality obliterated any points this garnered in his favour. His hair was almost black, and fell straight down to his shoulders; his skin was luminous brown despite the fact that it wasn't yet summer, as if he'd already been spending a lot of time out of doors. The cut on his eyebrow, the sleepless look he had about him, the slight bruising she now noticed on his temple; it all should have made him far less handsome, but instead it just added to his rakish charm. She was pleased to see that he was still no taller than her, at least.

The girls adjacent to her – girls all down the line, in fact – were looking at him, and he knew it. She couldn't imagine what they saw in him; this horrible boy who'd become a horrible man, sent here to torment her for the rest of her life. As soon as the music stopped, she walked away from him without a backward glance and went straight up to Gabriel, who was standing by the royal table, still talking to Lord Stafford. He took one look at her expression and excused himself.

'Are you all right?' he said, once Lord Stafford had walked away.

'What was Stafford talking to you about?' Gwen asked, keen to be distracted.

'War,' said Gabe, grim-faced.

'With who?'

'Amongst ourselves. The cultists are getting restless. The Catholics too. Father's keeping it all in check, for now.' Gabriel leaned back against the fretwork of an ornate oak pillar as they watched the dancers begin again. 'Although judging by the look on Arthur Delacey's face, if we do need to quash anybody – really crush their spirits – you're the woman for the job.'

Arthur had also retreated from the dancers. He was now sitting with Sidney, his stew-covered manservant – although, Gwen noticed, he had managed to locate and remove the stew – and talking quietly to him, glaring around at everybody as he did. When he saw Gwen looking at him he caught her gaze and then rolled his eyes like a child as Sidney laughed into his ale.

'Can't you go and rough him up or something?' Gwen demanded of Gabriel, who was still staring at Arthur.

'*What?* Er. No. Might cause a minor political incident.'

'Cause a major one. Do it for me. He insulted my honour.'

'Did he?'

'Well, no. But he was very snippy with me.'

Gabriel gave her a wry smile. 'You'll live.'

Two of the ladies who'd been next to Gwen in the dancing line came giggling over to them, ostensibly to talk to Gwen, but really to bite their lips and blush prettily in front of Gabriel, who was so unmoved that at one point he actually yawned. Gwen had to bite her own lip to keep from laughing; watching women throw themselves at Gabriel while he politely studied the flagstones, or cleared his throat only to make a comment about taxes or the unusual colour of the evening's soup, was one of her favourite pastimes. These ladies were surprisingly tenacious; mere yawning could not keep them away, and they hovered for an age before giving in.

'Hard luck,' she said to the retreating girls when they finally departed; both of them looked daggers at her.

'That's the sort of thing you're supposed to say inside your head, G,' Gabriel said distractedly. 'Why don't you go to bed? You don't have to stay.'

Gwen shrugged. 'I either submit to torture by dancing tonight or torture by Mother in the morning.'

'Well, why don't you go and get some air, at least? I'll distract her.'

She gave him a grateful pat on the shoulder and walked quickly from the hall and out into the south courtyard. It was mercifully quiet as she crossed it, the sounds of revelry muffled, the night air cool and steeped in wood smoke. She was just wandering in the direction of the stables – and her very patient and understanding horse, Winifred – when she saw somebody coming out of them, walking directly towards her.

There was no logical explanation for her reaction when she realised who it was. Before rational thought had been able to communicate with her limbs, she had ducked behind a low wall.

Lady Leclair was no longer armoured as Gwen had seen her the day before, but just as striking in a plain tunic and men's breeches; her hair was pulled untidily away from her face, her sleeves rolled up to expose the taut muscle of her forearms, and she had a smear of something dark – potentially mud, potentially horse manure – on her cheekbone.

Gwen had never seen something so magnificent in all her life.

Lady Leclair stretched her limbs until her bones clicked, eliciting a sigh of satisfaction that immediately turned Gwen's mind to jelly, and then she paused as if remembering something and turned abruptly to walk back into the stables. She looked less imposing out of armour – she couldn't have been any taller than Gwen, and she didn't have a particularly large frame – but there was still a solidity to her, as if she were made of something stronger than whatever Gwen was spun from.

41

Gwen continued to crouch in an undignified sort of way even after she was gone, frozen to the spot, only realising that she should move when she felt a cramp starting to creep up her leg.

She had just resolved to get a hold of herself and go back inside when she heard more footsteps approaching from the opposite direction.

They grew louder, and Arthur Delacey came stumbling into view. One of her father's men, blond, perhaps a Mark or a Michael, was tripping along after him and holding on to his arm in a very familiar manner. She tried to place him – assistant to the Master of Hounds, perhaps? As she watched, Arthur glanced around the otherwise empty courtyard, pulled the young man into the shadowy alcove between the stables and the gate, and *kissed* him.

Gwen's mouth fell open.

Arthur was smiling lazily through heavily lidded eyes, pressing his mouth to Mark or Michael's jaw while sliding one hand inside the other man's tunic. The dog-boy closed his eyes and allowed his neck to be kissed, tilting his head back so that his hair fell away from his face, looking completely at ease. Gwen was so astonished that she completely forgot she was attempting to stay hidden – and when Arthur looked up, his eyes locked directly with hers.

He pushed the young man away, muttered something sharply, and Mark or Michael was gone in an instant. Arthur stood alone, smoothing his hair, colour high in his cheeks. He looked back over at Gwen, his jaw working as if he were trying and failing to summon the right words – and then they both jumped.

42

Lady Leclair had re-emerged from the stables, a jacket slung over her shoulder. Moving without thinking, Gwen ducked back behind the wall, her face flaming, listening to unhurried footsteps as the knight walked away in the direction of the kitchens.

When she dared to straighten up again, Arthur was standing right in front of her.

'Nice night,' he said, in a very strained voice. His hands were clenching and unclenching at his side as he waited for her to respond.

'Arthur,' Gwen said eventually, in a whisper. 'That was a *boy*. You were kissing a *boy*.'

'Was it?' said Arthur, sounding a little panicked now. 'No, I don't think so. I'd have noticed.'

'I should think it would have been obvious. You practically had your hand down the front of his—'

'*All right*,' Arthur hissed. 'All right. It was a boy. Congratulations, you're a genius. Let's get this over with – would you like to tar and feather me now, or send me back to my father so he can do it? Either way, I'm sure you'll be allowed to watch.'

'Oh,' said Gwen. '*Oh*.' She was still trying to wrap her head around this; this brazen sneaking around where anybody could have caught him, this boy-kissing that he'd been doing so expertly, as if he did it all the time. He probably *did* do it all the time.

'What the hell were you doing *spying* on me, anyway?' he spat, with such vitriol that it immediately raised her hackles.

'I wasn't *spying* on you,' she said. 'I was just ...' She gestured in the general direction of the stables. Arthur's gaze followed her hand and then snapped back to her face, eyebrows furrowed as if he were puzzling something out. She realised her mistake immediately.

'Who was that girl?' he said slowly.

'What girl?' Gwen said, the note of hysteria that she had noticed in his voice making an unexpected appearance in her own.

'You know exactly which girl,' he said, eyes widening. 'You were spying on *her*.'

'I don't know what you're talking about,' Gwen said, but something had betrayed her – God, Merlin, the universe – because she sounded entirely unconvincing, and he looked triumphant. He *knew*. Of course he knew.

It wouldn't have crossed most people's minds, but – he'd just been kissing a *boy*, hadn't he?

'Right,' he said, the panic visibly draining from him. '*Right*.'

'I . . . Listen, I don't know what exactly you think you've discovered here, but—'

'Why don't we go and talk about this somewhere more private, hmm?' He turned on his heel and walked away across the courtyard.

With the air of somebody condemned to an extremely painful death, Gwen followed.

Arthur had thought the guards might stop him; they certainly looked suspicious as he strode through the servants' door with Gwendoline trailing reluctantly behind him, but she must have given them some imperceptible signal to fall back, because they didn't follow him or try to slap him soundly for daring to be alone with the princess. If they *had* considered the possibility that he might be leading her off to impugn her virtue, they didn't seem too bothered – perhaps they thought her virtue was in need of a little light impugning.

He located the door to the cellar and opened it with a flourish.

'What's this?' Gwen said with disgust, as he took a lit torch from the wall and started down the steps into the darkness.

'What do you mean, "What's this"? You live here, don't you?'

'I don't make a habit,' Gwendoline said, stumbling on the stairs as she hurried to keep up, 'of opening mystery doors and walking into dark tunnels with unreliable men.'

'You should give it a try, it might loosen you up a bit,'

Arthur said as they reached the bottom. 'Anyway, this isn't a *mystery door*. It's the wine cellar. Please tell me you knew about the wine cellar.' The glow from the torch illuminated rows and rows of enormous barrels, stretching on into the gloom. It smelt like aged oak and dust and alcohol, which was somewhat calming to Arthur's nerves.

'Why would I?' said Gwendoline, scowling. She had to stand quite close to him to stay within the torchlight, and she was clearly unhappy about it.

'It's where the *wine* lives,' Arthur said incredulously.

'Oh, well, *silly me*,' Gwendoline replied, wrapping her arms around herself and looking uncertainly around at the room. 'I don't drink. Can you hurry up and say whatever it is you want to say? It's cold down here.'

Arthur leaned back against a barrel with practised nonchalance and considered her for a moment. She always looked pinched and irritated, but right now her face actually seemed in danger of collapsing in on itself.

'Let's just agree to be straight with each other,' he said slowly. 'Can you manage that?'

'What do you mean?' Gwendoline said, clearly knowing exactly what he meant.

'You were lurking behind that wall—'

'I wasn't *lurking*.'

'Okay, fine, you were *reclining gracefully* – with poise and dignity, as befits your noble house – behind that wall, spying on that woman.'

'I was – taking some air,' Gwendoline said too quickly, 'and she just so happened—'

'What is she? Lady's maid? Scullion? Laundress?'

'She's a *knight*, actually,' Gwendoline snapped, bristling. 'Lady Bridget Leclair.'

Arthur bit back a laugh at her furious expression. 'Great name.'

Gwen put a hand to her forehead and closed her eyes. She seemed to be thinking painfully hard; her effort was palpable. When she opened them again, she fixed Arthur with an extremely icy stare.

'Whatever you *believe* you saw,' she said, choosing her words carefully, 'I saw something at least ten times as ... interesting. So I wouldn't be throwing accusations around here. If I were you.'

'I'm not *accusing* you of anything, you despotic little psychopath,' said Arthur. 'You know something about me, and I believe I know something – different in the superficial details, but actually rather similar – about you. It would be in *both* of our interests for that information to stay private.'

'If I told my father what I saw ...'

'I'd tell him I saw you lusting after *Lady Bridget*. Although – I might embellish it. Add a few sordid details.'

'He wouldn't believe you,' Gwendoline scoffed, but she was tugging nervously at her sleeve.

'He'd believe me enough to keep her away from you,' Arthur said, with a certainty he didn't really possess. 'And I think he'd believe me enough to keep an *extremely* close eye on you from now on.'

'Even if you had seen what you've dreamed up in your head – which you *didn't* – not all of us are stupid enough to go running around making our – our private feelings public, by putting our hands all over *Mark* from the *dog-house*—'

'Well, more's the pity for you,' said Arthur. 'And his name is *Mitchell*.'

'Is it?'

'Er . . . I think so.'

'Good *God*, Arthur. Go to bed. We'll talk about this tomorrow,' Gwendoline said. She snatched the torch from him and headed for the stairs, taking careful and deliberate steps that somewhat impeded her flouncing. He didn't move as he was swallowed by the shadows.

'I'm not sure you're in any position to be giving orders right now, Gwendoline.'

She turned at the door, her face illuminated in the flickering torchlight, looking at him with utter disdain. 'You can address me as *your highness*.'

'My apologies, your *fucking highness*,' Arthur called after her, but the door had already slammed shut – he was shouting into an empty room.

It was quite early in the summer for things to have gone so spectacularly wrong. The situation required quick thinking; usually it was Arthur's forte, but he had used wine as a crutch this evening, and his deductive reasoning skills had taken a hit.

'You're screwed,' Sidney said, as he watched Arthur pace around their quarters like a caged and tipsy hound.

'Helpful,' Arthur said, scrubbing a hand across his face. 'Here's the thing. This – *this* is the thing. If I had one tiny nibble of real, tangible dirt on her, one salacious little crumb, I'd be laughing. But she's so dull. She's just so, *so* dull. If she *has* been up to anything untoward, then the only person who'll know is her brother, and he was always her horrible sidekick when we were children.'

'So she wouldn't tell ... I dunno, a friend?'

'*What friends?*' Arthur said meaningfully.

Sidney scratched his neck and looked thoughtful. 'Not one measly friend? No princess clique she has round for sleepovers? Not even a pen pal?'

'No,' said Arthur. 'The only person she ever wrote to while I was here was ... Oh, hold on. Hold on a bloody second. I've got it. You're a genius.'

'I know,' said Sidney. 'Why?'

'Come on,' said Arthur, feeling freshly renewed with the vigour of somebody who might soon be holding priceless blackmail material. 'Put on your worst trousers. Oh – never mind, you're already wearing them. We're going *digging.*'

The next morning dawned irritatingly clear and sunny. Arthur hadn't managed much in the way of sleep, and the dazzling weather felt personal. A note had been brought to his chamber door and then read aloud to him by Sidney, requesting that he meet Gwen in the orchard with all possible discretion and haste.

'*Very* nice-looking girl delivered it,' Sidney said, cramming a sugared bun into his mouth as he did. 'Think I might be in love.' Arthur just biffed him feebly on the arm and demanded a bun of his own.

When they reached the gate to the orchard, which was walled on all sides, Arthur turned to Sidney with an expression of deepest agony.

'Christ, Art, it's a sixteen-year-old girl, not an hour on the rack,' said Sidney, rather unsympathetically.

'She's seventeen. And I'd take the torture in a heartbeat,' said Arthur, but he squared his shoulders bravely anyway and went inside. The orchard was large and regimented, neat rows of trees shedding swirling clouds of blossom every time the breeze picked up. Gwendoline was walking slowly down the middle row towards him with a short, delicate brunette woman, presumably the one Sidney had taken a shine to; she was quickly dismissed, and as she walked past him with her head bowed he flashed her a smile and saw her go satisfyingly pink.

'What's her name?' he said when he reached the princess.

'What?' She was wearing sky-blue today, her hair pulled back into an intricate braid across the top of her head that looked, if you were slightly hungover and squinting, like a crown. He wondered if that's why she was always so tetchy; too much strain on her scalp.

'*Her*. Brown hair. Grey dress. Nice little hands.'

'What the hell were you looking at her *hands* for?'

'I take an interest in people,' said Arthur, noticing that quite a lot of blossom had already landed in his hair and attempting to dislodge it.

'I bet you do,' Gwendoline said gravely.

'Oh, yes, very good, I'm a pervert and a criminal because I looked at a person's hands,' Arthur snapped. 'Shall we walk? While we talk? You did ask me here because you wanted to talk, didn't you?'

'Fine,' said Gwendoline, as if walking were beneath her,

despite the fact that she had just been doing it quite willingly. They started awkwardly down the row, as far apart as they could be from each other without either of them actually walking into a tree. 'I don't see any logical reason why I wouldn't tell my father what I saw last night. Whatever you try to tell him about me, he won't believe you. And then the engagement will be off, and we can put this whole thing to bed.'

'Right,' Arthur said, dread bitter on his tongue. 'Well. I don't suppose I could appeal to your sense of humanity, instead?'

'Oh, come *on*, Arthur. He won't necessarily tell your father *why*. Then we're both out of this mess, and free to part ways and never meet again . . .'

She was still talking, but Arthur wasn't listening. He knew with absolute certainty that it didn't matter one jot what reason Gwendoline's father did or didn't give for breaking the betrothal. His father would . . . well, Arthur couldn't begin to *imagine* what he'd do. As he had quite a vivid imagination, this was more than a little concerning.

'I thought you might say that,' he said, despite having no idea whatsoever what she'd just said. He fought to keep his voice steady. 'So I had a little think last night. And then I went for a little walk.'

'A little think and a little walk?' Gwendoline said. 'What on earth are you—'

Arthur presented his evidence with a flourish. The flourish was probably unnecessary, but gratifying nonetheless. Gwen flushed an interesting beetroot colour, and stopped walking.

'But – you – how did you—'

Arthur cleared his throat and opened the cracked leather binding with a reverence befitting the occasion. His prize had, after all, been quite hard-won. There had been absolutely no way to know for certain that the damned thing would still *be* there, after all these years, and they'd had to dig under quite a few trees before they'd found the right one.

'*Dear diary,*' he began to read. '*There is a new squire at the tourney. She is strong and brave, and she has black hair and brown eyes. I think she's very beautiful. They say she is an only child, and that her father saw no reason not to treat her as he would a son. Her name is Bridget Leclair and she is actually a Lady but she wants to be a knight* – Christ, didn't anybody ever teach you that you're supposed to show, not tell? – *so she has been travelling the country attending tourneys all year. I don't know why but I would like to kiss her.*' Arthur stopped then, not because he had run out of steam, but because Gwen had lunged for the diary and necessitated his taking a very quick step backwards.

'I didn't . . .' she said, still an alarming shade of purple. 'You can't—'

'Well, that's just the thing, isn't it?' Arthur said smoothly, tucking the diary into his trousers where he was relatively sure she wouldn't follow. 'I don't *want* to, but I can. And I've already torn out some particularly damning entries from that summer and given them to Sidney for safekeeping.'

It had been like striking gold. He had been fully prepared to discover that she had long ago burned it, or to find page after page of utter banality – and there *had* been plenty of that – but then, dated three years ago, just before Gwendoline's fifteenth birthday and the last summer she had put pen to parchment, there it all was in embarrassingly neat script.

'Don't do this,' Gwendoline said, finally finding her words.

'I won't if you won't.'

There was a very long silence, during which Arthur wondered if he may have miscalculated.

'Fine,' she said eventually. His shoulders sagged with relief before he remembered he was trying to give the impression that he was the one driving this carriage.

'Good. That's what I thought.' He started walking again, and after a pause Gwendoline followed. 'There's no need for this to get nasty. And, as a show of good faith, what if we agreed to . . . to help each other out? In this regard.'

'In what regard?' Gwendoline said, her voice still tight with anger.

'You know. Look out for each other. Or – not, as the case may be. I'll turn a blind eye to whatever you might get up to, and you do the same for me.'

'I don't *get up to* anything,' Gwendoline said, bristling.

'Well, that much is painfully clear,' Arthur said, raising an eyebrow at her. 'But if you did ever loosen your skirts for a night out on the town, I'd – I don't know – cover for you, if you'd do the same for me.'

'I don't need you to *cover* for me,' she snarled, but then she thought for a few seconds and seemed to reconsider. 'There is . . . My mother and father want this match to work. If we were to give them the impression that things are going well between us, it could make my life a lot easier. I'd be left alone.'

'So we just – pretend to get on?' Arthur said doubtfully. He supposed it wasn't actually much to ask, but as he couldn't look at her scowling face without wanting to flick it, it felt monumental.

'Yes. We pretend their grand plan is working, we are – *pleasant* to one another. It's classic misdirection.'

'My father will be ecstatic.'

'As will mine,' Gwendoline said gloomily.

'And what happens when they say, "Right, they're clearly not going to kill each other if left in the same room alone, let's celebrate by setting a date for the wedding"?'

'I don't know. We get married, I suppose.'

'Brilliant,' said Arthur. 'Glad this all has a happy ending. If we're lucky, some insurgents will rise up and kill us all in our beds before we have to say "I do".'

'Don't give me hope,' said Gwendoline. 'It'll only make reality all the more crushing.'

Arthur looked at her. She was staring listlessly up into the branches of an apple tree, looking almost as miserable as he felt.

'It's a deal then,' he said, keen to conclude the conversation as quickly as possible so that he could achieve his dream of being imminently horizontal.

'Yes – with some caveats. You can't get caught with . . . people. It'll undermine the whole thing. You can't do anything to embarrass me. If you must go out, try to be . . . I don't know, discreet.' She looked at him doubtfully, as if thinking that he'd never once been discreet in his entire life.

'You can't tell anyone. And we have to make it believable.'

'I have to tell Sidney,' Arthur said quickly. 'He's going to know something's up anyway, if we start batting our eyelashes at each other.'

'Yes. Well. I suppose . . . Gabriel will have to know at least part of it. I don't think I can trust Agnes, even if I swore her to secrecy—'

'*Aha*. Agnes. That's her name. The brunette.'

'Take this seriously, Arthur.'

'Fine,' he said curtly. 'We should pretend we're meeting in secret. Like we can't stay away from each other. But we should do a bad job of it, so word gets out. Quick and effective, and it means we don't actually have to spend much time together.'

'Fine. But the first events of the tournament start next week, and we ought to be seen there. Let's lay the ground-work then.' Gwendoline glanced over at the gate and Arthur followed her gaze; Sidney was clearly visible through it, talking to Agnes. She was holding a sugared bun and looking delighted.

'You can go,' said Gwendoline.

Furious that she felt she had the authority to *dismiss* him, Arthur half wanted to stay just to spite her – but his head was pounding, the sun was too bright, and he really fancied a bun.

'Whatever,' he snarled, turning on his heel and stalking away, worried that his magnificent display of anger may have been slightly undermined by the shower of petals that fell from his shoulders as he went.

Gwen had never been particularly interested in the occult, but at that moment she would have traded her father's entire kingdom for one tiny, pathetic trickle of Arthurian magic.

She just needed enough to turn back time, sprint to the orchard and remove that damned diary before Arthur could get his hands on it. She trembled with rage every time she thought about it, but she wasn't angry at Arthur – not more than usual, at any rate. She was furious with *herself*.

She should have burned it years ago, but it was the one place she had allowed herself to voice her most closely guarded secrets. Some part of her liked that she had a record of first sightings, brief encounters – every scrap of Lady Leclair that she had been able to collect. There had been precious few of them: a nod from across a courtyard when Bridget had still technically been a squire, shadowing a knight from a neighbouring county; brief glances in Gwen's direction when Bridget was paying her respects to the king during the tournament; an incident where Sir Blackwood, the Grand Marshal, had tripped over his own hem and they had been the only ones to laugh.

She had collected rumours too, throwaway remarks and the tail ends of stories she had overheard. People said that Lady Leclair could fight off two grown men by the age of twelve. They said she spoke six languages. They said that a stable boy had tried to grope her once at a regional tourney, and it had taken him six weeks to regain full use of his legs. Everything Gwen had heard about Lady Bridget Leclair just made her want to know more.

She had been there the first time Lady Leclair entered the lists, had watched with her heart in her mouth as she went out in the first round to a chorus of boos and jeers – it had just been all the sweeter the next year when she'd won, and kept on winning for weeks, until she'd been knocked violently from her horse and forced to retire. Gwen could have sworn that just once, during a golden August evening as she sat next to her father in the royal stands, she had caught Bridget staring at her intently when she thought Gwen wasn't looking.

All these memories were tainted now, thanks to Arthur.

It felt wrong to withhold the finer details of what had happened from Gabriel, but the sight of him sliding into the chair opposite her in their private dining room that evening, wan and exhausted from a day of royal duties, gave her pause. She had been pausing like this for years, never quite sure how to talk to him about Lady Leclair, occasionally testing the waters with a passing comment about the knight's choice of armour or prowess in battle, but never able to take the next step. She was sure that she *would* tell him everything at some point – she had to, she had never withheld anything from him for this long – but, as always, she told herself that it simply wasn't the right time.

Their parents had been called to a private dinner with the elderly archbishop of Camelot, so Gwen proceeded to tell Gabriel approximately half of what had transpired since they had last spoken, the cracks in her story conspicuous despite her efforts to paper over them.

'G, I don't really understand how this is some dastardly plan,' he said, rubbing at his temple.

'Do you need me to explain it again?' said Gwen, biting into a gooseberry and wrinkling her nose as her mouth flooded sour.

'No, I grasp the basic concept, I just ...You caught him kissing somebody? And now you're covering for him? Why?'

'Charitable spirit?' Gwen offered, and Gabriel raised an eyebrow. 'He's agreed to be civil, Gabe. It'll get Mother and Father off my back.'

'But if you just *explained* that he's up to no good, they'd probably call the whole thing off. What aren't you telling me?' He looked very, very tired, and it made Gwen feel even worse for lying to him. She stared down at the picked-at plate of fruit in front of her, her throat feeling suddenly tight.

'It's nothing,' she said, trying to smile at him and only managing a grimace. 'I just want a bit of peace, and ... this seems the easiest way.'

'All right,' he said slowly, reaching out and patting her arm so awkwardly that Gwen laughed. 'But, you know, if you need—'

'Yes,' she said. 'I know. Just ... It's fine, Gabe. I know what

I'm doing.' He considered her for a while, and then sighed, reaching for an apricot.

'So,' he said. 'You and Arthur? Besotted sweethearts?' Gwen put her head in her hands and nodded. 'Well. This should be interesting.'

'What *are* you wearing?'

Arthur was sporting an elaborate jacket that was all brushed velvet and polished gold hardware; walking next to him, in a simple peach dress, Gwen felt distinctly underwhelming.

'That's not a very good start,' Arthur said, smiling pleasantly at her. They were heading north, past the orchard, towards the drawbridge that would take them out of the castle and down to the tournament grounds. She saw her mother glance back at them and smile approvingly as they crossed the moat, and then they were being hustled through a back entrance by a fleet of guards and escorted to their seats in the royal stand. The king and queen sat first, taking pride of place in the hardy thrones constructed strictly for outdoor use; they were wildly luxurious compared to the tight rows of narrow benches in the other stands.

The ornamental sword Excalibur was already in place directly in front of her father on its own little plinth. It was large and ornate, modelled on the original, protruding from a slab of glittering rock. The winner of the tournament was allowed to hold it very briefly during the closing ceremony while the crowd cheered for them – and then it was hastily reclaimed, lest they drop it, or try to yank the sword from the stone and proclaim themselves king.

Gwen sat down with Gabriel on her right and Arthur, still smiling that infuriatingly benign smile, on her left. She saw a ripple of interest travel through the crowd, and resisted the urge to roll her eyes. Of course they were all muttering. She never came to the tournament escorted. Arthur was a novelty, and he was probably *loving* it. A quick glance at him confirmed her theory; he ran a deliberate hand through his hair and then turned slowly so that his face was in profile, stopping short when he met Gwen's glare.

'What?'

'Are you quite finished *preening*?'

This rebuke didn't seem to land. 'Put your hand on my arm,' he said quietly, and Gwen snorted.

'Thanks, but I'm really not that desperate.'

'I mean, I'd say you *are*, but that's a matter for another time – put your hand on my arm, and laugh as if I've said something terribly funny. For your parents. For the people.'

'Why don't you put *your* hand on *my* arm, and laugh as if *I've* said something terribly funny?' Gwen hissed back indignantly. 'It's more realistic anyway – it can't look as if I'm succumbing to charms of yours that don't exist.'

She expected a retort, but instead she felt Arthur's hand alight gently on her elbow; he leaned towards her, as if they were deep in private and amorous conference, and then tossed his head back prettily and laughed.

'He's good at this,' Gabriel said quietly in her ear on her other side. Gwen flinched.

'Stop watching,' she said, through gritted teeth.

'I am good, though,' Arthur said, winking at Gabriel,

who looked thunderstruck and quickly turned back to face the arena.

'Don't wink at *him*,' Gwen said. 'The point is to make it seem like *we're* getting together, not that this is some kind of ... mildly incestuous free-for-all.'

'You have a truly terrifying mind,' Arthur said, leaning back in his seat. 'God – is that – that's not Excalibur?'

'The real Excalibur was lost,' Gwen said slowly, as if explaining something to an infant. 'Surely you saw the replacement here when you visited as a child?'

'You'd be surprised how little attention I pay to things that don't interest me,' Arthur said, although he *did* seem interested in the sword; he was craning his neck to get a better look at it. 'Why *is* it in a stone? Didn't some odd woman chuck it out of a pond?'

'Reports differ about how it was obtained,' said Gabriel, sounding as if he were trying not to smile. Gwen was surprised that he was being so talkative – but then, he never passed up an opportunity to wax Arthurian. 'And we could hardly present somebody with a pond.'

Arthur's brow furrowed. 'So that's, what – Excalibur version two?'

'Actually,' Gabriel said, 'it's Excalibur Nine.'

'Excalibur *Nine*?' Arthur spluttered, as if this were the most hilarious thing he'd ever heard. 'What happened to Excaliburs two through eight?'

'They – I don't know, they kept losing them,' Gwen said crossly. 'In bets, or just ... in battle. Stop *laughing*, for God's sake. Someone stole Eight, probably sold it to some Arthurian cultists somewhere, but we've had Nine for years.'

'Oh my *God*. Can anybody just . . . pull it out, and bagsy king?'

'No,' Gwen said. 'Well, I think it might be made so that nobody can remove it – but then, they'd want Father to be able to take it out, if he had to. Seriously, Arthur, stop *laughing*, be quiet . . .'

Arthur's glee was drowned out as the first knights to face each other in hand-to-hand combat were announced by the Grand Marshal, to fanfare and applause.

Gwen listened intently, until she realised that two generic *Sirs* had been announced.

'She's second,' Arthur said, having finally recovered, and Gwen snapped around to look at him.

'What?'

'I walked through the competitors' encampment before I met you. She's second, fighting a rather elderly man with a duck's feather in his helm.'

'I don't know who you're talking about,' Gwen blustered.

'That would be a lot more convincing if there were more than one knight I could be referring to when I say "she",' Arthur drawled. Gwen felt herself blushing and straightened up a little to try to maintain her composure.

The two knights approached the royal stand, helms in their hands; unable to bend the knee in their armour, they bowed awkwardly, and Gwen's father genially inclined his head in response. A woman in the front row of the neighbouring stands threw out her favour, a posy of flowers; the knight it was intended for missed it spectacularly, and then stared sadly down at it, unable to reach for it without toppling over.

'Why were you even back there with the competitors?' Gwen asked out of the corner of her mouth.

Arthur grinned. 'Talent scouting.'

Gwen's horrified response was cut off by the roar of the crowd as the two knights were given the signal to raise their swords and fight; they circled each other for a few moments before the taller of the two stepped in to strike, and then suddenly they were grappling, landing clumsy blows that rang out even over the sound of the bystanders.

'There's no art to this,' Arthur sneered, leaning back in his seat and dangling one arm over the edge of it to look artfully fatigued. 'You might as well clad a couple of bears in tin and let them have a go at each other.'

'They do, in London,' said Gwen, watching as the larger man struck the smaller so hard on the head with the flat of his sword that the latter was driven down on to his knees. 'If you're so convinced it's *easy*, why don't you enter? I'm sure my brother will lend you his sword and armour. He gets little use out of them, and he has plenty of spares.'

'Er – no I won't,' said Gabriel on her other side.

The victorious knight had his sword at his competitor's throat; he looked, for a moment, as if he might be considering using it to lethal effect, but the trumpets quickly sounded and the stands erupted into cheers and boos as he was announced the winner.

'I didn't say it was *easy*, I said it was artless. Besides, I struggle to hold a sword – I wonder why that is ...' he pretended to ponder. 'Oh *I* know, it *might* have something to do with the fact that a little ginger sadist snapped my bloody arm in half when I was a defenceless young boy.'

63

'You were never a boy,' Gwen hissed back. 'You were a demon.' Her hand had gone to her mouth, and she realised a moment later that she was chewing agitatedly at the raw skin around her nail. She promptly removed it from reach by sliding her hand under her leg.

'I don't recall breaking any of *your* bones,' he replied hotly.

'Not as if you didn't *try*,' said Gwen, but the trumpets had started up again, driving a spike of excitement through her chest.

Lady Bridget Leclair was announced to a cacophony of jeers and laughter. She strode out across the arena, her posture and bearing betraying no sign of disquiet at her reception.

The Grand Marshal hadn't announced her competitor; there was an awkward pause, the noise dying down, and then he cleared his throat. 'Fighting her today – *Sir Marlin of Coombelile.*'

'The *Knife*?' Gwen turned to Gabriel. 'She wasn't supposed to be fighting the *Knife.*'

'Who the hell is the Knife?' Arthur demanded. The crowd bellowed as Sir Marlin, clad in armour so dark and lustrous that it almost looked liquid, walked out to take his place next to Lady Leclair. He was of a height with her – from here, he looked narrower, too – but Gwen still felt nervous on Lady Leclair's behalf as she watched them both approach the royal stand.

'Oh. That'll be him then,' said Arthur, as the Knife took off his helm and slicked his dark blond hair away from his pale face. 'He's quite short.'

'So are you,' snapped Gwen. She couldn't take her eyes off Lady Leclair, savouring the rare opportunity to stare openly at her; when she removed her helm she didn't look the least bit frightened, although on closer inspection her jaw was clenched rather tightly. Her hair was pulled back into a small bun, and Gwen thought fleetingly about how much she'd like to see it fall free from its tie.

'I'm taller than you,' Arthur said, his voice squeaking a little in indignation.

'You're the same height as me,' Gwen hissed. 'Now shut *up*.'

'You are freakishly tall for a woman,' muttered Arthur, just as both competitors reached them.

They bowed, Sir Marlin perfunctorily and Lady Leclair with her hands meeting as if in prayer, and the king gave them a nod and a smile that looked significantly more like a grimace than his previous one had; they were just about to turn away when Gwen caught Bridget's eye. Gwen was too slow to pretend she hadn't been staring, and she thought she saw one corner of Bridget's mouth quirk up ever so slightly, as if she found this somehow amusing.

'Lady Leclair,' Arthur called suddenly, halting proceedings. Gwen froze, her heart pounding wildly in her chest. 'Please,' he said, flashing Bridget his most charming smile. 'Fight for *me*.' He leaned forward and presented her with a single, slightly crumpled yellow flower.

Laughter rippled through the crowd. Bridget paused for a moment, and then reached up and took his favour. Gwen felt like she could actually hear her own blood rushing around her skull; as the knights walked away to take their positions everybody else settled easily back into their seats, but she stayed upright and rigid. Her father was frowning at her. Gabriel was frowning at Arthur.

'What the *hell* was that?' she said through clenched teeth.

'Audience participation,' Arthur muttered back, his smile unwavering. Gwen *so badly* wanted to push him out of his seat. 'What's the big deal about this *Knife* man anyway?'

'He hasn't competed for years,' said Gabriel, and Gwen turned to glare at him for engaging with Arthur when he had just been so terrible. 'Because the last time he did, he killed somebody. Apparently, it wasn't intentional – the man died of his injuries after leaving the arena.'

'He sounds like a delight,' said Arthur.

'He stayed on to try to win the tournament,' Gwen said reluctantly. 'It was in dreadful taste. And then when he reached the melee everybody turned on him and gave him a good kicking. A feeling I'm sure you're used to being on the receiving end of.'

'Who does he fight for?' Arthur asked, ignoring her. 'Who sponsors a *murderer* at a stabbing contest?'

'Our father's second cousin,' Gabriel said in a low voice. 'Lord Willard.'

'Ah. Yes. I'm told my mother hated the man. Apparently if it hadn't been for her, my father might have sided with Willard and the other cultists instead of *your* father when the old king died – and just think, we would never have been betrothed. I mean, you'd also never have been born, so ... it's not so much a silver lining as it is just silver all the way down.'

'What are you *doing*?' Gwen hissed. 'That's treason. You're talking directly to royalty about *treason*.'

'Calm down. I wasn't intending to *commit* any, although you do make it ever so tempting,' Arthur said lightly. 'Now, if you don't mind – my lady is about to fight.'

Gwen bristled at 'my lady', but she didn't want to miss a moment of the fight either; she turned back to watch as the trumpets sounded for Lady Leclair and Sir Marlin to begin.

Last year during the third bout Gwen had watched Bridget compete against someone much taller and larger than she was; Gwen had felt sick with nerves watching them square up to each other, sure that Lady Leclair wouldn't make it out of the arena with all of her limbs intact. Instead, she had been quick and light on her feet – had been able to use the much larger knight's weight and lack of speed against him – and had been triumphant. They had booed her anyway, of course. They *always* booed her in single combat.

She really excelled in the lists, and for some reason the crowds didn't seem to mind so much that she was a woman when she had a lance under her arm. Gwen wished they were watching her joust now. Instead, she had to watch as the Knife feinted to the side, then leaped forward to strike.

If the fight between the previous competitors had been undignified and fumbling, this was the exact opposite. Both Lady Leclair and Sir Marlin wore lighter, thinner armour; both favoured speed over power. Bridget didn't just lead with her sword. She used her entire body – elbows, knees, even a well-timed kick. She got a few good blows in, but it was impossible to be truly agile while wielding a sword and shield. When she next tried to land a hit, the Knife stepped neatly to one side, hooked her leg and sent her sprawling. She struggled to get up; he let her try for a few seconds before raising his sword and bringing it down on her helm with such force that many of the people in the crowd groaned.

'She's already down,' Gwen said, glancing over at her father, who was talking to the queen. 'They should stop.'

'They won't while she's still trying to get back up,' Gabriel said, nodding over at Lady Leclair, who was indeed struggling to get to her feet. The Knife glanced over at the Grand Marshal, who didn't react at all, and then lifted a foot almost lazily and stamped down hard on Lady Leclair's hand as she reached for her sword.

'Stay *down*,' Gwen said, her fingers tightening against the wooden barrier in front of her. 'Why won't she just stay *down*?'

'I suppose it's not in her nature,' Arthur said, with infuriating indifference. Lady Leclair managed to get up on to one knee; the Knife struck her again, and she dropped on to all fours in the dirt. Even from the stands Gwen could see that her chest was heaving under her armour. Sir Marlin considered her with acute, predatory interest, and then kicked her hard in the side.

'She's not even armed any more,' said Gwen, her voice rising, her hands flying to her mouth. The Knife took a slow and deliberate step back, and then kicked her again. Gwen felt the impact of it jolt through her body as if *she* were the one on the ground. Lady Leclair's helm had been knocked loose, obscuring her vision; she reached up with a shaking hand to remove it, and Gwen saw that blood was pouring down her face. The crowd were still baying for more. Sir Marlin reached down to grab Bridget by the hair, hauling her towards him as her feet scrabbled for purchase, his sword raised as if he intended to strike her bared neck. Gwen gasped behind her fingers – but then the Grand Marshal finally signalled for the trumpets to be blown, and the fight was over.

The ancient rules of chivalry dictated that knights would be gallant and modest in victory, but Gwen wasn't the least bit surprised when instead of helping Lady Leclair to her feet, Sir Marlin left her where she was. He walked over to the stands to remove his helm and give a curt final bow to the king before exiting with a profoundly smug smile on his face. Bridget got up very gingerly, her squire running out to help her. As they made their way back to the competitors' tents, moving at an agonising pace, Gwen caught a glimpse of Arthur's yellow flower, crushed and forlorn in the dirt.

'Pleasant sort of people, your subjects,' Arthur said; they were all, of course, laughing.

'Can I speak to you?' Gwen said, her voice tight. 'In private.'

'Of *course*, my love,' Arthur said, getting to his feet and putting out an arm; Gwen had no choice but to take it, although she was loath to touch him. She watched her mother look up at them as they went to leave, but she only smiled again at the sight of them getting along; she couldn't hear what Gwen was whispering furiously to Arthur as they exited to the back of the stands.

'You utter *bastard* – you brought that flower just to

irritate me and to humiliate her, as if people needed any other reason to *laugh* at her—'

'Steady on,' said Arthur, yanking his arm away at the exact same time that Gwen went to remove hers. 'I'll have you know that it was entirely for *your* benefit, not hers.'

'Oh, *fantastic*, well as long as you were only trying to humiliate *me*,' Gwen fumed. 'What happened to our agreement? You've as good as told the entire city that something strange is going on, drawing all that attention to her. *Have* you told anybody?'

'No! God, you are so delusionally paranoid, you need—'

There was a commotion over by the guards standing watch at the entrance; Gwen looked up and saw Arthur's body-man attempting to get past them, looking over at Arthur and throwing up his hands in exasperation when they refused.

'It's all right,' Arthur shouted. 'He's with me.'

One of the guards turned to look at him. 'And who the hell are you?'

'He's with me,' Gwen said reluctantly, stepping forward. The guards parted and let Sidney through. He took in Gwen's crossed arms and Arthur's smirk, and laughed quietly.

'Lovers' tiff, is it?'

'*Excuse me?*' Gwen said, glaring at him in disbelief. 'Who exactly do you think you're addressing?'

'My apologies,' Sidney said, bowing his head slightly. 'Lovers' tiff, is it, your highness?'

'Let's get one thing straight,' Gwen said, turning to Arthur and brandishing a finger at him. 'You are not to try to embarrass me, you are not to play *hilarious* jokes, you are not to involve –' she dropped the volume of her voice significantly – 'to involve *Lady Leclair* in any of this for your own sick amusement—'

'Hello,' said Gabriel, appearing at her side. 'I was sent to make sure you weren't alone unchaperoned.' He looked at Sidney. 'Who's this?'

'Sidney Fitzgilbert, your highness,' Sidney said, bowing deeply without any prompting.

'Oh, so *he* gets "your highness"?' Gwen said, rounding on him. 'You arrogant, impudent little . . .'

Sidney stepped sideways, behind Arthur.

'You're supposed to protect *me*,' Arthur said indignantly. 'What the hell do you call this?'

'Not in my remit,' he replied. 'She's not going to kill you, but she looks like she might be about to start poking.'

'I wouldn't be so sure,' Gwen hissed, stepping closer, 'that I won't kill you.'

'Oh dear,' Arthur said wearily. 'She's gone feral.'

Gwen really might have slapped one of them then – either would do – but Gabriel put a gentle hand on her shoulder and she just gave a quiet little scream of frustration instead.

'This is not helpful,' Gabriel said, looking directly at Arthur. 'Stop goading my sister.' Arthur looked back at him defiantly, raising his eyebrows in a wordless challenge.

Gwen had had enough. She turned on her heel and stormed away, two guards peeling off from the group and falling into step behind her as she made for the drawbridge.

She was so angry she wasn't looking where she was going; she had to pull up so suddenly when somebody stepped into her path that she almost tripped. Immediately there was a guard at her side holding her steady, and another throwing up a sword between her and her potential assailant.

Lady Bridget Leclair looked extremely done in. She had a nasty bruise already mottling her cheek, a split in her lip, and her eye was blackening in one corner where her helm must have made contact with the bone; she was wincing as she breathed, and Gwen could only imagine how battered she must be under her tunic. It took the knight a moment to realise whom she had almost collided with, and when she did, she straightened up despite her injuries; Gwen tucked one of her plaits behind her ear, hoping she hadn't gone bright red.

'Your highness,' Bridget said, bowing with a wince and then struggling to rise again; Gwen reached out without thinking, but Bridget held up a palm to stop her. The sleeve of her tunic had slipped down to her elbow, revealing smooth gold-brown skin and hard muscle underneath.

Hands, Gwen thought hysterically. *Hands* – and also *arms*.

'Bridg— er, Lady Leclair,' she said. 'How are you? I mean, you look—'

'I'm well,' Lady Leclair lied, grimacing around her split lip. 'Forgive me – Sir Marlin was very thorough.' Her hair, Gwen noticed, hadn't stayed confined for long; strands of it were escaping, curled and damp with sweat where they touched her neck.

'He shouldn't have kept hitting you,' Gwen said impulsively. 'While you were already down.'

'Well, perhaps not,' said Bridget, her voice edged with pain. 'But I entered to fight, and a fight was what I got.'

'I – I suppose,' Gwen said, knowing she was definitely blushing now. 'I'll ... Good luck, in the rest of your events.'

'Thank you,' said Bridget. That tiny smirk Gwen had noticed on her face before was back now, even though it must have pained her; it was so subtle that Gwen could almost have been imagining it. As she went to leave, Bridget held up a hand again – not touching her, not even close, but making Gwen stop in her tracks regardless. 'And – please, thank your suitor. For his favour.'

'He's not my suitor,' Gwen said quickly, before realising how ridiculous this would sound, given the fact that they were trying to convince everybody in Camelot of the opposite. 'I mean – yes. Thanks. I will.'

'He's not your suitor,' Bridget repeated, maintaining a steady eye contact that Gwen thought might perhaps kill her. She had no idea what to say in response to this. When Bridget removed her hand and stepped back, Gwen simply nodded awkwardly, and then continued up to the slope towards the drawbridge.

She spent the rest of the day wondering what on earth it could have meant.

6

Arthur liked his rooms at Camelot. The main space was cramped but cosy, filled with a table, Sidney's cot and two well-padded chairs by the fireplace. The adjoining bedroom contained a four-poster so large that it constituted gross overkill. The best feature was the tiny terrace, just big enough for him and Sidney to breakfast on. It certainly helped that the guest quarters were entirely separate from the royal family's wing; his rooms were, in fact, as far away from Gwen's as it was possible to be on this side of the castle. Arthur wondered if Gwen had chosen them on his behalf.

'This is nice,' Sidney said as they ate. 'Could get used to it.'

'What – waking up with me every morning? If you want to marry me, just ask,' said Arthur, through a mouthful of bread. 'It'd solve a lot of my current problems.'

'I meant the view,' said Sidney. 'You couldn't marry me. I'd be too much for you. Romantically speaking.'

'Sometimes I think you forget that I'm your boss,' said Arthur, swallowing the bread and reaching for a cup of ale to wash it down. 'I could have you roundly flogged for saying things like that.'

'Hmm,' said Sidney. 'On second thoughts, I think you could romance me just fine.'

Arthur snorted. 'Haven't you been running around after that lady-in-waiting, pelting her with sugared buns?'

'Ah, Agnes,' Sidney said, sighing dreamily. 'They won't let me anywhere near that bit of the castle. And anyway, I'm too busy running around after you, watching you get shouted at by pubescent princesses.'

'Well,' Arthur said, sighing for entirely different reasons. 'Consider yourself free of responsibility today. I won't be going beyond the castle walls. I'm being frogmarched to an audience with the king for lunch.'

'Sounds like plenty of potential for trouble, to me.'

'How much trouble could I possibly get up to without leaving the grounds?' Arthur said indignantly.

Sidney pointed a stern finger at him. 'Those words will come back to me in a moment of vivid clarity later as I watch you being clapped in irons or hauled out of the moat.'

'Fine, Sid, you're *not* free of responsibility. I task you to go into the city and locate the very best drinking establishments for our use at a later date. Scope them out, count the entrances and exits—'

'Sample the libations?' Sidney said hopefully, perking up.

'Sample all the bloody libations you want,' Arthur said, grinning. Sidney immediately got to his feet, disappeared back into their rooms and came back out seconds later wearing his cleanest coat. 'Oh, right. You're going now, then?'

'No time like the present,' said Sidney, reaching for his cup and draining the last of his ale.

'Sid, it's ten o'clock in the morning.' Sidney hovered, as if awaiting further admonition. 'No, I mean, I'm just *impressed*. Off you go. Try not to make the women weep.'

'At the sight of me?' Sidney said, patting his pockets to check he was sufficiently funded.

'You can't do my punchlines for me,' Arthur said crossly. 'They're quite literally all I have.'

At home Arthur's chief occupation had been responsibilities, the avoidance thereof; his father had given up on attempting to engage him in politics or the minutiae of running the family's affairs when he realised that no matter how much he screamed, threatened or threw things at him, his son remained determinedly uninterested. Instead of dragging him along to meetings or taking him to suppers peppered with influential people, Lord Delacey had contented himself with verbally flagellating Arthur whenever their paths crossed. As far as his father was concerned, his betrothal to Gwendoline was the only proof that he had ever made himself useful to another living person. Arthur had responded to all of this by being out of the house as much as possible without technically being classed as a runaway.

As a result, even a castle as vast as Camelot felt oppressive and claustrophobic. After dressing, Arthur started walking aimlessly around it, exploring the reaches he hadn't encountered during his first week, trying to find his way by memory alone. There were two courtyards in the north of the castle in addition to the larger one to the south; he thought he remembered that the armoury was attached to the one in the north-west, and was pleased with himself when he visited to check and found himself correct. Other times, his memory failed him; he kept running into dead ends around corners and at the end of long, dusty galleries, and every time he approached the rooms in the most northerly part of the castle the guards would send him back the way he'd come with a shake of their heads. Clearly Gwen had not let them know that he was meant to be enjoying special privileges.

There were quite a lot of people walking around, and they all seemed to have jobs; many of them nodded at Arthur as he passed, and he acknowledged them while wondering who the hell they were. He supposed a large cast of miscellaneous castle-dwellers was required to keep the whole thing running, but had no idea where, for example, the two young men carrying a crate of tiny horse statuettes could have been going with such urgency.

Arthur made his way out into the bailey, and immediately felt more lost than ever. Everything seemed to have swapped places since his childhood; apparently the orchard was one of the only things that had been immoveable. All manner of new buildings had sprung up or been relocated, and he set about trying to catalogue them. Ice house, dovecot, forge, buttery. Almost by accident, he opened a tiny and unfamiliar door in an unremarkable-looking exterior wall and stumbled into a garden so beautiful that it stopped him in his tracks.

It was a rose garden, partially shaded from above by wooden trellises that were covered in soft yellow climbing roses in bloom; raised beds were arranged in concentric diamonds, broken up with small sculptures and stone benches. It was completely private, with only one entrance in, and nothing that overlooked it. In the very centre of the garden there was a large statue; before he'd reached it, Arthur knew exactly who would be frowning down at him.

King Arthur had seen better days. His nose was chipped, and two of his fingers had broken off. His beard was still intact, rendered in startling detail; in fact, his face was almost entirely obscured by meticulously carved bristles, his beady eyes staring out from underneath enormous eyebrows. Arthur reached out a hand and touched the rough, well-worn surface of the stone sword clutched in the king's hands; it was almost as tall as he was.

'Hullo, you old bastard,' he said flatly. 'Shagged any of your sisters lately?'

He was startled when the statue seemed to make a sound in response; this mystery was solved by the sudden appearance of a skinny, battle-worn ginger tabby cat, which gave the statue an affectionate headbutt before abandoning it for the flesh-and-blood Arthur and wrapping itself around his legs.

'How the hell did you get in here?' Arthur said, crouching to offer a hand; the cat closed its eyes blissfully, and pressed its little pink nose into his palm. 'On your way to corrupt the royal purebreds, I imagine.' He gave it a scratch under the chin; the cat purred loudly and then bit down on his index finger. Arthur swore and retracted his hand, but the cat hadn't drawn blood. It looked extremely pleased with itself.

'I like you,' Arthur said approvingly. 'Try not to get exterminated.' A bell began to ring somewhere in the distance, and Arthur's stomach lurched. After an entire morning of aimless wandering to kill time, he was somehow going to be late.

As he rushed from the courtyard, he was nearly tripped up by a flash of orange fur slipping between his ankles. He sprinted towards the main buildings, trying to smooth down his hair and tunic as he did so; it was only as he reached the east door, out of breath from trying to maintain a loping half-jog, that he noticed the cat was still at his heels.

'Begone, tiny demon,' he hissed over his shoulder. The cat blinked back at him, and then sloped off in the opposite direction as the guards let Arthur inside. As he approached the labyrinth of rooms that made up the king's private cabinets and day chambers, he slowed down, hoping that he wasn't too visibly sweaty. He was admitted without ceremony, and moments later was standing at the end of a wood-panelled room dominated by a very large table. The king sat alone at the far end.

The table was rectangular. *Extremely* rectangular, thought Arthur, as if perhaps the king were making a point of it.

'I see you're admiring the furniture,' the king said, glancing briefly up from his papers.

'Your majesty,' Arthur said, remembering himself and bowing.

'Yes, yes, hello, Arthur. Sit down,' said the king. Faced with at least fifteen chairs and absolutely no idea what was appropriate, Arthur hovered for a moment before taking a seat about three places down from him, which felt a safe and respectful distance.

There was quite a long silence. Arthur, who distinctly remembered that the word 'lunch' had been bandied about, looked hopefully at the door to see if sustenance was forthcoming; it was not.

'The last time you were here,' the king said finally, 'you set fire to something.'

Arthur grimaced down at his hands. 'Yes. I mean – my apologies.'

'What was it, do you recall?'

Arthur pretended to think about it. 'Er – I believe it was your wife, sire.'

'That's right,' said the king evenly. 'It was only my son's quick thinking that stopped her entire dress from going up in flames.'

'It was actually *Gwendoline*, your majesty, who lit the candle in the . . . Never mind,' Arthur muttered, seeing the king's expression and thinking better of his protestations.

'There is a time and place for dwelling on the past,' the king said, observing Arthur thoughtfully. 'I firmly believe that we should respect what has come before, but be sure that we are always learning from it; to emulate the good, and acknowledge the bad, and always be striving towards progress.'

'Right,' said Arthur, not entirely sure where this was going. 'I agree.'

'I have heard from many sources – my daughter chief among them – that your general conduct since we last met has been less than exemplary. So much so that I am pleasantly surprised to find that in the few days you've been here, nobody I hold dear has been set aflame . . . yet.'

Arthur opened his mouth to respond, but realised he had nothing to say in his own defence.

'I have great respect for your family, Arthur, and I have been grateful for your father's continued support since your mother passed on. She and I were old friends and allies, and I felt her loss keenly – although, of course, not as keenly as you yourself. It was good of your father to stand with me after she was gone, being of ... well, more of Arthurian persuasion than anything else himself. The blood that runs in your veins made Camelot what it was—'

'Not really,' Arthur said, realising too late that he had interrupted, which was quite high on the list of things you weren't supposed to do to kings.

'Not—?'

'I only meant – if there is any of Arthur Pendragon's blood in me, sire, it's diluted well past the point of consequence.' To his surprise, the king let out a small exhalation of laughter at this.

'Well. Your father has always been very proud of where he came from, however distant that line may be now. You are part of the fabric of England, and you will help write her future. Which brings me to the matter at hand.' Arthur shifted uncomfortably in his seat. He always dreaded arriving at *the matter at hand*. 'Leave whatever battle you're fighting in the past, Arthur. You will be the Lord of Maidvale. You will be my daughter's husband. Do not make me live to regret the choice I made when Gwendoline was born. Because if I do, then make no mistake – *you* will feel that regret tenfold.'

There were quite a few things that Arthur considered

saying in response to this, but sanity prevailed. 'Yes, your majesty. I . . . Thank you. I understand.'

'Good,' said the king. He pulled his papers towards him again, and Arthur sat awkwardly for a second, watching him. The king glanced back up, seeming mildly confused that he was still there. 'You are dismissed.'

Arthur didn't need telling twice.

When Sidney got back to their rooms, Arthur had been lying face down on his bed for the best part of three hours. After retiring from his meeting with the king, he'd heard a strange scrabbling at his door, and upon opening it had been baffled to find that the little ginger cat had managed to track him down; he watched as it slinked into his room and hopped up on to the bed for a nap, and had come to the conclusion that it had the right idea about how to spend the rest of the day.

'Who's this?' Sidney said, poking Arthur on the shoulder and then gesturing at the cat.

'My cat,' said Arthur, as if this should have been obvious.

'Right,' said Sidney doubtfully. 'What's it called?'

Arthur turned his head and squinted at the cat, which was currently licking itself in unfortunate places on top of his silk pillowcase. 'Lucifer.'

'Good meeting then, was it?' Sidney said, producing a bottle of wine and putting it down on Arthur's desk. He took off his jacket, too, and then started relieving himself of a number of small daggers he liked to wear discreetly about his person.

'The king thinks that if I try *really* hard, I can become as great a man as my father,' Arthur said listlessly.

'Ouch,' said Sidney, with a sympathetic wince. 'Want to hear my review of the great city of Camelot?' Arthur nodded, and Sidney sat down on the edge of the bed. 'Shithole. Everything's falling apart. Few good inns though. Auditioned them all.'

'Don't let the king hear you call it a shithole,' said Arthur, reaching out to stroke the cat. 'It's his pet project.'

'Fine, it's *up-and-coming*,' said Sidney. 'He could have just settled at Winchester like everybody else for the past ten million years, or given London a go if he wanted to modernise, but he had to give this old relic one last gasp.'

'All right, well, you've really sold me on it,' Arthur said, retracting his hand as the cat attempted to shred it. 'I need you to carry a note for me. We're going out tonight.'

'Out,' said Sidney, 'or *out*?'

'What do *you* think?'

Sidney just sighed, picked up one of his daggers and slid it back into place in his belt.

Arthur knocked on the door for a second time, his brow furrowing.

'She knows we're coming,' he said to Sidney, who shrugged. 'The guard let us through.'

Arthur was about to knock for a third time when the door opened; a pretty face with a faint scattering of freckles over the bridge of its slightly upturned nose was looking warily at them through the gap.

'Good evening, Agnes,' said Arthur. 'I believe we were expected?'

'My lord,' Agnes said, with a little curtsy. She pulled the door fully open to let them in.

'Bloody hell,' said Sidney, as they walked into a room at least twice the size of theirs; it contained a dining table that seated six, a set of floor-to-ceiling bookshelves and an enormous fireplace carved all over with flowers and gurning cherubs. Soft, cushioned chairs were arranged regimentally around the hearth, which was carpeted with a plush and extremely expensive-looking rug. In the corner there was a thickly padded cot, with blankets and cushions stacked neatly. It was *too* clean. The only sign of life was a vase full of bluebells on the dresser by the window. 'This is a *very* nice room.'

'Her highness will be with you in a moment,' Agnes said, smiling shyly at Sidney and then retreating through an adjoining door.

'There's no way she's read all these,' Sidney said, straying over to the bookshelves and picking a book at random.

'I wouldn't be so sure,' said Arthur, throwing himself into one of the armchairs and immediately putting his feet up on the upholstery. 'She's got nothing else to do.'

'Hello,' Gwendoline said warily from the doorway. Her eyes swept over Sidney mauling her books and Arthur's boots on her armchair, but Agnes was watching them, so she just treated them to a very tight and unconvincing smile.

'Evening. Wine?' Arthur said, pointing at Sidney, who put down the book and presented a bottle with a flourish.

'Agnes,' Gwendoline said with some effort. 'Could you please pour the boys some wine, and then – and then you're dismissed.'

Agnes looked startled. 'But ... you want me to leave you *alone* with him?' she said, her voice dipping to a loud whisper.

'Yes,' said Gwendoline firmly. Agnes did as she was told and then left, glancing back over her shoulder with wide-eyed astonishment.

'Why did she have to leave?' said Sidney, sounding genuinely disappointed, knocking back most of his glass in one gulp.

'Get your feet off my chair,' Gwendoline snapped at Arthur. In the interest of temporarily keeping the peace, Arthur did. 'Sending her away is much more effective than having her sit here and listen to us pretend at being sweethearts. If the guards don't talk, then *Agnes* certainly will. She'll tell her noble friends at court; it'll be all over the castle by tomorrow that we're being hideously indecorous, because we're so *terribly* in love.'

'So you don't want any wine then,' Sidney said. Gwendoline gave him a withering look.

'I'm going to go back to my bedroom to read,' she said. 'You can sit out here and drink as much as you want. Just let me know when our great romance is over for the evening.'

'Ah – actually,' said Arthur, getting up and crossing to the mirror on the opposite wall so that he could check his reflection. 'We'll be heading out.' He took a length of ribbon out of his pocket and used it to tie up his hair, twisting it expertly into a knot at the nape of his neck.

'What do you mean, heading out?' Gwendoline said, crossing her arms. 'I thought the whole point was that we're supposed to be having a – a clandestine evening together. How does that work, if you're not even here?'

Sidney walked over to the windows and started methodically checking them, opening each one and popping his head out to peer around before moving on to the next. 'Got one,' he announced.

'I'd ask if you've ever climbed out of one of these, but that would be a silly question, wouldn't it?' said Arthur, reaching into his pocket and pulling out a rather squashed, wide-brimmed hat with a feather in it. He stretched it out with his hands and then pulled it low over his eyes.

'Out of the *window*?' Gwendoline said incredulously.

'That's what I thought,' said Arthur. He whipped off his jacket, turned it inside out and then put it back on again. The outside was dark green embroidered satin, but the lining was brown and nondescript.

'There's a tricky bit where the masonry's coming apart, but otherwise it's a piece of cake,' said Sidney. 'Do you want me to leave this, or can I take it with me?' He was holding up the bottle of wine.

'But – people will *see* you,' Gwendoline spluttered. 'The guards, for one thing—'

'Ah,' said Arthur knowingly. 'That's where you're wrong. Because we've timed it, and there's a tasty little break in the patrols that leaves just enough time for two dashing young whippersnappers to make a run for it.'

'Well, what about the guards at the gate?' Gwendoline countered. 'They'll certainly see you.'

'And say what?' said Arthur. Sidney had wedged the cork back into the bottle, tucked the wine into his jacket and hauled himself out on to the windowsill; he glanced down with the tip of his tongue sticking out in concentration, judging the distance, before dropping out of sight. 'A manservant and a nondescript man in a hideously unfash-ionable hat slipped past their defences and off into the night? The *horror*. Agnes and the guards outside will still think *I'm* here secretly meeting with you.'

'But . . .' Gwendoline tried again. 'Where are you *going*?'

Arthur climbed out after Sidney and then grinned back at her over the sill. '*Out*,' he said, enjoying the half-furious, half-baffled expression on her face before he found the next foothold and disappeared from her view.

The pure, unadulterated joy he derived from annoying her buoyed him all the way out of the gates, past the guards and down the hill until they reached the busy streets of Camelot. They were narrow and winding, turning back on themselves and producing dead ends with no rhyme or reason, ramshackle rows of houses suddenly and dramatic-ally interrupted by large statues of Galahad clutching the grail, or Gawain in his little sash. Everything smelt like blackened meat, soiled straw and woodsmoke; they seemed to be walking down another dead-end alley when they finally reached the inn Sidney had picked out for them.

They took up residence in a back corner on rickety stools, watching all manner of people competing for the innkeeper's attention, laughing and shouting and spilling their drinks on to the already ale-soaked floor. Arthur took a glass of wine, and then another, knowing he shouldn't but finding it difficult to care; he felt the day slide away from him until the conversation with the king could have happened to somebody else and been recounted to him second-hand. Sidney kept fetching him drinks, and he kept knocking them back, and when an elderly man started singing an extremely explicit drinking song he joined in heartily, raising his hands aloft as if conducting the crowd.

Just as he was getting tired, and the last glass of wine was starting to feel sour in his stomach, he saw a sandy-haired boy watching him from over by the bar. He looked painfully familiar; for a second Arthur thought that a ghost from his past had somehow followed him all the way to Camelot. He blinked a few times, and realised the boy *was* familiar, although he wasn't the ghost in question. Mitchell from the feast ducked his head and looked a little pink when he noticed Arthur staring back.

Sidney said something in his ear, but Arthur wasn't listening. When he glanced back up, Mitchell was looking at him curiously; as Arthur watched, he raised his eyebrows and then glanced towards the back door of the inn, which opened out into a cramped alleyway. Sidney looked from Arthur to the bar and took it all in remarkably quickly.

'It's . . . You know that's not him,' he said quietly.

Arthur shrugged. 'No, but – I know him. He works with dogs.'

'Does he now? Well, it's your funeral. Ten minutes,' said Sidney, swapping seats so that he had eyes on the door.

Arthur watched as Mitchell shouldered through the crowd to reach it and disappeared into the alley without a backwards glance. He drained the rest of his drink, smoothed down his jacket and then followed.

Gwen was desperate for her bed.

She had been pretending to herself that her book was just *so* scintillating she couldn't possibly retire yet, but in reality she had read the same line five times in a row and not taken in a word. The longer Arthur was gone, the more annoyed she became. She found herself listening for signs of his return – drunken shouting from below, perhaps, or the scream of somebody missing a foothold and plummeting to their very timely demise – and was surprised when her only warning that his arrival was imminent was the sound of somebody swearing faintly right underneath her window. A second later, Arthur tumbled through it. He was no longer wearing a jacket, and his hat was filthy, as if it had been dropped repeatedly and placed back on his head.

'Good evening,' he said from the floor. Gwen slammed her book shut and stood up.

'For God's sake, Arthur, you were gone for four hours. Where's your – where's Sidney?'

'Regrettably,' Arthur said, getting to his feet with considerable effort, 'he was too drunk to make the climb.'

'Oh, and you're not?' Gwen said, casting a disapproving eye over him.

'I'm here, aren't I,' he said bitterly, taking off his hat. Most of his hair had already managed to come loose from its knot, but he untied the rest and pushed it away from his flushed face.

'Tell Agnes she can come back in,' Gwen said, watching as he walked unsteadily towards the door. 'She'll be in the ladies' solar, just before the guards. And ... we're going to the joust together first thing tomorrow. Meet me in the entrance hall.'

Arthur made no sign of having heard this. 'A delight, as always, Gwendoline. Hope you enjoyed your book.'

'Just as much as you enjoyed *debasing* yourself, I'm sure,' Gwen hissed after him, reluctant to let him have the last word.

'You have no idea,' he said over his shoulder, before he closed the door behind him.

At breakfast, Gwen was practically falling asleep in her food. Her parents were conferring with Lord Stafford, who was standing at her father's shoulder dressed in scarlet and looking gaudily anxious; on a normal day their conversation would have been well worth eavesdropping on, but this morning Gwen was only capable of leaning her head on one hand and pretending to listen to Gabriel, who was talking to her about market fluctuations.

'It's amazing how much bread can tell us about society,' he was saying now, pointing to a passage in his book.

'Bread,' Gwen said, picking some up and shoving it into her mouth. '*Amazing.*'

'Gwendoline, please don't talk with your mouth full,' her mother said from down the table. 'And I'd like to speak to you when you're finished eating.' Gwen sat up a little straighter. She'd been expecting a conversation like this, but perhaps not so soon.

Ten minutes later her father got up from the table to leave with Stafford, kissing the queen as he went and passing a quick hand over Gwen's head in both greeting and farewell. Gabriel only noticed that he was supposed to be leaving too when their mother cleared her throat loudly. He snapped his book shut and slipped from the room with a curious glance back at Gwen, who rolled her eyes in response.

'I've just heard something troubling about a visitor to your rooms last night,' her mother said, steepling her fingers and considering Gwen evenly.

'I don't . . . Who told you that? Was it Agnes?' Gwen said, going red.

'No, it wasn't *Agnes*. Stafford was informed—'

'Lord *Stafford*? Did he have his ear pressed against the door to my chambers?' Gwen said hotly. It didn't matter that *she* knew she'd done nothing wrong, or that this had been the plan all along; she still felt horribly uncomfortable knowing what everybody *else* must be thinking. While she supposed this sort of thing did fall within Stafford's remit, he rarely paid this much attention to her – usually, she didn't need much managing.

'He had it from Sir Hurst, who was told in confidence. *Gwendoline*. Did Arthur visit you last night? In your *rooms*? Unaccompanied?'

'Um,' said Gwen, clenching both hands under the table. 'Yes, he visited me. But we *were* accompanied, Mother. His servant was there, and Agnes was – around. We just sat by the fire and . . . talked.'

Her mother sighed and sat back in her seat, her eyes roaming Gwen's face. She looked more thoughtful than angry, which was something.

'Gwendoline, I'm – I'm pleasantly surprised that you're getting along so well, but I must say I'm astonished at your behaviour. *Betrothed* is not *married*, and you must take every precaution—'

'*Mother*,' Gwen squeaked before this hideous sentence could continue. 'I assure you, there's no need – we really were just *talking*. I want to know the man who's going to be my husband. I thought you'd be pleased.'

'Well . . . I am pleased,' said her mother. 'But if I might recommend a modicum of propriety, Gwendoline? We don't need the entire castle talking about it.'

'Message received,' said Gwen, still bright red.

The queen sighed in a long-suffering way, and then put her hand to Gwen's cheek. 'Just think, all those years you spent resisting everything a future bride ought to be, hiding yourself away like a recluse – and it was all for nothing! I hope you see now how silly you've been.'

Gwen felt something in her chest harden as she pulled away. 'Right. Can I . . . I'm supposed to meet Arthur for the joust.'

'Yes. Your father and I won't be there, I'm joining him for an audience with the northern guard after his morning briefing – so please *behave*.'

'I always do,' Gwen said truthfully.

Arthur wasn't in the entrance hall when he was supposed to be. Gwen waited for what felt like an age, getting more and more frustrated, before stalking out of the door with guards scrambling to keep up with her.

Today the arena's tilting rails had been raised for the joust. The air was already pungent with the smells of horse shit, trampled straw and spilt ale warming in the sun. Without the king present, the atmosphere had shifted slightly. It was wilder – more celebratory, far less formal.

It felt strange to enter the royal stands alone. Even without her parents there, Gwen didn't feel comfortable taking one of their thrones, and she took her usual seat awkwardly, her gaze on her lap as she felt many eyes on her. She'd never adjusted to this, despite the fact that it had been happening her entire life; she still distinctly remembered when, aged seven, she'd asked Gabriel what everybody was staring at as they'd entered a feast in some viscount's great hall. He had shushed her with a wry smile, and later had gently explained that they were considered the most important people in any room; nay, in the whole of *England*. It was just as disquieting now as it had been then.

She was looking so determinedly at her hands that it took a while to notice a guard standing at the entrance to the stands trying to catch her attention; when she finally looked up, he seemed extremely relieved.

'Your highness, forgive me. There's a – a lady here,' he said, apparently struggling with some aspect of this sentence, 'who says she was sent a royal invitation to join you.'

Baffled, Gwen glanced behind him, and then froze; Lady

Bridget Leclair was standing there, flanked by guards, looking straight at Gwen. She was wearing men's clothes again, a dark tunic with a simple belt, a shortsword at her hip. The cut on her lip was beginning to heal, and one side of her face was covered in blotchy purple and yellow bruising. The guards were all staring at her as if she were a lost dragon.

Gwen realised she was also agape, and quickly closed her mouth. She certainly hadn't sent any 'royal invitation', but she could hardly turn her away now.

'Oh. Well – thank you.'

'Should I ask her to disarm, your highness?'

'No, no, it's fine. Let her through.' Gwen settled back into her seat and tried to look as if she were utterly *fascinated* by the knights currently being announced to raucous cheering as Lady Leclair made her way along the row.

'Your highness,' she said stiffly, with a tiny bow. Gwen just stared at her for a moment before realising that she was waiting for permission to sit down, and nodded awkwardly at the seat to her left. Arthur had lounged in it, as if born to sit there; Bridget settled in with perfect posture and quiet confidence. Gwen sat bolt upright in her own chair as if strapped into some kind of torture device.

Arthur. Of course. The only person who'd dare send an invitation on her behalf. She was going to *kill* him. It was incredible, really, that he hadn't managed to make it out of bed to join her, but *had* found the time to engineer another plan designed to humiliate her.

'You're not – you aren't entering the lists today?' Gwen asked eventually to break the silence, watching as one of the knights tried to calm his horse, which was currently walking jerkily backwards and rolling its eyes agitatedly.

'No,' Bridget said slowly. 'I need a little time to recover. But I assumed . . . you knew that. The note said—'

'Who brought it?' Gwen interrupted, mainly to avoid finding out how horrific the contents had been.

'Ah,' Bridget said. 'I see.' She rolled one of her shoulders back as if it were paining her, and Gwen heard something click. 'Cropped black hair. Stocky build.'

'Yes,' Gwen said darkly. 'I know him. Listen, Lady Leclair, I'm—'

She had to stop speaking suddenly when she realised that the knights were approaching her awkwardly to present themselves to her in her father's stead. When they bowed from their saddles, Gwen gave them a stiff nod in return, not quite managing to smile. The silence between her and Bridget felt very charged as they rode away to take their starting positions.

'You didn't send it,' Bridget said matter-of-factly. Gwen turned to her, imagining that she might be confused by this revelation, but she was just looking at Gwen expectantly.

'No, I think – I think an acquaintance of mine was trying to vex me,' Gwen spluttered, as the Grand Marshal signalled for the knights to make themselves ready. Bridget was still looking at her very intently.

'What about me,' Bridget said in a low, amused voice that sent a thrill up Gwen's spine, 'is so particularly vexing?'

Gwen was spared answering by the start of the event; the knights urged their horses forwards, the crowd increasing in fervour and volume until the two competitors met with a dull crack. One of the horses had spooked at the last moment, and while one lance had splintered, the other had veered wildly off target. The knight who had broken his lance had won the round without receiving a single blow from his opponent; he also, however, had a rather large piece of splintered wood sticking out of his cheek.

Gwen watched with grim fascination as he dismounted and his squire came rushing to his aid; he attempted to pull it out, and the crowd reacted with cheers and groans of sympathy as this only seemed to make him bleed more profusely. The sound of the knight's swearing – slightly garbled, as he was unable to move one side of his face – got fainter as he walked away towards the competitors' encampment.

'Not much of a victory,' said Bridget, watching him go.

'Well, I'm sure they'll be able to get it out, and then he'll be able to celebrate – although, might be hard to drink wine with a hole in his face, as it'll just all sort of . . . pour out of him, like a human thurible . . .' Gwen trailed off, wishing she had just said, 'Yes.'

'No,' Bridget said. Her eyes were smiling, even if her mouth wasn't. 'I meant . . . You want to have a few runs at each other. Get your blood up.'

'Is that why you do it?' Gwen asked. 'To get your blood . . . pumping?'

In retrospect the word 'pumping' did not seem an auspicious choice, but Bridget didn't seem to notice Gwen's compounding misery.

'That's part of it,' she said, one hand going to her mouth, her thumb probing gently at the bruising until she winced.

She looked sideways at Gwen, who was transfixed. 'I like some risk now and again, if what's at stake is worth having. Plus, it's nice to have a win. We don't get a lot of those.'

The Grand Marshal was announcing the next to joust: Sir Woolcott, an absolutely enormous man whose steed barely seemed to be holding him up, and . . .

'The Knife,' Gwen hissed as soon as she recognised him sitting astride his gleaming black horse, not bothering to raise a hand to the crowd, half of which was already booing him. She didn't temper her expression as both of the knights came to pay her their respects, their bows really no more than nods, and narrowed her eyes at Sir Marlin's back as he trotted away.

'You shouldn't call him that,' Bridget said mildly. 'The Knife, I mean. Giving him a sinister nickname elevates him. Makes him sound like he's more than a man.'

'I'll just call him *that bastard* then,' Gwen said, surprising herself with her own vehemence. 'To make it clear that I consider him significantly *less* than a man.'

Bridget laughed quietly. 'Ah. You're not fond of him, I take it.'

'Oh *yes*,' said Gwen heatedly, 'I have him over for sleep-overs in my chambers all the time. We eat sweets and talk about which of the knights of the round table we'd most like to marry if they were still alive, and then we laugh about his delightful propensity to hit people repeatedly over the head when they're already on the ground.'

'I told you that wasn't personal,' said Bridget.

'It was your personal face he battered,' said Gwen. 'Your lip he split. That feels pretty personal to me.'

'Spoken like a woman who's never been in combat.'

'You're the only woman who's ever been in combat,' Gwen countered.

Bridget's nonchalance faltered. 'God. You don't really believe that, do you?'

There was a burst of fanfare, and then the horse's hoofs were pounding the ground as their riders levelled their lances. *Knock him off his horse*, Gwen silently urged Sir Woolcott. *Knock him* off *and then* under *his horse.*

When they did come together, it seemed her prayers had been answered; Sir Marlin was hit so hard that the momentum threw him halfway out of the saddle. The horse was pushed off balance too, and they seemed to hover precariously at an impossible angle before both man and beast came crashing down into the sand. The stands erupted, screaming for Sir Woolcott, who had pulled up his horse and was holding his broken lance aloft in victory.

The Knife was still down; neither he nor his horse seemed able to get up, as they were thoroughly entangled with both each other and the tilting rail. Sir Woolcott dismounted and approached, walking with an exaggerated swagger; Gwen expected him to reach out a hand to help his opponent, to take the horse's halter and urge it up, but instead he looked around at the crowd, bathing in their adoration, and then slowly and deliberately unsheathed his sword.

'He wouldn't,' said Bridget quietly, her eyes narrowed.

'Wouldn't ... what?'

'Sir Woolcott was blooded in local tourneys. I have no idea how he came by his title – he certainly didn't have one the last time I encountered him. There are far fewer rules in those independent tournaments, and ... well, he's not the greatest thinker. And he enjoys the spectacle of violence. It's not a reassuring combination.' Bridget wasn't looking at Gwen as she spoke; she was leaning forward in her seat, body tense, hands braced against the barrier as if she were moments away from leaping right over it. 'If the people keep cheering for him, there's no telling what he might do. Why won't the Grand Marshal call to *stop*?'

Gwen craned her neck, looking for Sir Blackwood. 'He's not in his seat,' she said. It came out barely louder than a whisper. Sir Blackwood was often not where he was supposed to be; even Gwen had heard the rumours that the Grand Marshal had turned drinker and gambler in recent years. She knew her father had been too busy to push the matter, but if it came to light that he had left his post to settle his debts while needless blood was spilt in the arena, there'd be hell to pay. 'Oh, God. Look at the crowd.' They were all up in their seats, chanting Sir Woolcott's name. He had removed his helm and was grinning back at them, clearly emboldened by their frenzy.

'This is the king's tourney,' Bridget said, finally facing Gwen. Her expression was furious; it was hard to look at somehow, like trying to stare directly into the sun. 'Everybody here knows the terms. We fight according to the rules of chivalry.'

'My father isn't here,' Gwen said weakly, gesturing to the empty seats next to her.

Bridget's eyes tightened. 'Then this is *your* tourney.'

Gwen could see the logic in this, but in reality she felt no more in charge than the pageboys who put down fresh straw between tilts. Not even her own lady-in-waiting took her seriously; why would anybody else?

She watched helplessly as Sir Woolcott advanced on the Knife, who was still trapped beneath his panicking horse.

'Call the round,' said Bridget. 'Come on. Tell them to stop.'

Gwen looked up at her, horrified. 'I can't do that,' she said. 'It's not for me to . . . They won't *listen* to me anyway.'

'He's going to kill him if you don't,' Bridget insisted. '*Say* something.'

'I'm sorry,' Gwen said, paralysed by fear and guilt. 'I don't – I really don't think I can.'

How could Bridget not see that she was asking the impossible? And besides – somebody else would surely step in. If they just held on for a few more seconds, one of the other knights would intervene, or the Grand Marshal would return, and the trumpets would sound. The Knife would get up, Sir Woolcott would be reprimanded, and they'd call in the next competitors with no harm done.

'Fine,' said Bridget, flexing her fingers against the railing. '*Fine.*' Before Gwen could blink, she had jumped the barrier and landed lightly on the ground below. She unsheathed her sword from her belt and strode towards the two knights. The reaction from the crowd was immediate and deafening.

Bridget ducked under the tilting rail and placed herself squarely between the Knife and Sir Woolcott, shoulders back, hands steady. The latter looked at her, his chest heaving, almost vibrating with adrenaline, and then threw back his head and laughed.

'You won, sir. Put your sword away,' Bridget said, her voice low; Gwen had to strain to catch it.

'*You*,' scoffed Sir Woolcott. 'You make a mockery of this tournament.'

'If I do, then I'm about to have company,' Bridget said evenly. 'You and I both know there's no honour in fighting a man who's already down.'

'No?' shouted Sir Woolcott for all to hear, playing to his eager crowd. 'Let's see what honour I can find in fighting a mangey, jumped-up *bitch* who doesn't know her place.'

The crowd roared its approval. Gwen watched with her heart in her mouth.

Bridget pushed her hair away from her face and adjusted her stance ever so slightly, readying herself. *This is ridiculous*, Gwen thought faintly. *She's covered head-to-toe in bruises, and she doesn't even have her armour on.*

This thought was finally enough to get Gwen on her feet; she almost tripped over her hem in her rush to the end of the royal stand. The guard standing there was watching the fight, transfixed.

'Please go and fetch the Grand Marshal,' Gwen said. He couldn't hear her over the sound of the crowd, and leaned in as she tried again. 'You have to – please, get Sir Blackwood, *now*.'

The guard nodded, and called over another of her father's men. Gwen turned back to the arena just in time to see Sir Woolcott swing his sword at Bridget with such velocity that when she dodged neatly out of the way it stuck fast in the dirt. Bridget could have struck, but she didn't seem to want to hurt him; she attempted to take out his legs, to

101

unbalance him as he yanked at the blade, but he stayed standing, solid and immoveable as a brutish tree.

Gwen looked behind her desperately, hoping to see the Grand Marshal hurrying to his seat, but he was nowhere to be found. Some of the other competing knights had been drawn from their encampment, and seemed to be considering intervening; a few were already reaching for their weapons. She heard a clash of swords again; Bridget was on the ground, her weapon held above her head, Sir Woolcott's pressing down against it and eliciting a tortuous, shrill squeal as steel met steel.

Bridget was going to lose. He was going to wound her, perhaps mortally, and not even the knights with their swords drawn would be there in time to stop it. Gwen suddenly felt dangerously light-headed as the entire scene in front of her seemed to slide sideways, falling from her grip – but then she heard a voice ringing out across the arena.

'*Stop.*'

The crowd quieted, and all heads turned. Gwen sagged against the barrier in her relief. Her father was here. Her father had come, and Bridget was saved.

When she turned, however, it was not her father, but Gabriel – he was standing at the entrance to the royal stands, looking incensed and a little sick. The guards standing either side of him had their hands on their hilts, and it occurred to Gwen far too late that she should have ordered her own guards to step into the fray.

'Stop this at once,' Gabriel said again, his voice heavy with disgust. Sir Woolcott deflated, his grin faltering, and threw his sword to the ground. The Grand Marshal had finally returned; he was looking from Gabriel to Bridget with naked panic on his face. *Good*, thought Gwen, pressing her shaking hands to her chest. *You useless bastard. I hope you're dismissed without reference or pay.*

Bridget got to her feet with only a hint of difficulty, dusting herself off as calmly as if she'd been sitting down for a brief rest rather than moments away from abruptly and dramatically exiting this life; even injured as she was, she turned to offer a hand to Sir Marlin, who had finally managed to disentangle himself from his horse. The Knife squinted up at her proffered hand, barked a laugh and then spat loudly and deliberately at her feet.

Murmurs and mocking guffaws rippled through the stands. Bridget looked down at the Knife, and the Knife glared up at her, and then she gave the slightest of shrugs – as if to say, *Have it your way* – and sheathed her sword, before ducking under the rail and walking away towards the Grand Marshal.

Gwen was so preoccupied with the white-hot rage that had flooded every inch of her at the Knife's insolence that it took her a moment to realise that Gabriel had reached her.

'God, Gabe, thank you,' she said, putting a hand on his elbow. 'I don't know what would have happened if you hadn't . . . *Thank* you.'

'How did it get that far?' he said. Now that he was closer, she could see that his hands were shaking. 'Gwendoline. Why didn't you *say* something?'

'I – I was going to, but . . . I couldn't think, and they wouldn't have *listened* to me anyway.'

Gabriel took a few steadying breaths. 'If all I had to do was shout,' he said quietly, 'then all *you* had to do was shout.'

Gwen felt shame blooming darkly in her gut as he sighed and patted her on the shoulder, looking mildly apologetic, as if it were his fault for burdening her with his unrealistic expectations.

As if he knew, like she did, that at the end of the day – she just didn't have it in her.

8

Upon waking, Arthur immediately knew that it was going to be another Very Bad Day. Sometimes the bad days came out of nowhere, hitting him with the force of a battering ram halfway through some inane morning task, and sometimes they were easily predicted. A night of drinking, for example, usually precipitated an extremely gloomy morning, punctuated by roiling nausea and waves of self-hatred that left him dour and sullen and utterly useless to absolutely everybody, himself included. Since all that had happened last summer, his lowest lows had somehow intensified, as if he'd unlocked the door to new realms of misery.

Arthur hadn't gone to meet Gwendoline for the joust earlier in the week – he'd awoken late that morning and not bothered to mark the time, as he had absolutely no intention of being friendly *or* useful – and had instead spent the rest of the day in bed. And most of the day after. He'd received an extremely snippy note the next morning, delivered to Sidney by a blushing Agnes, but no amount of blackmail could make him a convincing suitor when he was feeling so dire.

Eventually he had decided that the best solution would

be to open another bottle of wine, and he and Sidney had stayed up late the previous evening playing cards until Arthur couldn't distinguish a queen of hearts from a six of clubs. Sidney had left some food this morning, but the sight of fruit and cheese turned Arthur's stomach; he wanted lovely, reliable bread, and Sidney had clearly already eaten through their supply. It was selfish, really; the man had an iron stomach, and Arthur's was famously delicate.

He dreaded the idea of leaving the room, but he dreaded life without bread more; he reluctantly slunk from his chambers and made his way down to the kitchens, keeping his eyes firmly on the floor. He refused to acknowledge anybody at all until he had to attempt a smile to barter with the cook, who handed over half a loaf with a suspicious look as if he might be about to do some dark, yeasty ritual with it. He tore into it as he walked, leaving a trail of crumbs in his wake. He was almost at the stairs when he felt something small and insistent bump against his legs with purpose.

'Hello, Lucifer,' Arthur said, bending down to stroke him and receiving overenthusiastic headbutts in return. 'I assume it was you who vomited next to the bed last night. Could have been me, I suppose, but I don't remember eating anything with a rat's head in it.'

'Arthur?' said a politely bemused voice from down the corridor; he glanced up to see Gabriel approaching, holding a stack of parchment and peering down at him. His curls were sticking up haphazardly, as if he'd been running his hand through them, and he had a smudge of ink on his chin. The general effect wasn't particularly regal.

When the cat, suddenly neglected, gave a scandalised

miaow, it occurred to Arthur that it probably wasn't the done thing to play with grimy strays on the castle landing. 'You needn't look so horrified, Gabriel,' he said, scratching the cat defiantly behind the ears. '*I* didn't let the damn thing in. He's been following me around for days making sad eyes at me – pitiful, really. I named him Lucifer.'

'Right,' said Gabriel. At the sound of his voice, Lucifer's ears twitched; he ducked underneath Arthur's hand and ran straight for the prince, rubbing himself against his boots and making little trilling sounds.

'Well. Why did he do that?' Arthur said, suddenly feeling ridiculous without a cat to stroke and straightening up from his squat.

'Probably because he's my cat,' Gabriel said mildly, bending down to scratch him and losing half the stack of papers as he did so. 'He's called Merlin.'

'*Merlin?*' said Arthur, equal parts miffed that the cat had already been claimed and horrified that it had such an awful name. 'Bet your Wizard *loves* that.'

'I think he does, actually,' Gabriel said, as the cat almost climbed up on to his shoulders in its attempts to get closer to him. The role of court Wizard was an ancient tradition reintroduced when Gabriel's father took the throne, and was entirely ceremonial. While cultists believed whole-heartedly in *real* magic – the type that could turn back armies, transform people into birds and heal the sick – even they had to admit that nobody had exhibited that sort of power since the days of Merlin and Morgana (and that was if you believed the legends, which Arthur decidedly did not). As a result, the Wizard took on an informal spiritual and advisory role on the council, and was never asked to produce so much as a spark of true sorcery.

'Little bit rough around the edges for a royal pet, don't you think?' Arthur said, watching Lucifer – he *refused* to call him Merlin – drop to the ground and then flop over so that he could writhe shamelessly around on his back.

'He's a free spirit,' said Gabriel, more to the cat than to Arthur. 'I found him when he was a kitten, looking rather lost, and he never really took to a life of leisure. Too wild, I suppose. You're a man of action, aren't you, Merlin? He scraps with father's hounds all the time, and they're about eight times his size. I just feed him and try to clean up his war wounds, when he lets me.'

This was without a doubt the most Arthur had ever heard Gabriel talk. It stood to reason that it was about a cat. Arthur scrubbed a hand across his face, and looked up to see Gabriel watching him.

'Are you all right?' he said, surprising Arthur again; the prince was looking at him closely, probably taking in his dark circles and the general air of despondence he wasn't alive enough to disguise today. He was frowning again. Arthur would have frowned back, but his face hurt.

'Not really,' he said, which was also a surprise. This was why he shouldn't have left his room; it was dangerous to be let loose like this, to be alarmingly honest to anybody who happened to stumble across his path and express a modicum of interest. He had a reputation to uphold, after all.

'You look . . . tired,' Gabriel ventured.

'So do you,' said Arthur.

It was true, but it was almost his default state. Gabriel had always been a serious, quiet child – Gwen was the only one Arthur had ever seen get a smile out of him – and it didn't seem like much had changed.

'Well. I'm expected at the . . . My family is attending the tournament again today,' Gabriel said slowly. 'I know Gwen has asked you to join her.'

Arthur felt immediately rankled by the suggestion that he had been *summoned*, and should therefore obey. 'I did receive that invitation. Many invitations, in fact, each more colourfully worded than the last. I actually thought that instead I might go and find a man with strong arms – you know, blacksmith, window cleaner – and ask him to hold me down in the moat until dead.'

Gabriel looked taken aback, and somewhere very deep down Arthur felt a little guilty. He put a stop to this at once. He and Gwen may have made a deal, but he was no royal lapdog; they were supposed to be equals in this arrangement, if nothing else, and he wouldn't come running on her every whim.

'Fine,' said Gabriel, starting away down the corridor. The cat attempted to follow; he glanced down at it, then back at Arthur, and said, 'Stay here, Merlin.' Incredibly, the cat stopped abruptly and sat down, tail twitching. They both watched as Gabriel disappeared out of sight.

'Uh-oh.' Arthur turned to see that Sidney had finally caught up to him; he was watching Gabriel walk away, with his arms folded and one eyebrow raised. 'I know that look.'

'What look? There isn't a look,' Arthur snapped. He strode over to the cat and picked it up, ignoring its startled little yowl.

'He's not bad-looking,' Sidney observed as they walked together by unspoken agreement back in the direction of their chambers. 'And I mean, you love a terrible idea. This one could be your worst yet.'

Arthur chose to ignore him.

They returned to their rooms and Arthur slept soundly all afternoon with Lucifer curled up on the pillow next to him, purring madly and digging his claws into Arthur's scalp whenever the mood took him. When Arthur finally opened his eyes, Sidney's face was inches away from his.

'Is this a seduction?' Arthur croaked. 'Because your breath smells like onions.'

'Believe me, you'd know if it was a seduction,' said Sidney, putting a bit of space between them. 'You wouldn't be able to miss it. You'd be like, *Christ, what a seduction I'm having right now.*'

'Lovely,' Arthur said dully.

'Was just checking that you're still breathing.'

'I regret to inform you: yes,' said Arthur.

'Do you want to come out tonight, or do you want to mope?'

Arthur considered. 'Mope.'

'I don't suppose there's much point asking what's wrong?'

Arthur sat up on his elbows and sighed. 'It's sort of general and specific at the same time. Life, the world, existential despair; my father, my blushing-bride-to-be, *her* father. It's all extraordinarily boring, Sid. I'm exhausted listening to myself talk about it.'

'Well, I think you should buck up,' said Sidney, pulling his jacket on. 'Living in a castle. Whole city of strapping young men to pine after. There are much worse things, Art. And you've got a cat.'

'It's not even my cat,' Arthur called after Sidney as he left. Lucifer looked at him reproachfully, and Arthur tapped him gently on the nose. 'I didn't mean that.'

A few hours later, Arthur found himself quite bored with sulking; he paced circles around the room, drank some wine, trailed bootlaces across the floor for Lucifer, and then felt genuinely hurt when the cat eventually got bored too and screeched at the door to be let out. Once the door was open, Arthur thought he might as well put on his coat and see about catching up with Sidney.

He paused when he reached the staircase; the royal wing was just beyond it. Gwendoline's notes had been getting increasingly crotchety in tone, and despite his reluctance, he could kill two birds with one stone if he exited the castle via her window. He half expected the guards to stop him when he reached them, but instead one of them gave his neighbour a just-perceptible smirk and then stood aside to let him through.

Arthur knocked on Gwendoline's door, wondering for a moment if she might be elsewhere, but when Agnes admitted him he saw that the princess was sitting by the fire, reading. Her hair, normally braided up out of her face, was already undone for bed; it softened her somewhat, although she ruined the effect immediately by scowling at him.

'Are you ever not ... here?' Arthur said, waving around at the room as he entered.

'Are *you* ever where you're *supposed* to be?' Gwendoline countered, closing her book. 'Agnes, give us the room please.' Agnes left, rather reluctantly. 'Thanks for not bothering to show up to the joust, Arthur. And for involving Lady Leclair *again* – does your selfishness know no bounds? You haven't been at a single event, or replied to any of my notes. You're a really *fun* person to fake a relationship with.'

'Oh, shit,' said Arthur thoughtfully. 'I completely forgot about that. The Lady Leclair thing, I mean. Glad it went off as intended.'

'Your sincere and heartfelt apology is noted,' spat Gwendoline. 'Why haven't you been at dinner either? I haven't seen you at all. Have you even been sleeping in this castle?'

'Wouldn't you like to know,' Arthur said airily, despite the fact that he'd essentially *only* been sleeping.

'This only works if you're actually *here*, Arthur, and if we actually pretend it's ... You are *so* infuriating.' Arthur shrugged in a way that he knew all too well was frustratingly insolent. 'We had a deal, and instead you're toying with me on purpose. Why don't you care?'

Arthur was slightly taken aback by the emotion in her voice; she looked a little grey around the edges, as if she'd been expending more energy than she could afford to give.

'All right,' he said, sighing. 'Fine. I'm here. I – I *care*.'

Gwendoline stared at him for a second, and then all the fight seemed to go out of her. 'Sit down,' she said heavily. Unable to muster the outrage required to disobey, Arthur did. He could feel her looking at him, so he kept his eyes fixed on the fire.

'Why do you hate me?' she said. This was startling enough to get him to lift his head.

'Does it matter?'

'Yes, it matters. I'd rather not spend my time with some-body who actively reviles me.'

'What if I don't want to tell you?'

'Well,' Gwendoline blustered. 'You *have* to.'

'And there it is,' said Arthur, rolling his eyes. 'Look – I don't particularly enjoy being ordered around, insubordin-ate as that might make me.'

'I don't give *orders*,' Gwendoline said quickly. 'One of us has to act like an adult, Arthur—'

'There is it again,' said Arthur bitterly. 'Can't you hear yourself? As convenient an excuse as it would be to break off this engagement, you're not my *mother*, Gwendoline.'

Gwendoline exhaled a quick huff of frustration. She drummed her fingers lightly on the arms of her chair, and then got to her feet and crossed the room to fetch a pitcher of something from her dresser and pour herself a small glass. Whatever it was smelt sharply of lemons – lemons and something slightly medicinal, like mint. She took a long drink, and then turned to lean against the dresser, eyeing Arthur thoughtfully.

'I never met your mother,' she said.

'What? No, you – you did. You just wouldn't remember.' *Arthur* barely remembered, and he clung to the scraps that were there so fiercely that he worried he'd made them up in his desperation. Long, dark hair; the smell of incense burning in her rooms; kisses pressed to his head when he was half asleep; his father actually smiling, his mother drag-ging him out of his study so that the three of them could eat dinner together every night, Arthur's legs not quite reaching the floor yet under the table. He'd been six when she died. Gwendoline must have been four.

That summer was utterly blank. He'd asked Mrs Ashworth about it once, and she'd said that he screamed so much and so continuously that his father had asked her to take him out of the house all day, every day, for weeks on end, returning only when he'd exhausted himself into silence.

'Oh,' said Gwendoline. 'What was she like?'

'She was ... I don't know, she was my mother,' said Arthur. 'She didn't live long enough to be disappointed by me, so all I have are pleasant memories.'

Gwendoline sighed. She picked up the jug again and filled her glass to the brim. She hesitated, and then poured a second. When she went to hand it to him, Arthur eyed it with deep suspicion.

'Oh for Christ's sake, Arthur, I'm not trying to poison you. Just drink it, it won't kill you,' Gwendoline said crossly, sitting back down in her chair. 'You were a nightmare every time you visited, you know. That's why *I* didn't like *you*, in case you're even remotely interested. You were awful to me. And you took pleasure in it. You still do.'

'You just make it so easy.' Arthur sampled his glass. It wasn't bad; sour, but infused with something gently sweet.

'I was a child! I was younger than you, I looked up to you, and you just ... I let you ride my new pony, and in return you put a *toad* in my bed.'

Arthur stared at her incredulously. 'That's not how it happened.'

'Yes it is, I remember—'

'You let me ride your pony as a display of your grand

benevolence, and then you got angry and started stamping your little feet because you wanted it back, and I was having too much fun, and then – you ran and told my father that you didn't like me, and that you'd *never* like me. That you wanted him to take me away.' He stopped to take a sip of lemons. 'My father didn't take that particularly well.'

'So you put a toad in my bed because your father scolded you?'

'No, *Gwendoline*, I put a toad in your bed because my father told me I was useless to him if your parents ended our betrothal,' Arthur said heatedly. 'I put a toad in your bed because my father said that it was my sole purpose on this earth to unite our families and to make myself agreeable to you, and that if I couldn't even manage that, I was even more of a waste of space than he'd previously imagined.'

'What?' said Gwendoline sharply. 'No he didn't. You were nine.'

'Oddly enough, I remember it distinctly – although he probably doesn't; he was drinking quite heavily by that point. Anyway, I didn't particularly enjoy that little chat.'

'Hence the toad,' Gwendoline said quietly.

'Hence the fucking toad.'

They sat in silence for a while, broken only by the sound of Arthur putting his glass back on the table. He ran a thumb round the rim of it, pressing a little too hard. He felt raw and exposed – he wanted to gather up everything he'd just said and push it back inside himself, not leaving anything for Gwen to hold on to or against him.

'I didn't know,' she said eventually.

115

'This is shaping up to be the worst hangover I've ever had,' he said irritably. 'Just so you know, that's the only reason I haven't already jumped head-first out of the window rather than continue this. I'm compromised.'

'You drink too much.'

'Yes, and to that point, the sky is blue.'

'Don't you care?'

Arthur pressed his thumb and forefinger against his eyelids, distantly hoping that he might push his eyeballs into his brain and put an abrupt and bloody end to this conversation. 'What else would you recommend?'

'I'm not sure,' Gwen said. She glanced over at the window. '*Are* you going out?'

'Yes,' snapped Arthur. 'No. I don't know.'

'Very illuminating,' said Gwen. 'You really don't have to let every single thing I say put your back up.'

'Pots, kettles.'

'God, can't we – can we just call a truce? For, I don't know, five minutes?' Gwen said. Finally too tired to argue, Arthur just shrugged. He regretted ever entering this room, but he was quite committed to this armchair, and Gwen was pouring him another glass of lemon water.

'Where do you go? When you go . . . out?'

'Oh, you know. Dens of ill repute. Gambling houses. Unregulated cockfights.' Gwen just looked at him over the rim of her glass. 'I don't know, usually . . . inns, taverns. The gutters outside inns and taverns. So far, Sidney is *very* disappointed by what your fine city has to offer – did you know that you've got *two* drinking establishments called The Round Table? They're only ten minutes apart.'

'No, I didn't,' said Gwen. 'I don't really go into the city. It doesn't surprise me though. I have four cousins named Lancelot. Two Percivals. Court is rife with noble ladies called Morgan, or Morgana.'

'No Mordreds?' Arthur said, and Gwen snorted. 'Shame. He always seemed the more interesting of my ancestors. They do love to gloss over all the sticky parts though, don't they? What's a little incest, between family.'

'It doesn't bother you, then? To think about ... where you came from?'

Arthur laughed drily. 'Er, no. If you go back a few hundred years, I'm afraid *everybody* was shagging their brother. It was weird if you *didn't* shag your brother. Don't make that face, nobody's asking you to do it *now*, although as brothers go—'

'*Arthur.*'

'I'm just endlessly thankful that my family ran out of attractive siblings and first cousins and branched out to other kingdoms. You probably weren't so lucky.'

'Well, Father wasn't a blood heir to the throne,' Gwen said, shrugging. 'Just related by marriage. Our line is Norman too, of course, like the old king's, but you can keep your inbreeding jokes – they don't hold water.'

Arthur sighed. He was fond of those jokes. '*I've* never understood why he dragged court to Camelot, when he has absolutely no ties to the place and it's practically demolishing itself.'

Gwen wrinkled her nose at him. 'Do you pay *any* attention to what's happening in this country?'

'Not if I can help it.'

'When Father took the throne, the people had just united behind him – your family included – to avoid the risk of becoming West Norway. But once that threat had passed, people stopped feeling quite so cuddly. The rift that Lord Willard had wanted to leverage to take the throne himself – the growing divide between Catholics and Arthurian cultists – was still there. Willard himself has long quietened down and made peace with my father, but the cultists are still unhappy.'

'So he dragged everybody to Camelot as a peace offering?'

'Well. Yes. He's trying to heal the divide. Make an England for everybody. There are lots of cultists on his staff, you know. Lord Stafford, for one. And of course we have a Wizard, Master Buchanan, which my mother thinks is completely ridiculous.'

Arthur laughed. 'It is ridiculous.'

'Your father is a cultist!'

'Yes. And my mother was Muslim, and your father is Catholic.'

Gwen finally seemed to notice that her glass was empty, and went for the jug again. 'What's your point?'

'That spiritually, our cup overfloweth,' said Arthur. 'Although my *actual* cup is quite empty.' Gwen rolled her eyes, but filled it for him anyway. 'My point is that I don't have to believe in what my father does. I don't know if I believe in *anything* in particular.'

'I'm Catholic,' Gwen said automatically. 'I mean – I don't go to mass any more, really. Father can hardly kick off about it when he's trying to encourage freedom of religion. And

I stopped praying when . . .' She trailed off, looking suddenly embarrassed.

'When?'

Gwen wasn't looking at him; she was picking at her nails instead, half of her lip caught between her teeth, as if she were attempting to devour and unravel herself in the least efficient ways possible.

'I used to pray for all the usual things. For my family's health, for the kingdom. And then one day I realised I'd been slipping other things in there too. Things I wanted for myself. Things I knew I could never have. And it got too . . . painful, I suppose, to keep asking and asking, knowing it was futile. And the things I wanted started to feel . . . wrong. So I stopped.'

Arthur was trying very hard not to pity her, but it was difficult when she was currently embodying the Platonic ideal of pitiful. 'I wouldn't say it's *wrong* to develop a crush on a dashing, lusty young knight of the realm. I'd say it's entirely normal.'

'Well, of course *you* would,' Gwen snapped. She closed her eyes and pushed her hair out of her face. 'Sorry. I don't really know how to talk about any of this. I haven't before. I'm not like you, Arthur. You do what you like, and kiss who you like, and damn the consequences—'

'I am living with the consequences right now,' Arthur said bitterly. 'I am drinking juice with the consequences.' His goodwill towards her was rapidly evaporating.

'How do you do it?' Gwen said. She was looking at him like he was some sort of patron saint of same-sex kissing, and he relented and shrugged.

119

'Nobody else is ever going to care as much as you do about the things that you want, Gwendoline. So it's up to you – you can put them aside forever, if you can live with that, or you can put on your big-girl girdle and demand more for yourself.'

Gwen looked deflated, as if this were not the answer she had been after. 'I don't think I can.'

Arthur grimaced at her and then abruptly stood up, scraping his chair back and stretching. 'Well. This has been depressing enough to make me feel *heaps* better about my own life, so for that, I thank you.'

'Oh – so you *are* going out?' Gwen asked, looking startled. It was disquieting to have managed civility for so long that she didn't look immediately thrilled at the prospect of him leaving. It made much more sense to him when he and Gwen actively loathed each other; this had felt dangerously close to a real conversation.

'No. I'm going back to my rooms. I'm tired, and I'm ill-tempered, and besides – my cat needs me.'

'What cat? You don't have a cat.' He ignored her, giving her a half-hearted wave of his hand on his way to the door. '*Arthur.* What *cat?*'

Two days later, the fragile truce still seemed to be holding. Arthur had nodded at Gwen from down the hallway when nobody else was around to require the pretence, had actually bothered to send Sidney back with a response when Agnes took him a note, and that evening when Gwen left her chambers for dinner he was waiting at the top of the stairs, clean-shaven and freshly washed and generally looking in much higher spirits than he had been the last time they'd spoken.

'What's that smell?' she said, as he held out an arm and she took it.

'Oh, lovely, that's just what a person likes to hear in lieu of greeting.'

'No, it's – it's nice,' Gwen said quickly, eager to keep the hard-won peace. 'You smell like something . . . I don't know, musky. And kind of like – a tree?'

'*Kind of like a tree*,' Arthur repeated despairingly. 'It's orange and sandalwood. You pain me. Kind of like a *tree*.'

'What part of anything you just said doesn't come from a tree?' Gwen said indignantly. Arthur sighed in exasperation, which Gwen thought wasn't particularly fair.

She had been *trying* to pay him a compliment. She just wasn't very good at them.

The hall was packed with guests once again, the tournament continuing to attract more visitors than Gwen had ever seen. As a lady of noble birth and Gwen's personal attendant, Agnes should have been sitting in her usual place with other ladies of similar standing, but Gwen saw her covertly slide in opposite Sidney instead, blushing as he leaned across the table to talk to her. Arthur had noticed too; he raised his eyebrows and shot Gwen a conspiratorial glance, making her snort. She stopped short when she realised what she was doing. Since when had Arthur made her laugh? Since when had she and Arthur had *inside jokes*?

Gabriel was running late for dinner; when he sat down next to Gwen, she noticed that they were wearing almost exactly the same shade of blue.

'Twins are very unnatural,' said Arthur conversationally.

'We're not twins,' Gwen said. 'As you well know.'

'You look identical,' Arthur said, spearing a bit of chicken with his fork and pointing it at Gabriel, 'and he can't have more than a few inches on you, height-wise, because you are – to put it delicately – some sort of giantess.'

'Arthur is very sensitive about the fact that we're the same height,' Gwen said to Gabriel by way of explanation. 'He exaggerates, because if I'm a gigantic woman, then he can pretend he's an average-sized man.' Gabriel just cleared his throat awkwardly, and picked up his fork.

The rest of dinner passed without incident. Arthur was on his best behaviour, and every time Gwen looked up she noticed people watching them; smiles, elbow nudges, whispers and nods in their direction. Arthur kept refilling her glass, leaning in and finding little excuses to put a hand on her arm. Gwen was surprised to find herself unbothered. He had mastered the art of making their conversation look intimate without actually stepping over the line into uncomfortable territory.

Towards the end of the meal, when people tended to drift from their places to find entertainment further afield, Sidney raised a hand to call Arthur over to where he was sitting with Agnes. Arthur left, giving Gwen a squeeze on the shoulder as he walked away.

'That's going well, then,' Gabriel said.

'Well – yes, I suppose so. Are you all right? You look ... squinty.'

'No,' Gabriel said. 'I mean, yes. I'm all right. Just sat in four hours of military strategy meetings, shuffling little pretend troops and horses around a map of England.'

'Cultists again?' Gwen said quietly, and Gabriel gave a small nod in response. 'Is it bad?'

'No,' Gabriel said. 'I don't think so. Just these little pockets of ... potential unrest, I suppose. They seem to be popping up all over the place, but especially towards the north. They look like they might boil over, so we're sending men. Too many men, I think, but then I've never really had a head for strategy.'

'If they send all our men north, who's left to protect us here?'

'I don't know,' said Gabriel. 'You, I suppose.'

'Well, did you tell Father what you thought? About the war chests?'

Gabriel had recently confided in Gwen that he thought they were spending too much money fighting their various battles; he wanted their father to divert some of it, to focus on helping the ordinary people of England, but hadn't yet found the courage to tell him.

'Somehow it hasn't come up,' Gabriel said. He wasn't looking at Gwen. He was watching somebody across the room. As Gwen finished her stewed pears, he excused himself to go and speak to the Wizard; lately Gwen had noticed him spending more and more time with Master Buchanan, who was probably thrilled that *somebody* in the royal family was taking an interest in Arthurian history, even if it was only academic. Arthur was still talking to Sidney and Agnes; he said something with a wry smile that made Agnes snort ale out of her nose. For a moment, Gwen imagined what it might be like to get up and join them.

'Good evening, Gwendoline.'

Gwen startled at the sound of her father's voice. He sat down in Gabriel's chair with a glass in hand, making a small groaning sound as he did; he wasn't that old really, but age seemed to have caught up with him in a rush recently.

'Evening, Father. Gabriel said you were with the war council most of the day.'

'Oh? Yes, yes. I suppose we were.'

'But you won't have to go?'

'North? No, I shouldn't think so. Not for some time anyway. Hopefully never.'

Gwen bit her lip. 'Gabriel said – I mean, he mentioned that you were sending a lot of troops, and I thought—'

The king chuckled, sounding very tired. 'Ah. Yes, that did take up quite a lot of the afternoon. Don't worry yourself about *that* . . . Tell me, how are things going with young Arthur?'

'Oh. Good,' Gwen said, which was mostly true. 'We're getting along much better.'

'I'm glad to hear it,' said the king, patting her on the hand. 'I really don't wish for you to be unhappy. I know I've put you in a difficult position – but I hope *you* know I wouldn't have done it if it weren't truly important. More so now than ever.'

'So it *is* bad?' Gwen said. When she was younger, he had often confided minor matters of state to her over their regular games of chess, when her mother wasn't there to hear him and tell him off for filling her head with information that was of no use to her; lately any one-on-one discussions about the running of the country had been reserved for Gabriel alone. 'With the cultists, I mean?'

Her father sighed, rubbing at his beard. 'The problem with compromise,' he said eventually, 'is that, often, everybody loses. You sit on the fence for so long that you discover you've built a kingdom on it.' He took a long drink of wine, and then visibly perked up. 'Ah, here he is. Been asking the Wizard to make ready the troops of magic birds, son?'

'No,' said Gabriel, shifting uncomfortably. The king nodded slightly awkwardly, and then got to his feet.

'Duty calls. The Earl of Northumberland wants to talk my

ear off about Arthurian miracles; apparently a magpie told somebody in the port of Blyth to beware of red-headed men.'

Gwen and Gabriel retired to her room to play chess after dinner. Gwen used the opportunity to quiz him further about the supposedly imminent cultist uprisings, while his answers got increasingly weary, most of them culminating in, 'I don't know, G. Come on, it's your move.'

It was quite late when Agnes, who had ostensibly been changing Gwen's bedclothes and arranging her outfit for the next day in the other room, emerged wearing her cloak and looking very much like a person who didn't want to be noticed. Gwen and Gabriel both turned to look at her, and she froze on the spot.

'Going somewhere?' said Gwen.

'No,' Agnes said, flushing very pink.

'Just thought you'd take your cloak for a turn about the room, then?'

Gabriel shot her a warning look – a look that said *be nice* – and she sighed. 'You're allowed to go out, Agnes. I don't particularly care what you get up to at night, as long as you don't wake me on your return.'

There was a soft knock at the door. Agnes looked even more guilty than she had before.

'Who's that?' said Gwen.

'Nobody,' said Agnes, bunching the edges of her cloak up in her hands.

'*Agnes*,' somebody hissed, in a very loud stage whisper. 'Ags, it's Sidney. Open the bloody door.'

'I don't know what he's doing here,' Agnes said, sticking

126

her chin out defiantly, still bright red. Gwen and Gabriel exchanged another look.

'Are we early?' Sidney said quietly to somebody on the other side of the door.

'She said a little before midnight,' said Arthur, not bothering to lower his voice. 'So actually we're right on time. Unless she had no intention of meeting you, and this is actually a jilting, in which case . . . Oh, hello, Gwendoline.'

Gwen had crossed the room and wrenched open the door. Sidney was bent over, apparently trying to look through the keyhole, while Arthur lounged behind him against the wall. Sidney straightened up immediately, looking slightly sheepish; Arthur just nodded in greeting.

'What *are* you doing?' Gwen demanded.

'Crimes,' said Arthur, at the exact same time that both Agnes and Sidney said, 'Nothing.'

'Well, you've certainly done an excellent job of getting your story straight,' Gwen said, crossing her arms.

'We're going to a party,' Arthur said, studying his fingernails and then looking up at her archly. 'Now, how do I explain what a party is? It's a place where people meet to have fun, and—'

'It's not a party,' Sidney interrupted. 'Right, Agnes?'

Agnes put a hand to her forehead and sighed. 'No.'

'Well, what is it then?' Gwen said. Gabriel had appeared at her shoulder, and was watching the proceedings with mild interest.

'It's Morgan's Day,' Agnes said, as if that explained anything.

'Morgan's Day? Morgan who? Le *Fay*?'

'*Yes*, le Fay,' Arthur said, as if she were being incredibly slow. 'It's a secret gathering for her birthday. Or ... something.'

'You're going to a witch's birthday party,' Gwen said. 'A witch who's been dead for hundreds of years, and who was considered morally questionable at best.'

'That's the crux of it,' said Arthur. 'Any more inane questions or can we leave?'

'Oh, I have questions,' said Gwen. 'Why is this party starting in the middle of the night? And what's the point of a birthday party for somebody who's dead?'

Arthur went to speak, but Gabriel got there first.

'The more progressive Arthurians celebrate the duality of her spirit. Her capacity for kindness and evil. The stories about her can't pin down whether she was good or bad, so people have decided she was a bit of both. The more devout cultists prefer Merlin, so she's become a bit of a symbol of resistance, especially for women. People confess their faults to her, and celebrate their strengths. It's a sort of ritual.'

Everybody turned to stare at him.

'I'm not a cultist,' he said. 'I've just read a lot about them. Their practices are interesting.'

'You are mad as a newt,' Arthur said, shaking his head. Gabriel looked down at his feet; the tips of his ears had gone very pink.

'We'll be off then,' said Sidney, offering Agnes his arm. 'Unless – do you want to come?'

'Me?' said Gwen. 'To a secret cultist gathering, at Camelot? In this political climate?'

'Gwendoline doesn't do fun,' Arthur said. 'Come on, I

128

don't want to get there after they've given out all the good dark magic.'

They were already halfway out of the door, and Gwen felt a pang of longing like she had back in the Great Hall; she couldn't help but think of all the times she had watched groups of young ladies laughing together at feasts and dances, telling herself she wasn't anything like them, burying the part of herself that quietly ached for companionship.

Perhaps she didn't need to act on *everything* she wanted; perhaps it was enough just to have this, and then be done with it.

'I'll come,' Gwen said.

'No you won't,' said Arthur, pausing in the doorway and looking mildly scandalised.

'Yes I will,' said Gwen. His indignation just made her want to double down. 'It's – it's not outside the castle, is it?'

'No,' Agnes said reluctantly. 'It's within the bailey, your highness.'

'Fine. I'm only coming to keep an eye on you, Arthur, so you don't do something rash. Agnes – just – fetch my cloak.'

'*Don't* fetch her cloak, Agnes,' Arthur said firmly. Agnes looked from Arthur to Gwen. Gwen narrowed her eyes.

'Fetch. My. Cloak.'

Agnes sighed, and ducked past Gabriel to go back into the bedchamber.

'I'm really not sure this'll be your sort of thing,' Sidney said slowly; Gwen suspected that Arthur had given him a pinch on the arm to inspire him to speak.

'If *people* like to celebrate this day, then I'm sure I'll find some part of it amusing. I'm *people*, aren't I?'

'No,' said Arthur, as Agnes reappeared and reluctantly helped Gwen into her cloak.

'I think it's probably best if I come too,' Gabriel said suddenly.

'*What?*' Gwen and Arthur said at the same time, managing to match each other in tone and pitch.

'Just – give me a second,' Gabriel said. 'I need to go back to my rooms and—'

'If you say *fetch my cloak*,' said Arthur, 'I am going to *scream*.'

Arthur insisted that Gwen and Gabriel put their hoods up as they walked, and that they weren't to take them down under any circumstances, as they would risk 'ruining the integrity of the event'.

'What's that supposed to mean?' Gwen said, rankled despite the fact that she had absolutely no intention of getting caught at some questionable cultist bacchanal.

'Do you think *anyone's* going to relax and take part in dark and terrible magic rituals if they think they're being observed by the heir to the throne and the heir to – hmm, what *are* you the heir to? The slightly smaller seat next to the throne?'

'Do you suppose people will notice?' Agnes said quietly to Sidney.

'Nah,' he said. 'They'll blend right in.'

'Oh *yes*,' said Arthur. 'Why wouldn't they? They're only about eight feet tall with flaming red hair, and act like they were raised in a haunted tower away from all human contact—'

'Well, we were,' said Gabriel. Arthur laughed in a strangled sort of way.

'What was *that*?' he said incredulously. 'Gwendoline, did your brother just make a *joke*?'

'Don't ask me,' said Gwen. 'Where the hell are we going?'

They had left the familiar confines of the inner castle and were now out in the bailey; Gwen knew the areas to the north and south of the main keep well, but they were currently walking east to the servants' domains, and in the darkness all the squat little service buildings looked identical. They ducked down an alleyway, following close at Arthur's heels, and it opened out into a small courtyard that Gwen knew she had never seen before in her life.

'Is that a *chapel*?' she said, frowning at the structure at the far end.

'What gave it away?' said Arthur. 'Was it the massive bloody cross on top?'

'I didn't know there was a chapel in here,' Gwen said, looking at Gabriel, who shrugged.

'Religion for the lowly masses,' said Sidney. 'Servants. Regular folk.'

As they watched, a couple of giggling serving girls burst from another doorway and crossed the courtyard, glancing back over their shoulders and talking in exaggerated whispers before opening the door of the chapel and ducking inside.

'No time like the present,' Arthur said, leading them on.

'We are definitely going to hell,' Gabriel said in Gwen's ear, as Arthur opened the chapel door, cocked an eyebrow and beckoned them inside.

It looked entirely unremarkable – rows of neat pews, that particular smell of tapestry dust and candle wax and wood in the air that Gwen recognised from every religious building she'd ever entered – but at the far end up by the altar a door was ajar, and candlelight was flickering in the space beyond. They followed it into a narrow corridor and down stone steps until they reached another door; on the other side, Gwen could hear voices and laughter.

'I'm not sure this is such a . . .' she started, but it was too late. Arthur herded Sidney and Agnes inside ahead of him, and then looked back at where she was hovering and rolled his eyes.

'And you were so excited about the part where you got to fetch your cloak,' he said, taking her firmly by the arm and yanking her inside.

They immediately encountered a problem.

'Before you enter, I must tell you – there are no men allowed in here,' said a grey-haired, stern-looking woman in a dark robe. 'Are any of you men?'

'We're very well-behaved men,' Arthur offered. 'Normal. Innocent.' Gwen snorted.

'I don't care what variety of man you are,' the woman said. 'We are here to celebrate the Lady Morgan le Fay – it's a sacred space on Morgan's Day.'

'Ah,' said Sidney. 'Well. Agnes, shall we . . . ?'

'Oh,' said Agnes. 'Well, I sort of want to . . . stay. If that's all right.' Sidney looked disappointed, but rallied quickly.

'I shall wait for you outside,' he said gallantly.

Agnes giggled horrifyingly, but Gwen was too

132

preoccupied to scoff – she was looking around at the room. She had expected a cellar about the size of the chapel above, but the space was cavernous, with pillars and arches running along the length of it and at least a hundred people gathered in hooded groups beneath them. The entire space was lit by a large open fire in the very centre, the smoke disappearing up into a hidden chimney. Beyond the flames, somewhat warped and rippling in the heat, Gwen could see a huge, mottled stone statue. It towered above them, gazing down dispassionately with both hands raised.

'Are you coming?' Gabriel asked, nudging her arm.

'Er,' Gwen said. 'Gabe. Are you seeing this? This – this is some sort of secret cultist *temple*. In the castle grounds.'

'I know,' Gabriel said, not looking nearly as horrified as he should have. 'It's *fascinating*.'

'Come on,' Arthur said insistently. 'Let's go.'

'I think – I think I'd like to stay,' said Gwen. Having braced herself for life-affirming adventure, she didn't want to turn back now; and besides, it was only a very little escapade, barely even deserving of the word.

'Oh,' said Gabriel. 'All right. If they do the ritual, can you make a note of everything? I want to hear about it later, especially the part where they—'

'Christ,' Arthur said. 'Even she didn't bring parchment and a quill to a *party*. Come on, you insufferable academic.'

Gwen just had time to see the expression of shock on her brother's face before he was being pulled back through the doorway they had just come through. Arthur did seem to spend rather a lot of time yanking them both around. *Like an ill wind*, thought Gwen. *Or a rip tide.*

'Is that her? Morgana?' Gwen said, pointing up at the enormous statue.

'Yes,' said the grey-haired lady. 'Now, hurry on in – the ceremony is about to begin.'

10

It appeared that Sidney was perfectly serious about waiting for Agnes all night, if he had to; as soon as they exited the chapel he located a promising stretch of wall and settled himself down on it.

'Look at that,' Arthur said to Gabriel. 'Sad, isn't it.'

'There are quite a few things I could say right now,' Sidney said. 'Quite a few stories I could tell, about the lengths you've gone to while *pining*—'

'Yes, well, I'm very pleased for you,' Arthur said quickly. 'Adieu, good evening, have a lovely wait, and I hope she's worth it.'

'She will be,' Sidney said, grinning.

'*So* unnerving,' Arthur muttered, as he and Gabriel started walking away across the courtyard. 'He's not usually like this. Maybe he's ill.'

'What lengths have you gone to while pining?' said Gabriel, his face obscured by his hood.

'Oh, he's just trying to . . . There was this thing with a song, I was never particularly good at the lute – not important,' Arthur blustered. Gabriel slowed down and glanced over his shoulder, back at the chapel.

'I don't really feel I should just leave her in there,' he said. Arthur could see the lower half of his face now; he was chewing anxiously on his bottom lip, which by rights shouldn't have been the least bit attractive.

'Oh, she's *fine*,' Arthur said, taking him by the arm. 'Come on – we're far more conspicuous lurking out here than she is partying in there.' Any other heir to the throne, Arthur thought, might protest at being hauled around by a minor member of his court; Gabriel seemed to take it in his stride, as if he'd just been waiting for somebody to tell him what to do next, and Arthur's direction was as good as any.

'I would have liked to see it,' Gabriel said, as they approached the alleyway.

'Yes. Well. It's not in my nature to leave a party early, but we were very much surplus to requirements,' Arthur replied. 'I feel at a bit of a loss, now. All worked up and nowhere to go.'

'Yes,' said Gabriel vaguely. They lapsed into an awkward silence, which to Arthur was tantamount to torture.

'Off to bed then?' he said, for lack of anything else.

'Actually, I – I'll probably go to the library.'

'In the middle of the night?'

'In the middle of the night.'

'Oh,' said Arthur. 'That's . . . admirable, I suppose.'

'Is it?'

'Well, somebody's got to do it.' The fact that this made no sense at all was not lost on him.

'I'm sort of . . . studying,' Gabriel said, and even in the dark Arthur could see that he was blushing. It was a shame not to be able to see it more clearly; his kingdom – or, Gabriel's kingdom, he supposed – for a well-placed brazier.

They reached the gate into the main castle, and Gabriel removed his hood for the guards, who quickly scrambled aside.

'Studying for what?' They were slowing down, and Arthur didn't know who had initiated it. He was usually a fastidiously fast walker; Sidney was forever complaining about it.

'Um. Everything? My future,' Gabriel said. Arthur's instinct was to laugh, but he managed to keep himself in check.

'You're studying for *life*? For *your* life? Is there a – is there a how-to guide for monarchs? Tips and tricks for subjugating the masses? Prevent a revolt in ten easy steps?'

'Yes,' said Gabriel. 'Well. Sort of. But it's chronicled in a thousand different volumes about the history of the kings of Britain, or written by the kings themselves, and they all disagree about precisely how to go about the ... subjugating.'

'So you're working on the pamphlet,' Arthur said. 'To make it snappy. Summarise it on to one piece of parchment, to instruct future generations.'

'I'm working on ...' Gabriel sighed. They had reached the middle of the north-west courtyard and come to a complete stop. 'I'm just working.'

'Well, I'm sorry we couldn't liven your spirits with a secret cultist party,' said Arthur. 'Clearly you needed it.'

'Right,' said Gabriel. There was another awkward silence.

'So you're going to the library?' Arthur said.

'Yes,' said Gabriel. His voice was much higher in pitch when he said, 'Are you – do you want to come?'

This was unexpected. Arthur couldn't imagine what could have precipitated the invitation, besides perhaps general panic.

'Better than going to bed, I suppose,' he said, shrugging. 'Or – probably about the *same* as going to bed, but at least it's a change of scenery.'

Gabriel just nodded, and Arthur followed on as he set off towards the main keep. He managed to restrain himself from talking for the sake of talking until they had made it to the library entrance.

'Wild in here past midnight, is it?' he said, peering dubiously around as Gabriel took up a lantern that had obviously been left for his use by the door. The room was packed with bookshelves, arranged back to back and bookended with large pillars, creating a dark and dusty warren. They had to take several hairpin turns, but eventually they made it to a corner that had clearly been furnished for extended stays. It contained a small linenfold table with a hard-backed chair behind it and a thick stack of books neatly piled atop it. There was also a large, well-used armchair; the velvet was slightly worn at the back and the seat, patches threadbare and faded.

Arthur immediately flopped down on to it, and Gabriel walked carefully around the table to pull out his chair and sit down. He seemed to lock into it, his spine curving forward, shoulders hunching up around his neck as he pulled the book at the top of the pile towards him. It was as if he had shed his outside self; in the library, he was the real Gabriel.

The real Gabriel had *terrible* posture.

'What are you reading?' said Arthur, pulling the next book on the pile down into his lap. It expelled quite a lot of dust; he promptly sneezed on it, and then wiped it apologetically on his tunic.

'They're first-hand accounts of how the early cultist factions formed,' Gabriel said. Arthur flipped open the cover of the book he was holding and found that it had been meticulously transcribed in dark brown ink that looked unnervingly bloody. 'It's useful to understand the original context, but it's also a bit of a – a personal project of mine.'

'Go on then,' Arthur said.

'Go on – what?'

'Tell me how the early cultist factions formed,' he said. Gabriel turned a page, and Arthur put his own book down on the table, and then rested his head on it, so that he could listen in the least taxing way possible.

'Well,' said Gabriel, clearing his throat. 'You'll know this part. Arthur Pendragon fell at the Battle of Camlann, at Mordred's hand. The cultists believe that Morgan le Fay oversaw the transportation of Arthur's body to Avalon, an uncharted island and the source of all of England's magic – and that one day he'll return.' Arthur could tell that Gabriel was much more comfortable recalling events from a book than having to come up with the words on his own; the awkwardness between them had dissipated almost immediately.

'After all your father's peacekeeping,' Arthur said, 'what would he do if they were right? If the bastard returned? He could hardly hop off the throne and say, "Sorry, old chap, I was just keeping it warm for you" – but the only other option is all-out war with King Arthur himself and all his cultist pals.'

'What would my father do,' Gabriel said slowly, 'if a man who's been dead for hundreds of years appeared and asked for his throne back? To be honest, I don't think he's really thought about it.'

'I bet you all the money in my pocket that somewhere in the depths of his war room there's a contingency plan for that exact occasion. Operation *Rex Undeadus*.'

'I can assure you, there isn't,' said Gabriel, but he didn't look entirely convinced.

'All right,' said Arthur. 'What's next? After the bit about the magic island.'

'Well, it's interesting – you would have thought that with all this magic supposedly out in the open, *everybody* would have believed in it, but plenty of people were sceptical at the time. Most of them only heard about it through stories, you see – it wasn't like Merlin was standing in the town square doing tricks for all and sundry. Then after the Saxons invaded, there was a bit of a muddle with lots of old gods in the mix, and then the country was Catholicised very rapidly. It wasn't until about a hundred years later that cultists really started practising in earnest; by that time it had been long enough for Arthur Pendragon to have become legend. A myth, not a man.'

'Well,' Arthur said. 'I suppose it's much easier to devote yourself to the idea of somebody, instead of the flesh-and-blood person. Much neater.'

'Exactly,' said Gabriel. 'What I'm reading now is this

man – this sort of Arthurian thought leader – talking about the power of people. The theory that with magic gone, it's up to the cultists to stand up for Merlin and Morgana's ideals, while they await the second coming of their king, and the magic that'll return with him.' He was talking earnestly, moving his hands; Arthur had never seen him so animated. It was clear that he didn't ensconce himself in the library out of a sense of duty – he actually really enjoyed this, all the reading and the learning and the inhaling of vast quantities of dust. 'Because the magic isn't enough, on its own. It doesn't just fix everything. They need people who are open to it, people who want to channel that power for good. And back when Arthur was king … he was that person.'

'So they follow a man they believe was Merlin's puppet,' Arthur said. 'Why not just worship the wizards?'

'Well, they are very fond of them,' Gabriel said, 'but look – read this.' He pushed the book towards Arthur again, and this time Arthur actually sat up properly to read it.

'This is written in Old English,' he said. 'I *hate* Old English. It's almost as bad as Common Brittonic. My father made me learn both.'

'Well, this man was hardly going to write it in Latin,' said Gabriel, pointing to a line of text.

'Arthur … *hygeclæne*. I don't know that one – what's *hygeclæne*?'

'Roughly translated, "pure of heart",' Gabriel said, using his finger to trace the word without ever actually touching the page. 'He wasn't their puppet – he was their *chosen one*. The only one good enough to take on all that power and not be corrupted by it. Cultists believe that Arthur's downfall came not because he wasn't strong enough, or *good* enough, but because of the people around him. I mean – in half the stories, Morgan le Fay is pitted against him, although the more progressive think that she took him to his final resting place, so they must have reconciled in the end.'

'Ah,' said Arthur. 'But they don't believe it was his final resting place, if he's coming back. Final *napping* place, maybe.'

'Well,' Gabriel said. 'Opinion is divided about whether he'll come back in body, or in spirit. Plenty of cultists believe that Arthur's return will be more of a . . . a rebirth. An awakening, inside somebody else who is as pure – as *hygeclæne* – as him. And then Merlin will return in some form too, and probably Morgana, and we'll have magic again in England and a true ruler on the throne.'

'But . . . you don't believe any of this,' Arthur said slowly. 'Right? Because that would be potentially problematic, seeing as your father is our true ruler. And, you know . . . because soon *you'll* be the one on the throne.'

'No,' Gabriel said, running a hand through his hair. 'I don't believe it. Or – no, not in the magic. But it is fascinating. And I suppose I do want to be . . . the kind of king these people want. Worthy. Even if the Catholics in this country don't believe that Merlin really existed, or that Arthur had some spiritual significance, they do all think he did a pretty good job of being king.'

'But it's like you said. They devote themselves to the *idea* of somebody. You can't live up to a legend. Not even the legend himself could do it, if he were here.'

'Maybe not,' said Gabriel, but Arthur wasn't buying it.

'Hang on – so you're modelling yourself on *Arthur Pendragon*? Is that what you're doing shut away in here all the time? Trying to read enough about him by the time you ascend to the throne that you can become the – I don't know – the chivalric ideal?' Gabriel didn't say anything, but he did look slightly embarrassed. Arthur let out a huff of laughter and collapsed back against his chair. 'Well, that's – that's nonsense, Gabriel. And entirely unattainable.'

Gabriel sighed, and rubbed at his cheekbone irritably. 'By all accounts, King Arthur was a good man. He truly cared about his people. People thought of him as fair. And, yes, he was the embodiment of chivalry – or at least, he tried. He knew what kind of England he wanted to live in. I don't see what's so wrong about trying to be a king like that.'

'There's no way to live up to the chivalric ideal,' Arthur scoffed. 'There are only three ways to attempt it – die on a religious quest, die for your true love, or die in battle. Regardless, you never get out of it alive.'

Gabriel looked up at Arthur, his thumb still pressed to his cheek. 'When I was ten I thought about running away,' he said, so quietly Arthur had to lean forward to listen.

Arthur nodded slowly. 'Yes ... I know. Because – don't you remember what you said to me, that summer? Things were going so terribly between your sister and me, and you had barely spoken a word to me for years, always shutting up like a clam when I was around, but then you came up to me one day in the courtyard and ...'

'Asked if you'd like to be king instead,' Gabriel said,

looking stricken. 'I remember. I didn't think ... well, I hoped *you* didn't. Remember, I mean. I had finally told Father how I felt, that it was all too much for me and I didn't want it, and he said ... he said I had to be the king the people needed, even if it wasn't the man I wanted to be. I was so desperate for a way out, and hearing that ... it felt like watching a door close, and knowing it'd never open for me again.'

'Ouch,' said Arthur. He tapped his fingers on the table, considering. 'You know ... fathers aren't always right just by virtue of being fathers. Or even ... just by virtue of being king.'

Gabriel didn't reply – he just took another book from the pile, opened it gently and began to read.

As much as Agnes had protested that the event wasn't a party, there *was* a sort of makeshift bar at one end of the cultist cellar, stocked with enormous cauldrons of a mysterious beverage that tasted strongly of liquorice and peppermint. Gwen and Agnes backed themselves into a wall to drink, entirely anonymous in all the hubbub.

'How did you find out about this?' Gwen asked. 'And why is it secret? Surely everybody knows that my father encourages freedom of beliefs by now. Doing it covertly just makes it seem ... suspect.'

Agnes looked suspiciously as if she were wishing that Gwen had decided to leave with the others.

'From another lady-in-waiting,' she said miserably. 'I was meant to meet her. And — I suppose it's all part of the fun.'

Despite the fact that Gwen had never voluntarily sought out Agnes's company, her obvious disappointment stung. Just moments ago Gwen had felt like one of the gang, sneaking around the castle grounds together in the dead of night — but suddenly things were right back to how they always were. 'Well. Don't let me hold you back.'

'I can't leave you alone,' Agnes said, wide-eyed and a little too hopeful.

'Don't be ridiculous,' Gwen said stiffly. She didn't actually want Agnes to abandon her, but it was better than feeling as if her presence were being suffered. 'Nobody here knows who I am – I'm quite safe. Go.'

'Well,' Agnes said, having the good manners to look briefly torn. 'If you insist.' She was off across the room looking for her friends a moment later. Gwen stood clutching her cup, catching snatches of conversation and laughter all around her, focusing solely on finishing her drink. Once it was done, she pulled her hood more securely around her face and went to refill it; she only managed to take two steps back towards the cauldrons before she felt a hand on her arm, insistent fingers pressing into the jut of her elbow.

'Could you not find them?' Gwen said, expecting Agnes – but when she turned, she almost dropped her empty cup.

'What,' said Lady Leclair, 'are you *doing*?'

'Um,' said Gwen, hearing her voice jump almost a full octave. 'Getting a drink?'

'No,' Bridget said, 'I mean, what are *you* doing *here*?' She gently steered Gwen back into a dark corner. She was wearing an inky-blue formal jacket, her hair pulled half up and secured with an ornate hairpin that was easily the grandest thing Gwen had ever seen her wear. 'Your cloak isn't quite the disguise you think it is. I'd call you *your highness*,' Bridget continued in a low voice, 'but I'm not sure that would be wise.'

'I'm here with – well, what are *you* doing here?' Gwen said. Or, squeaked.

'I'm here with friends,' Bridget said. Gwen felt immediately envious of these friends, whoever they were. Somehow, she hadn't pictured Bridget having any at Camelot, but of course she did – who *wouldn't* want to be friends with her? 'You didn't ...' Bridget started to say, but she broke off, looking uncomfortable.

'Didn't what?' said Gwen.

'You didn't follow me here, did you?'

Gwen gaped at her. '*Follow you?*' she said. 'What? I wouldn't – how would I even—'

'All right,' Bridget said, holding a hand up. 'My apologies.'

'Why would you even think of that?'

'Uh,' Bridget said, glancing around the room before answering. 'I thought I'd noticed ... Well, I'm just surprised to see you here. And – to be honest, it's not like it would have been the first time somebody's done it.'

'People just ... follow you around?' Gwen said incredulously.

'Girls ... follow me around,' Bridget said. 'Not often, but. It happens. Tournaments make minor celebrities of those who take part, as I'm sure you've noticed.'

'Right,' Gwen said stiffly. 'Well. I'm sorry to have given you that impression, I thought we were just ... Actually, I did want to tell you something, but I certainly wouldn't have *followed* you anywhere to say it—'

'What did you want to tell me?' Bridget said, cutting cleanly through what Gwen was sure would have been quite an extensive bluster.

'Oh. Er. I wanted to say – that it was very brave, what you did at the tournament,' Gwen said in a small voice. 'I'm not sure the Knife – Sir Marlin – in fact, I *know* he wouldn't have done the same for you. And I'm sorry you had to do it at all.'

Bridget nodded. 'Because you could have said something.'

'Well,' Gwen said defensively. 'It's not actually that simple, but ...' Bridget was looking at her expectantly. Gwen sighed. 'But, yes. I suppose ... I should have said something.'

She was rewarded with a dangerous little half-smile. If she were an artist, she would have rushed home later that night and attempted to commit it to canvas; embroidering it would probably lose a lot in translation.

Bridget went to speak, and Gwen thought she might be about to receive some sort of praise – was, quite frankly, desperate for some acknowledgement that while cowardly, her behaviour had been redeemable in Lady Leclair's eyes – but instead, Bridget's face smoothed over into something more neutral.

'Keep your head down,' she said.

'What?' Gwen said, confused – but a moment later she was ducking her head as two young women descended on them.

'This stuff tastes like pigswill,' one of them said, handing Bridget a cup. She was tall and Black, with deep dimples and closely cropped hair.

'Great,' said Bridget, squinting doubtfully at the drink. 'You needn't have bothered then.'

'Who's this?' said the other woman. She didn't wait for an answer before handing Gwen a fresh cup of her own.

148

She looked, Gwen thought, a bit like a mouse; colourless blonde hair and a fair, pointy face.

'Er,' said Bridget.

'I'm – Winifred,' Gwen said quickly, hoping she sounded convincing.

'Adah,' said the first woman, shooting her a grin.

'Elaine,' said the second. She had quite a lot of long necklaces on, and they clicked when she moved.

'Adah works in the mews,' Bridget said, 'and Elaine in the kitchens.'

'Oh,' said Gwen. 'The mews – with the falcons? How is it I've never seen you before?'

'Well, I've only been there a year,' said Adah, shrugging. 'Took a bloody age for them to come round to the idea that I might actually be good at it. Why? Where do you work?'

'Oh,' said Gwen again. She could think of no logical reason why she'd have business in the mews if she didn't house a bird there, and was struggling to come up with a lie. Door-cleaner? Or, perhaps – feather-collector? Was feather-collector anything close to a real job?

'She ... doesn't work here. She's my cousin,' Bridget said. Both of the other women looked from her to Gwen and then back again – Bridget, dark-haired and muscular and brown-skinned, Gwen willowy and red-headed and white – and then seemed to accept this explanation in good faith.

'Come to see Leclair crush the competition?' Adah said, grinning as Bridget rolled her eyes.

Gwen noticed that they seemed very comfortable with each other. As Bridget knocked back the contents of her cup, her nose wrinkling in exaggerated disgust, Adah clapped her on the back and laughed – and then left her hand there, resting easily on Bridget's shoulder blade.

Gwen was instantly, irrationally jealous.

'Have you thought about what you're going to say?' Elaine said, and it took Gwen a moment to realise that she was being addressed.

'Say? When?'

'During the ceremony,' Elaine said. 'Your offerings. You offer Morgan le Fay a strength and a weakness. It's all about . . . duality of self, you know? All your facets.'

'Elaine,' Adah said, 'is very into *duality of self*. And Morgan le Fay. And facets.'

'Are you a cultist?' Gwen asked Elaine; she smiled beatifically and nodded. 'Are *all* of you cultists?'

'No,' said Adah and Bridget at the same time.

'But – you know that about Leclair, of course,' said Adah, raising her eyebrows. 'As she's your cousin.'

'Distant cousin,' said Bridget.

'So you believe in magic?' Gwen said to Elaine, desperate to change the subject.

'Oh, yes,' she said breathily. 'If you think about it, some variety of magic turns up in the story of every country and kingdom in the world. It goes by different names, but it's always there. Other religions have their own magic words – their own rituals. It seems unlikely that magic never existed, and yet everybody came to the same conclusion of their own volition.'

'So you think . . . King Arthur will rise again?'

'Yes,' Elaine said brightly. 'When the right vessel comes along. Morgana will sort it all out. Merlin will help.'

'Where are Merlin and Morgana now then?' Adah said, goading her in a way that was obviously habit.

Elaine considered this for a moment. 'On sabbatical.'

'Brilliant,' said Adah. 'Glad I asked.'

'Honoured guests,' called the woman who had greeted them at the door, clapping her hands together importantly. 'Gather, please. It is time.'

A wave of excited muttering rippled through the room, and everybody moved towards the fire and the enormous statue above it. Gwen wanted to get a proper look at it, to gaze into the stone eyes of Morgan le Fay and see what all the fuss was about, but to do so would have meant exposing her face; she watched Bridget's back instead, noticing that Adah had fallen into step next to her.

'We are gathered here to celebrate the night that our lady Morgana's spirit claimed her body; she was born from magic, and to magic she returned. When the time is right, she shall once again grace us with a mortal form . . .'

Gwen felt somebody tap her on the shoulder; when she turned, Elaine nodded in triumph and mouthed, '*On sabbatical.*'

'. . . but until that day, *we* are the guardians of her legacy, here on this plane. To that end, we present our offerings in the knowledge that we are unfinished and imperfect; that we are ever-growing and inconstant, but always striving to become more *ourselves* with each passing year.' The woman smiled around at the crowd. 'Who will be first to honour our lady tonight?'

'I will,' said an elderly woman at the very front, taking down her hood; she shuffled forward without hesitation, her expression open and eager, and their host pressed something into her hand and then stepped aside to make space for her by the fire. 'To my lady Morgan le Fay,' she said in a clear voice, holding her slightly shaking hand out in front of her, 'I give my vanity.' She opened her fingers and dropped whatever she had been clutching directly into the flames; there was a brief, strong smell of something herbal, burned quickly to bitterness. 'And I give my love for life.'

Everybody clapped, and a few of the more spirited guests whooped as the woman stepped aside.

'Who will go next?'

Two people stepped forward at once; there was a slightly awkward moment when neither of them wanted to back down, and the woman at the front laughed.

'There's no rush,' she said. 'Everybody in this room will take their turn.'

Gwen's mouth suddenly felt very dry. The woman's tone hadn't allowed for argument, but there was no way she was going up there; for one thing, they'd recognise her as the princess, and for another ... she simply didn't want to. Bridget turned around, frowning, as if she was having similar thoughts.

'I think it might be time for you to leave,' she said quietly.

'What?' whispered Elaine, looking disappointed. 'But – but it's the whole point of the festival! You can't leave now.'

'I'll walk you out,' Bridget said in a low voice, putting her hand on Gwen's arm; the contact made Gwen's breath catch. She couldn't quite pinpoint why this felt like being claimed, and why being claimed felt so explicitly *good*, but she wanted the walking-out to be extended as long as possible – far beyond the length of the room. She tried to make herself small and inconspicuous as she broke away from the group, Bridget falling in behind her, but at that exact moment the crowd parted to let somebody else come forward.

'Ladies,' said the woman at the front. 'Surely you aren't leaving without making your offering?'

'I wasn't aware that participation was mandatory,' Bridget said immediately; she had turned to face the others and taken a small step backwards towards Gwen, as if trying to obscure her from view.

'Come now,' said the woman, disapproving. 'That is not in the spirit of the day. Make your offerings now, and then you may leave at once.'

'Or,' Bridget said, crossing her arms, 'we could skip straight to the part where we leave.'

Now that sneaking away without being noticed was off the table, Gwen realised that the longer this confrontation continued, the more likely it was that she was going to be recognised. 'It's all right,' she said to Bridget. 'Let's just do it, and then we can go.'

'Very good!' said the woman at the front, instantly all smiles, clapping her hands together. 'Come forward into the light, ladies, and tell us what you have for Morgana.'

Gwen thought she was a bit too cheery for somebody who was press-ganging them into a magical party game, but she walked forward anyway; she kept tugging at her hood, trying to get it to cover more of her face without obscuring her eyes entirely and leading to an unfortunate fire-pit accident.

'Here,' said the woman, pressing a soft handful of something into Gwen's palm when she reached the statue. When Gwen opened her fingers, she saw that it was a pile of dried sage leaves, twisted together and crumbling around the edges.

Her mind had been halfway out of the door, and now very suddenly had to snap back to where she was actually standing – in front of a crowd of expectant faces, waiting for her to impart some deeply held truths about herself that she hadn't yet identified.

'Er . . .' she said, holding her hand out in front of her as the other women had done. 'So it's – one good thing, one bad?'

'Ascribing "bad" and "good" to parts of ourselves isn't helpful,' said the woman, in a slightly condescending tone. 'Perhaps – one thing that helps you, and one thing that you feel hinders you.'

Gwen thought this was just a dressed-up way of saying 'good' and 'bad', but she had reached the end of her stalling; her thoughts were a blur as she tried desperately to think of something good to say about herself. She was – punctual? Organised? The crowd was getting impatient now, and in her panic, Gwen spoke without knowing what was going to come out of her mouth.

'I'm – I'm consistent with my embroidery,' she said, throwing the handful of sage into the fire and then coughing when it spat out a dark plume of smoke in return. She was still keeping her head firmly down to avoid detection, but she didn't need to look up to know how that particular observation had landed. 'And,' Gwen said, looking back into the flames and taking a deep breath, 'I'm – I'm a coward.'

A few people clapped, but the reaction was fittingly lacklustre.

'Well,' said the grey-haired woman, holding out another handful of sage for Bridget. 'You *are* actually supposed to do it the other way around, but I suppose—'

'I'm stubborn,' Bridget said, immediately tossing the leaves into the flames. 'And I know who I am. Come on.'

She took Gwen by the arm without another word, and they slipped from the glow of the firelight into the welcoming shadows beyond.

12

Having quickly ascertained that he wasn't the least bit interested in reading anything in Old English, Arthur had accidentally started to doze instead. The sound of Gabriel turning pages, his quill scratching against parchment when he went to make a note, and the distant footsteps that occasionally passed the quiet library were too strong a sedative to resist. It was all rather pleasant, until the moment when Gabriel shut a book too loudly, startling Arthur awake so suddenly that he almost fell off the chair.

'I'm finished,' Gabriel said.

'Right,' said Arthur blearily. 'Yes, me too.' He staggered up and stretched, noticing Gabriel's eyes flicker briefly to his midriff where his tunic had ridden up, and then away again. 'To bed, then?'

'I actually – I'm going to the mews,' said Gabriel.

Arthur had vague memories of the mews. Gwen had kept a tiny sparrowhawk when she was a child, although she seemed utterly terrified of it. Arthur would have given anything to have a bird, but had pretended to find the whole thing beneath him to disguise his jealousy, and once he had committed to his disdain it was hard to shake. He was still sneery whenever anybody talked about falconry. It certainly helped that when people really liked birds they became absolute bores about things like *feeding schedules* and *flying weights*.

'As you're up,' Gabriel said slowly, 'would you mind – you might be able to help me with something.'

'Ah,' Arthur said, taken aback once again. He had assumed that Gabriel was just tolerating his company – and yet now he was asking for more of it. Intriguing. 'Yes?'

'Right then,' Gabriel said, looking embarrassed but leading the way.

When they reached the building that housed the mews, a wonky stone structure near the orchard, Arthur expected Gabriel to ring for somebody – or for a servant to just appear out of thin air, anticipating his arrival even at such an unsociable hour – but instead he produced a key from his jacket and unlocked the door.

Inside it was dark and there was an odd, animal smell; a musty combination of wood, leather and bird droppings. As Arthur's eyes adjusted he started to see the shuffling, uneasy shapes of birds on their perches, housed behind slatted wooden gates. They were hooded and blind but could clearly sense the intruders, and Arthur felt a strange urge to hold his hands up to demonstrate that he was a friend, not a foe.

'Which one is yours?' he said, and the bird closest to him extended its wings a little in protest before shuddering and settling back on to its perch.

'She's a peregrine falcon,' Gabriel said quietly. 'The large one, at the far end. My father gave her to me when I was thirteen. Her name is Edith.'

Arthur peered into the gloom and glimpsed a bird further down the row, hunched over and somehow bristling with anger even in dingy silhouette. He shivered involuntarily.

'She looks friendly.'

'She's not,' Gabriel said shortly. 'Well – she likes *me*.'

'Are we – are we going over there?'

'No,' Gabriel said, approaching another door. Arthur followed closely behind him, reluctant to be left alone in this room full of sinister raptors. The door opened with a creak, and there was a sudden burst of flapping wings and strange, high-pitched shrieking.

Arthur jumped about a foot in the air, and grabbed Gabriel's arm without meaning to.

'Hello, sweetheart,' Gabriel crooned, and Arthur turned to stare at him; he realised a beat later that Gabriel was absolutely *not* talking to him, and released his arm. Gabriel closed the door behind them; it was lighter in this room, the moonlight filtering through a tiny, barred window, and illuminating the demonic creature that had attacked them.

'What's *that*?'

Gabriel laughed softly. 'She's a fledgling crow.'

'It doesn't have a hat on,' Arthur said warily. The crow wasn't tethered, either; it was standing in the middle of the small room looking up at them, turning its head rapidly from side to side as it tried to decide which eye it wanted to observe them through.

'No, she's not a hunting bird,' Gabriel said, still using the love-soaked, deeply affectionate tone of voice that Arthur had heard only once before, aimed at the cat. Gabriel leaned down and held out a hand; the crow hopped forward and then nibbled hopefully at his finger.

'Why is it in *here* then?' Arthur said, discomforted again by Gabriel's sudden transition from awkward silences and stunted half-sentences into easy confidence.

'She's not supposed to be. She fledged last week – they often leave the nest before they're ready to fly, they're too bold for their own good – and she hurt herself. I didn't want her to get into any more trouble, so I brought her inside, and since then she's just been hopping around here eating scraps and getting in everybody's way.' Gabriel twirled his index finger, and the crow followed it with her head, turning around in a jerky circle. 'She's got a wound on her side – there, you can just about see it when she lifts her right wing, with the white patch.'

'So she'll leave? When she's healed?'

'I hope so,' said Gabriel, as the bird tired of spinning and attempted to fly up on to his bent knee in a very unco-ordinated flurry of dark feathers. 'She's a wild bird. Not a pet.'

'Right. No name, then,' Arthur said, bending and reaching out for the crow, who smartly sidestepped him.

Gabriel laughed again, and Arthur felt a warm pull of satisfaction at the sound. 'No. You can give her one though. If you'd like.'

'What?' said Arthur incredulously, straightening back up. 'Christ, no, that's – that's *far* too much responsibility. It's your crow. You should name it.'

'I recall you had no trouble renaming my cat . . .'

'That's because your cat has a stupid Arthurian name.'

159

'Good point,' Gabriel said, looking up at him and raising an eyebrow, '*Arthur.*'

'Well, I didn't name *myself*, did I?' Arthur said, folding his arms and watching as the crow tried to decide whether it was pleased or furious that Gabriel was scratching it on the head.

'Can you . . . I need your hands,' Gabriel said. Arthur was so startled he just stared back at him. 'Just come down here for a minute, will you?'

'Er . . . All right.' Arthur knelt awkwardly on the hard stone floor, knocking his thigh against Gabriel's accidentally, and then briefly considering doing it again on purpose. The crow was assessing them both with utmost suspicion; Gabriel held out his finger for her consideration, and then suddenly grabbed at her, managing to press both wings against her sides so she couldn't escape. He turned her over on to her back, and her spindly legs stuck out ridiculously from her feathery little body as she glared at him accusingly.

'Hands,' Gabriel said, and Arthur held them out. Gabriel immediately pressed the crow into them, and Arthur jolted at the unexpected warmth of both bird and fingers. He felt strangely skittish, and tried to concentrate on the task of containing the angry ball of feathers now wriggling against his palms. 'Don't squeeze her, just hold her firmly. Turn her towards the window a bit, I want to get a look at her injury – she doesn't let me do it any more, I think she's quite tired of me.'

He gently pushed two of Arthur's fingers out of the way to release her right wing and then pulled it away from her body, leaning in closer to get a good look. He dipped his head so low that Arthur could feel Gabriel's breath, warm against his knuckles. The crow made a strange, hoarse squeaking sound and then turned her head to one side to study Arthur properly; she was looking at him as if she knew exactly what he was thinking, and was not particularly impressed.

'There we go,' Gabriel said to the crow, letting go of her wing. 'Healing up nicely. You can release her now.' Arthur opened his hands and the bird righted herself indignantly, then dropped down on to the floor to gather herself. 'Thank you. You were good at that – just the right sort of grip.'

'That's what they all say,' said Arthur, but they were still very close together on the floor, and it hung awkwardly in the air between them. He wouldn't have said it at all if he'd realised that Gabriel was looking right at him – well, *down* at him, even while kneeling – with the moonlight picking out the fine-boned features of his face. 'You don't have any freckles,' he said suddenly.

'Er – what?'

'Your sister has freckles,' Arthur said, as if this explained anything.

'She takes walks,' Gabriel said, his brow furrowing in a way that already felt very familiar. 'Every day, she walks . . .' He stopped abruptly, as if he'd been interrupted; as if Arthur had been doing something other than staring stupidly at him.

As much as Arthur liked to give the impression that he was some sort of seasoned rake, he rarely managed to follow through when actually confronted with an attractive boy.

161

Mitchell from the kennels was a recent and notable exception, and had been the one to make the first move. Flirting was easy – Arthur was never short of words or winks, and he parcelled them out freely – but hurtling head-first into anything more was an incalculable risk, and *this* particular risk was off the charts.

Nevertheless, Arthur felt the strange, quiet tension in the room building. Gabriel's eyes were still soft from looking at his damned crow, and – he really didn't think he was imagining it – they were soft from looking at him, too.

He tilted his head and looked quizzically at Gabriel, then gave a little shrug, leaned forward and kissed him.

Gabriel let out a muffled sound of surprise, and for half a breath he barely moved; Arthur could have sworn he felt the slightest bit of give, the *tiniest* touch of reciprocation, but suddenly he was being shoved away with considerable force. His back hit the floor and knocked all of the air out of him in a violent wheeze. The crow was apoplectic, screeching and flapping its wings, seemingly wanting to get in on the thrilling fight it was witnessing.

'Um,' said Gabriel, staring at him in wide-eyed panic. Arthur stared back, breathing heavily. 'Excuse me.' Before Arthur could respond he was up, and gone.

'Well, *shit*,' Arthur said, staggering to his feet, pushing his hair back and straightening his jacket as he attempted to regain some small semblance of his dignity. He felt shaken and slightly sick from the full force of Gabriel's rejection – although admittedly, part of it may have been from his impact against the floor. The crow blinked curiously up at him.

'Don't repeat that,' he said sternly. 'You're too young for that sort of language.'

He crossed to the door, closed it carefully behind him, then half jogged through the next room to avoid looking at the menagerie of menacing birds, grimacing as he heard them shake out their wings in agitation as he passed.

He was just wondering what he'd do about locking up when he stepped outside and found that Gabriel was still standing there, looking like a spooked horse.

'The key,' he said. 'I mean – the lock. I need to . . .' He gestured hopelessly at the door, and Arthur stepped aside. He seemed to be having a fair amount of trouble with it, which gave Arthur time to consider his approach.

'Er – I'm really sorry about that,' he said, trying to sound cheerful. 'It was . . . you know. A mistake. It's late, and . . . apparently all that talk about ancient magical deities really gets me going.'

Gabriel didn't say anything. He finally managed to turn the key in the door, but then just stood there staring at it, his back to Arthur.

'In my defence, I really did think—'

'Is this why you made a deal with Gwen?' Gabriel said quietly. 'She knows?'

Arthur squinted up at the starry sky and only momentarily considered lying. 'Yes.'

'She's protecting you. Because you're . . . you don't like women?' He said it slowly, as if the pieces were only coming together in his mind as he did.

'I like them just fine,' Arthur said. 'For strictly hands-free activities. Going to concerts. Book clubs. Turns about the hall.'

'*Why* did she agree to this?' Gabriel still hadn't turned around. It was making Arthur extremely nervous. The full repercussions of what he'd just done were hitting him as violently as he'd hit the floor. He had kissed the Prince of England . . . on a whim. Gabriel could be angry enough to tell his father – he could be angry enough to have Arthur *arrested*, for that matter, for losing his mind and attacking him in a shed.

'I can't – um,' Arthur said stupidly. 'You'd have to ask her.'

'Right,' Gabriel said. 'Right.'

'Are you going to . . .'

Arthur faltered, because Gabriel had finally turned to him with an expression of such uncharacteristically fierce determination on his face that Arthur strongly considered making a run for it.

He cleared his throat nervously and tried again.

'Is this the part where you—'

He had been about to say 'call the guards', but as it turned out there was no need for any further speculation to that end, because Gabriel had stepped forward and kissed him.

It was extremely clumsy – he had approached with far too much speed, and practically knocked their heads together – but Arthur pressed a hand to Gabriel's neck to steady him, feeling Gabriel's curls brush against the tips of his fingers as he held him in place. Gabriel had the element of surprise this time, but if there was one thing Arthur knew he was good at, it was kissing; his eyes fluttered closed as Gabriel tentatively put a hand to his chest, and then Gabriel was moving more insistently, surprising Arthur with the urgent press of his mouth and the fact that his fingers were fisting in Arthur's tunic.

Arthur was just really getting into it, deeply enjoying the hitch in Gabriel's breath when he let his mouth go all soft and yielding, when he was suddenly pushed away. Again.

'Sorry,' Gabriel said, pink and wild-eyed and breathless. 'I – damn.'

Arthur grasped for something to make the moment less awkward and failed. 'You should call your bird Morgana,' he said in a strangled voice. 'You know – Merlin the cat, Morgana the crow.'

'Right,' Gabriel said. 'Thanks.'

And then Arthur was looking at his back. Again. He stood watching the prince walk quickly away and then turned and kicked the wall of the mews, immediately feeling guilty when he heard an alarmed, avian shriek emanate from within.

'Well,' he said to his aching foot. '*That* certainly clears things up.'

'Where have you been?' Arthur said when Sidney finally came stumbling through the door a few hours later.

'You bloody well know where I've been,' Sidney said, wrinkling his nose in affront. 'You've been where I've been. You left where I've been. I was waiting for Agnes, and then I was with Agnes. Where have *you* been? You're all dusty.'

Arthur had been sitting and staring out of the window at the stars since he'd returned to his quarters. It had all felt rather romantic and dramatic at first, but after a while his neck had started to hurt.

'I was with Gabriel,' he said. 'And then I wasn't.'

'Uh-oh,' said Sidney, pulling up a chair and sitting down heavily next to him. 'What did you do?'

'Kissed him,' Arthur said matter-of-factly. 'In the bird shed.'

'Shit,' said Sidney. 'Is that some sort of slang for something I don't want to know about?'

'No, it was a literal – it was a shed full of birds.'

'*Shit,*' Sidney said again. 'Shouldn't we be packing? Shouldn't we be out the window and halfway across England by now?'

'Can't see why,' Arthur said, leaning back in his chair and looking rather smug. 'Because he kissed me back.'

Sidney gaped at him. 'In the *bird shed*?'

'You're awfully fixated on the bird shed.'

'You're right,' Sidney said, rubbing his eyes with both hands. 'Let's back up to – what happened?'

'He was showing me his birds,' Arthur said, feeling slightly hysterical now, 'and he had this crow, and he – he called it *sweetheart,* so obviously I had to . . . He ran off and I thought the bill had come due, the chopping block was calling, the noose was nigh, but then instead he – he asked me if I liked women, and then he kissed me.'

Sidney put his head in his hands. 'Is this treason?' he said, muffled by his fingers. 'Or is it just a regular crime?'

'I was wondering that. But *you* have an alibi,' Arthur said, patting him on the arm. 'You were lurking outside a secret underground party.'

'Please just . . . This was a one-time thing, right?' He peered through his fingers, looking very tired. 'Tell me it was a one-time thing.'

'Definitely,' Arthur said. 'Absolutely. He's not – you know. He barely talks. He *reads books*.' It was true; Gabriel was not his usual type, and he needed to be practical. It would be one thing to risk his neck for some confident, dashing prince with muscled thighs and witty repartee to truly die for, but Gabriel was quiet, and strange, and ultimately just – *not* worth the hassle.

Even if he was nice to birds.

'Ah, yes. His dusty looks and lack of personality have captivated you,' Sidney said, sighing and getting up. 'I'm going to bed. Suggest you do the same, instead of staring dramatically out of the window like you're in a poem.'

'I don't do that,' Arthur said crossly, and Sidney rolled his eyes as he went over to his cot and started taking his boots off.

Arthur left the window, went to bed and stared dramatically at the canopy for another hour instead. It was far less romantic, but much easier on the neck.

Gwen followed Bridget up the stairs and out into the quiet of the church in a daze. She had hoped that Bridget might forget that she was holding Gwen's arm – that they might make it all the way out into the night air and she'd still be in Bridget's sure, steady grip – but life had not been that kind.

'That was . . . forceful,' she said, as they walked through the rows of pews. Bridget winced.

'Er . . . Yes. My apologies. It seemed urgent that we remove you from the situation, before somebody recognised you.'

'No, no, I mean it was – brilliant,' said Gwen, more out of breath than their walking speed could account for. 'I wish I had that sort of . . . self-assurance, and strength, and . . . and *presence* like you do.'

'Oh,' said Bridget, visibly relaxing. 'Well. I've been training for combat since I was very young, and I suppose it instils a certain . . . confidence.'

'Confidence? You're magnificent,' Gwen said, too caught up in the moment to be embarrassed; Bridget's expression twisted into something unreadable, and she cleared her throat and looked straight ahead as she walked, clasping her hands formally behind her back.

'My family is from the Sukhothai Kingdom – there's a fighting style there that's very different to what they teach in England. It's targeted – efficient. I learned to fight with my whole body, with fists, elbows and knees, before I picked up my first weapons. My father never had a son, so he taught me instead. Learning to fight like that makes you very . . . aware of your body, and what it can do.'

Gwen was certainly very aware of Bridget's body, specifically the habit she had of stretching out her shoulders to loosen the muscles there. She was doing it now, and Gwen was so distracted by the shift of her arms under her jacket that she missed what Bridget said to her next.

'I was saying,' she repeated, taking in Gwen's baffled and flushed expression, 'I could teach you the sword. If you like.'

'Oh – no, I couldn't,' Gwen said automatically. Bridget nodded, and they kept walking in silence for a while, out across the courtyard where the only sounds were their footsteps and the gentle hooting of a perturbed owl. No good could come of spending more time with Bridget, no matter how much she wanted to. And learning to fight, with all the physical exertion involved, the intimacy and the *sweat* and seeing Bridget up close as she expertly handled her weapon . . .

'Actually,' Gwen said suddenly. 'Maybe – yes. I'd like that.'

Bridget appraised her solemnly. 'Well. Good. I'll come for you in the morning.'

They parted at the keep, and Gwen walked upstairs feeling stunned. She fell asleep thinking of Bridget, standing between her and the rest of the world with her arms crossed and her eyes blazing in defiance.

Morning brought fresh clarity, and Gwen was twisting her silken belt into knots when Gabriel sat down opposite her at the breakfast table on the balcony, looking as if he hadn't slept at all.

'Do you know what's happening?' she asked, and Gabriel looked confused for a moment. 'Mother and Father? I haven't seen either of them for days.'

'Oh. Yes. There was some kind of incident in Ruthin last week,' said Gabriel. 'They're meeting with the local guard now.'

'What's in Ruthin?' Gwen said, as a page rushed out bearing heaped plates of food. Gabriel thanked him as Gwen reached for the grapefruit.

'Maen Huail,' said Gabriel. 'It's a stone block where Arthur Pendragon apparently beheaded one of his enemies. Cultists treat it as a sacred site.'

'Lovely,' said Gwen, through a sour mouthful of fruit. 'So they . . . ?'

'Attacked a church there,' Gabriel said. 'Apparently. Although they say the church attacked them. Nobody was injured beyond scrapes and bruises.'

'Were you up late with Father, sorting it all out?' said Gwen. Gabriel twitched, and then rubbed at the back of his neck. He looked almost guilty.

'No,' he said eventually.

'But you were up late?' Gwen pressed. 'You look *wrecked*.'

'Oh, thanks,' Gabriel said, attempting levity. 'I went to

the library. And then I went to the mews, to check on that crow, and . . .' He took a bite of bread, as if trying to put off the rest of his sentence for as long as possible. 'Arthur . . . was there.'

'Arthur came with you to look at a bird?' Gwen said, both eyebrows raised. She distinctly remembered him renouncing all of birdkind when they were children.

'Yes,' Gabriel said miserably.

'Well,' said Gwen. 'How was the crow?'

'Fine. Much improved. Fine.'

'So if you weren't up late dealing with matters of state,' Gwen said, 'and if the crow is fine – fine twice over, in fact – what on earth is going on with you?'

'Tired,' said Gabriel, and Gwen snorted.

'You're not tired. I mean, you *are*, but you're always tired. You're . . . twitchy. What's going on?'

Gabriel rubbed his eyes, and then ran a hand through his hair; his copper curls were mussed and sticking up at the back, as if he'd been fiddling with them quite a lot already this morning. 'Why don't *you* tell me what's going on?' he said finally.

'You can't just repeat what I say back to me, that's not—'

'Gwendoline,' Gabriel said, slow and serious. 'Why don't you tell me what's been going on?'

Gwen's hands clenched around her grapefruit, which was quite an unpleasant tactile experience. The bottom had dropped out of her stomach, which was even worse. 'Why? Did Arthur say something to you?'

'This isn't about Arthur,' Gabriel said, although she

noticed that he was pink in the cheeks. 'This is about *you*. You don't keep secrets from me. Or at least – you never have before.'

He was right. She had always trusted Gabriel with everything – not that there had been much to tell, but still – and it had been difficult not to talk about this; not just for the past few weeks, but for years, ever since she'd first seen Bridget tie up her hair and stretch out her arms and wondered why it was so thrilling. Usually she'd have muddled through the problem with him, but it had felt too invasive, like she was offering up her own organs to be examined. It hadn't helped that when she was fifteen, Gwen had been foolish enough to ask her mother what it meant when a woman loved another woman; the queen had looked slightly alarmed, but then explained to Gwen that while some ladies experienced confusion brought on by close quarters and intimate friendships, it was always temporary, and nothing Gwen would ever need to worry about.

Of course, as Gwen's feelings refused to stay temporary, her mother's words had given her more to worry about than ever.

But Gabriel wasn't her mother. Gabriel didn't judge. Gabriel would understand.

Still, she felt seasick as she cleared her throat and began to speak. 'When I told you that Arthur and I had made a deal,' she said slowly, 'it was ... He knew something. He knew something about me. Or, he thought he did, and I told him he was wrong, but – he wasn't wrong. He was right.'

'Okay,' Gabriel said, looking even more confused.

'I've wanted ... for a while, I've wanted something I don't think I can have,' Gwen pressed on, desperation creeping into her voice. 'I mean, you must understand that – I know this isn't the life you would have chosen for yourself.'

Gabriel took a deep breath in and out through his nose. This wasn't going particularly well. Neither of them had actually ever said this out loud so plainly – had dared to voice that Gabriel really didn't want the throne. It went unsaid because to say it felt tantamount to treason, although Gwen couldn't tell who they were actually committing it against.

'I've never said that,' Gabriel said quietly, and Gwen leaned back in her chair and sighed.

'No, I don't – sorry. That's not what I meant. Let me start again. I'm not really in love with Arthur.'

'Yes. I know.'

'Well – I've never really liked anybody in that way. Not properly, anyway. But lately I've ... lately there has been someone. A person. That I think about.' Gabriel didn't say anything. His face had closed off somewhat though, and Gwen was desperate to break back through. 'For a long time I just tried to forget about it, but that's become a lot harder lately. I want to tell you. But ... I don't want you to think any differently of me, or for it to change things between us. I couldn't bear it.'

Silence.

'It's Lady – it's Bridget. Bridget Leclair. That's who I've been ... thinking about.'

She had expected him to look surprised. Some part of

her had hoped that he might relax, and soften into a smile; that he had noticed something was distracting her, and would only be glad that the mystery was solved and that she had finally shared this part of herself with him. If Gabriel knew, and *saw* her, and didn't mind, then it wouldn't feel so wrong. It would ease some of the panic and regret she felt every time she thought about her mother patting her on the head and reassuring her that the horror of *ladies who loved other ladies* would never darken Gwen's door.

But Gabriel wasn't smiling.

'But …' he said, breaking off and looking down at the table. 'Are you sure?'

'Sure? About what?' Gwen said. Her throat felt strangely tight, her cheeks hot. 'I don't know how I can be *sure* about anything, when I don't know what any of it means yet. But I do like her, Gabe. I have for a while. I know there's nothing I can really do about it, and soon I'll be married to Arthur with everything in its right place, but … that doesn't stop it from being true.'

Gabriel took a deep breath. Gwen was still waiting for reassurance, but it didn't come. Instead, Gabriel finally looked up at her with something that looked strangely like pain in his eyes.

'I don't think this is a good idea.'

'What?' Gwen felt like she had been slapped; the same shock, the same sharp sting, the ringing numbness that followed. 'What do you mean? I know it's not … ideal, but it's not an *idea* I've had, I don't actually think I have a choice in the matter—'

'I'm sorry, but I can't – I can't hear this,' Gabriel said,

standing up. Gwen stared at him, tears burning behind her eyes; he shook his head once, a brief, terse movement, and then abruptly turned and walked from the balcony.

Gwen was left gazing after him, letting her tears fall freely as her chest tightened like a vice. She pressed her thumb hard into the bed of one of her nails, where the skin was red and inflamed from worrying at it. The pain throbbed there, but it didn't help; the other hurt was far too big.

She made her way back to her rooms like a sleepwalker, and once inside saw that Agnes had returned; she hadn't come back to their chambers the night before, and the sight of her tired and happy and a little dishevelled was suddenly all too much.

'Where on earth have you been?' Gwen snapped. 'I had to dress myself, you know.'

'Ah – sorry,' Agnes said, blushing crimson. 'I was at the party until quite late, and then I was . . . Sidney and I went for a walk.'

'For Christ's sake, Agnes, he's a *body-man*. A common servant. Your position here is highly coveted by every noble lady at court, as you well know. Your father didn't send you here to throw it all away on a man who – who always has *soup* on his sleeves.'

'I'm sorry,' Agnes said again, before rushing away into the bedroom. Gwen sat down heavily in her reading chair, then picked up a book and stared at it, seeing nothing at all. She couldn't tell which was winning out – her utter devastation at Gabriel's lack of support, at the way he'd made her feel so *monstrous*, or the suspicion that she *was* monstrous; that it was somehow a dishonourable thing to look at Bridget the way she did, and that Gabriel was right to have reacted with revulsion. She wanted to scrub it all out. She wanted to take back everything she had said and go back to a time when she was still just the sister that Gabriel knew and loved, not this stranger he had looked at with such disappointment.

Shame. That was the feeling. She felt flooded with it, like it was curdling the blood in her veins and taking root in the pit of her stomach.

This is what comes of wanting things.

'Do you ... We could still go for our walk?' Agnes said, creeping into the room ten minutes later.

'It's too late now.'

'The weather is fair – there's still plenty of time before lunch, we could—'

'I said it's too late!' Gwen snapped. The day felt ruined. *Everything* felt ruined. Agnes was looking at her reproachfully, like a kicked dog, but it wasn't making her feel more charitable; it was just making her want to kick harder. Everything came so *easily* to Agnes; she had a close cabal of friends, she was generally beloved at court, and now she had this new, ridiculous romance with Sidney. It just wasn't *fair*.

They passed the next hour in stony silence, until there was a knock at the door; a guard had come to convey a message, and after hearing it, Agnes approached her tentatively.

'He said ...' She screwed up her face, looking as if the contents of the message were entirely indecipherable. 'He said a lady is here to take you down to the north-west courtyard? To – to teach you combat?'

'Oh *Christ*,' Gwen breathed. After how things had gone

with Gabriel, she had entirely forgotten. The idea of facing Bridget now was almost unbearable, but she couldn't turn her away when she had so graciously offered to give up her morning. 'Tell them she's allowed to come through.'

She glanced over at the mirror on the wall, taking in the hair she had braided inexpertly without Agnes's help and the pinched expression on her face. It would have to do.

Gwen unclenched her jaw, took a deep breath and went to find Bridget.

She was standing a little way past the guards, in breeches and a loose shirt, ignoring the fact that they were all staring openly at her. Gwen suddenly felt ridiculously overdressed, even in a simple gown.

'Er – hello.'

'Good morning, your highness. You ... don't have anything else to wear?' Bridget said, tilting her head slightly as she considered Gwen. If she were in a better mood, Gwen might have enjoyed being considered, even if her sartorial choices were being found wanting.

'Um. Not really.'

'Well – I suppose it doesn't matter. Probably best you learn in a dress anyway, if you're always wearing one.' They began to walk down the corridor, a couple of feet of space between them, Gwen falling into step with Bridget and then intentionally lengthening her gait so it didn't look like she was trying to do some sort of synchronised walking.

Gwen had attended combat training in the north–west yard before; she had watched Gabriel there, had sat on the wall eating buns and swinging her legs, waiting for him to be finished so that they could play. As she had grown older and fallen into her own daily routine, she had stopped going with him. It had never entered her head to ask for a training sword of her own.

She still wasn't sure she actually wanted to learn *now*; last night she had been giddy from proximity to Bridget, and desperate to elicit some more. In the cold light of day she felt sure the whole thing would be a disaster. As Bridget greeted the Master of Arms, Sir Dhawan, and requested a sword, Gwen picked at her fingers and tried to push down the mounting dread.

'A sword? For the princess?' Sir Dhawan said, frowning.

'Yes. She wishes to learn the basics of combat.'

'Well . . .' the Master of Arms said slowly, looking around as if expecting Gwen's father to appear out of thin air. 'I'm sorry, but I would need to ask the king. Get special permissions. It's not the sort of thing we usually—'

'It's for a play,' Gwen said suddenly, desperate to end this conversation as quickly as possible. 'It's for a play I'm putting on. For Father's birthday. You wouldn't spoil the surprise?'

'No,' said Sir Dhawan, clearly not convinced but unwilling to call her a liar. 'Well. I suppose – no.' He handed Bridget the blunted practice swords she had requested without any further complaints.

'Have you ever held a sword before?' Bridget said when they had relocated to the centre of the courtyard.

'No,' Gwen said miserably. She was holding it gingerly, letting the point trail against the cobblestones. 'I suppose that's obvious, isn't it.'

Bridget smiled, arching an eyebrow. 'You're gripping it like it's going to bite you.'

'Isn't it?'

'Unlikely,' said Bridget, adjusting her own grip. 'Unless it's a cursed, *magical* sword.'

'Well, how do I know if it's cursed?'

'Hold it like this – that's it, watch my fingers – there you go. Now give it a swing. If you don't open a portal to hell, then you're probably fine.'

Gwen laughed despite herself, encouraged by Bridget's firm, good-humoured guidance; she didn't know what she'd been expecting, but it wasn't this. She gave the sword an experimental swing.

'Good. You need to get used to the weight of it first. Feet shoulder-width apart, and bring that leg forward. Watch me – do what I do.'

Gwen *was* watching her. Bridget had transitioned easily into the fighting stance that she had seen many times during the tournament; it looked entirely natural on her, like she had been born to do it. Her eyes were fixed on Gwen's, her expression serious as she waited for Gwen to mirror her movements. *God*, Gwen thought wistfully. *I hope she stabs me.*

Bridget straightened up slightly. 'Er . . . you're just standing there.'

'Oh. Yes. Sorry,' Gwen said, lifting her sword again and trying to hold herself like Bridget, knowing that she probably looked ridiculous.

'Good. Don't lean forward on your front foot. Keep your weight evenly distributed – look at my feet, not my face, your highness.'

Gwen blushed and shifted slightly, hoping she was distributing something. 'Please, just call me Gwen. Like this?'

'Yes. Gwen. Now, just – give it a go. Try to hit me.'

'Um. Okay,' Gwen said, attempting a clumsy forward swing; she tried her best to put some force into it, and when Bridget's sword came almost lazily up to meet hers they collided loudly, a shockwave reverberating down Gwen's arm. Her reward was a proper smile from Bridget, briefly dazzling and then gone. That reverberated too.

'That's good. Make sure you don't swing too wide. Let's do it again.'

'Your father really didn't mind teaching this to a girl?' Gwen said as their swords came together, already breathing harder than usual. 'Or – you becoming a knight? Any of it?'

'No,' Bridget said, in perfect control of her own breathing. 'My parents might be the only people in England who didn't.' There was a brief pause, as Gwen had dropped her sword entirely; she retrieved it and tucked her hair behind her ear, trying to remember where her feet were supposed to be. 'People were very ... difficult about me becoming a squire, let alone entering the lists. I was turned away for years. Even at the local tourneys, where they'd let a dog compete if it could stand on its hind legs for long enough to meet the marshal.'

'God,' said Gwen. 'Then – why did you do it?'

'Because it was what I wanted,' Bridget said, as if that were the simplest thing in the world. 'I attended my first tournament when I was four, sitting on my father's shoulders, and I knew at once it was what I wanted to do with my life. We trained together for years; I wasn't going to back down just because somebody told me *no*. Hold your arm a little higher.' Gwen did so, and Bridget paused for a

180

moment. 'Well, it wasn't just somebody, it was actually quite a few somebodies – but what did they know about me, other than what they assumed just by looking at me? I knew I could do it. So I did.'

Gwen's sword sagged. 'You're . . . incredible.'

Bridget's expression did something strange, like she was suppressing multiple emotions at once. 'I thought I told you to raise your arm.'

Gwen forgot about Gabriel. She forgot about the Master of Arms, watching from the other side of the courtyard. She lost herself in the satisfying ache of using muscles she had never engaged before in her life; chased the glow that burned in the pit of her stomach every time Bridget smiled, or told her she was doing well. When Bridget stepped in closer to repel Gwen's meagre attacks, with her eyes bright with satisfaction, or stopped to press her sure, rough hands to Gwen's and shift her grip on the pommel, it was impossible to think about anything else.

Half an hour later, when Bridget was distracted looking at Gwen's stance rather than her sword, Gwen actually managed to get past her guard; she tapped the point of her sword lightly against Bridget's chest and grinned, genuinely thrilled.

'I win.'

Before she'd even finished speaking she felt something hook around her ankle, a hand supporting the small of her back to soften her fall, and then she was lying flat on the cobblestones looking up at the blunt point of Bridget's sword.

'Congratulations, your highness – ah-ah, wait.' Gwen had tried to get up, but Bridget kept her pinned at swordpoint.

Gwen narrowed her eyes; Bridget responded by raising her eyebrows and letting the end of the sword make gentle contact with Gwen's chin, lifting it ever so slightly as Gwen met Bridget's gaze and tried to hold back a smile. 'Stay down, and I'll show you how to get back up again.'

A short while later Gwen was breathless and laughing, pushing a sweaty strand of escaped hair away from her face as Bridget once again tried to show her how to do the ankle trick, when she heard a voice cut across the courtyard and froze immediately.

'Sidney,' said Arthur. 'I seem to be having the most *vivid* hallucination.'

He was leaning against the archway, Sidney next to him with his arms folded.

'Nah,' said Sidney. 'I see it too.'

'Can you go and do this bit somewhere else?' Gwen said, wiping her forehead with the back of her hand in a manner so undignified that her mother would have pitched a fit if she'd seen it.

'She speaks,' said Arthur. 'Is this really the Princess of England I see before me, with a massive bloody sword?'

'It's not bloody yet,' Gwen said, in what she hoped was a menacing tone.

'I seem to have interrupted the inaugural meeting of the convention for abnormally tall women. What happened here? Who threw down the gauntlet? About money, is it? Or did one of you insult the other's wife?'

'Ah. Terrible when they involve the wives,' Sidney said, shaking his head seriously. Bridget looked from Arthur to Gwen and then back again, her expression inscrutable.

'Why don't you come over here,' Gwen said sweetly, 'so I can pit you like an olive?'

Arthur straightened up.

'Sidney,' he said pompously. 'Fetch my sword.'

Sidney looked unconcerned. 'You didn't bring a sword.'

'Fetch *a* sword then.'

'Righto.' Sidney went gamely over to Sir Dhawan; there was a quick flurry of discussion, but he eventually returned with a weapon. 'Don't poke your face off.'

'I'm not going to poke my— Give it here,' Arthur snapped, grabbing it from him.

'You can't fight the princess,' Bridget said. 'It would hardly be fair, she's only just picked up a sword. But I'll second for her.' Gwen flashed her a smile – the unexpected wink she received in return turned her insides molten.

Arthur paled. 'Er . . .' he said. 'I'm going to duel Sidney, actually.'

'No you're not,' said Sidney. '*Sidney* is going to lean against this wall here and have a nap.'

'It's okay to be afraid,' Bridget said, lowering her voice as if to preserve his dignity; Gwen snorted with laughter.

'Oh fine, fine,' Arthur said, straightening up and pushing his long hair back over his shoulders. 'But you're not to cry after.'

'I won't if you won't,' Bridget said, as she watched him approach. Gwen hastened to the wall, to stand by Sidney and watch.

At first it seemed like Arthur might actually hold his own, but this illusion was shattered as soon as he attempted to land a hit; in a movement so quick and sudden that

Gwen felt she had somehow missed it, Bridget had disarmed him and knocked him flat on his back, with none of the gentleness she had shown Gwen.

'Would you like to go again?' Bridget asked.

'I want to schedule an exorcism,' Arthur said bitterly, as he scrambled to his feet. 'You're clearly possessed by the spirit of a – a massive bloke with a sword.'

'I just practise,' Bridget said, shrugging, clearly enjoying herself. 'A *lot*.'

'Well, in any case, it's not fair,' said Arthur imperiously. 'I have to hold back, because you're a woman.'

'A terrible shame. Perhaps his highness would be a more worthy opponent,' Bridget said, gesturing with her chin. Gwen turned and saw Gabriel standing in the opposite doorway with a book in his hand, watching them, looking stricken. Bridget dropped into a quick bow, and Gabriel waved the book at her distractedly, indicating that she should be at ease.

Gwen felt bile rise in her throat at the sight of him, and he looked just as horrified as she felt. She had managed to forget about their conversation for an entire, glorious hour, but the look on his face was bringing it all back with painful urgency.

'What do you say?' Sidney said, pushing off from the wall to stand up straight. 'Shall I fetch you a sword, your highness?'

Gwen resisted the urge to roll her eyes. He was *never* this polite to her.

'No,' Gabriel said, glancing over his shoulder. 'I was just—'

'Your highness,' said Sir Dhawan, somehow managing to bow as he walked. 'I'm delighted to see you, it's been weeks. We'll just . . .' He clicked his fingers, and a boy came running with a sword.

'Right,' Gabriel said, automatically taking the sword out of politeness and then staring at it as if he had no idea what it could possibly be for.

'Your father told me just yesterday that he would encourage you to return to practising daily – we have new-made armour too, if you'd care to give it a try. Gold-plated, just as Lord Stafford requested.'

'Ah – yes,' Gabriel said, looking trapped.

'Would you like to train with me, your highness? Or . . . I can fetch a squire—'

'It's all right,' Sidney said, smiling affably. 'He'll fight Arthur.'

Arthur was looking at Sidney with a murderous expression, but Sidney seemed entirely nonplussed.

'Splendid!' said Sir Dhawan. 'Very well, your highness. Show him how we fight at Camelot.'

Gabriel threw one more desperate glance back at the keep, like he was hoping somebody would appear and call him away to attend to urgent business, but then sighed and lifted his sword.

14

Arthur was feeling quite confused about the situation he found himself in. The sight of Gabriel wielding a sword certainly wasn't helping matters.

A need to be near-constantly entertained was, he believed, one of his few personal failings; up until very recently, the most entertaining thing about Gabriel had been that he was an oddly quiet and reluctant royal.

Now he was a person who played nursemaid to crows, gripped his sword like an expert, and kissed people in the middle of the night before promptly running away. Watching him raise a sword now with a form that must have been ingrained through years of practice, he was imagining the lean muscle that must be hidden somewhere beneath Gabriel's clothes.

It was all a bit distracting.

'You're meant to hit him with it,' Sidney called.

'Yes, thanks, Sid,' Arthur said. To his right, Gwen and Bridget were sparring again; the sound of Bridget urging her on, giving little corrections and light ribbings that seemed to Arthur to be *very* flirtatious, just made the silence between him and Gabriel all the more pronounced.

Arthur raised his sword. His bad wrist buckled slightly; he tried to compensate by tightening his grip.

'All right then,' he said. 'Shall we—'

Gabriel had already advanced, his every movement by the book; Arthur managed to parry, but it was clumsy, and a few seconds later Gabriel had tapped his swordpoint lightly against Arthur's shoulder.

'Oh.'

Gabriel's expression was completely neutral; Arthur raised his arm just in time as he lunged again, and deflected weakly. '*Shit*. This isn't the sort of thing you look like you'd be good at, you know. It's misleading.'

'Why?' Gabriel asked quietly.

'Well. You're built for reading,' Arthur said, his words punctuated by the sound of blade against blade. 'Reading – in a darkened room – until covered in a fine layer of dust.'

'I'm good at that too,' Gabriel said, attempting to knock Arthur's sword completely from his hand; Arthur blocked him, then pushed in closer, forcing Gabriel's weapon back towards him.

'I know you are,' Arthur said in a low voice. 'Among other things.' Arthur distinctly heard Sidney make a quick, strangled noise behind him.

Gabriel immediately pushed away from him, threw his sword down on to the cobblestones with a clatter and walked away.

'Guess you win,' said Sidney. Bridget and Gwen had stopped fighting to watch Gabriel leave; Gwen seemed to be making a meal of one of her fingers as she frowned after him.

'Your highness?' the Master of Arms called, looking rather disappointed.

'I'll go,' Arthur said. 'Sid, why don't you fight Lady Bridget for me while I'm gone, hmm?' He pressed the training sword into Sidney's hand and took off at speed after the retreating prince.

Gabriel had much longer legs than Arthur; he had made it as far as the south entrance courtyard by the time Arthur caught up.

'Going for a spontaneous walk?' he asked breathlessly. Gabriel stopped, but didn't turn to look at him. 'Or . . . a ride?' They were almost to the stables; as Arthur watched, a stable hand led a handsome palomino out of a stall to be tacked up in the yard.

'No,' Gabriel said, sounding a thousand miles away.

'I think we should talk,' Arthur said decisively. Gabriel didn't agree with him, but he didn't leave, either; Arthur reached for his arm, intending to steer him towards the stables. Gabriel shied away from Arthur's grip, but followed him anyway.

They located an empty stall. It was cool inside and smelt sweetly of hay and horse; Arthur closed the door firmly behind him and then realised somewhat comically that he had to close the top half too, leaving them in near darkness.

'It's always sheds, isn't it,' he said thoughtfully.

'What?' said Gabriel.

'Don't worry,' Arthur said. 'Um. Hello.'

'Hello,' Gabriel said warily. There was quite a long silence, accompanied by the sound of horses snorting and stamping their feet in neighbouring stalls. 'You wanted to say something?'

'Yes,' Arthur said, neatly sidestepping a pile of manure and crossing his arms. 'You keep running away.'

'Do I?' Gabriel said, shifting from one foot to the other and looking determinedly at the door.

'That's twice in as many days,' said Arthur.

'I don't know if that counts as a pattern.'

'You're trying to do it now,' Arthur pointed out.

'Well, I'm standing in horse manure, and I'd rather I weren't,' Gabriel said, suddenly sounding irritated. 'What do you want from me, Arthur?' He seemed to realise immediately just how charged this question was, because Arthur saw him go bright red, even in the relative darkness of the stable.

'I mean – nothing, really. I just thought – you seemed a bit torn up about last night. And there's no need, honestly. It's not a big deal. I'm not expecting a proposal of marriage. I am, famously, otherwise engaged.'

'A proposal of . . .' Gabriel trailed off, glancing at Arthur and then quickly away again.

'I'm not going to tell anybody,' Arthur said. '*Obviously*. So whatever crisis you're having right now, there's no need.'

Gabriel looked at him properly, face screwed up in disbelief. 'You can't be serious.'

'Rarely,' Arthur admitted. 'But right now, yes.'

'Maybe it doesn't seem like a problem to you,' Gabriel said, pressing the heel of his hand to his forehead, 'but I've had a lot of time to think about this. And it *is* a problem. Just because you're not . . .'

'Heir to the throne?' Arthur supplied. 'No. But that's not what I'm talking about.'

'It's not?'

'*No.* I mean – yes, there is the slight issue of things like marriage and succession, if ladies don't take your fancy—'

Gabriel huffed incredulously. 'The *slight issue?*'

'Listen,' Arthur said impatiently, 'I'm not trying to pretend there aren't ... pitfalls. But what I'm saying is, you can't decide how you feel about who you might spend your evenings kissing –' Gabriel winced at this and looked away again – 'because of what it means for *England.* You have to decide based on how it feels ... to you. Surely? I mean, I don't know, I'm just improvising here.'

'There's no separating the two,' Gabriel said quietly. 'I *am* England.'

'And I'm your sister's fiancé,' Arthur said meaningfully, raising an eyebrow. 'We've all got our crosses to bear—'

'She's not your *cross,*' Gabriel said sharply.

'Well. All right. But you know, you can be king and still have what *you* want. There are plenty of ways to—'

'I am not having this conversation,' Gabriel said, crossing to the doors and wrenching them open, having none of the trouble Arthur had experienced in closing them. 'Just forget about it, Arthur. It doesn't matter. It was ... Let's just pretend it didn't happen.'

'Okay,' Arthur said, left alone with the gold-flecked dust motes that were spiralling all around him, already knowing he would do no such thing.

When he got back to the training yard, Gwen and Bridget were gone. Sidney actually seemed to have fallen asleep against the wall; the borrowed sword lay forgotten at his feet.

Arthur leaned in as close as he could to Sidney's face without touching him and then unleashed a wordless yell; Sidney awoke instantly, cracked his head against the wall with a muffled '*Christ!*', and then slid down until he was sitting.

'Didn't go well?' he said peevishly, rubbing the back of his head and wincing.

Arthur sat down next to him. 'No.'

'Thank God you don't really like him then.'

'No,' Arthur said, sounding unconvincing even to himself. 'I don't. But he intrigues me. And he feels like one of my own, you know? I ought to help. Tell him he doesn't have to be a lost lamb, stealing kisses in secret and then agonising over them afterwards.'

'Ah,' Sidney said wisely. 'You just want him to hold you like a baby crow.'

'Oh, go to hell. It's not *like* that.'

'I mean, for one thing, I don't really believe you,' said Sidney. 'And for another – don't you think you should meet people where they are?'

'I like to meet people where *I* am,' said Arthur, as they got to their feet. 'I'm already there. Saves on the commute.'

'Good morning!' the king said to Gwen the moment she sat down at breakfast a few days later. He looked exhausted but was smiling through it, his usually all-consuming stack of correspondence resolutely untouched. 'Glorious day for a hunt.'

She knew that her father was trying to reframe the day's hunt as an opportunity for family bonding because they'd seen so little of each other of late; in reality, it was a political exercise, a way to entertain an influential duke, who was visiting with his household. Nevertheless, she tried to smile back at him, even though her heart felt leaden in her chest every second she sat opposite Gabriel, with the chasm between them enormous and impassable.

She missed the easy rituals of past breakfasts, before her parents had become so busy and her life had started to crumble. The fact that her father knew how much she liked sour fruits, and would push the bowls of gooseberries and cranberries down to her end of the table. The way he would glare down at some list or ledger until she plucked it out of his hand and handed it to Gabriel, who would make sense of it at once. She even slightly missed the way her mother would tut over Agnes's handiwork and insist on replaiting Gwen's hair herself.

'We're hunting?' Gabriel said, looking up from what he'd been reading.

'The Duke of Lancaster is coming,' said the queen. 'He's bringing his son, a young Lancelot, I believe – and his three daughters.'

She looked meaningfully at Gabriel; under usual circumstances, Gwen would have met her brother's eye, united with him against their mother's attempts at matchmaking.

'Right,' said Gabriel, looking back down at his book. 'Very well.'

'You'll come too, of course, Gwendoline,' said the king, and Gwen pulled a face.

'To entertain his parade of daughters? You know I'm absolutely no good at that, Father.'

'Not just his daughters,' said the queen. 'We've invited many of the other families visiting court, too. There will be lots of young people in attendance.'

'Oh,' said Gwendoline. 'I see.' She waited for what she hoped was a safe amount of time, taking a long sip of lemon water to stop herself from speaking too soon. 'Will, er . . . is Lady Leclair going to be there?'

She saw Gabriel's hand slip from his book out of the corner of her eye.

'Yes,' the queen said with a sigh. 'I suppose she will.'

'Oh. That's . . . good.'

Gwen didn't enjoy hunting. She liked a brisk walk as much as the next person – unless that person happened to be Gabriel, in which case she enjoyed them far more – but hunting involved a lot of waiting around, and long, dull conversations with whichever of her father's friends' daughters she had been brought along to accompany.

Normally if she and Gabriel suspected a set-up, she might have amused herself by intervening on his behalf; interrupting private moments, stepping very intentionally on the handkerchief that some viscount's daughter had conveniently dropped for her brother to retrieve. They felt very far away from all of that right now.

They had never gone this long without speaking – had never really argued beyond gentle reproval from his side when Gwen was feeling particularly irascible, and tough love from hers when Gabriel was sleeping in the library and forgetting to eat lunch – and every second that it continued, Gwen felt it gnaw at her insides.

Really, she had no idea how to proceed when *he* had hurt *her*, because he had never done it before. It was completely unprecedented. There was only one thing she knew for certain: if she had to wait for him to work out exactly how he felt and approach her to talk things through, she'd likely be waiting a very long time.

Gwen's father had finally given in and picked up the first letter on his pile; as Gwen watched, his expression grew puzzled.

'What is it?' she said. Gabriel looked up too, his gaze flickering from the king's face back to the letter in his hand.

'My cousin has been sighted near Skipton Castle,' her father said, exchanging a look with Gabriel. 'We'll never hear the end of this from Lord Stafford.'

'Why?' said Gwen, her fork hovering.

'Stafford raised concerns,' the king said carefully, 'that somebody might take advantage of the northern cultist uprisings to rally the discontented. He's been keeping a close eye on any unlikely movements. Skipton is a little too far north for comfort, and certainly nowhere near Willard's lands.'

'You think Lord Willard is up to something?' said Gwen. 'But you made peace years ago!'

'I *don't* think he's up to anything,' the king said, sighing. 'He wrote to me recently, in fact, to warn of unrest near Carlisle, and thanks to him we were able to nip it in the bud. For all we know he has friends in the area and was simply invited to dine at the castle – but Stafford has been near-obsessed with the north lately, and this certainly won't improve matters.'

'He'll want to meet before the hunt,' Gabriel said reluctantly, closing his book.

'Yes,' said the king. 'Well. Off we go, then. And Gwendoline – please see Rowan about your bird before we depart. I saw the poor man yesterday, and apparently it's gone rather . . . feral.'

'He doesn't like me,' Gwen said, eyeing the agitated-looking merlin with great trepidation.

'That's because you never visit,' said Rowan, the tanned, brusque middle-aged Head Falconer who always looked pained the moment he saw Gwen approaching. 'Birds like to get to know you. He hasn't seen you for six months, you're practically a stranger to him.'

'Right,' said Gwen, nervously extending a hand. 'Hello,

Beowulf.' She had named the bird after a long visit from a travelling bard; the name seemed ridiculous now, attached to this small and furious bundle of feathers, but it was too late to change it.

'No sudden movements,' said Rowan disapprovingly. 'I'd keep your fingers out of reach, if I were you.'

'Great,' said Gwen miserably. 'Is there any part of me I *should* allow close to him?'

The falconer considered her. 'No,' he said firmly. 'You can take one of my boys with you. They'll fly him for you.'

'Fantastic.' Gwen didn't feel any affinity with animals, unlike Gabriel, and her interest in falconry had started and ended with choosing her new bird when she was fourteen. As soon as she discovered that they required rather a lot of training, as well as the ability to cope with sudden, incomprehensible bursts of violence, she had given up.

The visiting nobles were starting to fill the courtyard, and Gwen sidled into the shadow of a wall so that she wouldn't be dragged into conversation with somebody unforgivably dull before she absolutely had to. She saw an overdressed man who must have been the Duke of Lancaster talking to her father, and three dark-haired, pretty girls all dressed in various shades of red and pink trailing after; Gwen immediately glanced over to see if Gabriel had noticed them.

Her brother was at the other end of the yard, Edith the peregrine falcon perched on his gloved arm; he was talking to her in confidential tones, his expression serious. Usually the sight would have made Gwen smile.

'Your highness,' somebody said, very close to her ear;

Gwen jumped, and turned to see Bridget's friend Adah from the Morgan's Day party smiling expectantly at her. 'Sorry – were you hiding? I can pretend not to have seen you, if it helps.'

'Oh,' said Gwen. 'No. I mean – yes, I suppose I was hiding.' Adah was wearing something as functionally unlike a dress as possible while still technically being one; she had heavy leather gloves on her hands, and a feather stuck to her shoulder. A brief look of recognition passed across her face, and Gwen suddenly remembered that the last time she'd seen Adah, she had been pretending to be Bridget's distant cousin.

'Right,' said Adah. 'Winifred.'

'Er . . . Yes,' said Gwen, giving her an apologetic grimace.

'Well, you did a really awful job of pretending,' said Adah cheerfully. 'I knew you weren't *really* Leclair's cousin. Anyway – yours is the merlin, isn't it?'

'Yes,' Gwen said. 'He hates me.'

'Oh, I wouldn't say that,' Adah said, smiling again. 'He hates everybody. Equal-opportunity loathing. I'll fetch him, and we can remind him that you're the keeper of the snacks.'

She went in search of Rowan to claim Beowulf; left alone, Gwen was equal parts relieved and terrified to see Bridget walking across the yard towards her, looking distinctly uncomfortable in a simple, dark green dress. Somebody – surely not her *squire*, but then, who else? – had braided most of her hair, so that it was pulled back from her face.

'Good morning. Feeling sore?' she said, immediately upon reaching Gwen.

'What?' Gwen said, startled.

'From the training yard,' Bridget said slowly. 'You must ache.'

'Oh! Oh, yes,' Gwen said, extending her hand and making a small circle with her wrist. 'A little.'

She had ached quite a lot, actually. Muscles she hadn't known existed seemed to have been torn asunder by just an hour or two of activity, leaving her stiff and wincing for days. But each twinge had reminded her of Bridget's hand on hers – Bridget raising an eyebrow and granting her small smiles when she had done something right, Bridget's swordpoint kissing her chin – so Gwen had treasured them as souvenirs.

'You should stretch,' Bridget said, reaching for Gwen's hand and then pausing at the last second. 'May I?'

'Er,' Gwen squeaked. 'Yes?'

'Like this,' Bridget said, gently bending Gwen's hand back until Gwen let out a hiss from between her teeth. 'Sorry. Does that hurt?'

'No,' Gwen lied. 'It feels good.' The second part, at least, was true.

'I was told I could acquire a bird,' Bridget said, letting go of her hand and glancing over at the falconer's assistants, who were bringing out various disgruntled-looking hawks and matching them to temporary owners. 'Well. I was told *knights* could acquire a bird. They most certainly didn't mean me, but I have them cornered on a technicality.'

'Oh, don't worry about that,' Gwen said. 'You can fly mine. He hates me.'

'Enough with the dramatics,' said Adah; she had returned

with Beowulf on her arm, and Gwen took a step away from him instinctively. 'Morning, Leclair. Listen, your highness – he's a bird. His only requirements for feeling absolutely neutral towards you are that you feed him, and you're not a much larger bird who might try to kick his arse. He doesn't hate you.' Delivered by anybody else, this may have felt like a scolding, but it was all said with warmth and good humour. Beowulf, on the other hand, was looking decidedly less friendly.

Over in the centre of the yard her father was comfortably supporting his enormous gyrfalcon, Viviane. He must have given some signal to the gathered crowd, because all at once they started making their way towards the drawbridge across the north side of the moat, led by the exuberant hounds. At a different time of year they would have been able to begin their hunt from almost right outside the castle walls, but the tournament grounds and the large area set aside for visiting participants and spectators to camp had split the land beyond the castle; a copse of trees, which expanded into a proper forest the further they travelled north, formed a natural barrier between the campgrounds to the left and the open meadows to the right. The falconer and his men were trying valiantly to keep the birds happy and calm as they walked towards the woods; Beowulf seemed perfectly content to sit on Adah's arm and glare.

'I've never seen so many people come for the tournament,' Gwen said, nodding towards the spectators' camp through the trees.

'Me neither,' said Bridget, frowning at the closely packed tents thronging with people. She looked pinched, as if in pain; Gwen wondered if she had slept poorly the night before, or if it was just her natural reaction to wearing a dress. 'I wonder what has made the difference.'

'I don't know,' Gwen said, shrugging. 'Perhaps it's all for Gabriel. The older he gets without being betrothed or married, the more fascinating he seems to be. Everybody wants to catch a glimpse of him.'

'Perhaps they come to catch a glimpse of you,' Bridget said, and Gwen snorted.

'Right. Because *I'm* so fascinating.'

It dangled in the air between them, but Bridget didn't take the bait; she seemed suddenly distracted, her jaw tense.

'They've come to see the first woman to win the whole damned thing,' Adah said, and Bridget flashed her a quick smile that Gwen wished she could have earned instead.

When they reached the dark, mossy hush of the deeper woods, Adah was just trying to convince Gwen to put on a glove and fly Beowulf herself when the queen appeared at Gwen's side, putting her hand gently but firmly on her shoulder.

'You're needed, Gwendoline,' she said.

'Oh,' said Gwen, 'but – Mother, Lady Leclair is just going to borrow my bird—'

'That's fine,' said her mother, with a smile that didn't quite reach her eyes. 'She can borrow the bird, and I can borrow you.'

Gwen grimaced at Bridget, whose face remained politely blank, and then allowed her mother to guide her away towards the Duke of Lancaster's daughters, who were whispering together in a tightly knit flock. Gabriel was as far away as possible, talking to their father.

'Hello,' Gwen said awkwardly, after her mother had patted her on the shoulder and walked away. 'I'm Gwendoline.'

They all curtsied briefly and introduced themselves: Celestina, Clement and Sigrid.

'Do you like hunting, then?' Gwen asked desperately.

'No,' the youngest said firmly.

'Sigrid!' said Celestina, shooting daggers at her. 'That's not how you speak to a member of the royal family.'

'Ah. Sorry,' said Sigrid. 'No, *your highness*.'

'Oh, that's all right – I don't much like it either,' Gwen said, encouraged.

'I don't mind the birds,' said Clement, who was by far the prettiest. 'But I like rabbits, and I can't stand it when they catch one. They've got no fight in them, you know. They're cowardly little things – they just want to survive.'

'I suppose so,' said Gwen, who hadn't put much thought into the motivations of rabbits.

'Does your brother like to hunt?' Sigrid asked, attempting and failing to sound casual.

Gwen didn't have the heart for her usual mischief, and felt strange discussing Gabriel at all at the minute. 'I don't know. He loves Edith, no matter how awful she is to him. Edith is the falcon,' she added by way of explanation, when all three girls looked confused.

'Ah,' said Celestina, and they all turned to look as Rowan released Edith from his arm and she flew elegantly to Gabriel's fist, where she immediately and savagely started

201

tearing into the dead mouse that was waiting for her there, spraying blood as she did. 'How . . . lovely.'

Gwen rolled her eyes. The very best of luck to them in gaining his attention; they'd just need to sprout wings and talons first.

'Is your friend all right?' said Clement, staring past Gwen's shoulder.

Gwen turned, confused – and then she was stammering excuses, rushing to Bridget's side without a backwards glance.

Bridget was leaning against a tree, her head bowed, her back heaving with effort; Adah was carrying Beowulf away, trying to calm him as he shrieked and flapped his wings, straining against his tether. There was a large scratch on Bridget's right cheek, oozing a slow trail of blood down to her chin.

'What happened?' Gwen said, going to put a hand on Bridget's shoulder and then swerving at the last minute and letting it hover uselessly in the air.

'Nothing,' said Bridget, but her eyes were squeezed tightly shut, and she looked alarmingly bloodless. 'I'm fine.'

The hunting party was starting to move further into the forest; nobody seemed to notice that Gwen, Bridget and Adah were being left behind.

'You need to sit down,' Gwen said firmly, actually putting a hand to Bridget's arm this time. She was surprised when Bridget allowed herself to be steered gently towards a fallen tree trunk. They sat down, and Gwen watched as Bridget stared at the forest floor and breathed shakily in and out through her nose, fists clenched tightly in the fabric of her dress.

There was silence for a moment, broken only by the sound of Bridget's laboured breathing and the occasional flap of Beowulf's wings, as Adah came walking back towards them.

'I think he's done with his tantrum now,' she said, Beowulf still comically incensed on her arm. 'You all right, Bridget? Can I do anything?'

'Could you go and fetch the guards, please?' Gwen said. 'We need to go back to the castle.'

Adah looked as if she wanted to give Bridget a comforting squeeze on the shoulder, but when she tried to shift her arm Beowulf looked incredulously furious; instead, she hushed him, and walked quickly off in pursuit of the group.

'Did Beowulf try to murder you?' Gwen asked seriously, and Bridget gave a short, pained laugh.

'No,' she said. 'It wasn't his fault.' Her blood had formed a scarlet line from cheekbone to chin, and was dripping into her lap. 'I felt faint, and . . . I almost dropped him.'

'Here,' Gwen said, reaching out and blotting it with her sleeve. Bridget barely seemed to notice; her blood blossomed purple on the blue silk. 'Are you ill?'

'Er – no,' said Bridget, opening her eyes with a grimace. 'Not really.'

'Well, you're doing a very impressive impersonation of an ill person then,' said Gwen, watching as Bridget seemed to be struck by a fresh wave of pain.

'I'm fine, you don't need to baby me,' Bridget snapped, and Gwen raised her eyebrows.

'Are you embarrassed?'

'I'm not *embarrassed*, I'm just – I'd rather not be seen like this.'

'Oh,' said Gwen. 'Well, I don't mind. But I would like to know what's wrong. Have you been poisoned? Cursed?'

Bridget squinted over at the trees beyond Gwen, and then looked down at her hands.

'It's my bleed,' she said bluntly. 'It hurts. A lot.'

'Oh,' said Gwen, somewhat relieved that Bridget wasn't in danger of dying imminently of some obscure illness. '*Oh*. You should have said something! Is it always like this?'

'Yes,' said Bridget, through gritted teeth. 'Or worse.'

'I didn't know it could be that bad,' said Gwen. Inconvenient, messy, yes – but not bad enough to render somebody whey-faced and shaking. She'd seen Bridget walk away from being literally beaten with the blunt side of a sword with her head held high, so she couldn't imagine how bad the pain must be for her to almost collapse during a stroll in the woods.

'Well – apparently it isn't,' Bridget bit out.

'What do you mean?'

'I've tried to speak to physicians about it,' Bridget said, tentatively sitting upright, bracing her hands against the log. 'I actually thought when I came here that the castle doctor – well, I thought he'd probably know more than my doctor at home. But he said what they all say. It can't be as bad as all that, it's *normal*, and something about ladies and a low threshold for pain – and then a lot of blustering noises until I . . . until I go away.'

'But – that's awful,' Gwen said, outraged. 'Do they give you something? For the pain?'

'No,' Bridget said, with great effort. 'They say it would interfere with the natural order of things.'

'Does anything help?'

'No.' Bridget blinked up at the sky as she tried to even out her breathing. 'Well – yes. A . . . friend of mine used to knead my back. Her mother was a healer.'

'Oh,' Gwen said. There was a long silence while she worked herself up to saying something potentially very foolish. 'Well – I can do that. If it would help.'

'Don't be ridiculous,' Bridget said, pressing her hand to her forehead. 'Sorry, I mean – you don't have to do that. I'll ask Adah when she returns, or . . . It comes and goes, so perhaps in a few hours . . .' She broke off, wincing, and Gwen immediately got to her feet.

'No, I'll do it,' she said, sounding braver than she felt, walking around the fallen tree so that she was standing behind Bridget, looking at the broad planes of her back with trepidation. She had spent quite a lot of time thinking about touching Bridget, and now she was being given an open invitation – *but it's purely for medical purposes*, she told herself sternly. *So don't go getting any ideas.* 'What should I do?'

'If you just – my lower back, both hands,' Bridget said, 'as hard as you can. And – dig your thumbs in around the spine. This is really – you shouldn't have to—'

'No, please, it's okay,' Gwen said, putting both hands lightly on Bridget's back. 'Here?'

'Er – a bit lower,' Bridget said reluctantly. '*Yes.* There.'

Gwen pressed into the hard muscle and felt Bridget immediately relax a little at her touch; encouraged, she dug her palms in deeper. Bridget sighed and seemed to melt into her hands, the back of her head resting ever so slightly against Gwen's chest. Her hair smelt like something rich and nutty and sweet, and she was warm under Gwen's fingers; Gwen knew she must be blushing scarlet, and had absolutely no idea where to direct her eyes. She settled on staring at an innocuous and entirely platonic bit of tree.

'Who – um, who was the girl who used to do this for you?' Gwen asked, shifting a fraction lower and repeating the movement; she was rewarded with another sigh, and focusing on the specifics of the tree became even more pressing. 'It wasn't . . . Was it Adah?'

'*Adah?* No. She was the daughter of a neighbouring lord,' Bridget said, her words coming much easier now. 'Until – she left. To marry.'

'And – you were close?'

'You could say that,' Bridget said; Gwen couldn't see her face, but somehow she sounded as if her eyes were closed. 'I was courting her.'

Gwen stopped moving her hands. She felt like she had stopped functioning altogether. Her head was full of an odd rushing noise, like a river gone berserk, only one word audible over the uproar: 'courting'.

'Ah. Right,' she said stupidly. 'Lovely.'

Lovely?

'You don't have to carry on,' Bridget said, a slight edge to her voice, 'if you don't want to.'

'Oh, no, it's fine,' Gwen said quickly, very glad that Bridget couldn't see her expression. She worked away in silence, feeling her wrists begin to ache.

'She wanted me to come with her,' Bridget said quietly. Gwen didn't pause; she didn't want Bridget to stop talking.

'When she left. She was marrying a lord, and she asked if I'd go too, as a member of her household.'

'But you didn't want to?'

'No.' Bridget stretched, catlike, her back rolling under Gwen's fingers. 'No, that didn't sound like much of a life to me. Can you – just up under my ribs, if you can.'

'Is it helping?'

'Yes. It is. But you're not quite – if you just ...' She reached around and closed her hand over Gwen's, her palm against Gwen's knuckles, so that she could guide her into position. She turned to the side to make it easier and they finally made eye contact. The colour had returned to Bridget's face, and her eyes were dark and heavy-lidded, lips parted slightly in what must have been relief; for a moment Gwen just stared down at her, captivated and useless, for all intents and purposes holding her hand.

'Er – hello.' At some point Adah had apparently returned with a handful of guards in tow. Gwen immediately removed her hands; she saw Adah bite her lip and look away, as if trying hard not to smile. 'Your highness. Lady Leclair. I've brought ... aid.'

'Lady Leclair is unwell,' Gwen said, with as much dignity as she could muster, addressing the nearest guard. 'I need assistance taking her back to the castle. Thank you for your help, Adah.'

'I can walk,' Bridget said, but the moment she stood up she looked in imminent danger of falling over; Gwen quickly braced her with her shoulder, and a guard propped her up on the other side. They all started slowly walking back through the woods.

208

When they finally reached the castle, they made it as far as a private antechamber on the ground floor, and then sent for the doctor; when he arrived, he took one look at Bridget lying on a chaise clutching her abdomen and tried to turn around and leave again.

'I've already discussed this with – er – with her ladyship,' he said, looking anywhere but at Bridget. 'There's nothing to be done but – rest. Rest, and fortitude of spirit.'

'Fortitude of . . . ?' Gwen said disbelievingly. 'Surely you can give her something for the pain?'

'It wouldn't be appropriate, your highness,' the physician said. He was actually inching towards the door. Gwen looked at him, retreating, then looked back at Bridget, who seemed to be biting down on her lower lip to keep the pain at bay. There was an odd kind of panic rising in her chest, battling with disbelief and indignation.

'No,' she said suddenly, her voice cracking. 'No, I'm sorry – I would like a second opinion.'

'It's all right,' Bridget said heavily.

'I assure you, your highness,' the doctor said, 'I am the king's physician – with all due respect, I have a fair knowledge of ailments of the body, and this is not the sort of thing that requires medical attention.'

Gwen faltered, feeling her chest thrum with nerves, but one glance at Bridget's furrowed brow strengthened her resolve. 'I am – I am *ordering* you to either give her something for the pain or fetch somebody else who is willing to see reason. The Wizard has a good knowledge of herbalism, does he not? Fetch him.'

The physician looked outraged, working his jaw but

seeming unable to find the words, and then abruptly left the room. A few minutes later he was back, with the Wizard, Master Buchanan, in tow. He was an old, pale man with a smiling face, closely shorn grey hair and robes that were surprisingly simple, based on Gwen's limited knowledge of cultist tradition; he took one look at Bridget and frowned, putting down the small case he was carrying and walking over to her.

'The good doctor was a little light on specifics – is it your bleed that troubles you, Lady Leclair?'

Gwen had never in her life heard a man be so matter-of-fact about the intimate details of a lady's health; even Bridget looked slightly taken aback.

'Yes. I experience fatigue, extreme pain, nausea—'

'Fainting,' Gwen added. 'You nearly fainted.'

The Wizard rummaged in his case for a few moments, mumbling to himself under his breath as he searched, and then rose and handed Bridget a cup stuffed with herbs.

'Ginger, fennel and cinnamon bark. Have them add some hot water in the kitchens.'

'Thank you,' said Bridget, taking the cup and looking at it with tentative hope.

The Wizard smiled, his eyes crinkling. 'It is my pleasure to be of use – please call for me any time.'

The physician flounced from the room, and the Wizard followed; Gwen sat down in the chair next to Bridget's, heart still hammering.

'Thank you, too,' Bridget said, giving Gwen a tired smile and briefly pressing a grateful hand to her wrist. 'For saying what you said. I thought the doctor's head might fall off.'

Suddenly, Gwen wasn't sure she could blame her racing pulse on her altercation with the physician.

Arthur was uncharacteristically quiet when he and Sidney visited Gwen that evening. He perused her books while she went through the charade of sending Agnes away – she and Sidney gazed at each other like one of them was being sent off to war – and then simply gave her a half-hearted salute before exiting through the window.

Gwen had intended to do some reading or embroidery, but instead she found herself sitting by the fire all evening thinking herself in circles, returning to the memory of her hands on Bridget's back; the fact that Bridget had courted a woman; that Bridget had trusted her enough to *tell* her that she had courted a woman; Bridget's hands on hers, guiding her into place; the possibility that she may not have invented this pull she felt between them, that her feelings might be somewhat reciprocated. But then she pictured Gabriel's face when she'd told him – Gabriel backing away from her like she was something repellent. She *hated* him for ruining something as good as Bridget.

'Incoming,' said a voice at the window, barely an hour or two later. Gwen startled; she hadn't been expecting Arthur home for a while yet. His face appeared, hair a mess, eyes unfocused; suddenly he pitched forward and landed hard on the floor, barely reacting as bone thunked against stone. 'Oops.'

It was Sidney who had spoken; he summited the sill, looking almost as drunk as Arthur, then made a hideous belching sound and clasped his free hand to his mouth.

'If you're going to vomit, you can climb right back down,' Gwen said warningly as she rose from her chair.

'Prob'ly for the best,' he said, disappearing again. Gwen heard the sound of clumsy descent and then, after a pause, the distinct heave and splatter of vomit hitting the cobblestones below.

'I've died,' Arthur said dramatically from the floor. Gwen snorted.

'Not yet. But if I kill you now, I can just say you choked on your own vomit and nobody will be any the wiser.'

'Do it,' Arthur slurred. 'I'm over. I'm done. And I've drunk – I've drunk all the wine.'

'In the country?' Gwen said, watching as he turned over on to his back like an elderly beetle.

'God, I really hoped I'd climbed through the wrong window,' Arthur slurred, squeezing his eyes tightly shut. 'Clearly. Over-corrected. To the right one.'

'What *are* you talking about? Can you get off my rug?'

He turned to squint at her, looking violently unimpressed. 'I know you're you, so it's hard, but can you at least dredge up – I dunno … one *shred* of human emotion? Empathy? Pity?'

'Arthur, you *chose* to drink too much wine. And you're getting mud all over everything.'

'So … that's a no, then.' He pulled himself into a sitting position with difficulty. He and Gwen noticed the blood on his sleeve at the exact same time.

'You're bleeding,' she said bluntly.

'No I'm not.' He rolled up his shirt and looked down at his arm. The blood was flowing quite profusely, and he had

212

gone a very strange colour; Gwen had seen that expression on somebody once already today, and couldn't quite believe it was happening again.

'Don't faint,' she warned. He looked at her scathingly, clearly meaning to say something pithy in response, but betrayed himself by doing exactly what she had forbidden and fainting clean away instead. 'Oh for Christ's *sake*.'

It was lucky that he'd already been so close to the ground; he hadn't hit his head too badly, and Gwen rather thought he was hard-headed enough to take it. She reluctantly crouched down beside him and turned him over on to his side so that he wouldn't, in fact, choke on his own vomit. His hair fell into his face, and she swept it away impatiently; his skin was uncomfortably warm, and sticky with sweat. She wanted to call for Sidney, demand that he come up and deal with his charge, but she could still hear him vomiting in the distance.

'Arthur. Wake up,' she said, giving him a shake on the shoulder. He just moaned; blood was still dripping from the cut on his arm. 'Ugh. *Fine*.' She cast around for something to stop the bleeding; her half-finished embroidery was on the table by the fire, and she hesitated for a minute before tearing off a long strip of the pearly-white fabric and returning to Arthur so she could wrap his arm.

Arthur stirred as she did so. He made a little sound of discomfort, and then reached for her. Gwen stared down at his fingers, which had closed around the narrow jut of her wrist. He didn't seem to be conscious. She supposed it must have been a reflex. A desire to hold on to something steady.

'Arthur? Are you alive?'

He mumbled something, and she leaned down to catch it.

'No. Better off,' he muttered, the words sounding heavy in his mouth.

'What?'

'Better off dead.' He said it with such violent self-hatred, even half-conscious, that Gwen winced.

'Don't say that,' she said uncomfortably; she'd certainly wished him gone many times, had joked about murdering him endlessly, but it was one thing for her to say it and another thing entirely for *him* to do so with such sincerity. 'You just need to rest, that's all.'

She thought about calling for Agnes, or the guards, and having him carried back to his rooms – but instead she went and fetched the half-finished wedding blanket from its place on the dresser and arranged it over him, careful not to get it bloody. When she sat down next to him his fingers twitched; he seemed to be reaching for her hand again.

She sighed, and took it.

17

Arthur had woken up on floors before, but there was rarely anybody other than Sidney curled up next to him. It was dark outside, with a stillness that suggested the later hours of the evening. Gwen seemed to be fast asleep in a deeply uncomfortable position, her cheek pressed against the stone floor, the well-chewed fingers of one hand resting next to his arm. He lifted his pounding head, confused, and realised he had been woken by Agnes, who at that very moment had given up on knocking on the door and opened it to peer inside.

'Oh,' she said. Arthur shushed her, gesturing over at Gwen. 'I'm sorry,' she continued, in a whisper. 'I thought – it's so late, I thought you'd be gone. Where's Sidney?'

'Outside drowning in his own vomit,' Gwen muttered. Oh. Not sleeping, then. 'I'd give him a wide berth if I were you, Agnes.'

'Right,' said Agnes. She was holding a tray with a pot of tea on it, and put it down on the side table. 'I'll just – er – I'll leave you to it.' She closed the door again.

'She thinks we're passed out after an evening of rapturous lovemaking,' Arthur said, letting his head fall gently back on to the rug.

'I like to think that either she's not that stupid or she knows that *I'm* not that stupid,' said Gwen, sitting up and pushing the blanket off her legs. 'How's your arm?'

'What's wrong with my ...' Arthur trailed off as he saw the makeshift bandage. 'Oh.'

'Oh is right,' Gwen said, rolling her eyes. 'You must have caught it on something during your climb.'

'Yes,' said Arthur. 'Or perhaps during my daring getaway.'

'Your what?'

'Try not to think about it,' Arthur said, turning over on to his side with a groan. 'You'll sleep better that way.' It had actually been more of a pathetic getaway than a daring one – the innkeeper had threatened to have him arrested for *loitering*, of all things, but he probably wasn't *actually* going to call the guards – so all that running and falling over things had likely been just for fun. 'You don't have anything to drink?'

'Arthur, you are not in need of any *more* to drink.'

'Oh, come on. It's hair of the dog.'

'It's not hair of the bloody dog if you're still drunk, it's – I don't know, *dog* of the dog,' Gwen said crossly. 'You can have some tea.'

Ignoring his protestations, she got up to fetch him some. Arthur used the time to sit up gingerly, assessing his critical faculties, and when it seemed safe to do so scooted slowly across the floor until his back was against the base of the large dresser. Gwen sat down next to him, handing him a cup.

'Cheers,' Arthur said despondently. 'To a long and happy life together.'

'Don't say that,' Gwen said, wincing and taking a sip of her own tea. 'I'm already depressed enough as it is.'

Arthur tried the tea and found it surprisingly fortifying.

Gwen put her cup down on the floor between them. 'It's not healthy, you know. Drinking that much wine.'

'Really? I had no idea.'

'There's no need to take that tone, Arthur, I'm just saying—'

'Fine, yes, yes, I know. Forgive me for wanting to have a little fun before my life is over.'

Gwen shrugged. 'It doesn't really seem like you're having fun.'

This was far too astute; it was true that Arthur had been partaking in more drinking than usual since his return to Camelot, and equally true that it didn't really seem to help matters. He had only agreed to split a bottle with Sidney tonight because he was feeling maudlin about the crush on Gabriel he was now carefully cultivating, and things had gone steeply downhill from there.

'Are *you* having fun?' Arthur said. He was clutching his tea like a lifeline, even though it was scalding his fingers.

Gwen looked very tired all of a sudden. 'Listen,' she said, tilting her head back so that her hair tumbled over her shoulder, and fixing him with a very pointed look. 'Our agreement still stands, yes? We keep each other's secrets.'

'I suppose so,' Arthur said, feeling a very faint tug of guilt; he *had* kept Gwen's meagre secrets, but he'd also been adding to his own collection with no intention of telling her any of them.

'Your certainty is comforting.' Gwen picked up her cup

217

of tea, and then, rather confusingly, put it down again without having taken a sip. 'I told Gabriel. I told him how I feel about Bridget. And he – well, he all but told me I was a horrific abomination, and fled. He's not spoken to me since.'

'Ah,' Arthur said. 'Did he now.'

'Thanks for the moral support,' Gwen said bitterly. 'I'd have thought that you of all people might understand.'

'Well,' Arthur said slowly. 'People aren't always ready to know things when, er . . . when we need them to be known.'

'Very philosophical,' Gwen said. 'But he's my *brother*. He's the best friend I've ever had – the *only* friend I've ever had – and I thought that even if it's not what he'd choose for himself, he'd want me to be happy.'

'Christ,' Arthur said. He was too tired for this. It was one thing for Gabriel to be uncomfortable in himself – to run away, and hide, and try to pretend he didn't feel things Arthur was almost certain he *did* feel – but it was another thing entirely to hurt Gwen in the same way he was hurting himself. 'I don't think he's, er . . . coming from where you think he's coming from.'

Gwen shot him a sideways glance. 'Why are you talking like you know something I don't?'

'What? I've never known anything,' Arthur said. 'It's well documented, you can ask anybody.' He disappeared into his teacup for a while, trying to neutralise his expression. 'Incidentally, why *don't* you have any other friends?'

'Oh, thanks,' Gwen said, sounding so dour that Arthur laughed. 'I suppose . . . I don't want any. I always had Gabriel, and that seemed enough. All the ladies at court are dreadful anyway, blithering airheads busy transforming into exact copies of their horrible mothers. They all laugh at me behind their hands and think I'm odd.'

'Er . . .' Arthur said, raising his eyebrows. 'Are you sure they're not talking behind their hands because they're terrified of you? Perhaps because you call them "blithering airheads"?'

'They're not, Arthur. I mean, you've been spending time with Agnes, I'm sure the two of you have had many laughs at my expense—'

'*Agnes* would never say a word against you. Loyal through and through. And I think she actually quite likes you, when you're not being impossible. Which I suppose must happen once in a blue moon.'

'Agnes doesn't like me,' Gwen said, as if the matter were closed.

'Well,' said Arthur, stretching and then wincing as he knocked his injured arm. 'I think you're wrong. And you can hardly say you have no friends, now that you have Lady Leclair, your *very special* friend.'

Gwen let her head fall to her knees. 'God, don't. I don't know if she thinks of me that way, and I – I feel awful about it all.'

'Well, you shouldn't,' Arthur said. Gwen snorted into her kneecap. 'I'm serious. You know, the more progressive cultists believe that in the days of Arthur Pendragon, it was perfectly acceptable for a man to love a man, or a lady a lady, et cetera. Problem is, there's no proof. Probably because once Catholicism took hold they burned it all in a big friendly bonfire and pretended it had never happened.'

'Really?' Gwen said, her head lifting slightly. 'I didn't know that. Gabriel never said.'

Arthur almost swallowed his tongue in his attempt to look normal. 'No? Strange.'

'The thing is,' Gwen said, muffled again against her dress, 'I think I could love a man. I just ... haven't. I don't notice many people in that way. And if I *could* love a man, then surely I should try. It would make everything so much easier.'

'You could,' said Arthur. 'You could fall in love with a man, and know that you once liked Bridget, and neither of those things would change the other. They would both be true. But right now you *do* like Bridget. So I don't think you should settle for a life that denies that particular truth.'

'Well – aren't we shining examples of living truthfully right now?' Gwen pointed out, gesturing at Arthur with her teacup. 'Could you ... fall in love with a woman, do you think?'

'No,' said Arthur immediately. 'Although I assure you that if I ever find myself on the turn, you'll be top of my list.'

'Much appreciated.' There was a comfortable silence between them, during which Gwen sat up properly, leaning against the dresser and squinting up at the ceiling. 'Bridget told me she courted a woman once.'

Arthur practically spat out his latest mouthful of tea. '*Well* – there you go, then! Why would she tell you that if she hadn't noticed you desperately mooning after her and decided to give you some encouragement?'

'I don't know, maybe she was just telling me as a – a friend. And ... I don't moon,' Gwen said sternly, before her expression turned to worry. 'Do I?'

'You moon, I'm afraid. But she must find it endearing.

220

Can't say I understand the appeal. I like my men emotionally repressed and unavailable.'

'How many men have there *been*?'

'When you say things like that,' Arthur said airily, 'you sound exactly like your mother. Look like her, too.'

Gwen narrowed her eyes. 'There's no need to get defensive. You're clearly . . . experienced.'

Arthur winced. 'Why does the word "experienced" sound like it means "an unstoppable harlot" coming out of your mouth?'

'Well,' said Gwen. 'All those stories about you – I mean, they said you were with women, but I suppose that was some sort of cover – and then I'm sure you've been blazing a trail through the castle since you arrived—'

'How many people do you think I've kissed since I got here?' Arthur demanded.

'Oh. Er. I don't know. I don't really know what a normal week is like for you, and it's been almost a month. Five people, maybe? Six?'

'It's two,' Arthur said. 'Actually. And that's been an uncharacteristically busy month, for me.'

'Oh,' Gwen said. 'I suppose two is . . . Well, you can't blame me for *thinking* it. I mean, the sort of things I've been hearing, you sounded as if you'd been very . . . busy.'

Arthur snorted. 'If you want me to tally everybody I've been *entangled* with since last summer, excluding Camelot, I can give you a pretty good estimate.' Gwen just watched him, clearly eager. 'None. Zero. Nil.'

'*What?*' Gwen looked genuinely shocked. 'Then . . . where did all those stories come from?'

'I am a very effective wingman for one Sidney Fitzgilbert,' Arthur said, with genuine pride. 'I'm usually on distraction duty while he's wooing some ... I don't know, some innkeeper's daughter or married minor lady.'

'And before that?'

'Ah,' Arthur said. He had done a relatively good job of not talking about this – barely even *thinking* about it unless he was in exceedingly low spirits and it managed to sneak around his defences – and it seemed a shame to break his record now. 'I was ... courting someone. In secret, obviously. Up until last summer. His name was Gawain – *don't* laugh – and he was the son of one of my father's friends. He never quite came to terms with himself, or with the idea of *us*, so it was all very dramatic. Pyramus and Thisbe, mulberry trees, that sort of thing. Anyway. That's all over now, and he's disappeared off somewhere – Normandy, I think – to ruminate on his sins.'

It almost opened the floodgates – Gawain's smile, Gawain's blond curls, Gawain kissing him with spiced wine on his tongue at a Christmas feast and then throwing him out into the snow ten minutes later when they were almost discovered – and Arthur had to push back very firmly to retain control of his senses. It had been a full year now, but Arthur supposed some hurts ran so deep that they became part of your foundations; he had been relentlessly optimistic about his doomed romance until it had lived up to its name and imploded spectacularly one June afternoon, leaving Arthur stranded twenty miles from home as Gawain rode away on his horse, and he still cringed whenever he thought about it now. How foolish it had been to get attached to somebody who wasn't even particularly nice to him; how idiotic he must have looked to Sidney, the only person who knew, every time he returned from a clandestine rendezvous, going on as if he and Gawain were the romance of the century.

'God,' said Gwen. 'I'm sorry. I had no idea.'

'Well, of course you didn't. I'm an expert at subterfuge,' Arthur said, giving her a grim smile. 'I'm a dreadful romantic, I'm afraid. Sidney gives me hell for it.'

'I'm really ... not. I think that's why I'm feeling so ... overwhelmed.'

'You should just fall in love with me,' Arthur said, in an attempt to lighten the mood. 'I couldn't love you back, but I might grow fond of you. I am partial to being adored.'

'What an attractive proposition.'

'Well, it could be considered a plus to be attracted to your fiancé. I wouldn't know, of course, because everything in my life is completely backwards, but I hear it helps.'

Gwen tilted her head and studied him, as if willing herself to feel something for him. 'It's no good. You're a swaggering idiot, and you think far too much of yourself.'

'Ouch,' Arthur said. 'I'll have you know that I have extremely broad appeal. I'm easy on the eyes, I'm *very* funny – plus, I'm a fantastic kisser. If you'd kissed me, you'd be singing a different tune.'

'That's not a tune,' Gwen said. 'That's the sound of retching.'

'You can't knock it until you've tried it.' He was just goading her, but as soon as he said it he noticed a slight shift in her expression, which was ... interesting.

223

'Shut up. I'm not going to kiss you,' Gwen said, but she had gone a little bit pink in the cheeks, and as Arthur laughed she wet her bottom lip with her tongue.

'It's not a big deal, Gwendoline. People kiss each other all the time. I've kissed Sidney.'

'You have? How was it?'

Arthur considered. 'Very damp,' he said. 'Although admittedly, we were in the River Tamyse at the time.'

'Of course you were,' Gwen said. She shifted uncomfortably, putting down her cup. 'I mean. I haven't kissed anybody before. I don't know how you do it. And I suppose there *is* merit in – practice.'

Arthur could see that she was suddenly very tense, although whether she was clamming up with nerves or girding her loins, he couldn't quite tell. 'Well. That's the most erotic speech I've ever heard.'

Gwen was suddenly very close to his face. 'Shut up.'

He did. Having made it this far she seemed reluctant to go any further, so Arthur rolled his eyes and grabbed her by the back of the head, pressing a kiss to her closed lips. Instinct took over as she opened her mouth; he leaned in, deepening the kiss, his hand slipping through her lightly perfumed hair. She tasted like sweet tea and lemons. It was perfectly pleasant, kissing her, but in the manner of a satisfying stretch or eating a well-baked bread roll. In other words – not quite earth-shattering.

Arthur pulled away first. 'Well?'

Gwen bit her lip and then shook her head. 'Nothing.'

'No. Me neither,' Arthur said. 'Shame.'

'How was I?' Gwen said, trying and failing to sound

casual. 'At kissing, I mean.'

'You're a natural,' Arthur said, patting her arm. 'If only you had a beard, I'd have been swooning.'

'I'll work on it.' Gwen climbed to her feet, placing her cup on top of the dresser. 'I should go to bed.'

'Right, right. Plied with me tea and had your way with me and now you're done and I'm dismissed.'

'You plied yourself,' Gwen said. 'And it wasn't with tea.'

'Oh, bore off,' said Arthur, getting up too. 'I'll send Agnes in, shall I?'

'If you can find her. She's probably run off to find Sidney and nurse him in his time of need.'

'Ah, yes. They're truly disgusting, aren't they?' Arthur made his way to the door and then paused. 'Night, Gwen.'

She gave him a small smile in return. 'Goodnight, Arthur.'

18

Having already been unconscious once that evening, Arthur found himself in no hurry to do it again. He stood outside Gwen's chambers for a while, listening to the distant sounds of the guards talking to each other in low voices, and then suddenly made up his mind – instead of heading for the stairs, he continued further down the corridor towards the rest of the royal bedrooms. He didn't know exactly where Gabriel slept, but took a chance on the next door he came to, knocking softly with ill-gotten bravado and hoping he wasn't about to come face to face with the king in his nightclothes.

It took a while for the door to open, but when it did, Gabriel peered uncertainly through the crack, his bright hair mussed and pushed back from his face.

'If you tell me to go away, I will. I'll go at once,' Arthur said, holding his hands up in pre-emptive surrender. 'I want to talk to you about your sister.'

Gabriel sighed, his hand on the door, seeming moments away from shutting it again – but then he stepped back, letting it open wider. 'Come in.'

Gwen's rooms had a couple of large bookshelves by the

fireplace, but Gabriel's seemed to be made entirely out of books; shelves obscured the walls, and stacks of tomes and papers cluttered every surface. There were yards and yards of used parchment on a desk by the window; Arthur couldn't see into the bedroom, but he imagined it too would be more paper than furniture. There was an apple on the table with one bite out of it, the flesh browned, as if Gabriel had noticed his hunger for long enough to acquire it but then immediately become distracted.

'Why are you ever in the library if your rooms look like this?' Arthur asked, picking up the piece of parchment at the top of the nearest pile. '*Siege supplies in the Battle of Badon, 501*. Scintillating stuff.'

'The books in the library have been passed down through generations,' Gabriel said, rubbing his eyes and sighing. 'They belong to the crown. These are mostly my own.'

'I can see why you never sleep,' Arthur said, sitting down in an armchair. 'I too would lie awake worrying that my bookshelves would buckle, and I'd be buried alive by books about the proper amount of flour to bring to a siege.'

There was a sudden trilling and a blur of orange fur; Lucifer had clearly been sleeping, but he came rushing over to greet Arthur, who bent down to administer enthusiastic scratches behind the cat's frayed ears.

'What do you want, Arthur?'

'I'm touring the castle giving advice to every member of the royal family I meet who has a conundrum,' Arthur said brightly, as Lucifer headbutted his knuckles. 'Lucky you, you're next. If I'd bumped into your father, I'd be talking to him about tax evasion.'

'Oh,' said Gabriel. 'So – so you've spoken to Gwen recently?'

'I have,' Arthur said heavily. He leaned back in his chair and the cat seemed to abruptly give up on him, padding over to the far wall instead and then leaping up on to the windowsill. Arthur watched its tail lashing, fiddling with the makeshift bandage on his arm as he considered delicacy and decided against it. 'Gabriel. I know about her.'

'What do you know about her?' Gabriel said stiffly.

'I know what *you* know, even if you're pretending you don't.'

Gabriel turned away but seemed to have no idea where to go next. He stopped by his writing desk, with his back to Arthur. 'She doesn't really know what she wants.'

'Er – who does? I'm not talking about what she *wants*, I'm talking about who she *is*. She's confused and trying to work things out right now, and you've made her feel like some kind of – well, like she's done something dirty and wrong.' Gabriel didn't reply. 'Come on – the two of you have always been irritatingly attached at the hip. Whatever you're feeling right now, this isn't *about* you. She told you something big – something important – and you turned it against her.'

'I didn't say she'd done something wrong,' Gabriel said quietly.

'It doesn't matter what you actually said,' Arthur said, raising his voice more than he had intended. 'Jesus, Gabriel – why are you punishing her for who she is because you're scared of who *you* might be?'

The silence from Gabriel suddenly seemed extremely loud.

'I'm just saying,' Arthur continued, 'you should be happy that this is something you two can share. Not everybody gets to have family who might actually *understand* them.'

'I don't want her to understand,' Gabriel said finally, his voice shaking a little. 'I don't want this for either of us. Not with our titles – what's expected of us. It's too difficult, it's too—'

'Well, hard luck,' Arthur said. 'I'm sorry it's so abhorrent to you, so disappointing that you might be like *me*—'

'I could never be like you,' Gabriel said, turning to him, and Arthur was surprised by his furious expression. 'You don't . . . There are so many things about this that you can't comprehend. My father trusts me with his legacy. He has worked so hard to win over the hearts of the people of England, to prove himself a worthy heir – everything he does is a careful balancing act, in the hope that he can create the kind of monarchy people can believe in. That's the only future there is for me, because otherwise – otherwise we might lose *everything*.'

'Well,' Arthur said, taking a breath before cocking an eyebrow at him. 'That's certainly a convenient excuse for running away from yourself, but I'm afraid I don't buy it.'

'*What?*' He seemed to have shocked some of the anger out of Gabriel, whose mouth was hanging open.

'There are ways to do both, you know. To be king and also have what you want. And besides, has it never occurred to you that being king means you'll have the power to *change* things?'

'No,' Gabriel said, red-cheeked and frowning. 'It's not

that simple. And . . . it's not what I want. Because I want to do this *right*.'

'I don't necessarily think that's true,' Arthur said, getting up and taking a step towards Gabriel, who shrank away from him towards the desk. 'I think it's what you've told yourself you want, to make it hurt less when it's all you get in the end. I think you'd rather try to make yourself into an *ideal* than accept that you are a real person, because it feels safe. You'll still be you, even when you're king. So what do *you* want to do with your one slightly dull but nonetheless precious life?'

Gabriel flinched. He opened his mouth and closed it again, and then gave it another try. 'I thought you came here to talk to me about Gwen.'

'Well, if it were really *about* Gwen then I would have stayed on course, but I'm afraid it's not at all, is it?'

'How am I supposed to know what I want?' Gabriel said quietly. 'There's only ever been room for what I'm . . . destined to have.'

Arthur sighed. If only both siblings could have had their crises in the same room, he could have halved the evening's work. 'Come on. You must have some idea about how you'd like to live your life. Very deep down, somewhere under about sixty layers of ink and parchment, you must have a beating heart.'

'I don't see how being rude to me is going to—'

'Well, if you'd stop being so *avoidant* and just—'

'Fine,' Gabriel snapped, finally losing his temper. 'Fine! If I got to choose . . . I'd like to do things differently. I'm not criticising my father, I'm not – I just think we have different priorities.'

'Like?' Arthur prompted.

'Like . . . there's this library at Tintagel Castle. It's enormous. It houses the largest collection of books in England, including almost all of the remaining cultist texts, and there are academics who've been living and studying there all their lives. If it were my choice, I'd leave Camelot. I'd go there. And . . .'

'And?'

'It's stupid.'

'I'll be the judge of that. I'm very familiar with stupidity.'

Gabriel sighed. 'I want books to be available to everybody. Not just people like us. I want – I'd like to help educate people. To train academics at Tintagel, and send them out across England. Not just to . . . teach Latin and hymns to nobility. Do you know how few people can read and write in this country? I think – when people are given the chance to learn for themselves, they're not forced to think that everything that happens to them is due to the whims of some higher power. They have *real* choices.' He exhaled, half-terror, half-relief. 'I've never told anybody that. Anybody other than Gwen.'

'Well,' Arthur said, briefly speechless for once. 'That's – that's *brilliant*.'

Gabriel looked irritated. 'It's not. It's not how things are done, and it's unrealistic and idealistic and . . . foolish.'

Arthur snorted. 'It's how things *could* be done, if you just told somebody about it.'

'What happened to your arm?' Gabriel said, as if Arthur hadn't spoken.

Arthur glanced down, surprised at the question; he had managed to forget about it. Gwen's bandage was unravelling, coming loose at the end. 'I fell. Or – I think I did, anyway. It's all a little hazy.'

Gabriel shook his head. 'You're a careless person, Arthur.' Arthur liked how his name sounded in Gabriel's mouth, even if his tone was weary. 'That's not who Gwen and I are. We're careful. And – I don't want things to be difficult for me, or my sister. I want her to be happy.'

'I don't think doing a difficult thing and being happy are mutually exclusive, Gabriel. I think you could *both* have some of the things you want, if you're brave enough to ask for them.' He crossed his arms, feeling a bit combative. 'Would I be invited to this giant library at Tintagel?'

Gabriel shrugged. He was leaning against his desk, fingertips pressing into the wood.

'Are you really going to try to pretend that you haven't thought about me at *all*?'

To Arthur's great satisfaction, Gabriel blushed deep scarlet at this, and then shrugged again.

'Come on. I'm waiting for a real answer. You can kiss me again while you consider it, if you think that might help swing it.'

The slightly choked sound Gabriel made at this was worth the risk Arthur had taken in saying it. It was starting to feel familiar to him now, how quickly Gabriel went from stern and distant to suddenly being very present – to seeming very aware of exactly how far apart they were standing from each other.

'I don't think I can,' Gabriel said, his gaze hovering

somewhere in the vicinity of Arthur's shoes. It was far more encouraging a response than Arthur had been expecting.

'You did before.'

'Yes, but it wasn't ... premeditated,' Gabriel said. He looked up and seemed unable to stop himself from glancing at Arthur's lips, which were now quirking upwards into a smile.

'Well, it was a kiss,' he said, staying exactly where he was. 'Not a violent crime.'

Gabriel opened his mouth like he meant to laugh, but no sound came out.

'Do you need me to talk you through it?' Arthur said, half joking – but Gabriel looked so genuinely at sea that he followed it up with, 'Put your hand on my shoulder.'

'Why?'

'So I can flip you like a wrestler,' Arthur said. 'Why do you think?' Gabriel looked wary, but approached anyway, looking as if every sensible bone in his body was telling him to jump out of the window instead.

'I have thought about you,' he said, in barely more than a whisper. 'Not . . . just this summer.' He reached out a slightly shaking hand and put it on Arthur's shoulder. Arthur thought it was probably the bravest thing he'd ever seen Gabriel do.

It had the desired effect. As soon as they were touching it felt natural for Arthur to lean into him, to let Gabriel's face blur out of focus as he half closed his eyes; he waited for so long that he thought he might need to open them again to give further instruction, but then he felt warm breath ghost across his lips. There was another pause. He gave an impatient little huff before bridging the last couple of inches between them to solve the problem himself.

He half expected Gabriel to pull away when he put an arm to his waist to press him closer, so that they could kiss without leaning across a ridiculous expanse, but he didn't; he just kissed him back. It was gentle and uncertain at first, but then he seemed to relax into it, sighing into Arthur's mouth in a way that made his nerves sing. It sounded like *relief* more than anything – the sound of somebody finally at rest after a too-long day – and Arthur was amazed that kissing could feel like that, like both a blessing and a comfort, instead of like the inevitable meeting of two people who were reaching desperately for something they couldn't quite grasp.

Gabriel's hand skittered down Arthur's arm, as if it didn't have permission to land anywhere but desperately wanted to, eventually deciding on Arthur's wrist; Arthur felt Gwen's bandage give up the ghost and flutter away to the floor, felt the sting and shivered as Gabriel inadvertently ran his thumb over the fresh wound there, but he didn't flinch away. It occurred to Arthur as he tentatively lifted his hand to find the fine curls at the nape of Gabriel's neck that this was the second royal sibling he'd kissed in one evening. It was potentially the sort of thing that might need declaring.

'In the interest of full disclosure,' he said, breaking away but leaving his hands where they were, 'I actually kissed your sister tonight. About ten minutes ago, actually.'

'You – *what*?' Gabriel looked pink and breathless and absolutely baffled. Arthur was reaching for an explanation that didn't make it sound ten times worse when they heard a shout in the corridor outside, followed by the clang of something heavy hitting the ground at speed.

'What in the hell ... ?' Arthur turned to the door, his heart pounding. He still had one hand on Gabriel, and some part of his brain registered that if there was any danger it would almost certainly be heading in their direction. The next second he was pushing Gabriel towards his bedroom.

'What are you doing?' Gabriel said, flustered and struggling to keep his balance as Arthur bundled him in – floor-to-ceiling books, just as he'd predicted – and then left him there, rushing back to the main door. He listened for a second, glancing back at Gabriel's red and very confused face, before wrenching it open.

'Shit,' he said loudly before he could stop himself, a hand flying to his mouth.

Lady Bridget Leclair was standing in the corridor, sword raised, shoulders heaving. On the floor at her feet lay a man who seemed to have recently been clutching a dagger. He had dropped it, largely due to the fact that he was dead.

Arthur considered his options, and then, with one hand braced against the door frame, bent at the waist and vomited.

Gwen was roused from her bed by guards bursting through the door; once they had ascertained that there was nobody imminently threatening to harm her, she was marched into her father's private solar and told to wait. The longer she sat there, running her fingers over the notches and whorls of the table over and over again, the more convinced she was that something terrible must have happened to *some* member of her family to warrant all the panic.

After what felt like an age, Gabriel walked into the room – closely followed, for reasons unfathomable, by both Arthur *and* Bridget.

'What's happened?' Gwen said, immediately getting to her feet. 'Where's Father? Is that *blood*?'

'He's fine,' Gabriel said, sounding very weary. 'So's Mother. They told me – he's talking to Sir Hurst right now.' Sir Hurst was her father's Captain of the Guard, which surely indicated that either all was lost or everything was in hand. Arthur pulled up a chair opposite Gwen and sat down in it, rubbing circles into his temples and looking as if he'd rather be anywhere else. Gabriel and Bridget didn't move.

'Sit down,' Arthur and Gwen said at exactly the same

time; under different circumstances Gwen might have laughed, but she was still thrumming from head to toe with spiky, nervous energy.

'What *happened*?' Gwen said again, as Gabriel took a seat.

To her surprise, it was Bridget who spoke.

'I was coming to your chambers to bring you something,' Bridget said from where she was still standing by the door. Arthur, whose eyes had been closed, immediately snorted with laughter. Gwen gave him a long, incredulous look, and he bit his lip – and then snorted again.

'I think it's the shock,' Gabriel said, looking at Arthur with no small amount of horror.

Arthur pressed a hand to his mouth and made a muffled squeaking noise, but appeared to be attempting to compose himself.

'I noticed something further down the hall,' Bridget said, ignoring Arthur. 'It turned out to be a man, with a knife. He attacked me, so I – intervened.'

'You *killed* him?' Gwen said, her eyes travelling from Bridget's face, which did not seem to have any new scratches, to the sword in her hand and the surreally lurid streaks of blood on her breeches. *It's not her blood*, Gwen thought distantly. *That's where she wiped the sword clean.*

'Yes,' Bridget said heavily. 'I killed him.'

They sat in uneasy silence as these words sank in.

'Wait,' Gwen said slowly, once the initial shock had worn off somewhat. 'Arthur – where were you?'

She was sure she wasn't imagining it; Arthur's eyes flickered briefly over to Gabriel before he looked at her. 'Walking.'

'Walking? Walking in the royal wing?' Gwen said. 'Why did you all come in together? I thought you were going to bed.'

'I didn't say I was going to bed,' Arthur said petulantly. 'I said I was leaving. If you assumed I was going to bed, that just demonstrates your utter lack of imagination.'

'All right,' Gwen said, narrowing her eyes. 'So just say I *were* to use my imagination—'

The door opened, and the king and queen walked in, followed by a handful of panicked-looking attendants. Gwen's mother crossed to her immediately and pressed a kiss to her forehead before walking around the table to do the same to Gabriel, who closed his eyes tightly shut as her lips met his head. Their father walked the length of the room to take his customary seat at the head of the table, leaning back in his chair and sighing heavily as they all waited for him to speak.

'It seems it was only one attacker,' he said, as a page fetched and poured him some wine. 'Although God knows how he was able to get as far as the royal wing.'

'What happened to the guards?' Gabriel asked.

The king, who had been staring into his cup, looked up – and suddenly seemed to realise that the room was far more populated than he'd expected.

'To what do we owe this pleasure?' he asked, nodding at Arthur and then looking pointedly at Gwen.

'Um,' said Gwen. She tried to meet Gabriel's eye, but he was staring at the table. His hands were tensed against it, as if he might need to push up and flee at any moment. 'Arthur and I were just – talking.'

'Oh, *Gwendoline*,' her mother sighed. 'Again?'

'Again?' the king said in a dangerous tone.

Arthur looked distinctly uncomfortable. 'Well, it's been lovely,' he said, getting to his feet, 'but I think I'd better be going. Very glad you're all alive, of course – good job, and keep it up for the foreseeable. Good evening, your majesty, your highnesses . . .'

As Arthur practically sprinted from the room, the king turned his gaze to Bridget. 'And you?'

'I was on my way to speak to the princess, your majesty,' Bridget said without a moment's hesitation. 'She rendered me a service and I wanted to bring her a token of thanks.'

'And what token was this?'

Bridget did hesitate this time, just for a moment, before lifting the sword she had used to apprehend the man in the hallway and dropping it on to the table with a clatter that made Gwen wince. 'This.'

'You were bringing my daughter a *sword*?' the queen said, sounding utterly horrified.

'The guards let you through to the royal chambers, late at night, with a weapon?' said the king, equally unimpressed.

'I told them she had my permission to enter earlier this week,' Gwen said, trying to keep her voice steady. 'They were only following my orders.'

'Gwendoline, this is highly inappropriate,' her mother said, frowning down at the sword as if it too had disappointed her as a daughter.

'I agree,' said the king wearily. 'Although I can't ignore the fact that if she hadn't been in exactly the right place at precisely the right time ... I owe you my thanks, Lady Leclair.'

Bridget inclined her head, and the king waved her away, her eyes meeting Gwen's briefly as she backed out of the room. Lord Stafford was coming in the other direction; he was wearing a garish magenta jacket over his nightshirt, which he had stuffed into navy breeches, and an expression of deep anguish. He looked, Gwen thought, a little bit like a depressed jester.

'No dead,' he said. 'Except the assassin himself, your majesty.'

'So, what – somebody let him in?' Gwen said. Gabriel did finally look at her then, but she reciprocated too late; he had already turned away.

'My guess is that he was a recent hire to the guard,' Lord Stafford said, very pale. 'A lone actor, with some imagined score to settle. We vet everybody fastidiously, of course, but sometimes you just can't tell. I expect Sir Hurst will confirm as much when he comes to brief you, your majesty.'

'A lone actor?' said Gabriel. 'So you don't think this was something to do with what's been happening in the north?'

Stafford grimaced sweatily. 'Not on this occasion, no. Unfortunately people do things like this for all kinds of reasons.'

'But I thought you were obsessed with the north,' Gwen said, forgetting that this sort of thing was best said in private and earning herself a furious look from the steward.

'Obsessed? Not at all. Not at all. I simply wish us to react appropriately to the situations at hand. In fact, just the other day I was telling his majesty – we need not panic *every* time somebody wanders north of Nottingham.'

'You mean like Lord Willard?'

'Yes,' said Stafford. 'Yes! Exactly. Visiting family, up in Skipton. His majesty is well aware of the concerns I have about cultist uprisings, but that does not mean that everything is part of some grand conspiracy.'

'Well, we'll soon know for certain. Sir Hurst is exploring all the options,' said Gwen's father. 'He's even asked the damn Wizard to come for questioning, not that it'll help. I know Master Buchanan, and this isn't of his doing, cultist or not. Just – don't do anything foolish, either of you. Stay vigilant. Gabriel – get some rest, we'll be convening the council early in the morning.'

'Of course,' said Gabriel. Gwen was itching to go after Bridget, but she could think of no excuse to rush from the room that wouldn't seem very odd and downright danger-ous if there was any chance that more assassins were roaming the halls.

The door opened yet again, and the grizzled, mousta-chioed Captain of the Guard entered. He was olive-skinned and very handsome for his age; he had the kind of face that people liked to ascribe to great knights and princes in their portraits, although right now it looked deeply troubled. 'Your majesty. I can brief you now, if you're ready.'

If it had in fact been a guard recently hired by Sir Hurst who had attempted a little late-night regicide, Gwen could only imagine how tense that briefing was going to be.

'Stay together tonight,' said the queen, reaching over to touch Gwen's shoulder. 'We'll post extra guards right outside the door.'

'Guards we *trust*,' said the king. 'We won't make the same

mistake twice.' He got to his feet, nodding to Sir Hurst. 'Let's get this over with.'

'Be safe,' their mother said to Gabriel, before both of their parents hurried from the room.

Gwen considered Gabriel from across the table. He looked genuinely wretched – as grey-faced and hollowed-out as if the assassin had, in fact, succeeded.

'Come on,' she said with a sigh. 'I'll sleep in your room.'

Gabriel followed Gwen without complaint or comment, shrugging off his jacket once they reached his room and hanging it neatly off the back of one of the chairs, which he sank into with a very resigned expression on his face. It was only when Gwen sat down in the other and put a hand to her still-braided hair that it occurred to her to miss her lady-in-waiting.

'I don't know where Agnes is,' she said, anxiety plucking at her chest. 'I don't – she went to find Sidney, but—'

'Father said everybody's fine,' Gabriel said evenly. 'They're probably both being interrogated though, if they were loitering outside. About where they were. What they saw. Sidney might be a suspect, for all we know.'

'Poor Sir Hurst,' Gwen said, her pulse slowing. 'I can't imagine interrogating Sidney will be a particularly fruitful task.'

'I don't know,' Gabriel said. 'I've always found him perfectly pleasant.'

'That's because you're a man,' Gwen said bitterly. 'He doesn't talk to me as he should.'

'Perhaps he just doesn't know how to talk to you,' Gabriel said, ignoring Gwen's exasperated sigh.

'Well,' she said, crossing her arms. 'That makes two of you.'

Gabriel ran a hand through his hair, starting to look like a bird that had misjudged the voracity of the wind, and seemed to be working up to saying something. Gwen fought her urge to press him and just waited, her fingers working steadily at a loose thread in the hem of her sleeve.

'Gwen, I'm sorry. I shouldn't have said what I said, I wasn't – I wasn't expecting you to tell me ... what you told me,' he said eventually.

Gwen just looked at him. She was always the one who spoke first; helped Gabriel fill in the gaps when he couldn't find the words. It wasn't her responsibility this time. He'd have to find them on his own.

'I don't want things to be more difficult for you,' he said slowly. 'For you to spend your life longing for something that you could never have in any real way. Isn't it better to just ... make peace with what you *do* have? Try to forget about the rest?'

'What does that even mean?' Gwen said despondently. 'In any *real way*? What part of my life is real, at the moment? I'm betrothed to a man I'm not the least bit attracted to, and I know he feels the same about me. But I've been thinking ... and, Gabe, if we might all be stabbed in our own beds at any moment, it seems ... Well, there might be a way to let a little bit of my life be my own. Even if it's secret, even if it's hard, it'll be *mine*. What's not real about that?'

'What do you imagine you'll be allowed to have?' Gabriel

asked; it could have sounded confrontational, but he genu-inely seemed to be asking her.

'Well, I'll marry Arthur, obviously,' Gwen said, noticing the slight twitch in Gabriel's hands as she did. 'I'll marry him and we'll find a way to live together without killing each other, and then Bridget ...' And then what? She'd offer some tiny slice of herself to Bridget, who might not even want it?

'Does she feel the same way about you?' Gabriel said, seeming to read her mind. 'Because there's too much at stake if you're not sure. I can't even begin to imagine what they'd say about our family if this ever gets out. They might even come for our heads.'

Gwen glanced away from him to the floor, and then paused when she realised what she was looking at.

'Gabe. Why was Arthur still in the royal wing?' she said slowly.

'I haven't the faintest idea.'

'I know that's his bandage under your chair. I know because it's actually a bit of my blanket, and I did a pretty good job of tying it. Why are you lying? What was he *doing* in here?'

Gabriel looked completely and utterly defeated; he glanced up at the ceiling as if he were trying to spontan-eously vacate his body. 'Oh God.'

'Oh God *what*?' Gwen pressed.

Gabriel was so red he seemed on the verge of erupting. He cleared his throat, still unable to meet Gwen's gaze. 'I ... look, maybe there's something I need to—'

'No,' she said, comprehension dawning. She thought of

245

Gabriel putting on his very best jacket the night Arthur arrived at court, and looking thunderstruck every time Arthur spoke to him; the improbability of Arthur going to look at a *bird* with someone, without ulterior motives. 'Wait.'

'He started it,' Gabriel muttered wretchedly, and Gwen let out an incredulous half-laugh.

'You're not serious,' she said, as reality tilted on its axis. Gabriel looked like his face was imploding. 'Oh my God. Oh my *God*.'

'I'm sorry. Gwen, I'm so, so sorry. This was certainly not my idea, and I—'

'But – you *like* him?'

'Like is perhaps not the word,' Gabriel said, looking utterly miserable, and Gwen laughed again, out of pure shock. The tension between them had broken, the air suddenly easier to breathe.

'Oh. *Oh*. So that's why you were so ...' Gwen trailed off, waving a hand at him. She had felt so betrayed. She hadn't understood how he could be so terrible to her, but she was beginning to – because it hadn't really been about her at all. Perhaps she still should have been angry with him, but watching him now as he stared anxiously at her on the verge of tears, she just felt *sad* for him.

'I really didn't mean to do it. It just ... happened.'

'Well.' Gwen couldn't tell if she was under- or over-reacting; the evening's events had left her with very little remaining in her emotional repertoire. She supposed – why *shouldn't* Arthur like Gabriel? Gabriel was wonderful, most of the time. And as for him liking *Arthur* – just because she hadn't expected it didn't mean that it didn't make sense. In fact, it made more sense to her than it would to almost anybody else. When she took a deep breath and reached for his hand, he looked ready to collapse with relief. 'God, Gabe. I'm sorry you felt you couldn't tell me.'

'*You* shouldn't be apologising to *me*. Please know it's not that I didn't want to tell you, I barely even – I've tried very hard to make sure that you would never *need* to know. I wasn't ever going to act on it. I know some people might be able to live one way in public and another in private, but I think the stress of it would kill me. It's not like I need any more distractions if I'm going to attempt to lead this country.'

'Oh, Gabe,' Gwen said softly. 'They're going to be so lucky to have you. *All* of you.'

'They'll never have all of me,' he said, and she squeezed his hand. They sat quietly with the weight of this, until Gwen let go.

'So, just to be clear – did you *kiss* Arthur?' Gwen said, and Gabriel winced.

'Er . . . Yes. So did you, apparently.'

'Ha! No. Well, yes, but we were just . . . trying something. Didn't work.'

'Oh,' said Gabriel, letting go of her hand so that he could rub at his chin distractedly. 'Well.'

'But you . . . ?'

Gabriel looked pained. 'It worked,' he said. 'But I can't let it happen again.'

'Great. So . . . you're going to carry on as if nothing has changed. And you're going to do exactly what everyone expects, and never have anything for yourself. And you're going to be miserable.'

'And I'm going to be miserable,' Gabriel repeated. 'But – I was always going to be miserable.'

Gwen sighed heavily. 'Is there something in the water here?' she said, raising her hands in exasperation. '*Both* of us?'

'Perhaps we were cursed,' Gabriel said, with an attempt at a smile. 'Morgana's revenge, for not tearing down the cathedrals and putting up temples in her name.'

Gwen didn't laugh. 'I don't think it's a curse.'

'Sorry. I know. I'm sorry if I made you feel – if I made you feel how *I* feel.'

'You were awful,' Gwen said. 'But you're so rarely awful, Gabe. I think you're allowed three days of being an unfeeling bastard, after almost two decades of being perfectly pleasant.'

Gabriel nodded solemnly. 'You look shattered. You can take my bed, I'm going to sit up a while longer.'

'I know you're only saying this to stop me from asking you more questions ... but yes. Bed,' Gwen said. She was suddenly so exhausted that it took every ounce of her strength to heave herself out of her chair and walk the fifteen feet to his bedroom.

Despite the very real and present danger of men with knives lurking in the hallways, something inside her had lightened, and she fell asleep almost instantly.

When Gwen awoke, Gabriel was fast asleep in his armchair by the dying fire. She slipped silently out of bed, pulled on one of his cloaks and walked barefoot into the antechamber, making sure not to wake him. She studied his profile, the purplish smudges under his eyes and the frown lines that didn't completely disappear even when he was sleeping, and felt a rush of fondness towards him.

Arthur had told Gwen to demand more for herself, once. She wondered if he'd told Gabriel the same thing. She had barely been listening at the time, so sure that no wisdom he could impart could possibly apply to *her* life, but some of what he'd said must have caught and held, because after the previous night's panic and revelations Gwen had woken up feeling different. Reckless.

Brave.

It wasn't quite day yet, the pinkish dawn light warming the flagstones as Gwen slipped on her shoes and then walked quietly from the room before she could think too hard about where she was going. The guards outside seemed mildly startled, but only watched silently as she passed them; she crossed through four more human barricades before she reached the stairs, and it was only when she reached the ground floor and walked out into the north-west courtyard that two of them peeled off to follow her.

It was almost like she had dreamed Bridget into existence, a light sword in each hand and her hair wild, wearing the same bloodied shirt and breeches Gwen had last seen her in; she was standing on the other side of the courtyard squaring up to a training dummy, her shoulders heaving. The dummy had been given a shield, and there was a small pile of discarded swords on the ground, as if Bridget had been working her way through them.

'I'm fine,' Gwen said to the guards, her mouth dry. She cleared her throat. 'Leave me, please. I'd like some privacy.' They fell back and out of sight as Gwen walked the rest of the way alone.

Bridget genuinely didn't seem to have noticed her. She was pure focus, unrelenting as she ran her drills, her swords finding their target again and again, but as Gwen approached she could see the sweat curling the hair at the back of her neck, her breathing ragged with effort.

'Bridget,' she said softly, trying not to startle her; Bridget turned abruptly, her swords still raised, and for a split second Gwen thought she had miscalculated herself out of a face.

'Gwen?' Bridget looked bewildered at the sight of her, as if she found her entirely incongruous with the surroundings. Gwen supposed she sort of was, in just her shift and a borrowed cloak, with her hair loose and God knows what expression on her face. Bridget finally seemed to realise that she was holding weapons dangerously close to a royal throat, and lowered them.

'I wanted . . . I wanted to come after you when you left last night,' Gwen said. 'I wanted to see if you were all right. Are you? All right?'

'I'm fine,' Bridget said – but as she spoke she turned to the dummy and lifted her swords again, as if she couldn't bear to stand still for another second.

'Have you been here all night?'

Bridget didn't pause for breath. 'Yes.'

'Right,' Gwen said, watching as she struck with renewed vigour, wondering if these were the actions of a person who was fine. 'I mean . . . you know yourself best, after all, but—'

'I've been – training,' Bridget said, her words punctuated by the sound of sword on shield, 'to fight – since I was young. I knew this day would come – and it has. I wanted to be a knight, I wanted – *everything* that came with it. And I got it. And I'm fine.'

'Okay,' Gwen said, taking a step back, her bravado leaving her. 'Well. I suppose I'll just—'

'*Shit*,' Bridget spat, a sword dropping from her grip and clattering against the cobblestones. She wasn't wearing a gauntlet or gloves, and when she pulled her hand in against her chest Gwen saw that her knuckle had split, blood trickling down into her clenched fist. She stretched out her fingers, wincing, and then wiped the blood on her already ruined tunic before readying herself with her remaining weapon.

'Bridget,' Gwen said, alarmed. 'Stop.'

'Is that an order?' Bridget said, as her sword found its target once again, hand still bleeding freely.

'No,' said Gwen. 'It's not. But I think you should stop anyway.'

If anything, Bridget only seemed to hit the dummy harder. Gwen's gaze dropped to the discarded pile at her feet; she picked one up, and then without thinking at all about what she was doing, put herself squarely between Bridget and her target and clumsily raised the sword. The blow she caught seemed to vibrate all the way down to the base of her spine, but she managed to hold her ground.

'That was stupid,' Bridget said furiously from behind her guard. She didn't lower her sword, so Gwen didn't either; they stayed locked together, weapons crossed, neither willing to concede an inch. 'I could have hurt you.'

'You're already hurt,' Gwen countered. Bridget sighed, looking mutinous – and then gave Gwen a little push, disengaging them, and threw down her sword.

'I've never killed anybody before,' she said roughly, wiping her brow with the back of her unbloodied hand and addressing a point somewhere past Gwen's shoulder. 'It's not something I ever wanted to do. Taking somebody's life. It all just happened so *quickly*. He was going for my throat, and then I . . .' She raised her fist and then let it fall again.

'You only did what you had to,' said Gwen. She was used to thinking of Bridget as older and wiser, but at that moment she looked exactly as she was: eighteen and shaken, too young to have watched a man die at the end of her blade; too young to have been the only thing standing between the heir to the throne and the knife meant for his throat. Gwen hesitated for a moment, and then reached out to touch Bridget's face with her free hand, her thumb grazing her temple.

Bridget's gaze snapped into focus. 'What are you doing?' she said.

'I don't know,' Gwen said, wondering why her voice had dipped so low. 'I thought it might help.'

'Damn it,' muttered Bridget, as if she had made an unforgivable mistake – and then she followed through by leaning forward and kissing Gwen so fiercely that Gwen made a noise of surprise into her mouth. She had just recovered enough to reciprocate – to close her eyes and let her hand fall to clutch at Bridget's shoulder, to taste salt on her tongue and go in search of more – when Bridget broke off, briefly

252

pressing her forehead to Gwen's before wrenching herself away.

Gwen stared open-mouthed at her, then let go of the sword she hadn't realised she was still holding, reached out and *pushed* her. Bridget looked suitably confused, but allowed herself to be pushed backwards until she hit the stone wall, where they were out of sight from any prying guards or passers-by.

'Do you have any plan for what comes next?' Bridget said, looking down at Gwen's hands, which were still pressed against her collarbone. 'Or did the forethought start and end at pushing?'

'Shut up,' Gwen said, surprising both of them. 'I'm going to kiss you.'

'All right,' Bridget said. 'Carry on, then.'

If she had been paying more attention to the finer details, Gwen might have noted that Bridget's skin was slightly damp and hot to the touch beneath her fingers; that her hand was still bleeding, leaving tiny smears of blood on Gwen's dress, and that her dark hair smelt faintly of smoke and leather.

As it was, her attention was primarily engaged elsewhere. Bridget's muscled arms had immediately encircled her, fingers sliding up and coming to rest on her shoulder blade and the small of her back; she was kissing Gwen with a hunger that seemed entirely at odds with the careful way she was holding her, somehow both steadying and wrecking her all at once. Not even in her dreams had kissing Bridget been this good – she hadn't been able to imagine that Bridget might reach up to slip her fingers into Gwen's hair, wrapping a coil of it around her hand to draw Gwen closer and making a little *humming* noise of approval that made Gwen desperately curious about what else Bridget's hands could do.

'Um,' Gwen said, breaking away, noting distractedly that even when Bridget's eyes slowly opened, they lingered on Gwen's lips. 'Was that . . . okay?'

'Okay?' Bridget said, her gaze flicking up to meet Gwen's. 'Yes. Yes, that was okay.'

'Well, that's – I just . . .' Gwen stalled. 'I haven't really done that before. I mean I did kiss Arthur, actually, but that was more of a joke than anything else, and I didn't – I wasn't sure if you liked me. I mean, I like *you*, but I didn't think you'd . . . noticed.'

Bridget considered her, her head cocked slightly to one side. 'I noticed. It just seemed . . . impractical. And unlikely that you'd ever do anything about it. It didn't seem like a good idea. I suppose it still doesn't.'

'No. Well. I've done something about it now,' Gwen said stupidly, as if Bridget may not have realised.

'Yes,' Bridget said, with a hint of a smile. 'You have. You are, in fact, quite proficient at *doing something*.'

A door opened on the other side of the courtyard and Gwen jumped about a foot in the air; Bridget had reversed their positions in an instant, pressing Gwen into the wall and craning her neck to assess the intruder. It was just a servant attending to early-morning duties, whistling their way towards the Great Hall.

Gwen tried not to look too disappointed when Bridget released her.

'This is all ... very odd,' Bridget said, reaching up and brushing the tiniest smear of blood from Gwen's jaw. 'I'm so tired. It feels like a dream.'

'It's not a dream,' Gwen said. 'Trust me. In the dream, you're always on a unicorn.'

21

'You look suspiciously perky,' Arthur said, frowning at Gwen when she sat down next to him in the royal stands, 'for somebody who was just *perilously* close to being murdered.'

'Don't be ridiculous,' Gwen said breezily. 'Nobody's going to bother killing me. I'm of no consequence; I'm barely in the family portraits, they put me really small in the corner.'

'That's the spirit,' Arthur said. 'Any update on the malevolent forces attempting to end your father's line?' The atmosphere in the castle for the past few days had been extremely charged; Arthur had been seized by some over-enthusiastic guards on his way to the tournament, and it had taken quite a lot of shouting (on his part) and menacing posturing (on Sidney's) to get them to un-seize him for long enough to explain who he was.

'Yes. It seems it was just as Lord Stafford said – a recent hire to the guard who slipped through the cracks. It wasn't coordinated or anything, no co-conspirators. I suppose they'll just be paying *much* closer attention to who we employ.'

'How neat,' said Arthur.

'That's what Gabriel said. He's not entirely convinced. But Stafford has been so paranoid about the north lately that there's no way he'd let this go if he weren't absolutely certain.'

The king and queen entered the royal stands, waving at the crowd as they settled into their seats. Arthur glanced over at them and then back at Gwen. He fidgeted with the hem of his sleeve for a moment, then cleared his throat. 'Is your brother not . . .'

'No,' Gwen said placidly. 'He's not. What particular business do you have with my brother?'

Arthur felt prickly heat travel up from the collar of his shirt to the tips of his ears. 'It's a . . . you know, I wanted to ask him about – being a lord and everything, and managing lands, there's a chance I might not know the first thing about—'

Gwen snorted. 'Christ, don't hurt yourself. You look like Merlin is in your breeches clawing holes in something vital.'

'The cat's name is Lucifer,' Arthur said, sounding pathetic even to his own ears.

'Art,' Gwen said. 'I *know*.'

'Then why did you just call him Merlin?'

'No, you *imbecile*,' Gwen said, rolling her eyes and leaning in closer as she lowered her voice. 'I *know*. About you. And – and Gabriel.'

'Oh,' Arthur said, crumpling back into his seat and sighing. 'Right. Well. I mean. *What* do you know, exactly? Because to be frank, Gwen, I feel like *I* hardly know. And I'm somewhat involved.'

257

Gwen chewed on her lip as she considered her answer, and seemed to risk losing a large chunk of it when a fanfare of trumpets announced the start of the joust; Arthur raised his hands in affront, feeling that Gwen had somewhat skipped over his attempt to gather Gabriel-related intel, but the true source of her distraction became clear when the first competitor was announced.

Lady Bridget Leclair emerged, resplendent in her armour. Her squire was far less composed, struggling to carry her lance and keep up with her horse.

'Excuse me,' said Arthur. 'We were talking about me, and then you got a little sidetracked, but just to recap—'

Gwen actually *shushed* him; she hadn't taken her eyes off Bridget, who was approaching the stands as her competitor closed in from the other side of the lists.

After bowing as much as was possible from horseback, Bridget turned her steed back in the direction she'd come – but not before making brief and burning eye contact with Gwen, who was practically vibrating out of her seat. Arthur watched as Bridget gave her a tiny smirk of greeting, and then turned his entire body around to face Gwen, who was red-cheeked and slack-mouthed and practically giddy with longing.

'Oh my God,' Arthur hissed, the truth suddenly bestowed upon him like an early birthday present. 'You *did it.*'

'I – what?' Gwen said, finally distracted, whipping around to look at him with an alarming expression on her face.

'You – you got your lance wet, didn't you?' Arthur said, probably not as quietly as he should have done; he was feeling a bit giddy himself. 'You gave her the green gown!

258

You ground her corn! You—'

'Shut your *damned mouth*,' Gwen said, her jaw clenched tightly.

Arthur mimed sewing his mouth shut and throwing the needle away with a flourish; he stayed silent just long enough for Bridget and her opponent, a stout and well-worn-looking man on a bay mare, to take up their positions. 'You did though, didn't you?'

'Did *what?*' Gwen hissed. 'I have no idea what anything you just said actually *means.*'

'Did you kiss her?' Arthur said, having the presence of mind to lower his voice to a mutter. 'Did she kiss you?'

'No comment,' said Gwen, but despite the fact that she had been spitting mad at him only seconds ago, she had to press her lips together to keep from smiling.

'Oh no,' Arthur said, gripping her by the shoulder and giving her what he hoped was a friendly little shake. 'I'm actually proud of you. I don't . . . I don't really know what to do with that.'

'Please,' Gwen said, 'do absolutely nothing with it. It does not require action. And stop shaking me like a maraca, people will think we're odd.'

'We *are* odd,' Arthur said happily. 'I can't believe it. I honestly never thought you'd do it. And to think, you're my protégé; I taught you everything I knew, and sent you off into the world. Did you slip her the—'

Gwen was spared the conclusion of this sentence by the blare of the horns; her eyes were glued to Bridget, who was lowering her visor and urging her horse into motion. It all looked rather impressive, Arthur had to admit; as she picked up speed she sat perfectly balanced in the saddle, bringing her lance into position as if it weighed no more than a longsword, tucking it tightly into her arm and leaning forward with easy competence and nerves of iron.

The ground was soft from recent rainfall, and he could smell the freshly churned mud under the horse's hoofs mingling with the smells of mead and metal that always permeated the air on jousting days; Arthur almost closed his eyes at the point of contact, but he was glad he didn't.

Bridget's aim didn't waver; her lance splintered, and the crowd roared. The man she was competing against hadn't even managed to strike a blow.

'*Yes*,' Gwen hissed, applauding wildly, bouncing in her seat as if she had wanted to leap out of it in celebration; Arthur raised both eyebrows at her, nodding towards her parents, who were clapping politely. Gwen raised her eyebrows back, giving them a little waggle that was so uncharacteristically saucy Arthur snorted with shock.

'I knew you just needed a good tonguing to cheer you up,' he said in her ear over the sound of the crowd, and she elbowed him quite hard in the side but kept smiling. She was watching Bridget come, helm in hand, to accept the king's congratulations.

They probably thought they were being subtle, but even feet apart from each other, the tension between them was palpable. They might as well have had a proclamation drawn up: *Behold, kissing hath recently taken place betwixt this lusty knight and this passing good woman.*

'She was brilliant,' Gwen said breathlessly as Bridget walked away, and Arthur laughed.

'Why don't you go and see her in the competitors' encampment, and ask her to show you that thing where she knocks people to the ground?' Arthur said, and Gwen grimaced.

'Can't,' she said, gesturing to the guards at the end of the stands. 'They're my shadows right now. They interrupted and insisted on walking me back to my rooms, when Bridget and I were ... talking. It's my birthday tomorrow and I thought I might ... Anyway. It's impossible.'

'Well, that's no good,' Arthur muttered, as he watched one of the aforementioned guards break his composure and attempt to squash a bothersome fly between his pinched fingers. 'How are you supposed to enjoy illicit affairs and birthday debauchery under these conditions?'

'I'm not,' Gwen said resignedly.

It was hard to argue with her logic.

'It's a letter,' Sidney said, as they both stood either side of the small table in their chambers the next day, considering it. 'Not a rabid dog.'

'It's a letter *from* a rabid dog,' Arthur said, circling it as if it really might bite. He had to stop abruptly when he reached Sidney, who had refused to be part of this strange dance. The letter had arrived at breakfast, along with an assortment of Arthur's things that he had requested from home, including some of the many books from their library on Arthuriana, which he had procured with the vague idea of giving them to Gabriel.

'Do you want *me* to read it?' Sidney said, folding his arms.

'No, you'll do the voice all wrong,' Arthur said. It was a weak joke, and earned him an appropriately lacklustre snort in response.

'Come on,' Sidney said impatiently. 'Reading it? Not reading it? Tossing it into the fires of hell?'

'Ugh,' Arthur said, which wasn't really an answer. He picked the letter up gingerly and stalked off into his bedroom with it, throwing himself down on the embroidered coverlet with a sigh. His father's handwriting was as spiky and uneven as always, Arthur's name inked on to the page as if he'd been trying to drive his quill right through to the other side. Arthur broke his seal – the ridiculous three crowns he'd lifted directly from King Arthur's own coat of arms, with the addition of the traditional Delacey raven – and unfolded the letter. Better to get it over and done with.

My son Arthur, the letter began. That was enough for Arthur to need a quick break; he rolled over on to his back and considered the hangings for a few seconds, taking the deep, calming breaths Sidney often told him he sorely needed. He turned over and took up the letter again.

My son Arthur,

It pleases me to hear that your relationship with the Princess Gwendoline is proceeding as planned. The king has written to express that we should set a date for your nuptials at this time, and I concur.

Now that you have become closely acquainted with the princess, it would be greatly beneficial to be brought into the prince's confidences as well.

Remember, Arthur: any information you can provide should be sent with haste, as agreed before your departure.

Yours,

The Honourable Lord of Maidvale

'Honourable,' Arthur spat, throwing the letter down and laughing humourlessly before snatching it back up again. 'Honourable!'

'Who's honourable?' Sidney said, appearing in the doorway holding the stack of paper and parcels the letter had arrived with, visibly bracing himself.

'Well, I can tell you who's *not*,' Arthur shouted, discarding the letter once more. 'He pretends he's *pleased* for me when actually he just wants me to cosy up to Gabriel to collect information and gossip, anything that he might be able to trade – anything at all to make him feel like a *big man*, like he's important, like he's not just a drunk, addled, friendless old *bastard*.'

'Oh dear,' said Sidney. 'Was that all?'

'Oh,' Arthur said, pausing. 'No. Apparently we're setting a date for my wedding.'

'Ah,' said Sidney heavily. 'Well. Congratulations. Do you think Gwendoline knows?'

Arthur shrugged, and Sidney came to sit down next to him on the bed, relinquishing the packages. 'You know,' Arthur said bitterly, 'a month ago I'd have *loved* to have been the one to tell her. Misery loves company, you know? May as well have some fun, dance on the deck if the ship is going to sink either way. But somehow I don't find it particularly funny any more.'

Sidney bit his lip. 'What if you told her it's a tradition in your family to get married on top of a mountain?'

'No, no,' Arthur said despondently, stacking the letter on top of the parcels and throwing them carelessly on to the windowsill, before turning back to Sidney. 'Well. Actually.

Maybe? Let's workshop it a bit. And then we'll see.'

Arthur insisted he wasn't going to answer the letter, listing his reasons as he paced circles around his chambers, but an hour later he was doing exactly that, tapping his quill rapidly against the table top as he glared down at the slightly crumpled, blank piece of parchment in front of him.

Sidney sighed. 'Watching you do this isn't as fun as you might imagine.'

'Go and look at something else then,' Arthur snapped. 'I'll not stop you.'

'Nah,' said Sidney resignedly, tilting his chair backwards and balancing it momentarily on just two legs before letting it swing back into place.

Arthur knew why he wouldn't leave, and it thoroughly irritated him; Sidney was worried that if he left him alone he'd explode, pick up a bottle of wine, drop something expensive off the roof, or find some other self-sabotaging way to distract himself from thoughts of his father, his wedding, or his father *at* his wedding. Arthur wondered if Sidney thought he was being subtle with his attempts at damage control; wondered if Sidney knew that of course he recognised these moods in himself, could isolate the particular prickling in his chest and the bile at the back of his throat that heralded them. Knowing that the way Arthur responded to stress wasn't exactly healthy didn't mean he could stop himself once he'd started.

It was like pulling a bowstring taut, Arthur thought; once you'd begun, all that *something* had to go *somewhere*.

'You don't have to write to him tonight,' Sidney said. 'You don't have to write to him at *all*.'

'And let him have the last word?' Arthur said, fingers knotted in his hair as he glared down at the parchment, feeling affronted that the perfect comeback hadn't materialised in front of him without his nib touching the ink.

'It's a bloody letter. It's impossible to have the last word, because he can just send one right back. You'll go on for ever and ever trying to one-up each other until one of you dies.'

Arthur laughed mirthlessly. 'I see you're finally beginning to understand the true nature of my relationship with my father.'

In the end, Arthur wrote a quick, messy missive – he'd worked himself up into a rage by that point, and rather than being a perfectly crafted, immaculately polite refusal to participate in whatever games his father was playing, it may have included a few choice phrases that insulted both his father and the horse he rode in on – and then, ignoring Sidney's protests, immediately went to find a servant to arrange its passage.

'Probably should have slept on that,' Sidney said as they both watched the serving boy hurry away.

'Oh, shut your mouth, and the rest of you,' Arthur said, somewhat nonsensically. 'Come on. Fetch my trunk. We have work to do.'

The nature of their work led them, half an hour later, to the royal wing.

'Every time I open this door,' Gwen said, 'you're standing behind it.'

'You lucky thing,' said Arthur, pushing into her room; he

265

beheld a large blanket spread out over the table, needle and thread dangling precariously from one end. 'What the hell is this?'

'It's my embroidery.'

'Wait, I recognise that blanket – I think I *bled* on that blanket,' said Arthur, going to fiddle with it.

'You did,' Gwen said. 'I had to remove a whole section.'

'This is what you're doing on your birthday?' Arthur said, aghast. 'Your *eighteenth birthday*?'

'It was thought unwise to throw a banquet only days after a security breach,' Gwen said, shrugging. 'Father offered to send his Fool, but I thought it might be a bit depressing, just Gabriel and me sitting here watching a grown man pretend to fall over his own bollocks.'

'Oh, well, Art can do that for you,' said Sidney.

'Have you heard they're setting a date for the wedding?' said Gwen, sitting down heavily.

'Ugh. Yes. I know we always knew this day would come,' Arthur said, dropping the piece of blanket, 'but I sort of hoped I might be dead by then. No offence.'

'Er ...' said Agnes, appearing in the doorway from the bedroom, where she had clearly been hovering for some time. 'Good afternoon, Lord Delacey.'

'Oh,' said Arthur. 'Damn. Did you hear any of that?'

'No, no,' Gwen said, with the air of somebody who had long given up hope. 'It's all right. Agnes – Arthur and I have been feigning attraction to each other in hopes of distracting our families and various other onlookers from the fact that we harbour certain ... romantic inclinations that might get in the way of us forming a harmonious union.'

266

'Oh,' said Agnes, taking a step into the room. 'Yes. I know.'

'You *know*?' said Gwen, swivelling around in her chair to gawk at her lady-in-waiting.

'You're very loud in your sleep,' said Agnes, shrugging. '*And* when you and Arthur argue with each other. You talk about it all the time. And – I saw Arthur kissing Mitchell, the assistant to the Master of Hounds, at the feast.'

'You did?' Arthur said, mildly confused. 'I didn't *see* you seeing me – although to be honest, my memories of that night are somewhat hazy.'

'You *knew*,' Gwen said again. 'And you ... You haven't told anybody, have you, Agnes? Because if you have—'

'Of course I haven't,' Agnes said, looking affronted. 'I wouldn't.'

'We know you wouldn't,' said Sidney, in tones of such love-soaked adoration that Arthur mimed gagging behind his back, managing to get a smile out of Gwen.

'Right. Get up,' he said, clapping his hands together. 'We have plans tonight. Where is your ... Is Gabriel ... ?'

'He's in the library,' Gwen said. 'Under heavy guard. He was with me most of the day.'

'Ah,' said Arthur, feeling disappointed for a moment before rallying. 'Right. No matter! We'll go without him.'

'Go where? Wait ... Arthur,' Gwen said slowly. 'Are you wearing two hats?' Arthur was; he swept the first off with a flourish. '*Why* are you wearing two hats?'

'They call me Little Arthur Two-Hats,' he said.

'No they don't.'

'No, they don't,' Arthur agreed, pressing one into Gwen's hands. 'But that's because one of them is for you.'

'When you notice a flaw in security during a time of heightened peril,' Gwen said, crossing her arms, 'you tell the Captain of the Guard. You make sure nobody else can utilise it. You *do not* exploit said security flaw as a means to ... *party*.'

'You make a good point,' Arthur said diplomatically. 'Unfortunately, I'm not actually in the market for good points, so – shut up and put your moustache on.'

Gwen would have pressed this further but for two things: the first was that the attacker in the royal wing had been conclusively determined a deeply unfortunate one-off, a point that Lord Stafford had been making repeatedly and at length since the incident in question. The second – which she never would have admitted aloud to Arthur – was that since his arrival at Camelot she had found herself falling prey to a creeping dissatisfaction with many aspects of her life.

Her mother had sat her down at breakfast – on her *birthday*, no less – to tell her that the date for the wedding had been set for the end of the summer, and had proceeded to lay out plans for a packed schedule of meetings, fittings and mind-numbing conversations about the guest list and which meats they should serve at the feast. All semblance of her usual schedule would be thrown entirely out of the window, her days filled to the brim with other people making plans for her and talking over her and poking at her, with absolutely no room for what *she* might want – namely, time to sit in a quiet room by herself or to slip away and see Bridget.

As she listened to the queen, something inside her had finally snapped. It must have been a key part of her brain that looked after all of her more sensible faculties, because Arthur's terrible plan for the evening actually seemed quite appealing.

As a result, they were going *out*.

It was, apparently, still possible to escape the keep by means of climbing down the outer wall, as long as the initial portion of the climb was done at great speed between guard patrols. Sidney had done reconnaissance to perfect the timing. Gwen thought that, on the whole, it shouldn't have been quite so easy for Arthur to convince her and Agnes to dress in some of Arthur's clothes, adhere false moustaches to their top lips and shimmy out of the window to their almost certain doom.

'Whose hair is this?' Gwen said as she dubiously inspected the moustache in question. 'Did you pick it up off the ground?'

Arthur flashed her a grin. 'Don't worry. It's Lucifer's.'

In truth, Gwen thought that almost nothing could survive the ferocity of Arthur's energy when he turned it against other people's wills; given another half an hour of arguing when he was this fired up, he probably could have convinced her that the whole thing had been her idea in the first place.

The climb went surprisingly smoothly. Sidney had fashioned a very basic sort of rope ladder, which he knotted expertly to a pillar in Gwen's room so that she and Agnes were spared the true perils of mountaineering, and then removed for his own descent. They were waved through the castle gates, nobody particularly caring who they were due to the fact that they were going rather than coming.

As soon as they were on the main road into the city it became a little too real; Gwen felt slightly sick with panic, and started muttering an almost constant stream of regrets – *Oh my God, we're going to get caught, we're going to die, we're going to get caught* and *die* – until Sidney handed her a bottle of something and told her to take a nip of it to fortify her nerves. It tasted like she was being scoured by fire from the inside out.

'You shouldn't make a habit of that, you know,' Arthur said, as Sidney took the bottle back from her.

'A thief knows a thief as a wolf knows a wolf,' said Agnes, and everybody turned to look at her. She shrugged. 'I don't know. It's something my mother used to say.'

'Am I the thief, in this scenario?' Arthur enquired with mild interest. 'Or am I the wolf?'

'You're the man with the suspected alcohol problem,' said Gwen.

'Christ, not that again. I'm not drinking tonight, am I? Bone dry. Practically a saint.'

The closer they got to the city proper, the busier it

became. There were street hawkers selling what they claimed were genuine pieces of knightly armour, scavenged from the tournament; crowds of drunkards, overflowing out of the taverns and into the squares, which were packed; children rushing about underfoot, selling blackened buns and bone whistles and small bundles of dried flowers. Gwen realised once again with a rush of embarrassment that despite living in Camelot for most of her life, she had never really *seen* it; on parade days, or when the royal party left the castle en masse to travel to a nearby city or noble estate, the streets were cleared before they arrived. She had never seen what her father's people actually *did* when they hadn't been told to stand up straight, comb their hair and not come within twenty feet of a member of the royal family; it involved a lot more spitting than Gwen could have imagined, but a lot more chatter and life and laughter, too.

'Walk more like a man,' Arthur said to Gwen, jostling her with his elbow. She had his hat pulled down low over her face, and despite the fact that they were the same height, his tunic felt all wrong on her, tight across her stomach and loose about the shoulders.

'I don't know how to do that,' Gwen replied through gritted teeth, narrowly dodging a pile of vomit that had collected on the cobblestones. 'Surely men don't all walk alike.'

'Just walk like you own the street,' Sidney advised.

'I practically *do* own the street,' Gwen said.

'Fair point,' said Sidney.

'Walk like you don't care where your limbs are,' Agnes said, doing a much better job of it than Gwen. 'As if it's of no consequence to you where they end up. Like this. See? Swing them about. And you should act, at all times, as if your crotch is a burden.'

'Now hang on,' said Arthur. 'I'm a man, and my crotch isn't a burden.'

'Maybe not to you,' said Gwen. 'But it's a burden on the rest of humanity.'

'I made you a false moustache!' Arthur said, outraged. 'I did *crafts* for you! The least you can do is act grateful.'

'Thank you for my cat-hair moustache,' Gwen said, rolling her eyes. 'It's truly disgusting. I hope you washed it first.'

Arthur winked at her in a way he probably imagined was roguish and charming. 'I can guarantee you that I did not.'

At that precise moment they emerged from a question-able alleyway and into a square full of sound and colour. A dilapidated inn that seemed to be half sinking into the ground was the source of the revels; a band had set up their instruments just outside the door, and people had gathered to drink and dance in the warm evening air.

'This is more *like* it,' Arthur said triumphantly, as the fiddler struck up a new tune and the crowd cheered in drunken approval. 'Come on, Sid. Drinks.' He and Sidney shouldered through the crowd, leaving Gwen and Agnes hovering at the edge of the merriment. Gwen was sure that at any moment somebody would ask her why she had lint stuck to her upper lip, or arrest her for wearing breeches, but nobody noticed them at all.

A slightly awkward silence descended between the two women as they watched the dancers.

'I'm sorry I didn't tell you earlier,' Gwen said suddenly. 'About Arthur and me. I mean, you knew, but I should have told you. I didn't trust you with it, because ... well, I felt like I didn't really know you.'

Agnes looked at her, biting her bottom lip. 'Can I be honest?' Gwen shrugged. 'You *still* don't know me at all, and we've spent every day together for years. I think you just wrote me off as some silly giggling *woman*, off gossiping about you, and – I never did any of that. Well, the giggling and the being-a-woman part, yes. But there's nothing wrong with that.'

Gwen tried to grapple with this – her instinct was to be rankled, to try to deny what Agnes had just said, or at least reprimand her for her tone if she couldn't disprove her logic – but she realised that, on the whole, Agnes was right. 'Fair enough,' she said eventually. 'My judgement hasn't always been ... Well, I'm sorry. For being so rude to you. And ... I'd like to know you better.'

Agnes gave her a wry smile. 'Would you like to dance?'

'Not really,' Gwen said bracingly, 'but in the interest of getting to know you—'

Agnes had already taken her by the arm and pulled her towards the dancers; Gwen laughed, stumbling and almost losing her hat, buoyed by the freedom of dancing without skirts or her mother or leering men to put a damper on her enjoyment. There were no formal lines, no set dances; people were simply throwing themselves about to the music however they saw fit, and Gwen did her best to imitate them.

'You're being too delicate!' Agnes called over the pipes. 'Men don't dance like that!'

'Mouse in your trousers, is there?' Arthur enquired, appearing at Gwen's shoulder and handing her a cup of sage water. 'Come on, then. I'll show you how a real man dances. I'll teach you the hurdle-girdle. The dirty dog. The polyphonic rhapsody.'

'None of those are real dances,' Gwen said, clumsily sipping at her drink without pausing.

'Of course they are,' said Arthur. 'This is the – whatever it was I just said,' and he proceeded to do something so vulgar with his hips that Gwen sent up a quick prayer for her soul.

'I'm not doing that,' she said, and Arthur laughed and grabbed her free hand, waving it about in the air like she was so much seaweed.

It was wildly different from any birthday Gwen had ever had before – so different from what she had ever *wanted* before – and yet somehow, it was perfect. Everybody was laughing. Sidney kept trying to impress Agnes with misguided attempts to spin her around. When Arthur approached Gwen as if he might be about to do the same, and was rebuffed, he said, 'All right then, *you* spin *me*,' and she actually did. The crowd seemed to be growing every minute, morphing and changing and opening up to make room for them whenever they needed it. When Arthur let go of her hands and started craning his neck to look across the tops of many laughing and shouting heads, Gwen tried to follow his gaze.

'*What is it?*' she shouted, and Arthur turned back to her looking frighteningly pleased with himself.

'Your birthday present,' he said, grabbing her by the shoulders and turning her towards the inn, 'has arrived.'

'Oh *God*,' said Gwen, dreading to think what Arthur might consider a suitable gift for an eighteenth birthday – but when the crowd parted slightly, she caught a glimpse of a dark fringe, broad shoulders and a carefully neutral expression. She was off immediately, ignoring Arthur's laugh of surprise when she rocketed out of his grip, pushing her way through the crowd until she could properly see Bridget, who was wearing a simple, silken jacket and holding on to her drink like it was keeping her anchored as she stared suspiciously into the crowd. Her friends were standing with her, talking; Adah said something to make Elaine laugh and Elaine briefly put an arm around Adah's waist and squeezed, her hand safely back on her tankard only a second or two later.

'*Bridget*,' Gwen called, half laughing; she had the immense satisfaction of seeing Bridget turn towards her, her expression clearing, one side of her mouth quirking up in a smile that threatened to buckle Gwen's knees. Elaine and Adah excused themselves, Adah raising her eyebrows at Gwen and grinning in greeting as they crossed paths.

'Happy birthday,' Elaine whispered, before they were swallowed up by the crowd.

'Nice moustache,' Bridget said when Gwen reached her, touching it very gently so as not to dislodge it. 'Very convincing.'

'Really?' Gwen said, feeling excitable and giddy and more than a little stupid.

'No, Gwendoline,' Bridget said, her thumb still resting on Gwen's jaw. 'Not really. It's horrible. But everybody here is far too plastered to notice.'

'So in that case, do you think they'd mind terribly,' Gwen said, fingering the trailing end of her sleeve as she glanced back at the crowd, 'if we . . . ?'

Instead of answering, Bridget used the hand curled under Gwen's chin to gently turn her head so that she could kiss her. Having kissed Bridget before, all the terrifying newness was gone, and in its place was something better; a slow, familiar ache instead of heady, breathless panic. She liked the way that Bridget seemed to smile into her mouth as she kissed, as if she were pleased to have discovered something; she liked the feeling of strong arms and sure hands pulling her closer; she *especially* liked the small, frustrated noise Bridget made in her throat when she reached for Gwen's hair, which was carefully plaited away under her hat.

'These are ridiculous,' Bridget said in her ear, fingers pulling very slightly at the braids; Gwen could only make an undignified squeak in response. Her exhalation seemed to dislodge some of her moustache hair, and Bridget had to turn away to sneeze into her sleeve; it was high-pitched, not at all the kind of noise Gwen had ever expected to emanate from Bridget, and she stared at her disbelievingly, and then laughed as Bridget rolled her eyes and hauled her back in by the collar for another kiss.

They were interrupted by the sound of cheers. Gwen turned, with Bridget's hand still pressed to the back of her neck, to see Arthur and Sidney raising their drinks aloft in celebration, Agnes giggling into Sidney's shoulder; Arthur must have pounced upon Adah and Elaine and made introductions, as they were standing there too, laughing as they were jostled by the crowd. A red-faced man dancing next to

Arthur almost lost an eye to Arthur's wild gesticulating as he applauded in Gwen's direction, but Arthur mollified him with a friendly clap on the shoulder, shouting, 'Sorry – sorry, mate, sorry – just pleased for my friend over there, he's terrible with the ladies, barely knows which end is which – but he's found himself a lovely obliging girl and he seems to have located the correct end for the sake of public decency.'

'*Stop it*,' Gwen mouthed with narrowed eyes, but Arthur just saluted her with mock sincerity and then turned to Adah and Elaine and began talking to them animatedly.

'Your friend is deranged,' said Bridget.

'I can't argue with you there,' said Gwen, too happy to be peeved. 'I'm sorry we haven't spoken, I wanted to come and find you, but everything's been so . . .'

'You don't have to explain,' Bridget said, shrugging and removing some cat fur from Gwen's shoulder. 'I really wasn't expecting to see you again.'

'You weren't?' Gwen said, frowning, feeling some of her elation dissipate.

'Hey,' said Bridget, gently touching her chin. 'Not like that. Just – being practical. Didn't see how we could possibly swing it, with everything going on. But your pal Arthur came to see me, and he was very . . . insistent.'

'He does tend to be.' Gwen bit down on her lip, still feeling as if she'd somehow misjudged things. 'So – you're happy? To see me?'

'What do *you* think?' Bridget said, drawing Gwen towards her again.

'Just checking,' Gwen said, leaning back just enough to

feel herself held in place, and thinking that, ideally, Bridget would never let her go.

In the end, she did – but only because Arthur was pulling so insistently at Gwen's sleeve that she might have lost an arm if Bridget had tried to retain it. Bridget didn't *dance*, exactly, but she was willing to move as long as she was next to Gwen, who was in turn being goaded on by Sidney – who kept telling her that as the *man*, she was supposed to be leading. It didn't matter; in the chaos, the stamping of feet and the spillage of yet more drinks and the cacophony of raised voices and pipe and fiddle, nobody cared that she was anything other than another warm body; they didn't even notice when the last brave wisps of Gwen's moustache finally gave up the ghost and fell to the floor to be trampled into the stones.

Agnes danced with Adah and Elaine, attempting to keep up as Adah shouted instructions. Sidney and Arthur danced together, trying to one-up each other with little kicks and pirouettes that got increasingly violent. Gwen danced with Bridget and smiled and smiled, and Bridget smiled back as if she were trying very hard not to, and Arthur kept coming over and clapping them both on the back and shaking their shoulders vigorously as if they'd won a bet or just announced the birth of a healthy heir. Bridget tolerated him, although her eyebrows seemed to raise higher every time, until Gwen thought he was approaching dangerous territory – but then she went for ten minutes with her shoulders unshaken, and when she looked for him, she realised that Arthur was gone.

'I'm just going to . . . You stay here,' Gwen said, ignoring the uncharacteristically panicked look Bridget shot at her as she backed away and Agnes held out a hand to Bridget instead, shimmying her hips suggestively. Gwen shouldered her way through the crowd until she reached the edge of it, and there she found Arthur leaning against a very lopsided well, watching the festivities with an empty cup in his hand and a melancholy smile on his face.

'Hiding?' she said, and he shrugged.

'Taking a moment to replenish my youthful strength and vigour so that I may continue until dawn. And also, Sid stepped on my foot.'

'A tragedy,' Gwen said, taking a seat next to him. 'Are you all right? You look a bit . . . morose. Not usually your speed.'

'Hmmm,' Arthur said, peering down into his cup. 'He's not a dainty lad, our Sidney. They may have to amputate.'

'I didn't mean about your bloody *foot*.'

'I know you didn't,' Arthur said, sighing. 'You are terribly nosy and far too discerning for somebody who should currently be caught up in celebration, being thrown about the dancefloor by Lady Muscles over there.'

'I've done plenty of celebrating,' Gwen said, nudging his elbow with hers. 'If it's my brother you're moping over—'

'I know you think *everything* is about you and your blood relatives, but it's really not,' Arthur said, wrinkling his nose at her, which softened the blow.

'He wouldn't have come, you know, even if he hadn't been busy in the library under ten types of guard.'

'Oh, I don't know,' Arthur said, shrugging. 'I can be pretty persuasive.'

'Urgh,' Gwen said, pulling a face. Arthur smiled grimly back. 'I'm sorry, Art. I know he's not . . . I know it's not easy, with him. He's got it into his head that he must be everything our father is, and more – and that if he doesn't manage to unite the country and smooth over hundreds of years of bloodshed and squabbling, it's because he didn't work hard enough. There isn't space inside his head for . . . for much else.'

Arthur put his cup down, smoothing his hands over his hair and turning to look at her properly. 'Don't be silly. I'm fine. I'm always fine.'

'All right,' said Gwen, finding his hand where his fingertips were pressed into the bricks and giving it a squeeze. 'Well. If you're sure.'

'Lady Leclair must like you an awful lot,' he said, instead of replying. 'Sidney is currently trying to spin her, and thus far, she hasn't killed him.'

'I like *her* an awful lot,' Gwen said. 'Thanks for doing this. For inviting her. And bringing me here. And just – for all of it.'

'Christ, I must be going soft,' Arthur said, shaking his head. 'I mean really, what was in this for me? Practically nothing. It's shocking.'

'Art,' Gwen said, as she leaned clumsily into him and rested her tired head on his shoulder. 'I know we didn't get off to the best start – don't laugh at me, I just want to say something, and you're not to interrupt.' She felt Arthur nod, and gathered her thoughts before continuing. 'Before you came here . . . I spent a very long time feeling confused. I didn't know why I was feeling the way I was, or what it meant, and . . . you were the first person who knew. And all right, you used it to *blackmail* me, which wasn't ideal, but I suppose it was in self-defence . . . What I'm trying to say is, you knew, and it made perfect sense to you even when it didn't to me. I didn't have to try to justify it to you, or beg for your understanding – it wasn't something that even needed explaining. I had no idea how much that would mean to me. When I talked to you about it, even when you were being a bit of a nightmare, you always made me feel like it was . . . completely ordinary. Something I should be allowed to want and to have, without question. And this might sound foolish, but it felt like you were somehow on my side, even when you hated me. It . . . it made me braver. That's what I really want to thank you for.'

Arthur didn't say anything. When Gwen lifted her head from his shoulder to squint up at him she could have sworn that before he casually swiped at them with his sleeve, there might have been tears in his eyes.

'We've *both* gone soft,' he said, his voice a little scratchy. 'What sort of a marriage is this going to be? One of us has to wear the metaphorical breeches. Oh, here – I have a gift for you.' He rummaged inside his jacket pocket and then dropped something small into her lap. 'Should have given it back ages ago, but . . . anyway. It's all there, even the parts we tore out. I checked.'

Gwen looked down at the diary in her hand, all that childhood longing and sadness and *loneliness* pressed between a few hundred pages, and then back up at Arthur.

'Good birthday?' he said, and she smiled, turning to watch as Sidney did indeed try to lift Bridget off her feet; Bridget stopped him with a very serious look and one hand held up in warning. Adah had managed to pick up Elaine, who was shrieking happily, while Agnes threw her head back and laughed at them all.

'The *best*.'

281

23

After her birthday, Gwen seemed to vanish from Arthur's life.

He ascertained that she had been swallowed whole by wedding planning, which had yet to touch him; apparently for ladies it was an all-consuming occupation. He occasionally caught glimpses of her being frogmarched somewhere by her mother, and caught up with her at dinner once or twice, but she wasn't free to entertain him in her room by night or watch the tournament by day. Arthur and Sidney attended the latter frequently, Sidney pretending not to know that Arthur was primarily there to try to catch glimpses of Gabriel, who had been studiously avoiding him; unfortunately the men of the royal family were also busy, locked away in endless conference as their soldiers marched north, and Arthur was getting antsy.

'What the hell is going on here today?' he said one afternoon, feeling short-tempered, as he and Sidney wandered the busy courtyards, having already attempted to go into the city for lunch and found it so packed with people that it was entirely unnavigable. He was convinced that it had never been like this in the summers of his youth, although he had to allow for the fact that he had been quite small and not particularly observant.

'There's some . . . thing tonight,' Sidney said reluctantly. 'According to Agnes. A parade of England's most eligible daughters, specially imported for the prince to ignore.'

'Right. Well. Fantastic,' Arthur said, pushing a door open so hard that it made an ominous cracking sound against the wall. 'Good for him.'

'So you're going to come to the orchard with me and Agnes, right?' Sidney said doubtfully, following him through the doorway. 'And we're going to play cards and frolic and enjoy ourselves, and *not* get all pissed off and punchy and do something foolish. Right, Art?'

'Mmm,' Arthur replied distractedly.

'I need you to say it.'

'Ah – actually,' Arthur said, gazing down the corridor as if he might find some solution to his restlessness at the end of it. 'I'm going back to the rooms. To get changed.'

'Of course you are,' Sidney said with a sigh as Arthur departed.

Lucifer had been sleeping on Arthur's bed at least every other night, and he had apparently been making himself at home in their absence; when Arthur entered he discovered that there was a smear of fresh blood on the flagstones by the window, probably the last remains of an unlucky mouse, and the stacks of books and papers that had been sitting on the sill since they had been delivered from Maidvale had been tipped unceremoniously on to the floor.

'Bastard cat,' Arthur griped, leaning over to pick them up. The heaviest and most dull-looking of the obscure

Arthurian books Mrs Ashworth had included in the package had fallen open, some of its ancient pages bent beyond repair, and when he lifted it a few fell out and fluttered to the floor.

He was just going to leave them where they'd fallen, but his eyes landed on a beautifully scrawled line of Common Brittonic. He started translating despite himself – and then froze, staring down at what he was sure he must have misread. He gathered up the rest of the pages, his heart thudding in his chest, then spread them out on the bed and hunkered down to read.

An hour later, he was doing exactly what Sidney had been trying to warn him against.

It was none of his business, of course, if Gabriel wanted to ignore him and to go along with this charade, maybe even *marry* one of the poor girls. Arthur could hardly hold it against him, with his own wedding on the horizon. And besides, Arthur had done this before – had found himself caring too much about somebody, somebody who thought the only thing they could be together was a mistake – and look where that had landed him.

Completely, *utterly* none of his business . . . so it was difficult to say why he was still walking towards the Great Hall. He wasn't dressed for dinner, but he didn't care; he felt hot and itchy all over, determined to rid himself of this mood by taking a more direct course of action.

Peering through the doorway, he found the trestle tables full of the usual motley assembly of lesser nobles, although there were far more women present than usual. He had to argue quite sternly with the guard to even be let in, as apparently there was some sort of guest list that he definitely wasn't on.

Gwen wasn't sitting at the royal table, which meant he couldn't really approach it.

Gabriel was.

He looked beautifully exhausted in light, silvery blue, his curls combed and carefully arranged, a hand wrapped so tightly around his goblet that it looked as if his knuckles might be about to rupture. He didn't look up when Arthur entered, so Arthur just stood there and watched him – saw him duck his head and nod seriously as a pretty young brunette in violent shades of crimson said something in his ear, observed the way his brow furrowed and his teeth caught on his lower lip as he tried his hardest to look interested.

'Well,' Arthur said to nobody in particular. 'Great.'

He sat down and found himself looking at an unattended cup of wine; he hesitated for a moment, thinking of Gwen's remonstrations about his drinking habits, but one glance back over at Gabriel obliterated his self-control.

'Bad night?' said a rather reedy young man sitting next to him, sounding glum. 'Join the club. That's Lady Clement of Lancaster sitting next to him. She was supposed to be *my* betrothed. I've known her since we were children. I used to write her poems.'

'Chin up,' Arthur said, knocking his cup against the morose lad's. 'Perhaps he won't want her after all, and you can – you know – snuffle up his leavings.'

'Fat chance,' he said, ignoring the unkind framing. 'I mean – look at her.'

Arthur did. She was slight and pretty, and her eyes were darting around in a way that indicated actual shyness rather than affected timidity for Gabriel's sake. In another life, perhaps she *would* have been perfect for him. In this one, Arthur had to concede, she might be too – albeit in a very different way.

He drank steadily until it was time for the music, ignoring the little voice in his head that sounded suspiciously like Gwen and was telling him to slow down, and then watched as Gabriel very much did not ask Lady Clement of Lancaster to dance. There were two other ladies at the royal table with him, and plenty more vying for his attention even from the cheap seats; when Gabriel finally stood, all of them froze, and there was a silence so ridiculous that Arthur wanted to laugh.

He only realised he actually *had* laughed when all of his neighbours' eyes turned to him. He didn't have time to regret it – he was looking at Gabriel, who was finally looking back.

Arthur didn't think he imagined the flush that crept into Gabriel's cheeks, or the way his hand shook ever so slightly when he gestured for the music to resume. The prince awkwardly made his way over to Lord Stafford, deftly sidestepping his mother, who was clearly attempting to corral him towards the dancefloor.

Arthur put down his drink, then picked it up again and finished it. He loosened the collar of his shirt and looked around, half expecting Sidney to appear and stop him from doing whatever he might do next. When nobody intervened, he felt his mind had rather been made up for him.

He approached Gabriel with a pleasant smile affixed to his face, as if they were simply old friends, and certainly not two people who had ever had their tongues in each other's mouths.

'Nice-looking girl, that Lady Clement,' Arthur said to Gabriel, who was trying very hard to avoid his gaze. 'Just your type.'

'Arthur,' Gabriel said quietly, barely moving his mouth. Lord Stafford was wearing a hideous lime velvet jerkin and frowning at them both. 'This really isn't the time.'

'I'm just being friendly,' said Arthur, picking up a fresh cup of wine from a passing tray and raising it. He knew he was being belligerent, but he was so full of directionless energy, it was hard to stop. 'I've been wanting to speak to you, but you've been strangely difficult to track down.'

'Gwen said you weren't drinking,' Gabriel said, looking pointedly at the cup. Arthur sighed and put it back down.

'Come outside with me? I need to show you something.'

Gabriel looked horrified; he glanced at Lord Stafford, shook his head and walked away, as if Arthur were a complete stranger who needed taking care of.

Arthur couldn't pretend *that* didn't sting.

'Lord Delacey,' Lord Stafford said, with a painfully false smile on his face. 'Is there anything I can help you with?'

'*I'm* not the one who needs help,' Arthur said, wiping some wine from his chin. '*I'm* fine. You know – you're the one who's supposed to look after them all, aren't you? That's your job. Steward of the whatsit. He's too afraid to tell you, but he's got some bloody brilliant ideas about how to run this country, if you'd just be willing to listen.'

'Right,' said Lord Stafford, looking baffled. 'Such as?'

'Such as – Tintagel!' Arthur said, not entirely sure he was getting the point across, but feeling that for Gabriel's sake, it was very important that he tried. 'Like ... like putting all your gold into education instead of endless soldiers marching up and down the place, and – he's going to move to Tintagel and make it a school for teachers, and ... you should *know* all this, if you were any good at your job.'

'Tintagel Castle?' Stafford said, still minutes behind.

'Sort it out,' Arthur said, pointing an accusatory finger at Stafford before going to seek more chaos.

Lady Clement of Lancaster happened to be standing alone, looking crestfallen.

When he asked her to dance she agreed easily enough, although she did glance over at an older woman who Arthur could only assume was her mother. Clement was a good dancer, light on her feet and clearly relieved that *somebody* had finally asked her. He saw her look to Gabriel a few times, checking to see if he was watching.

Arthur only looked once. Gabriel was standing with his goblet still clutched tightly in his hand, ostensibly talking to an elderly man, looking deeply concerned as he tracked them across the room. Arthur felt a pang of something dangerously close to guilt, so he resolved not to look again. The edges of the room began to blur, the dancers speeding up and becoming nothing more than vague shapes in his periphery, Clement's pink face the only thing he could still see clearly – and then the music paused and another, equally excellent idea occurred to him. If Gabriel wouldn't come to him, maybe he just needed a little encouragement.

He leaned in close to Clement's ear and asked her if she wanted to step out into the courtyard for some air. He expected her to say no, but she was flustered and overheated from all the dancing, so she nodded and allowed herself to be escorted away across the hall and out.

'Thank you,' she said, smiling earnestly at him. 'I'm supposed to be talking to the prince. My mother ... Well, I don't know why he wouldn't just ask me to dance. He was looking. He *kept* looking. He wasn't dancing with anybody else. I don't understand him.'

'No,' said Arthur grimly. 'Me neither.'

'We shouldn't go far,' said Clement. 'I'm not supposed to be alone, and people might think ...' She trailed off, blushing. Arthur suddenly felt extremely tired.

'Don't worry. I'm engaged to be married. Although – you could kiss me, if you like,' he offered half-heartedly. 'Might ... I don't know. Make him jealous?'

'Er – no, thank you,' she said, patting him awkwardly on the arm. 'Thanks anyway, though.' She turned to go, and in that moment her face lit up. He followed her gaze and saw Gabriel, standing in the doorway with the light from the hall glowing behind him, casting his face in shadow.

'Your highness,' she said, with a half-curtsy. 'Lord Delacey and I were just—'

'I'd like to speak to Arthur alone, if you don't mind,' Gabriel said, his voice clipped. Arthur watched Clement visibly wilt in front of him, before ducking her head and hurrying back into the party. 'What are you doing?' he said, when they were alone.

'Invading Normandy,' Arthur said flatly. 'Come to help?'

'This isn't funny,' Gabriel said, ignoring him. 'You shouldn't have come.'

'*You* shouldn't have come.'

'It's my feast,' Gabriel said incredulously. 'They threw it in my honour.'

'Well, you seem to be having heaps of fun,' Arthur said, leaning against the wall, partially to look as if he didn't care but partially out of necessity. 'If you got any more lively you might reach the vivacity of a plague victim, or a recently deceased mouse, or – or—'

'Arthur,' Gabriel said, suddenly standing in front of him. 'Go to bed.'

'Make me,' Arthur said, hating himself a little bit for sounding so sneery. Gabriel looked all pinched and piqued; it was exactly the sort of expression he always wore just before they kissed. Hardly a good sign, but regardless, it was making Arthur's fingers itch.

'Go to bed,' Gabriel said again, and suddenly Arthur was at his limit.

'Leave with me,' he said. 'Come on. Do something you actually *want* to do for a change.'

Gabriel let out a frustrated huff that was half-laugh, half something else, and stared up at the star-strewn sky as if he couldn't bear to look at Arthur for another second.

'What?' Arthur said, knowing he sounded petulant and not even the slightest bit alluring. 'Is that really so mad a proposition?'

Gabriel looked back at him, entirely serious, and suddenly Arthur felt a bit sick. 'What makes you think that leaving with you would be what I *actually want*?'

290

'What?' Arthur scoffed again, but his certainty was wavering. 'You're not going to pretend—'

'You've been drinking. You're making a fool of yourself, and – you're making things too *hard*. I'm going to stay here, where I'm supposed to be. And I know you probably can't fathom this, but I thought I'd made myself clear – *I don't want you here.*'

Arthur felt something akin to a fist clenching in his chest, wringing the breath out of him and then releasing him just as suddenly.

'That's a shame,' he said, tilting his head to the side, knowing that his smile was more cruel now than anything else. 'Because I really do have something for you. A present.'

'I don't want it,' said Gabriel, shaking his head. He turned to leave, but before he could, Arthur grabbed his arm and pressed the thick wad of folded parchment he'd been carrying all night into Gabriel's hand. He half expected Gabriel to open his fingers and let it all fall to the ground, but he didn't.

'Had a book sent from home,' Arthur said, noting that his voice was trembling slightly and trying to temper it. 'It's been in my family for a very long time – I can only assume that my father never actually read it, because there was a little something extra inside. I know he certainly wouldn't want these getting into the wrong hands. Mine, especially. Go on. Read them.'

'What is this?' Gabriel said, not looking at the parchment, choosing to stare at Arthur instead. 'I don't have time for this.'

'I think you'll want to *make* time,' Arthur said. 'Because

it's something you've missed, in all your research. Something everybody has. Such interesting *letters* our fair Lancelot used to write to the great and noble King Arthur.'

'What are you *talking* about?'

'Read them,' Arthur said, shrugging. 'And then tell me if you're still ready to be a king as bold as Arthur Pendragon.'

Arthur left before Gabriel could, knowing that he was still standing in the courtyard, gaping after him, with secrets hundreds of years old crumpled in his shaking fist.

'Oh,' said Gwen. '*Oh.*'

'Wait until you get to the part about the feast,' Gabriel said, sounding slightly delirious. He was standing by the window of the east solar, his arms crossed. It was very late, and by rights they both should have been asleep long ago, but when Gabriel had knocked on the door Gwen had called him in from atop a footstool while a very sour-faced seamstress stuck pins in the blossom-pink fabric that was being shaped into her wedding gown. Agnes was fast asleep in one of the armchairs, and the room was lit in stripes of light and shadow from low-burning candles. Once the seamstress had finished her adjustments – and her furious muttering about ladies who were *far too tall* – Gwen had sat down heavily on the stool and asked her brother why his neck was sweating.

He hadn't said anything; he'd just handed her the letters.

'What?' Gwen whispered, having reached the aforementioned part about the feast. 'Sir Lancelot wrote these? *The* Sir Lancelot? To *Arthur Pendragon*?'

'I suppose they might have been forged,' Gabriel said, rubbing his bloodshot eyes. 'I wouldn't put it past him to do it, just to . . . toy with me.'

'Him who? Oh – *Arthur* gave you these?' Gwen said, glancing up at him and then turning the page over. 'No, I don't think he'd have had the patience or the endurance to fake all of this. They're so . . . earnest. Although I suppose I am translating very literally.'

'I just don't understand,' Gabriel said, finally sitting. 'I mean, Arthur loved Guinevere, Guinevere loved Lancelot, everybody's made their peace with that particular discretion, but this is . . .'

'*God*,' Gwen said again, before finally pushing the letters away, which was very difficult to do. They weren't particularly well written – there was quite a lot of repetition, and Lancelot didn't seem to have much of a poetic imagination – but they were captivating nonetheless, and actually quite sweet in their sincerity. 'He's responding to whatever Arthur wrote to him, so it looks . . . you know. Reciprocal. And *public*, too, if they danced all night at this feast. The other half must be out there somewhere, unless somebody had them destroyed. In fact, they must have had to destroy a *lot*, if they were courting in public for everyone to see.'

'Nobody's who I thought they were,' Gabriel said brokenly, and Gwen sighed, patting him uselessly on the arm as he slumped forward with his head in his hands.

'I mean,' she said tentatively, 'it's sort of . . . good news, isn't it? Here you are, trying to keep up with the great King Arthur, heir to a country where at least half the population thinks he's going to make a dramatic reappearance, and it turns out we've been . . . well, we've been accidentally living up to some of his ideals all along.'

'It doesn't matter,' Gabriel said, slightly muffled. 'Because obviously we can't *release* them.'

'What? Why not?'

'Because it'd be chaos!' Gabriel said, as if this should have been obvious. 'Everybody would assume they were fake, for one thing. They'd certainly suspect an agenda, if we ever – but we won't. And we can't. For another – well, it's hardly going to help heal this rift between Catholics and cultists, is it?'

'You don't know that,' Gwen countered. 'You don't know for sure how people might react. Catholics love Arthur, even if they don't worship him. Shouldn't we just ... tell the truth? And let everybody make up their own minds?'

Gabriel made a noise of disbelief and raised his head. 'I don't think so. I wish ... I wish I'd never seen them.'

'Why?' Gwen said, clutching the letters close to her chest as if he might be about to snatch them from her and chuck them into the fire.

'Because ...' Gabriel cast about, looking hopeless. 'Everything just got far more complicated, and it's already complicated enough. Knowing about them means ... having to make a decision.'

Gwen bit her lip, hard, to hold back from saying something slightly too unkind for his delicate state.

'What did Arthur say, when he gave them to you?' she said instead, hoping that perhaps he might have given one of his infamous lectures on bravery.

'He just sort of threw them at me,' Gabriel said, and Gwen rolled her eyes.

'It's going well, then.'

'There is no *it*,' Gabriel said. 'As you well know. You were just being fitted for your wedding gown, for God's sake.'

'Yes, and an hour before that I was kissing Bridget in the armoury,' Gwen said, causing Gabriel to choke on what Gwen could only assume was his own saliva.

She'd had to make all manner of excuses to get away from her mother, and Agnes had been dragged in to help with the complicated logistics, but it had been worth it for ten glorious minutes pushed up against a wall next to one of Gabriel's many suits of armour, every inch of Bridget's body pressed into hers – until somebody had walked past the doorway, and she had been forced to wrench herself away and run from the room without even saying goodbye.

'You're *kissing* now? When did that happen?'

'Um. After that security breach, and then again on my birthday,' said Gwen. 'It happened. It . . . continues to happen.'

'Well, I suppose . . . I'm happy for you.'

Gwen snorted. 'Thanks. *I'd* be a lot happier if I didn't have to sneak around. And I never would have thought it possible, but Gabe . . . these letters could change *everything*. Not just for us, but for a lot of people. Have you thought of that?'

Gabriel was quiet for a while, apparently trying to process this, and then he sighed. 'I found some poetry tucked away in the library once. Written by Mordred.'

'*Mordred?* He wrote *poetry*?' Gwen said, delighted and horrified in equal measure.

'Yes. It was awful, all about how misunderstood he was and how terrible his father was and . . . anyway. It was so strange. I've seen so many things written about him, by him, but all of it so formal – even his letters.' He jerked his head towards the ones grasped in Gwen's hand. 'Anyway. They don't seem like real people, do they? Any of them. And even knowing Father as well as we do, he's never just our father. Not entirely. He's . . . untouchable. Different. He can never actually take off the crown, even when he does. But this God-awful poetry Mordred wrote, it was so very . . . human.'

'They *were* real people,' Gwen said. 'And Father is a real person. And you can still be a real person, Gabe. You can be king and still be you. It doesn't have to be a . . . well, a crown you can't take off.'

'I wish that were true,' Gabriel said sadly. Gwen was suddenly exhausted by everything, head heavy and aching for her bed, thinking that they could untangle this mess in the morning – but before she could say anything, Gabriel's head snapped up. 'Do you hear that?'

'Hear what?' she said, but he shushed her; when she tilted her head and strained to listen, she *could* hear something. Strange, muffled moans coming from the corridor just outside.

'I'll call the guard,' Gabriel said immediately, reaching for his dagger, but Gwen held up a hand.

'No, it's not . . . Gabe, I think that's *Arthur*.'

'Damn it,' someone – Sidney – swore, accompanied by the sound of something falling to the floor. Agnes was up and out of her chair, squinting sleepily towards the sound.

'Sid!' she said; a second later she was rushing from the room. Gwen and Gabriel exchanged a glance, and then went after her.

In the hallway by the east stairs, they found Arthur collapsed on the rug, Sidney crouching over him while a couple of guards watched dispassionately from their stations, clearly used to Arthur's antics and unimpressed. 'Oh, for God's sake,' said Gwen as they approached. 'I thought you were in *real* trouble. Sid, how much has he had to – oh *God*.'

She had assumed Arthur very drunk, but as his hat fell from his head she saw in the torchlight that he was hurt. There were dark bruises blooming on his face, gashes where the skin had split open, and there was a terrifying amount of blood splattered down the front of his shirt under his jacket; he looked for a moment as if he might be able to open his eyes, but instead Gwen only briefly saw the whites of them before they rolled back into his head.

'Shit,' she said, dropping to her knees and running a shaking hand over his hair, pushing it back from his swollen face. 'What happened? How did you even get him back here?'

Sidney glanced up at the guards and then leaned in towards them, his voice low. 'He was – attacked. They jumped him outside an inn, he was ... I don't know, he went out there with some boy, I thought it was that blond one from before, Mitchell. When I got out there he was down, and they were kicking him. He was conscious at first, he even managed to do most of the walking by himself on the way back, but then he just ...'

Gwen glanced over at Gabriel, whose jaw was clenched so tight he looked in danger of breaking a tooth.

'Why weren't you *there*?' he shouted at Sidney, who flinched backwards as if he were the one who'd been hit in the face. 'Isn't that your *job*?'

'Why are you just standing there? Go and fetch the physician, *now*,' Gwen said to the guards. They had already scrambled away to do her bidding when something else occurred to her. 'Damn it. Agnes – can you please go too, and fetch the Wizard?'

'Why wasn't I tagging along with him into some alleyway?' Sidney was saying to Gabriel. 'Why do you *think*? I was inside, I was making sure nobody followed them out there. By the time I got outside they had him on the ground, and they ran, and I thought I'd better . . .' Sidney looked *spitting* mad, but somewhere underneath it all Gwen could tell that he was extremely upset. 'It was an ambush. I don't think they knew who he was, I guess he just looked – wealthy. But they didn't take anything. He didn't have anything worth taking.'

Except chunks of his face, thought Gwen. *Except a body upright and unbroken.*

She gently touched Arthur's shoulder, trying to see where he was hurt. He had crossed his arms over his torso protectively, as if expecting to be kicked again. Sidney took off his jacket and eased it under Arthur's head. Gabriel just stood there, staring down at Arthur.

'Hold his hand,' Gwen said. Gabriel looked at her, startled, hardly seeming to be awake. 'Hold his *hand*, Gabe. Sidney, grab the other one. I want – I need to see if he's still bleeding.'

They crouched down and did as she asked. Arthur moaned as they gently pulled his arms away from his torso. Gwen gestured for Gabriel to hand over his dagger and then cut open Arthur's tunic with it; it was so stiff and wet with blood that it fell heavily to the floor, revealing a chest already so swollen and bruised that Gwen couldn't imagine how bad it would look in the morning. The blood didn't actually seem to be coming from anywhere on his abdomen, so there was no wound that needed urgent staunching – it must have come from his split chin or temple or cheekbone, Gwen thought grimly as she tentatively touched the swelling at his ribs.

'Something in there might be ... broken,' Gwen said, thinking of fallen tournament knights and the mysterious internal injuries that sometimes killed them, and feeling very, very sick.

Somebody was approaching quickly from down the hall; Gwen looked up, expecting to see the grim face of the doctor – but it was Bridget. Clearly just out of bed, a thick nightshirt stuffed into a pair of breeches, her hair sticking up all around her face. For the first time, Gwen thought she might cry.

'What happened?' Bridget said, striding over and putting a hand on Gwen's shoulder. 'Agnes sent someone to fetch me, she said—'

'Robbers. Outside the inn,' Sidney said, clearly too exhausted to repeat the story in its entirety. Bridget didn't seem to need it.

'Which inn?'

'The Round Table. The – the smaller one. But they'll be long gone.'

'I know it,' said Bridget. 'What did they look like?'

Sidney described them, although they sounded so generic that it felt hopeless. Gwen watched Bridget as she took all of this information in, her expression focused and serious.

'All right,' she said, giving Gwen's shoulder a firm squeeze. 'I'll be back.' Before Gwen could react, she glanced around to check that the coast was clear, then leaned down and pressed a kiss into her hair. Gwen closed her eyes tightly and felt hot tears escaping from beneath her eyelashes. When she opened them, Bridget was gone.

The doctor arrived at last with two apprentices and the Wizard in tow, and Gwen saw Gabriel instantly let go of Arthur's hand. They had brought a makeshift litter, and Arthur's head lolled horribly as he was hoisted up on to it and then carried up the stairs towards his own room, Sidney at his side.

'We should go with him,' Gwen said, looking at Gabriel still sitting on the floor, his shirtsleeve soaked through with Arthur's blood. 'Come on.'

'I can't,' said Gabriel. Gwen wanted very much to say something to him then, but she knew it wouldn't help – so she left him there alone and made for Arthur's rooms, trying hard not to look at the trail of splattered blood leading the way.

25

Arthur tried not to breathe too much. It hurt to breathe.

He kept wanting to ask Gwen to stop scowling – she looked bloody *terrible* when she scowled, all haughty and imperious – but then he saw that she was also crying, so it felt rude to say. A thoroughly horrible man kept waking him up and poking him and making him drink things. Sometimes Gwen or Sidney would get angry if he did it for too long, and shout at him to go away. He wanted to cheer them on, but there was the whole issue of breathing to contend with. Cheering would use up an awful lot of air.

Sometimes in the middle of what felt like a long night, when he could feel darkness and pain pressing against him from all sides – when he felt like his chest was going to break under it, that no mortal body could possibly withstand it – he knew Gabriel was there, and if he squinted very, very hard, he could just about see his face, a single point of light in the black. Gabriel didn't cry. He looked dreadful, though.

Who hurt you? Arthur wanted to ask, but every time he tried to get the words out, the darkness swallowed him.

He dreamed of golden-haired boys who kissed him hard

and left him bleeding; of a murder of crows bursting from the treeline, hundreds of them flying overhead, until they blacked out the sky; of his mother, who was less a person and more a feeling, singing to him in a familiar language he didn't understand, holding something soft and cool to his head while he sobbed and clutched at her skirts. He dreamed of Gabriel sitting on a horse, the crown on his head white-hot and burning – he tried to cry out, to warn him, but Gabriel knew and smiled sadly and did nothing as he was engulfed in flame. A hand emerged from the inferno and Arthur stepped towards him to try to grasp it, but instead Gwen appeared, and calmly slipped her hand into Gabriel's so that they could go into the fire together, leaving him behind.

The first time Arthur truly woke up – opened his eyes and understood exactly who and where he was – he knew something was off, but couldn't quite place it. Things began to make sense when he turned his head very slightly, ears ringing with the effort, and saw a tangle of red plaits on the pillow next to him. His head hurt. His chest hurt. It was hard to pinpoint everything else that hurt, but he knew it tallied up to be almost all of him.

'You're in my bed,' he said, noticing that his voice came out strangely quiet and raspy. Gwen shifted, then turned over to look at him.

'Correct,' she said, frowning. She was fully clothed and pink in the cheeks.

'Are you lost?' Arthur said, trying to clear his throat and then closing his eyes tightly, as cruel, aimless pain shot through every part of his body, sending strange patterns of light skittering across his eyelids.

'I thought Sidney needed a break. He's been sitting in that chair staring at you non-stop. I don't think he was even blinking.' She sat upright, careful not to jostle him.

'Your reputation will be torn asunder,' Arthur said with great effort, opening his eyes again and watching as she slid gingerly from the bed and went to fetch him a cup of water; he tried to reach for it and realised that his hands weren't obeying him. He didn't understand how he could be so bone-tired when he'd only just woken up, his limbs heavy and weak. Gwen tried to press the cup to his lips but he choked and spluttered, feeling cold water slide down his neck. It wasn't unpleasant. In fact – he could hardly feel it at all.

'Too late for that, everyone thinks we've been at it all summer,' Gwen said, giving up on the water entirely. 'As long as I don't walk out of here pregnant, I think I'll be fine.'

'Come on then,' Arthur croaked. 'Lift up your skirts. May as well do the whole thing properly.' He had meant it to be a joke, but it was coming out strangely quiet and unconvincing. He couldn't really feel his hands now, which he thought might be a bit of a concern.

'Arthur,' Gwen said, but it sounded as if she were talking to him from very far away. He couldn't tell if he'd closed his eyes, or if everything had simply gone dark around him. Somewhere nearby, it sounded as if a cat might be purring. 'Art, are you all right?'

'They were . . . they gave me a message,' he said, with no idea what he was talking about.

'Art,' Gwen said again, sounding quite panicked. 'Look at me.' He tried — nobody could say he didn't *try* — but he couldn't quite reach her any more.

Bridget didn't try to make Arthur drink anything. She certainly didn't climb into his bed. She sat in the chair next to it, not reading or writing or even indulging in a little humming; simply staring straight ahead as if she'd vanished to some other plane of existence, with Lucifer asleep on her lap. After five minutes of observing this through half-closed eyes Arthur was about to announce himself awake when she spoke instead.

'You are very bad at pretending to be asleep.'

'No I'm not,' Arthur said, his throat dry. 'I've been awake for an hour.'

'No you haven't,' said Bridget, raising an eyebrow at him.

'No,' Arthur agreed. 'I haven't.'

Bridget got to her feet, displacing Lucifer. 'I'll fetch Sidney,' she said, rubbing her eyes.

'Bridget,' Arthur said just as she reached the door. 'Did I dream it, or did you . . . ? The other night Gwen was talking to me, when I was half asleep, she said you went back to the inn and — knocked some heads together.'

'In a manner of speaking.'

'She said you found one of the guys who did it and cracked him open like a walnut.'

'That's an exaggeration,' Bridget said, opening the door and pausing. 'He wasn't that tough to crack. Like an egg, maybe. A really puny little egg.'

Arthur laughed and winced, and then a thought struck him.

'They wanted to tell me something,' he said. What they'd told him was insubstantial, already floating away from him. 'Did he say anything?'

'No. Do you mean they said that to you . . . to get you to come outside?' Bridget said. 'To rob you?'

'No, it was . . . I don't know what it was,' Arthur said. He tried to reach for the thought one last time, and then almost instantly fell asleep.

Arthur only noticed that Gabriel was in the room at all because he moved so quickly trying to leave it.

'Coward,' he said, turning to look at him. He felt hot all over; he wondered if the shutters had been left open, if he was trapped in an unrelenting patch of afternoon sun, but then he realised far too slowly that it was, in fact, the middle of the night. That accounted for the darkness, and the quiet, and the fact that Gabriel was standing there in his nightclothes looking grim about the mouth. Lucifer was curled at the foot of the bed, seeming unconcerned.

'You've got a fever,' Gabriel said. 'They've been sedating you. It seems to come and go.'

'What's wrong with me?' Arthur asked, and he was irritated to hear how small and scared he sounded. He couldn't stop shivering. It was extremely embarrassing.

'Broken ribs. You took some very serious blows to the head, and they thought maybe your skull – but the swelling seems to have gone down. Your wrist was broken. The one you broke when we were children. The physician said he set it better this time, but it might . . . it might not be much use to you, broken twice. Your legs seemed to just be badly bruised. Your nose was broken, and you bled quite a lot.' He made as if to take a step towards the bed, then thought better of it. He looked excruciatingly uncomfortable, his eyes darting from the floor to the ceiling to the door, but never landing on Arthur. 'It was your head – at first they said you might die. And then that you might not be able to talk. Or walk. Or do anything, really. You managed to speak to Gwen and Bridget coherently a couple of weeks ago, but then – then you got that fever. They don't know why.'

'A couple of weeks ago?' Arthur said, panic constricting his throat. 'How – how long have I been here?' Gabriel didn't reply. In the darkness, his vision blurring and his eyes feeling strangely hot, Arthur couldn't be entirely sure that he was still there. 'Gabriel?'

'It's been a month,' Gabriel said, and Arthur released a breath that sounded suspiciously like a sob. 'Don't cry,' Gabriel said, suddenly a lot closer. He was sitting on the edge of the bed. He seemed to be holding Arthur's hot, sweaty hand.

'I'm not crying,' Arthur said, but if that was true, why was his face so wet? And why was it so hard to breathe? It really was *unbearably* warm. His lungs were on fire. He wanted to ask Gabriel to open a window – to throw him *out* of the window – to throw him in the moat and let him sink to the cool, blissful bottom.

'I'm here,' Gabriel said quietly.

'No, you're not,' Arthur said, crying in earnest now, feeling each laboured breath rattle through him until his bones hurt.

'Yes I am,' Gabriel said, putting a hand to Arthur's

forehead. Arthur had no idea how he was alive, with a hand that cold.

'Don't go,' he muttered, closing his eyes. It felt like a spell, or a prayer; like repeating it would make it so. 'Don't go. Don't go. Don't go.'

Of all the disturbing sights the world had to offer, Sidney crying had to be the worst of them. It was so disarming that Arthur felt annoyed; how *dare* Sidney cry, how *dare* he do something so utterly unlike himself when Arthur was the only one who should be allowed to be afraid?

'Shut up,' he said through chattering teeth. Sidney roughly wiped the tears from his cheeks, and didn't laugh. His eyes were bloodshot, the skin underneath them so dark it looked bruised. 'You look like shit.'

'You look like a skeleton,' Sidney said, his voice hard, his eyes cast downwards. 'You look like you've already been dead a week.'

'Maybe I have,' Arthur said, feeling a wave of nausea rush over him. He felt hollow. He had no idea when he'd last eaten; he had a vivid memory of somebody helping him to the chamber pot though, which he'd quite like to forget. 'I don't really want to know the answer to this question, but – did somebody cut off my hair? Do I have any ... left?'

'A bit,' Sidney said grimly.

'Damn it,' Arthur said wistfully. It was only hair, but it was *very* nice hair.

'I messed up,' Sidney said quietly, still staring at his hands. 'I really messed it all up, Art.'

'No you didn't,' Arthur said mildly.

'Don't say that,' Sidney said, standing up. 'Don't tell me what I didn't do. I know exactly what I didn't bloody do.'

'You can shout at me all you want when I'm dead,' Arthur said. Sidney kicked the chair he'd been sitting in, and it ricocheted loudly off the bed frame. '*Ow.*'

'Shit,' said Sidney. 'Shit. Did I hurt you?'

'Head,' Arthur said, feeling pain erupt through it. 'Can you – whatever they were sending me to sleep with, can you . . .'

Sidney was already striding from the room to fetch it.

Gwen wasn't sleeping. She wasn't doing much else, either. All wedding planning had been put on hold until they could be absolutely sure there would still be a groom, and even her mother was leaving her alone. This should have been a relief, but Gwen found herself with far too much time on her hands and nothing to fill it with. Once, she had longed for nothing more than her life of solitude, but now it felt somewhat hollow; the only bright spots in her day were the times when Bridget could get away from the last events of the tournament and come to sit with her.

'Who's with him?' Bridget said now, as Agnes let her into the room. She was holding a plate of spiced buns studded with currants. 'Elaine sent these for you, from the kitchens.'

'Oh. Oh – thank her, for me,' Gwen said from her armchair. Her eyes felt raw and swollen from crying. She was wrung out and useless, incapable of doing even the smallest task. 'Sid is with him. He needs a proper break, though.'

'He won't take one,' said Agnes, sighing. 'Even when he's not there, he's not sleeping.'

Gwen could have asked *how* exactly Agnes knew that

Sidney wasn't sleeping, but by this point, it was pretty self-explanatory.

'Did they say anything more about his head?' Bridget asked, putting down the plate and coming to sit with Gwen. The bruising hadn't seemed too bad at first, but when they'd cut away all his hair – Gwen had cried watching, as if they were cutting all of *her* hair, not that it really mattered compared to everything else – his head had looked oddly swollen, and the expression on the physician's face hadn't given Gwen much hope.

'No,' Gwen said. 'They didn't say anything.' And then she burst into tears.

She didn't see Agnes leave the room, because she couldn't really see anything – she felt Bridget's hands on her though, tentatively smoothing her hair away from her face and stroking her back. Gwen reached for her, feeling foolish and lost and small, and found herself being hauled into Bridget's arms properly so that she could cry there.

'You need sleep,' Bridget said eventually, when Gwen's sobs had gone more the way of sniffles. 'Bed.'

Gwen allowed herself to be steered into her bedroom and sat down on the end of her bed; she watched through blurry eyes as Bridget knelt to untie Gwen's boots, easing them off, precise and careful. Gwen's heart hurt, watching her; she leaned forward to kiss her, and Bridget caught her by the wrists, holding her steady.

'That's not sleeping.'

'Stay,' Gwen said, knowing she sounded desperate and only slightly caring. 'Please.'

Bridget considered Gwen; she must have looked

completely pitiful, because a moment later she was taking off her own boots so that she could climb up on to the bed.

It should have been awkward, but Gwen was too exhausted to care; she lay down, and Bridget lay down next to her, both fully clothed and staring up at the canopy ceiling.

'I don't even *like* him,' Gwen said eventually, and Bridget laughed quietly.

'He grows on you.'

'Like mould,' said Gwen. 'Like one of those plants that strangles trees.'

Bridget turned her head to look at Gwen, her expression knowing. 'Keep slandering him if it'll make you feel better.'

'It won't,' said Gwen. 'Can we talk about something else, please?'

'Like what?'

Gwen shrugged. 'Anything.'

Bridget hummed thoughtfully. 'I won again yesterday. At the lists. It's as far as I've ever made it in a royal tourney. Only a few events left.'

'You did?' Gwen said, turning over on to her elbow so she could look at Bridget properly. 'That's – that's wonderful. You should have told me.'

'It didn't seem important, considering.'

'Well, it is. You're incredible. Glory to House Leclair, honour upon your family name, et cetera, et cetera.' Bridget laughed quietly up at the ceiling. 'Has anybody else in your family ever competed?'

'No,' Bridget said. 'My father would have, but he has a

knee injury from a bad fall. And House Leclair has only been around for three generations, so there isn't a particularly wide pool of applicants. My grandfather picked the name himself.'

'Oh. Didn't he want to use a Tai name?'

'They don't have family names in Sukhothai. I think he chose Leclair from a book.'

'Which one?'

'*The Big Book of Vaguely French-Sounding Names*,' Bridget said seriously, making Gwen snort with laughter. 'I do have a Tai nickname, but it means *frog*, so I'd rather it didn't catch on at court.'

'*Frog?*'

Bridget gave her a hard look and refused to elaborate. 'Sir Marlin was knocked out yesterday too, so it was an excellent day all round.'

'Good,' said Gwen, thinking of the Knife having to leave Camelot in disgrace and finding that it instantly lifted her spirits. 'Bridget, if you won the tournament, would that be it, for you? Would you feel like you'd done it?'

'What do you mean?' Bridget said. Without her seeming conscious of it, one of her hands had found the end of Gwen's braid, and was very slowly pulling it loose.

'I mean ...' Gwen said, slightly losing track of her train of thought as Bridget's fingers tugged gently at her hair. 'I mean, would you stop touring the tourneys all year? Find ... something else to do? It can't be easy, the way people treat you because you're a woman. I imagine it must get quite wearing.'

'No,' Bridget said, her fingers briefly stilling. 'No, I don't think I'd stop. I enjoy it. It's a lot of hard work for very little glory, but you can find joy even in the worst and the most mundane parts of it, if you approach them with the right attitude and surround yourself with good people. Besides, I know I'm not the best I can be, yet. I'd like to get there.'

There was a brief silence while Gwen pondered this. She was trying to gather the courage to say something, and felt her heart start to beat very rapidly, a rush of blood in her ears, as she opened her mouth to do it.

'What's going to happen when summer is over?'

Bridget had finished unpicking one braid, and moved on to a second. 'I imagine we'll throw conkers at Sidney's head.'

'I'm serious.'

'So am I. Though it won't be a particularly challenging target, his head is enormous.'

Gwen pulled away from her hand to sit upright. 'Bridget. When summer is over, and the tournament is over, and everybody leaves . . .'

Bridget looked up at her, impassive. 'What are you asking me?'

'I don't know.'

'What do you want me to say?'

Gwen threw up her hands. 'I don't know!'

'Yes you do,' Bridget said, calm and infuriatingly correct.

'Fine,' said Gwen. 'Fine. I want you to stay. Stay at court with me.'

Bridget closed her eyes for a moment; when she opened them, Gwen found it difficult to look at her. 'Stay with you and do what?'

Gwen shrugged hopelessly.

'Be your ... lady-in-waiting?' Bridget said evenly. 'Wear nice dresses and go to dances and watch you from across the hall every night at supper?'

'No! I mean – yes, you might have to do some of that. All right, all of that. But would it really be so bad?'

'We don't even know each other that well, Gwen,' Bridget said, in such a kind and understanding tone that Gwen wanted to punch something inanimate.

'But I like what I *do* know about you. I want to know more. If you leave ... we won't even get the chance. Tournaments will always be there, you can put them off for a year or so, you can—'

'Let's not talk about this now,' Bridget said softly; to Gwen, it sounded like a death knell. She had assumed that Bridget felt exactly the same way as she did, but suddenly she had no idea why. All they had been doing was kissing – a *lot* of kissing, whenever they could, precious minutes snatched in quiet corners where Gwen lost herself entirely in Bridget's gentle mouth and firm grip – but that didn't mean Bridget really *liked* her. The thought of this – that she had misjudged everything, right from the start – felt like being plunged into ice water and left there to burn.

'I want to talk about it now,' Gwen said, trying to keep her voice as calm as Bridget's was, and failing. 'Would it really be so bad? To stop competing for a while? To see if we might ... be something?'

Bridget sighed up at the canopy, scrubbing a hand across her face. 'Yes. Yes, it would. I want ... more than that, from

315

my life. I've been fighting for that for a very long time, I've had to bruise and break myself and bleed for it, so what you're offering . . . I'm sorry. I care about you. But it's not enough for me.'

Gwen lay back down, feeling leaden. She squeezed her eyes tightly closed and felt fresh tears break free to slide slowly down her face.

'But I know what I want now,' she said, her voice cracking.

'Gwen,' Bridget said, reaching for her hand. 'Summer isn't over. I'm still here, and I'll be back next year. I could come at Christmas.'

'Christmas?' Gwen whispered, horrified. 'I can't wait until Christmas.'

'Please don't cry. Just – come here.'

Gwen allowed herself to be pulled into Bridget's arms, but she felt completely unmoored, even when Bridget pressed a kiss to the top of her head and told her again to get some sleep. She wanted to respond properly, to try to argue her case, but she was exhausted and heartbroken and really . . . what else was there to say? Bridget wasn't going to stay. Bridget didn't feel the same way about her, and never had. It hurt and hurt and hurt, each second suddenly steeped with melancholy, as if they were already saying goodbye.

It seemed like Gwen had only just drifted off when she was woken by a frantic knocking at the door – she experienced a moment of confusion, followed by her stomach dropping through the floor. It felt as if it could only be bad news, and she was light-headed with panic as she scrambled out of bed, Bridget close behind – but when she reached the outer chamber, she saw that Sidney had already been admitted, and was currently enthusiastically kissing Agnes by the fire.

'What?' Gwen said, and they broke apart. 'Don't tell me you knocked like that because you were just so desperate for—'

'Fever broke,' Sidney said, grinning at her; she found herself smiling back, her eyes just as misty as his were. 'They think he's going to be okay.'

'Fever broke,' Gwen repeated, sitting down heavily in a chair, Bridget letting out a long whistle of relief behind her.

He was going to be okay.

If nothing else in her life was going to go right, perhaps it was worth it, just for Arthur to live.

Agnes and Sidney were already kissing again.

27

They stopped giving Arthur anything at all for the pain, or to help him sleep. He realised that they'd cut him off when he spent an entire day awake, Sidney sitting stoically at the end of the bed, unsmiling, saying nothing when he made demands. He raged and raged against the physician, tried to drag himself out of bed to really make a point of it, but all they'd give him was endless broth.

Gwen visited and insisted on hugging him, even though he was grumpy and sweaty and generally unpleasant to behold.

'Get off,' he grunted, unable to defend himself. 'You're embarrassing yourself.'

'I don't care,' Gwen said, smiling at him fondly. 'God, I'm so glad you're still alive to be horrible to me. It won't last. Get your digs in now, while you're all pathetic and I feel sorry for you.'

She insisted on hugging him again before she left. He breathed in the clean, now-familiar smell of her hair, and felt strangely calmer.

He got better in increments, the days beginning to take shape and form. He even voluntarily drank some damn broth in the end, even though it was late at night and the serving girl had been sent away, and Sidney had to spoon it into Arthur's mouth himself.

'This is weird,' Arthur said, as Sidney used one hand to tilt his head up and the other to feed him.

'I've been doing this for weeks,' he said. 'It was weirder when you had no idea who I was, or what a spoon was.'

'Right,' Arthur said, taking a deep breath. 'So I suppose it wasn't the ghost of my dead mother cradling me and cleaning me and weeping all over me for nights on end.'

'No,' Sidney said grimly. 'That was me. D'you want some wine?'

'No,' Arthur said quickly, surprising himself. The thought of it turned his stomach, but it wasn't just that. 'No. I think . . . might be as good a time as any to try life without. Seeing as it was never much help before. What do you think?'

'Christ,' said Sidney. 'Is that all it takes, to knock some sense into a person? I need a head injury.'

'You *are* a head injury.'

Sidney eventually fell asleep in the chair, which looked uncomfortable; Arthur woke him up by shouting his name as loudly as he could – which, as it turned out, wasn't particularly loudly – and told him to go and sleep on a horizontal surface. He looked as if he might be about to argue, but then shrugged and walked into the adjoining room to collapse on to his cot.

Arthur took this as a good sign. If he were in any imminent danger of dying, Sidney wouldn't have fallen asleep at all.

Hours later, as Arthur lay awake feeling simultaneously exhausted and as if he'd never sleep again, he heard the door open. He knew who it was by their footsteps alone. He'd certainly heard them enough by now.

'You're up,' Gabriel said, seeming surprised. He looked so tense and drawn into himself that Arthur wanted to reach up and push down his shoulders.

'Not by most definitions of the word,' Arthur said, and Gabriel gave a humourless exhalation of a laugh.

'Are you in pain?' he said, sitting down carefully in the chair.

Arthur tried moving his limbs experimentally. It felt like he was dragging them through thick treacle, but they didn't hurt.

'No,' he said. 'Just . . . feel like I've been stampeded. By horses. Extremely large horses.'

'And that doesn't hurt?'

'The stampede was a month ago.'

'Ah,' said Gabriel. 'Right.' He didn't seem to know what to do with himself. He certainly wasn't looking at Arthur. 'Your father is here,' he said eventually. 'I saw him at dinner. I suppose he came to see you today.'

Arthur didn't think he had it in him to feel angry, but he managed it anyway. His *father* – here. His father, inside the castle, presumably to visit his deathly ill son, but inexplicably absent from his bedside. He simultaneously wanted to rage his way through the hallways until he found him, and ask for him to be barred from entering the room.

'Not yet,' was all he said.

'Well . . .' said Gabriel uselessly.

'How do I look?' Arthur bit out. Gabriel reluctantly looked down at him. His expression could have been

320

mistaken for dispassionate, if not for the slight tightening of his eyes.

'We thought you were going to die,' he said quietly. '*I* thought you were going to die.'

'Yes,' Arthur said, trying to sit up a little straighter and managing it at an agonisingly slow pace. 'Well. I didn't.'

'I didn't think I'd – that I'd get the chance to speak to you.'

'Anything you want to get off your chest? The last time we spoke properly, I recall you saying something about not wanting me around, and yet here you are again—'

He stopped talking abruptly, because Gabriel had shifted infinitesimally towards him and put a painfully gentle hand to his jaw. Arthur stayed perfectly still, every nerve in his body seeming to migrate to his cheek, so that he could feel the minute detail of the pads of Gabriel's fingers on his cheekbone, his chin, the corner of his mouth. Gabriel considered him for another second and then leaned down to kiss him. It was infuriatingly soft, just the faintest brush of his lips against Arthur's – there for a second, and then gone again. Arthur tried to chase him as he pulled away, reaching out for him with a shaking hand to bring him back and force him to stay there, but Gabriel just interlocked Arthur's outstretched fingers in his and took a deep, steadying breath.

'Sorry,' he said, looking down at their hands.

'For which part?' Arthur said, pressing his thumb into the creases of Gabriel's palm. 'Before? Or this, now?'

'All of it,' said Gabriel.

'That's not really the answer I was looking for,' Arthur

321

said faintly, closing his eyes, suddenly too bone-tired to look at anything at all. They sat in silence for a moment.

'I know that you and Gwen think this should be so easy,' Gabriel said quietly, as if he'd been planning to for some time. 'Now that we have . . . what we have. Those letters. But it *wouldn't* be easy. I'd have to give them to my father. I'd have to explain to him why . . . why they matter so much. To me. To Gwen. And he's a good man, Arthur, but he's keeping this country together by a thread, and he's not going to throw all of that away for something like this.'

'You don't know that,' Arthur said, his mouth dry. 'Because I don't think you've ever even tried to tell him what you actually think. What you really want.'

'That's not fair,' Gabriel said instantly, but then he sighed. 'Maybe not. But it would be an enormous battle to pick. And I'm not brave like you. Like Gwen.'

'Ha!' Arthur said, with such volume that he surprised them both. Lucifer, who had apparently been sleeping at the end of the bed again, looked up in annoyance. 'I'm not *brave*. I don't know what gave you that idea.'

'Arthur. Come on. You . . . you go after what you want. You don't let anything stop you. What's that, if it isn't bravery?'

'Some might say – your sister chief among them – that it's stupidity,' Arthur said, raising a hand to meet Lucifer as he stalked up the bed looking resentful. 'I'm a selfish bastard, Gabe. I do it all for me, and when things don't go my way, I'm . . . *deeply* unpleasant about it, as you've discovered. That's not bravery, it's just – ego. And I'm a coward when it matters. You'd never find me really risking my neck for anybody else. That's not who I am.'

Gabriel considered him. 'I think you're wrong. I don't think that's who you really are at all.'

'I'm afraid it is,' Arthur said, trying to laugh but finding himself incapable. 'I'm a self-centred, arrogant, *worthless* excuse for a—'

'Who told you that?' Gabriel said insistently. Arthur faltered.

He knew the answer. He just didn't want to say it out loud.

'Well, aren't we a sorry pair,' he said shakily instead. He squinted towards the window; it was getting lighter outside, the clouds picked out in grey and gold. 'I suppose you'll need to be off.'

'What?' Gabriel said, confused by this sudden change of direction.

'Sun's nearly up,' Arthur said, smiling tightly at him. 'We're out of time.'

He wanted so badly for Gabriel to disagree with him – to tell him that he'd stay – but they truly were a pair of cowards; Gabriel left, and Arthur didn't do a thing to stop him.

It was so hot during the last week of the tournament that spectators kept pouring ale on themselves to cool off, which led to a rather unfortunate olfactory experience as it mingled with the general fug of sweat and horse manure.

Gwen was there to watch Bridget joust. It was the last day of events to determine who would make it through to the final melee, and the stands were rowdy with anticipation. Both the king and queen had made time to attend, and were sitting in all their state trying to ignore the flies that plagued commoners and royalty alike. Gwen had debated not going, considered sulking in her room instead or going to bother Arthur, but in the end she couldn't stand to miss it – to sit elsewhere and be agitated and crotchety as she wondered what was happening at the tilting rail.

A very childish part of her had wanted to stay away just so that Bridget would notice her absence and miss her. Unfortunately it was exactly the sort of thing Bridget would see right through, so instead Gwen put on a sage silk dress and sat with her mother and held her head high. She thought she was doing a fair job of pretending to be somebody mature and reasonable, and not somebody who had cried herself to sleep the night before thinking about how empty life would feel by the time winter came.

Bridget's competitor was ferocious, an enormous knight who looked like he couldn't have been unseated by a direct hit from a battering ram. They each shattered a lance during their first run, Bridget's horse almost losing its footing due to the sheer force of their collision, and Gwen almost jumped up out of her seat before remembering herself. Bridget calmed her horse as she took up a new lance, and then set off thundering towards the gigantic knight again, but it was all over a moment later; she had to duck to avoid the risk of decapitation as the end of her competitor's lance snapped almost completely in half against her shield, and she didn't land a blow at all. The trumpets sounded for the winner, and Gwen was already standing.

'Gwendoline? What's wrong?' the king said, turning in his seat and frowning over at her.

'Nothing. Well – actually, I feel a bit faint,' she said, pressing a hand to her forehead. 'From the heat. I'm just going to . . .' She waved a hand up towards the castle.

'Go,' said the king, smiling wearily. 'I know your mother and I have neglected our tournament duties, but you are officially relieved until the finale. Get some rest. You've had a lot on your mind.'

Gwen really did intend to walk back up to the castle, but at the last moment she veered right instead, towards the competitors' encampment, a guard swearing under his breath as he half jogged after her. The tents were swarming with knights half-armoured and shouting for their squires. She stopped one to ask where she might find Lady Leclair.

'Little one on the end, your highness,' said a pink-faced squire. 'You can't miss it, it's – well, it's the only one with a lady in it.'

She left the guard standing outside the tent and entered to see Bridget's squire at her side, trying to relieve her of her armour as she poured water down her throat; when she saw Gwen enter, she handed the flask back to him, wiped her mouth with the back of her gloved hand and said, 'Leave.'

'But, you're supposed to—'

'Neil,' she said, in a tone that invited no argument. 'Leave.'

'Well, fine,' Neil the squire said crossly, 'if you want to get *rusty*.' He fussed around far more than necessary putting the flask away, then gave Gwen a brief and wide-eyed look of appraisal, before scurrying out past her and letting the tent flap fall back into place behind him.

'Hello,' Gwen said awkwardly.

Bridget just nodded. She was still trying to catch her breath.

'Sorry you lost.'

Bridget started taking off her gloves, and then her vambraces, throwing them one at a time into an open trunk.

'His lance was pre-cut,' she said. 'That's why it split so neatly. He was cheating.'

'What?' said Gwen, instantly outraged. 'We should say something!'

'Nah,' Bridget said, shutting the lid of the trunk so that she could sit on it and unbuckle her greaves. 'I'll sound like a sore loser. The Grand Marshal must have seen, it wasn't cleverly done, but if he didn't say anything then, he's not going to. It doesn't matter – I know the truth. It's just one tournament.'

'How can you be so calm about it?' Gwen said. She had known the Grand Marshal was hardly a saint, but to allow outright cheating at the king's tournament was no minor offence. Bridget shrugged. As she bent down, a necklace swung free from her neck; a plain silver chain with a dark stone pendant. Gwen had never seen it before. 'What's that?'

'What?' Bridget said, glancing up. 'Oh. It's . . . Elaine gave it to me. For protection. Apparently it's magic.'

'Of course it is,' Gwen said, watching as Bridget caught it and tucked it away. 'Do you need help? With your armour?'

'No,' Bridget said, pulling a larger piece loose and placing it carefully on the trunk beside her. 'I can manage most of it, and Neil will do the rest.'

In the ensuing silence, Gwen fully realised what had been set in motion the night Arthur's fever had broken. It was clear from the sudden distance between them, the slight coolness, the fact that Bridget suddenly felt untouchable.

Summer wasn't over – but whatever she'd had with Bridget already was.

'When will you leave?' she said, trying to swallow down the nausea that had risen in her throat.

Bridget put down the armour she was holding. 'After the final melee. I'll go home for a while, get some rest, eat some real food and train with my father, and then I'm travelling to a tournament in Cumbria, meeting some friends. Are you crying?'

'No,' Gwen said, even though she probably was.

'Gwen,' Bridget said gently; she sounded sad. *Good*, thought Gwen. 'We both knew this was—'

'Please don't,' Gwen said, her voice shaking. 'I really don't want to hear it. Maybe it was stupid of me, but I thought this ... meant something. It did to me. Obviously I was mistaken. I feel suitably foolish.' She was definitely crying now, tears rolling steadily down her face. Bridget looked stricken.

'It meant something to me too,' she said, and Gwen laughed.

'Not enough to stay.'

Bridget's jaw was working, as if she were trying very hard not to rise to this. She failed. 'You can tell yourself, if you like, that I showed up and flirted with you, and kissed you back when you kissed me, and led you to believe that I would stay forever if you only asked me – and then turned around and broke your heart. I know that's what you think is happening right now. But I didn't say no to you, Gwen. I said no to giving up my whole life to wait around for moments with you, whenever you could spare them. That's not who I am, and it's not what I want, and I think that, given some time, you'll realise that it isn't what you want either.' She got up and tried to take a step towards Gwen – but Gwen stepped back, knowing that if Bridget touched her right now, all would be lost. Bridget sighed, letting her hands fall to her sides in defeat. 'I'll see you next summer.'

'Fine,' Gwen said. And then she fled.

The last thing Gwen wanted to see as she rushed through the courtyard, eyes blurry with tears, was one of Bridget's friends; she reluctantly slowed down as Elaine approached, looking bright-eyed and cheery with a smear of flour on her forehead.

'I have something for you,' Elaine said earnestly with a quick curtsy. 'Bridget said your friend ... your *betrothed*, I mean – she said he's doing much better.'

'Oh – yes, thank you,' Gwen said, attempting to smile. 'Thank you so much for *all* the food, Elaine.'

'Oh, it's nothing – and this isn't food,' Elaine said, reaching into her pocket and pulling out a little package. 'They're protective wards. I had the ladies from the Morgana meetings help. Give it to Arthur, all right? I already gave one to Bridget, for the tournament.'

'Ah,' Gwen said woodenly. 'Right. The necklace.'

'It's not a *necklace*,' Elaine said breezily. 'It's a spell. Or – I think it is, anyway. Just have him wear it.'

'I will,' Gwen said, closing her hand tightly around the paper. 'Thanks, Elaine.'

Elaine peered at her thoughtfully. 'Hmmm. Perhaps I'll make you one as well. You don't look at all well.'

Gwen just nodded. She managed to hold herself together until Elaine had left, and then she turned towards the stables, walked as calmly as she could into an empty stall, and then sat down on an upturned bucket and let herself burst into tears. She felt like her chest was breaking open, tectonic shifts exposing the softest, most vulnerable parts of her. She hated that she'd cried on Bridget's shoulder so often while Arthur had been unwell; that she'd let her guard down completely and made it clear how much she needed Bridget, when all the while Bridget must have just been humouring her, holding her hand to get her through it, one foot already out the door.

Voices suddenly flared up just outside the stall; Gwen stopped crying, holding herself very still, dreading discovery. Instead of retreating, the voices grew closer, and then she heard a door swinging open and slamming shut. Somebody was in the stall next to her; two somebodies and a horse, Gwen surmised, after a quick foot-and-hoof count.

'Is this really necessary?' hissed a man's voice, sounding as if he had just stepped in something unpleasant. His voice was vaguely familiar to Gwen, but she couldn't quite place him.

'I don't care to be overheard. Now – *what* exactly have you learned since Skipton?' a second man muttered, as the horse shuffled warily in the hay.

'There's no need to take that tone with me,' said the first man.

'I've heard rumours that you have misled us about the nature of your relationship with your son – that in fact, he despises you,' said the second man sharply. 'That outside of this farce of a marriage he openly defies you, and his loyalties lie elsewhere—'

Gwen suddenly felt light-headed and sick. She leaned towards the wall, trying not to make a sound, both wanting and dreading to hear what Lord Delacey might say next – because she had placed him, now. It was Arthur's father, and her own farcical marriage they were discussing.

'Ha! That is a lie. And one we've told convincingly, if it's so widely believed. He came here under my instruction. He writes to me often. He recently obtained private, personal information that I believe will prove invaluable.'

'What information?'

'Well, I can't possibly divulge *everything*, you understand – let's just say the prince is very unhappy with his current circumstances, for a variety of reasons. He intends to abandon Camelot, decamp to Tintagel – divert huge amounts of gold into his pet projects, leaving the country undefended. He and the princess have proven to be ... *extremely* malleable.'

Footsteps were approaching from the other end of the stables; a servant was coming, whistling to himself as he walked, and Gwen heard both Lord Delacey and his confidant make a hasty exit. Gwen stayed where she was, staring down at the package in her hands; eventually she got stiffly to her feet and walked out into the courtyard.

She stood there for so long, her mind racing, a strange ringing sounding in her ears, that eventually a stable hand came to ask her if she required medical attention.

In the end, it was almost too easy to find proof. Arthur was sleeping, dark circles under his eyes, the chair that usually held Sidney empty; Gwen had hoped that it would be impossible, that she'd find no evidence at all, but all she had to do was quietly sift through the messy stacks of papers on his windowsill until she found a letter signed '*The Honourable Lord of Maidvale*'.

She read the letter three times, just in case there was some nuance she had missed – something that could undo all this, fix it, make it untrue – but it was all there, in scrawling black ink.

It was like a punch to the gut, and it left her dizzy and

reeling. In the next room, she heard Arthur moving around in his sleep, and she gathered herself and fled before he could wake up and see her there.

Gabriel wasn't in his rooms when she knocked for him, so she walked with leaden feet down to the library and traced her usual path through the stacks until she found him in the corner, books and ledgers piled so high either side of him that it looked like he had been methodically building himself a fortress. She had to take down a handful of books to slide the letter through to him.

'What's this?' he said, frowning down at it and carefully pushing the inkwell aside to make room as he unfolded it. 'G? Wait – have you been crying?'

Gwen couldn't answer. She simply sat down on the chair next to him, put her head in her hands and braced herself for impact.

29

Arthur awoke to a very strange sensation. He couldn't pinpoint it at first, but he knew for certain that something was very, very wrong. It seemed to be morning outside, which made sense – if he craned his neck, he could see Sidney asleep on his cot in the next room; so far, so normal.

It was only when he sat up in bed and reached for a drink to wet his parched lips that he realised what it was.

'Sid,' he called scratchily, clearing his throat and then trying again. 'Sidney. Come here.'

'Wha—?' Sidney said, falling out of bed and attempting to get to him even as his blankets twisted around him. 'Whassappening?'

'Start again,' Arthur said. 'Retrace your steps. You have to get out of bed before you can do anything else. You're currently trying to bring the bed to me.'

'Right,' Sidney said, flopping back on to his bed like a fish before managing to extricate himself and rushing to Arthur's side. 'What's wrong?'

'Well,' Arthur said. 'That's the thing, isn't it. Look at me.'

'I am looking at you,' Sidney said, his eyes darting all over

333

Arthur as if searching for some new injury or evidence of impending death. 'You look fine.'

'Exactly,' said Arthur, nodding. 'I *feel* fine. Dare I say – I think I *am* fine.'

'What?' Sidney said, looking genuinely baffled. 'That can't be right.'

'Watch this,' Arthur said. 'I'm going to do a trick.' He pushed off the covers, then pulled himself upright and swung himself around so that he was sitting on the edge of the bed.

'Jesus,' Sidney said, impressed. 'What else can you do?'

'Well, I don't know,' Arthur said, as they both stared down at his legs. They looked thinner and ropier than usual, less sturdy, and he wasn't entirely sure they'd hold his weight. He tried anyway, and found them to be strangely shaky and useless underneath him; Sidney caught him before he made a mess of his kneecaps.

'Good trick though,' Sidney said, trying to get him back into bed; Arthur was having none of it.

'The only way to get better at walking is to walk,' he said, throwing an arm around Sidney's shoulders and leaning heavily on him as his thighs started to shake. 'So let's walk.'

They completed a few very wobbly laps around their chambers before Sidney insisted on depositing Arthur in a chair and calling for breakfast; the novelty of it all, of being able to sit opposite Sidney at the table and spill runny egg all down the front of himself and nibble at pieces of bread and laugh almost as if it were any other day, made Arthur feel giddy.

'We should call for Gwen. Show her what I can do. She'll

probably weep with joy, poor lamb. Actually – where *is* Gwen? I haven't seen her or ... well, nobody's visited me for days.'

'Yeah,' Sidney said, wiping crumbs from his mouth and leaning back in his chair. 'Funny thing, that. Tried to go and see Aggie yesterday afternoon when you were conked out and the bloody guard wouldn't let me into the royal wing.'

'Odd,' said Arthur. 'Might be a security thing.' He dropped his knife, and when Sidney tried to grab it for him, he held up a hand to stop him and insisted on doing it himself. As he leaned down, he noticed a small brown package on the floor, as if it had been dropped and forgotten. 'What's this?'

'Dunno,' Sidney said, following Arthur's nod and then leaning over to pick it up. He unwrapped the paper and extracted a long pendant. They both watched the cut black stone rotate slowly between them at the end of its chain. 'I've seen these before, they're meant to be ... I dunno. Charms. Spells. They keep you safe.'

'Well. Excellent. I suppose somebody brought it as a gift,' Arthur said cheerfully, taking it from Sidney and looping it over his head. 'I like it. It's hard and black, like my heart.'

'Your heart is soft and yellow,' said Sidney. 'Like marzipan.'

'I have the heart of a lion. And the legs of a horse. I'm going back to bed, but tomorrow let's show everyone what these shapely pegs can do.'

He felt even better the next morning; shattered, with aching limbs as if he'd run a marathon rather than taken a hundred steps around the same fifteen-foot radius, but it was such a novelty to feel tired from physical exertion that he was in an extremely good mood. Not even the sight of his closely cropped hair in the mirror, or the fact that he could now barely bend his wrist, was enough to put a damper on the pure joy of being somewhere other than his bed. He had never felt so emotional about a chair before.

It was slow going, the business of getting back on his feet, but he was powered by determination and the strange, insistent twist of anxiety he felt in his gut every time Sidney attempted to glean any news from the royal wing, and heard nothing.

'What the hell is going on?' Arthur demanded, when Sidney returned once again without news.

'I wouldn't worry,' Sidney said, obviously very worried. 'Focus on getting all your parts in working order and then we'll sort it out.'

He reported back to Arthur that the castle was absolutely packed with people; hundreds were turned away every evening for dinner in the Great Hall, and the crowds attending the tournament as they approached the finale were enormous.

'And I saw your father,' Sidney said hesitantly, as they sat down to eat dinner on the day Arthur managed to walk the length of the corridor outside his room mostly unaided.

Arthur tried not to wince, but realised too late he'd done it anyway. 'Joy of joys. Did he offer any explanation as to why he hasn't been up here yet? A note expressing his concern, perhaps?'

'Er . . .' said Sidney. 'No. He pretended he hadn't seen me, actually.'

'Of course he did,' Arthur said, sighing. It was a

particularly frustrating conundrum; he had absolutely no desire to see his father, but his imagined, shadowy progress around the castle beneath Arthur's feet was almost as intrusive as if he were standing in the room. 'And the others?'

'Haven't had a reply to those notes yet,' Sidney said, through a mouthful of bread. Increasingly annoyed by the lack of visitors, Arthur had asked him to send messages to Gwen and Gabriel, informing them that he was out of bed, and had expected them to appear immediately to rejoice in the miracle; in a moment of madness he'd also asked Sidney to deliver one to Bridget. That had been yesterday morning; they had all gone unanswered.

'It's starting to feel somewhat personal.'

'Nah,' said Sidney, impressively unconvincing. 'They're probably just busy. With the tournament.'

'Let's pay them a visit, shall we?' Arthur said suddenly, trying to get up and managing more of an undignified stumble, during which he had to grab on to the table for support.

'What, now?'

'Yes,' Arthur said insistently. 'Now.'

'You have to let us in,' Arthur said to the least threatening-looking guard.

His eyes darted sideways, and then he gave a minute shrug. 'Can't.'

'Well, why not?' Arthur asked, trying to look intimidating and probably only succeeding in looking a bit miffed.

'You do not have access to the royal wing,' said a different guard with an impressive moustache.

'Under whose orders?' Arthur demanded.

'The princess,' said the unthreatening guard; the moustachioed one narrowed his eyes at him, as if he'd said something he wasn't supposed to.

'Let me talk to her,' Arthur said. 'This is clearly a mistake, we'll have it fixed in a—'

Two very sharp swords were suddenly within scratching distance of his chin.

'Oi!' Sidney said, pulling Arthur roughly backwards. 'No need for any of that. We'll be going.'

'But,' Arthur said, twisting in Sidney's grip, 'if they just—'

'If you don't come with me now,' Sidney muttered sternly, 'I'll just walk off and leave you here. And you can't really stand up on your own, so you'll just flop straight over and lie here on the floor waggling your limbs in the air like a dying bee until someone else takes pity on you. So. You coming?'

'Fine,' Arthur said belligerently, allowing himself to be pulled away. 'But – take me to the library.'

The library was apparently not included in the parts of the castle that had become mysteriously off-limits; there was, however, a pair of very listless guards standing at the door, which confirmed Arthur's suspicions about who might be within.

'I need you to distract them,' he said to Sidney, ducking out of sight. 'Just – get them away from the door, and I'll slip inside.'

'You'll "slip inside"?' Sidney scoffed. 'You going to slither in on the floor like a snake?'

'If needs must,' Arthur said, with as much dignity as he could muster.

'Fine,' said Sidney, looking resigned. 'Which distraction, do you reckon? Number four? Number six?'

'Modified 1.5,' Arthur said, grinning at him.

'I hate modified 1.5,' Sidney said darkly, but he gamely walked away. Arthur waited for a minute or two as he took the long way around, and then he reappeared at the far end of the hallway as if coming from the courtyard, and dramatically listed sideways, swearing and half collapsing to the ground.

'All right down there?' one of the guards called, clearly thrilled that something vaguely interesting was happening on his shift.

'Oh God,' Sidney moaned. 'I don't know, I don't know – what sort of rash do you get if you have a lover's disease?'

'A lover's . . . ?' the guard said, exchanging an amused look with his counterpart.

'Just, I don't know if you can get it, doing what we did – oh *God*, it's gone such an unnatural colour, I think it might be about to fall off—'

'Fall *off*?' Distraction 1.5 never failed; hilarious and disgusting human misery was too strong a lure. The guards glanced back into the library to check their charge was safely within, and then headed for Sidney, intent on seeing what may or may not be about to detach itself from his person.

Arthur didn't have to slither into the room like a snake, but it did take rather a lot out of him to get through the door before they turned around. Once inside, he slowed

339

down, leaning on the shelves for support; he grappled his way towards the back corner, where a candle was burning low.

'Boo,' he said flatly, when Gabriel glanced up in alarm from the book he was reading. He looked dreadful – as if *he* had been the one ill in bed for over a month.

'What are you doing?' Gabriel said, closing the book and immediately looking around, as if for backup.

'That's a funny way of saying "*Glad you're not dead, Arthur*",' Arthur replied, trying to steady himself as dark spots encroached on the corners of his vision.

'You can't be here,' Gabriel snapped. It was so unexpected that Arthur's mouth dropped open; he was unsure whether the pain in his lungs was due to overexertion or the fact that Gabriel was looking at him like he was some horrifying spectre.

'Tell me what's going on,' he demanded; Gabriel stood up, and actually seemed to back away from him, further into his corner.

'How did you get past the guards?'

'Oh – killed them all in cold blood, obviously,' Arthur said incredulously. 'I didn't do anything to them. Sidney's distracting them – with a little something we call the "bachelor in distress".'

'Leave now,' Gabriel said slowly, 'or I'll call them to have you removed, Arthur. Stay away from me, stay away from my sister—'

'Are you *possessed*?' Arthur shouted, accidentally knocking one of Gabriel's books to the ground, and feeling a horrid jolt of unease when Gabriel flinched. 'What have I done, Gabriel? Because *I don't understand.* Tell me—'

Gabriel hadn't needed to call for the guards; Arthur's shouting had done the job for him. They came up behind him and grabbed him quite forcefully by the arms. What little strength had powered him to the library was long spent, and he didn't even attempt to struggle as they started to drag him away.

'Gabriel,' he said, knowing he was pleading now and finding he didn't care. 'Please. Come on. Shit. *Please.* Tell me what I did.'

Gabriel said nothing, his face stricken. In the lamplight, he looked strangely young – not like a future king at all, just a boy, being swallowed whole by the dust and the darkness and the thousands of words of history closing in all around him.

One more day.

Gwen just had to make it through one more day, and then the tournament would be over; Bridget would be gone; the people filling the city of Camelot to the rafters would start to make their way home. Her life would shrink, and she and Gabriel could sit down and work out what on earth they were going to do about Arthur.

The letter had spelled it all out for her, damningly clear. The Delaceys had planned this together; her friendship with Arthur, his closeness with Gabriel. Arthur had been sent to charm them. It was all political, a game – and she and Gabriel had walked right into it willingly, ready to spill their secrets the moment somebody showed them the slightest bit of kindness.

After Gabriel had read it for himself, she'd told him exactly what she'd overheard – Lord Delacey's bragging, Gabriel's secret hopes for the future laid bare. He had sat for at least two minutes in complete silence going over the letter again, Gwen feeling as if she were going slowly mad as she waited for him to say something, until he had suddenly crumpled it in his hand, looked up at her and said 'Well. That's that then.'

'How can you be so calm? He knows *everything* about us. Me and Bridget. You, and—'

'Yes.' Gabriel was very pale. 'He does. But let's think about this rationally. His father won't use this information now, because he still wants you and Arthur to marry. Lord Delacey likes to feel powerful, and I know Father has been brushing him off – he wants more than Father is willing to give.'

'How do we know he won't use it now? He was telling that man plenty.'

'He likes to let his mouth run away from him, but he's not going to ruin the chance to marry Arthur into royalty,' Gabriel said. 'That's the highest position available to him, and we know that's what he's after. No . . . I think he'll use it later. For leverage. He can hold it above our heads – and Father's – whenever he pleases. Use it to get a higher title, perhaps, or a position on Father's council.'

Gwen put her head back in her hands, where it felt less likely to fall off her shoulders and plummet right through the floor. 'Oh God. Do we have to tell Father about this?'

Gabriel rose to his feet very slowly, as if every ligament in his body were resisting. 'No. Not yet. He might not even tell Father, he might come straight to me. I just need a little time to . . . think this through.'

'Gabe,' Gwen said. He was approaching all of this with careful pragmatism, as if they hadn't both been thoroughly, ruthlessly betrayed in the worst way possible. 'You're allowed to be . . . I don't know . . . angry. Upset. What he did to you . . .'

Gabriel sighed, rubbing at his forehead until it looked pink and painful. 'Yes. Fine. I am both of those things. But more pressingly, I need to work out what we're going to do about this.'

They both looked despondently down at the letter.

'How could he do this?' Gwen whispered into the silence.

Neither of them had an answer.

A clean, bright rage had come over Gwen that night. She had told the guards that circumstances had changed, to prevent Sidney or Arthur from snooping around the royal quarters at their leisure, and then cornered Agnes in the ladies' solar and told her to cease all contact with Sidney immediately.

'Why would I do that?' Agnes had said, chin lifted in defiance.

Gwen had given her a brief summary of events, but to her utter disbelief, Agnes had refused to accept her explanation.

'It must be a misunderstanding,' she kept saying, shaking her head. 'If you'd just talk to him—'

'I'm not going to talk to him!' Gwen had shouted. 'I'm not going to give him a chance to worm his way back into my brain when I've just managed to get him out. He's obviously a very ... a very skilled *liar*, a very good manipulator – I'm not going to talk to him, and neither are you. To either of them.'

'Is that an order?' Agnes said, her eyes glossy with furious tears.

'Yes, Agnes. It's an order,' Gwen said, turning and marching from the room.

As she lay sleeplessly in her bed that night, counting down the hours until dawn and the final day of the tournament, she wondered what Bridget would say if she knew. She pictured her there, lying next to Gwen in the gloom, the two of them talking in the kind of hushed tones only used between people tentatively mapping the foundations of each other in the middle of the night.

When she'd finally slept, she had dreamed of Camelot silent and empty, besieged by enormous drifts of snow.

One more day.

Gwen had never seen so many people packed into the courtyards of Camelot. As they descended towards the tournament stands, the true scale of the turnout became apparent.

'I can't believe there are this many people in *England*,' she said to Gabriel, who had joined her as she walked under the portcullis. 'What are they all *doing* here?'

'It's a tournament,' Gabriel said disinterestedly. Gwen looked at him properly. She was convinced he hadn't slept a wink since they had read Arthur's letter, and one glance at him seemed to confirm her suspicions.

'You look like hell,' she said, and he didn't even attempt a smile.

'Let's just get today over with,' he said grimly. 'And then all these people will leave the city, and I'll have room to – to think.'

'Gabe, are you . . .' she said, reaching out to put a hand on his arm, but their little cavalcade had suddenly collided and merged with the king and queen's.

'Hullo, Gwendoline,' her father said, giving her an absent-minded kiss on the head before straightening up, squaring his shoulders and ascending the stairs to the royal stands, his family in tow. Gwen couldn't help but scan the makeshift rows in front of the competitors' encampment, which were populated by a handful of knights who hadn't made the cut for the day's event. Many had left, helms and prides dented, but there were still a few standing shoulder-to-shoulder on the left side of the grounds. She wished her heart hadn't jumped so violently in her chest at the sight of Bridget, who was standing at the very end, dressed in soft browns and whites, talking to another knight and shielding her eyes from the watery sun.

The melee was the grand finale of the tournament; after months of competition, the highest-ranking knights were to gather in two teams and fight until the Grand Marshal judged the battle over and called to stop. From the victorious side, the king was to choose the ultimate winner of the tournament.

Excalibur – Gwen couldn't help but hear the word '*Nine?*' when she looked at it, in Arthur's incredulous tone – was sitting, freshly polished and gleaming, awaiting presentation to the winner. The weather was being suitably dramatic, the wind chivvying the clouds along so that the grounds kept alternating between weak sunshine and gloom, banners and flags whipping violently against their restraints.

The crowd was chattering excitedly, the tension so thick Gwen felt strangled by it; she was just settling into her seat when Gabriel touched her on the arm.

'Lord Willard is here,' he muttered in her ear.

Sure enough, her father's cousin was sitting in the raised stands opposite, where they had crowded some of the nobility due to overflow, watching them. He saw her startled glance, and gave her a perfectly polite and perfunctory nod of greeting. His hair was longer than she remembered, and he was grandly dressed in silver and black.

'What on earth is he doing here?'

'He and Father have been more cordial lately – he wrote to warn about an uprising in the north,' Gabriel said, shrugging. 'I suppose he was invited, as he always is, and decided to be friendly.'

This didn't quite make sense to Gwen; after all, Willard's only real stake in the tournament was the Knife, who was no longer competing.

'Who's he talking to now?' Gwen said, narrowing her eyes. 'Is that – Arthur's father?'

'Yes,' Gabriel said quietly. 'Yes, I believe it is.'

The Lord of Maidvale was standing at Lord Willard's shoulder, talking insistently in his ear. The sight of the two of them with their heads together stirred a vague memory, but Gwen couldn't quite grab hold of it.

'Gabe, did we have a conversation about Lord Delacey and Lord Willard?' Gwen asked, frowning. 'I feel like there was something . . .'

Gabriel just shook his head, barely listening.

There *was* something, Gwen knew it. Something about a trip, or a meeting . . . for some reason she thought of Lord Stafford, and then suddenly it clicked into place.

'Skipton Castle. Gabe, wasn't Willard seen at Skipton?'

'Yes,' said Gabriel slowly. 'But Stafford looked into it, and he has family near there. There was no reason to suspect anything untoward.'

'But – in the stables, the man talking to Arthur's father . . . he said that Lord Delacey had been to Skipton.'

'Are you sure?'

'Yes,' Gwen said impatiently. 'Yes, he said . . . "What have you learned since Skipton?" Surely that can't be coincidence. What would Arthur's father and Lord Willard have to talk about? Why would they both have travelled to North Yorkshire?'

Gabriel shook his head. 'I don't know. Perhaps they're friends.'

But Gwen was suddenly seeing the conversation in the stables in an entirely new light. Surely the exchange of idle gossip didn't require such confidentiality – and if Lord Delacey had attended some sort of meeting at Skipton Castle, a meeting kept secret, from which he had departed with instructions to gather more information . . .

'Father,' Gwen said, standing up to try to catch his attention. '*Father.*'

'Not now, Gwendoline,' he said, dismissing her with a wave of his hand – but Gwen refused to be dismissed.

'Father, please – your *cousin* is here. Lord Willard is sitting right over there, look.'

The king didn't appear the least bit surprised. 'I know he's there, Gwendoline. Keep your voice down. He was invited, and has decided, on this occasion, to take me up on the offer. We're trying to keep up friendly relations, a show of unity at this difficult time, so please stop *pointing* and *shouting* about him and sit down.'

'But . . .' Gwen said, glancing without meaning to back at Lord Willard, and finding that he was still looking directly at her. 'Why is he only here now, at the end of the tournament? And – he's talking to Arthur's father. He's talking to Lord Delacey.'

'And?' the king said, sounding exasperated.

'And – I need to tell you something,' Gwen said, her voice reduced to a nervous sort of high-pitched trill. 'I . . . I recently discovered that Lord Delacey wrote to Arthur and asked him to keep an eye on us. He wanted Arthur to ingratiate himself with us – with Gabe and me – and report back to him.'

Her father shrugged. 'And why shouldn't he, Gwendoline? He's going to be your husband after all. And we all know Lord Delacey is overfond of knowing the – ah – particulars of everything that goes on at court. Now –' he lowered his voice, sounding stern – '*sit down.*'

'But – listen, that's not all,' she said, not sitting. 'Lord Delacey was at Skipton Castle recently. Just like Lord Willard.'

'My cousin was seen *near* Skipton,' the king said. 'Not *at* Skipton. And Stafford confirmed with two sources that he was visiting family. The man is so paranoid about uprisings in the north, he'd certainly have spoken up if he thought nobles were convening secret meetings. Please sit, Gwendoline. Two people may visit a place without—'

'You don't understand,' Gwen said. 'I was there, I heard him telling somebody – if you'd just heard the way he was talking, I think—'

She was cut off by the sound of trumpets, an elaborate fanfare that went on for so long that her father had asked her twice more to sit down by the time it ended. She finally complied, throwing herself back into her chair and exchanging a look of desperation with Gabriel, who just shrugged helplessly.

A steady stream of knights, their armour polished and their weapons freshly sharpened, was entering the small arena. Cheers and boos greeted each one, and they raised their swords and shook their fists in return. The crowd was ravenous, boiling; in some places it looked as if the stands might fail completely, split at their seams and send the spectators pressed up against them tumbling down into the freshly raked sand.

The noise was reaching fever pitch as the last of the competitors appeared and they started splitting into their two teams, denoted by a knotted handkerchief in either regal blue or knife-slash red about their wrists. It all seemed good-natured, if a little rabid, which didn't account for how antsy Gwen was feeling as she shifted in her seat; the cheers and screams grated on her nerves, and her fingertips kept jumping against the guard rail. She chanced a glance over at Bridget and saw that she was looking back, frowning slightly as if she'd been watching her exchange with the king.

'I don't *like* this,' she said in Gabriel's ear. He still didn't seem quite with her, as if sleep had given up on waiting for him and come to claim him then and there. 'Gabe. This thing with Willard and Delacey. It feels ... off.'

'If Father isn't worried ...' Gabriel said, trailing off. 'You could go back to your rooms to rest. I'll tell Father – I'll say you were unwell.'

'No,' Gwen said, turning her frustration on her brother. 'That's not it, Gabe, it's not just a ... Wait.' She had turned back to look at the two teams of competitors, now arranged in relatively neat rows either side of some invisible line in the sand Gwen couldn't see. 'Wait, is – where's Arthur's father gone? Gabe, pay *attention*. Where the hell is Lord Delacey?'

31

'We've been doing this all summer,' Sidney said to the surly guard at the tournament grounds. Arthur had noticed that they'd been spending a lot of time bargaining with guards lately; it felt like a waste of their many talents. 'Come *on.*'

'Can't do that,' said the guard. He was blocking the only entrance to the royal stands, and Arthur quite desperately needed to be on the other side of him. Sidney flexed his hands at Arthur's side; his knuckles cracked ominously.

'Well – why *not?*' Arthur said. 'What on earth have I done, specifically, to incur your wrath? I want to go to the tournament. I like watching people hit each other. If you don't let us through, I'll gladly demonstrate, with the help of my slightly unhinged friend here.' He knew without looking that Sidney was rolling his eyes.

'Lot of people here today,' said the guard, ignoring his threat. 'Security's tight. 'S'not personal, boy. Lord Stafford said nobody's to come through this entrance except the royal family themselves.'

'I'm going to *be* in the royal family in a matter of weeks,' Arthur said through gritted teeth. 'Come on. Everybody knows who I am. Just let me through, I need to see my – my *betrothed*.'

'Sorry, pal. General stands are full too, so you won't get in there,' said the guard. Arthur did seriously consider doing something very stupid for a few seconds, but Sidney seemed to sense his rapidly increasing appetite for chaos, and pulled him gently away.

It was Sidney's fault that they were here anyway. After the altercation in the library Arthur had been perfectly content to lie in his bed and stew, wondering how he could have possibly ruined everything between himself and the royal siblings without even leaving his room. Perhaps, he thought wildly, the wedding had been called off for some reason? Maybe the king had changed his mind and, now that they were free from obligation, Gwen and Gabriel had been extremely relieved to cut him off at the first opportunity?

Sidney had insisted that it *wasn't* simply that Arthur was an innately unloveable person, as he often suspected, and had finally shed his reluctance and demanded that they go in search of answers.

'This is, quite frankly, bullshit,' Arthur said now, noticing that he was leaning heavily on Sidney and making an effort to straighten up and bear more of his own weight.

'Chill,' Sidney said, steering Arthur around the perimeter of the tournament grounds. 'Bet you a gold noble the guards care a lot less about who gets chummy with the *competitors*.' He pointed to the entrance that led to the knights' tents and enclosures.

'You don't have a noble,' Arthur said, but he was pleased to discover that Sidney was right; there wasn't even anybody standing guard at the entrance, and when they got inside, it was almost deserted.

Sidney jerked his head towards the arena. 'Hear that? Reckon they're about to start.'

The crowd was indeed growing louder every second, and they picked up their pace as much as they could, Arthur setting his jaw against the pain.

'So the plan is . . .' he said, breathing heavily. 'Out through the competitors' entrance – don't get dragged into the melee – wriggle our way towards Gwen. I reckon if we can just get her attention, we can— Oh.'

He had walked straight into his father.

'Ah,' said Lord Delacey. 'Arthur.'

Arthur had no idea where to begin with his response; in his determination to get to Gwen, he was completely baffled by this sudden and considerable obstacle. Sidney, however, gave a quick and curt sort of bow, taking Arthur with him.

'It's fortuitous, actually,' his father continued slowly, eyes darting from Arthur to Sidney and then back again, 'that I have run into you.'

'Odd that you should say so,' Arthur said tightly. 'If you wanted to come and find me, I've actually been pretty stationary. You know. Nearly *dying*.' Next to him, Arthur felt Sidney stiffen; quite a few large men had just walked through the entrance, and were now standing menacingly at Lord Delacey's shoulders.

'Arthur,' his father said, raising his eyebrows and continuing to speak as if Arthur were a stray dog that needed to be approached with caution. 'There's no reason to be difficult. Come with me now, and I'll explain on the way.'

'Actually,' Arthur spat, 'I can think of quite a few reasons to be difficult. *One*—'

'Seize him,' his father said, in a tone so light that for a moment Arthur was sure he had misheard. His father's men clearly hadn't; they immediately moved towards him, and Sidney took a step forward, pulling out his shortsword and putting himself squarely between Arthur and danger.

'Er . . . what the hell is happening?' Arthur said, as two of the men also raised their weapons, and Sidney moved back to accommodate them, his shoulders pressed against Arthur's chest.

'Get out of the way,' Arthur's father snarled at Sidney. 'I pay your *wages*, boy.'

'Now that you mention it,' Sidney said evenly, 'I resign. In disgrace.'

'Father,' Arthur said, his voice wavering. Even Sidney couldn't expect to hold off the half-dozen men who were now advancing on them, and Arthur had no desire to see his head removed from his body. 'Can we take a moment and go back a few steps? I think there's been some sort of—'

It happened so quickly that Arthur couldn't have explained how it had transpired with a sword to his throat – and certainly not with six. One of the men towards the back of the group let out an extremely loud grunt as something in his body made the sort of cracking noise that healthy bodies shouldn't, on the whole – and then he was toppling sideways; another managed to turn and raise his sword just in time as Lady Leclair, wielding only a dagger, brought her arm up to meet him.

'Bridget!' Arthur said, genuinely delighted to see her.

'You seem to be –' Bridget grunted, pushing hard against the man who was attempting to suppress her – 'in a spot of bother.'

'I don't have time for this,' Arthur's father hissed. 'Get him, and let's go.'

The first man who tried to grab Arthur discovered very quickly how reluctant Sidney was to let anybody get within touching distance; he was dispatched with a rather nasty stab wound to the thigh and a blow to the head that sent him tottering sideways until he collapsed quietly to the ground. The second, third and fourth were not quite so hasty; they attacked en masse, and it became clear almost immediately that this was a fight that Arthur and Sidney weren't going to win.

Within approximately ten seconds, Sidney had been knocked from his feet, a sword pressed to his throat, and Arthur was holding up his shaking hands in surrender. Behind his father, he could see Bridget locked in combat with a much taller man who was trying very hard to keep out of dagger-swiping range.

'Stop,' Arthur said raggedly, as the man who had Sidney at his mercy lifted his sword as if to get a better angle on Sidney's jugular. 'Father. Stop. I'll come with you – we both will. Sid, drop your sword.'

Sidney swore, but immediately did as he was told, opening his hand and letting it fall to the ground.

'Fine,' Lord Delacey said; the man who had been about to kill Sidney instead roughly hauled him to his feet, and then turned him to bind his hands crudely behind his back.

'What about ...?' One of the men gestured at Bridget, who had been pushed back against the fence but was still giving her all.

'Leave them. He'll finish her. We must go *now*,' Lord Delacey said impatiently. Arthur found himself practically lifted from the ground by the two men, who each grabbed one of his shoulders to frogmarch him away.

It was just as well, really; his legs had almost given out the moment Sidney had been forced to the ground.

If his father's men hadn't been so unforgivably rude, he might have thanked them for the lift.

Gabriel didn't seem at all interested in the fact that Arthur's father had disappeared. In fact, he wasn't paying Gwen the slightest bit of attention.

'Gabe,' Gwen said urgently. 'Why are you – *what* are you looking at?'

Gabriel was gazing up at the stands, his eyeline high above the competitors. 'That's – I'm sure that's Morgana.'

'*Morgana?*' Gwen said, momentarily convinced that he had started hallucinating due to extensive sleep deprivation. 'Morgan le Fay? The *witch*?'

'No,' Gabriel said distantly, still squinting. 'No. Morgana – my crow. The one I was raising. I released her about a month ago. Look, she's on top of the competitors' stands – she has that flash of white, on her left flank.'

'Are you even listening to me?' Gwen demanded, feeling rather than seeing her father's eyes cut across to her as her voice raised in pitch and volume.

'She looks very agitated,' Gabriel said, tilting his head to one side in a very birdlike way.

'Gabe. Look at *me. I* look very agitated,' Gwen said. 'Will you come with me? I want to see where Arthur's father went. I just want to make sure he's not—'

'At the sound of the trumpet,' the Grand Marshal called, 'our two teams of distinguished knights – the best that England has to offer – will fight for honour, for the long-held ideals of chivalry, and for their king!'

'Not what?' Gabriel said, finally looking away from the crow.

'I don't know! Plotting something! Perhaps he's ... Hang on, where's Bridget? Where does everybody keep *disappearing* off to?'

'Ready yourselves,' called the Grand Marshal. 'On the count of three. *One . . .*'

'Don't worry,' Gabriel said. 'We'll speak to Father properly when this is done.'

'*Two . . .*' called the Grand Marshal.

Morgana the crow cawed, and then set off across the arena. Some of the competitors looked up to watch as she passed just over their heads and then vanished from sight.

'*Three . . .*'

'Wait,' Gwen said, her thoughts seeming to accelerate as she watched the front line of the knights to her left ready themselves for battle. 'That's the Knife.'

'Is it?'

'Gabe, the Knife didn't qualify! He shouldn't *be* there!' Gwen stood up now, abandoning all propriety, no longer caring if her father was angry with her or if she embarrassed herself. '*Father.*'

'*Begin!*' shouted the Grand Marshal.

Gwen looked at the Knife. The Knife looked at Lord

Willard. In the split second before the howl of the trumpets, Gwen saw Willard nod.

Instead of converging on each other, most of the knights turned in unison towards the royal stands.

There were two very distinct seconds of confusion, during which everybody seemed frozen in place; in those seconds, Gwen had done something she had never in her life imagined doing and thrown herself bodily at her father, half succeeding in knocking him out of his chair.

A moment later, a knife that had been thrown with deadly precision from the arena had struck the wooden post just above the throne – and chaos was unleashed from all directions.

Gabriel and her mother were suddenly on the ground next to her. Gwen pressed herself into the wooden boards, her eyes squeezed shut as she braced for the sting of a knife or a sword. Numerous boots thundered past her as her father's guard moved towards the fray.

'*Move!*' her father was roaring in her ear. 'You have to *move!*'

Gabriel had her by the shoulder, was pulling her along as they half crawled towards the exit of the royal stands; there were so many people screaming and shouting that they became a wordless wall of sound, a noise that Gwen couldn't have imagined in her worst nightmares. She felt a splinter catch in her forearm, her eyes watering in pain as somebody hauled her to her feet; somehow, miraculously, they had made it out before anybody could breach the stand.

'*Bridget,*' Gwen choked out. 'Gabe, Gabe, I don't know where she is, I need—'

'*Go,*' shouted her father, more to the guards than to anybody else; at least twenty of them had formed a protective ring around the royal family, but Gwen was still pushing against them, mindlessly attempting to move back towards the violence. She thought of Bridget out there somewhere, with no armour on. Bridget, who would surely rather risk death than walk away from a fight like this one.

'Come *on,*' Gabriel shouted, pulling at her shoulder.

Gwen cast one last desperate glance over at what she could still see of the tournament grounds through the stands – people fleeing, swords clashing, bodies crumpling – and in that moment she saw Bridget, completely impossible and yet entirely real, putting her foot up on to the wooden rail where Gwen had been sitting just moments ago.

In one swift movement she reached over, grasped the hilt of Excalibur Nine and pulled.

The sword slid neatly out, with a ringing rasp of metal on stone that Gwen heard even over the mayhem.

Bridget's eyes darted across to where Gwen was standing but didn't seem to see her; she just wiped a sleeve across her bloodied forehead before jumping back down into the fight.

There was nothing more Gwen could do except let herself be borne away, across the drawbridge and back towards the castle.

They were crossing the threshold when it began to rain.

'They must have been filling up the camps for weeks,' Sir Hurst, the Captain of the Guard, was saying, as the king was strapped into his armour. They were standing in her father's war room, his council around him – or at least those who had made it back from the tournament grounds. Gwen knew she was only still in this room – sitting by the door, her hands shaking uncontrollably against her knees – because nobody had noticed that she was in there. 'No one thought to monitor the attendees, there's been no reason to suspect in the past . . . It's been busier, yes, but the tournament is popular. They've been concealing themselves in plain sight. The stands were half full of traitors.'

'And we're . . . *sure* it was Willard?' said Gwen's mother, looking stunned.

Sir Hurst ducked his head. 'Yes, your highness. He was seen giving orders.'

The king breathed in and out slowly through his nose, clearly trying to keep his temper in check.

'Hellfire and damnation to traitorous cousins.'

'We sent him casks of wine,' the queen said faintly. 'On his birthday.'

'And how is it that most of the best knights of the realm also happen to be murderous turncoats?' the king asked.

Sir Hurst winced. 'I believe – Sir Blackwood, the Grand Marshal, was bribed. We know he gambles, but his debts must be worse than we imagined. It would have been easy enough for a man in his position to mismatch opponents, overlook lances that had been tampered with . . .'

'Damn,' said her father softly, his hand curling into a fist and then quickly releasing again. 'All right. Where are we now? And – where the hell is Stafford? Did he make it inside?'

361

Somebody rushed from the room, presumably to try to find out.

'When it began,' Gabriel said, his voice quiet but steady, 'the knights who hadn't bought their place in the finale rushed to our aid, and I saw some of those watching from the stands do the same. They haven't all been turned, Father. Far from it.'

Bridget hasn't been turned, Gwen thought, a wave of nausea rolling through her. *Bridget is out there, fighting for us.*

'How many of our people have made it back into the castle?' her father said, as his gauntlets were eased over his hands.

'A good many. They're gathered in the Great Hall,' said the Captain of the Guard. 'We have hundreds fit to fight, not including the castle guard.'

'And my cousin has?'

'Impossible to say – they may not have brought their full force to the first wave. I imagine there will be more coming from the campgrounds.'

'The guard stays here,' the king said, holding his arms up so that he could be fully equipped with sword and dagger. Somebody else had hurried into the room carrying yet more armour – it was dropped unceremoniously on the table. Gwen tried to place it; it was pale gold, with the royal crest emblazoned across the breastplate.

'No,' she said, turning to Gabriel, who was standing with both palms flat against the table. '*No*. Not you as well.'

Gabriel tried to smile at her, but it looked instead like an apology she didn't want to accept. A messenger came rushing in, his chest heaving.

362

'Your majesty, the rebels didn't succeed in pushing up the hill – they've fallen back and they're regrouping with more forces for a fresh assault.'

Gabriel straightened up, clearing his throat, and the king looked at him. 'What?'

'We could ...' He broke off, swallowed, and then continued. 'We could bring up the drawbridge. Shelter in place until the nearest troops reach us. Perhaps—'

'No,' the king said immediately. 'That'll take days. If we didn't have men out there already, I might – but, no. We cannot protect ourselves and leave them cut off. Camelot does not hide.'

'Your majesty,' the messenger said apprehensively. 'I was told to inform you – Lord Stafford is with them.'

A stunned silence followed this, and then the king slammed a hand down on the table so hard that everybody jumped.

'But then ... that assassin ...' Gabriel said slowly. His father glanced sharply at him. 'He was so insistent that it was just a lone wolf with some personal, invented vendetta. But it wouldn't have been too hard for him to have a person with ill intentions hired to the guard. He was constantly throwing us off the scent. He was one of the loudest voices when it came to sending our troops north, leaving us unprotected, but when Willard was sighted he about-faced and told us it was all paranoia ...'

'After everything you did for him,' Gwen's mother said. 'After the trust you put in him, *knowing* he was a cultist and giving him a chance.'

'But ... he had plenty of opportunities to just kill you himself,' said Gwen. 'Why did he not take them?'

'Because the man is a coward,' Sir Hurst said. 'I suppose that assassin was a last-ditch attempt to prevent all-out warfare.' He turned to the king, shaking his head. 'This is my fault, sire. I take full responsibility. I should have—'

'Let's not waste time on regrets now,' said the king. Sir Hurst nodded bracingly, then took him aside. The rest of the room lapsed into anxious muttering.

'Gabe, stay,' Gwen said desperately, as a page lifted the breastplate of his armour and attempted to secure it. 'Somebody needs to, in case—'

'G,' Gabriel said quietly, fumbling to help the page; the small shake in his voice as he attempted to be reassuring broke Gwen's heart. 'I have to go. We need everybody we can get, and besides, Father is right – how would it look if we just sat here and hid, while we sent other men out to fight for us?'

Gabriel was shrugging on his pauldrons so that the page could buckle him into them. With every new piece of armour added to him, it felt as if Gwen were watching him being entombed – his narrow, breakable body gradually encased until she hardly recognised him any more.

'Gabe,' she said quietly, desperate now as she felt them running out of time, moving closer so that only he and the boy dressing him could hear. 'If Arthur's father – if he was working with Willard this whole time, then that means Arthur must have—'

'Yes,' said Gabriel, briefly closing his eyes. 'Yes, I know. I can't quite believe it of him, that he could have sat in our rooms and laughed with us, all the while knowing he was working to send us to our deaths, but . . . I suppose I didn't really know him at all.'

'He didn't deserve you,' Gwen said tearfully, gripping the shoulder that had not yet been plated. 'He didn't deserve either of us.'

'Well. Nobody does,' Gabriel said, smiling weakly; a moment later her hand was being waved away so that his armour could be completed, and then everybody seemed to be moving at once. The king signalled for them to exit, and they all walked briskly from the room and down the stairs, a clamour of steel and tense voices and boots on stone. They reached the Great Hall and were greeted by the sight of hundreds of men pulling on armour, swords being pressed into hands, helms placed on heads.

It was all happening too quickly. Gwen felt like a child clutching at handfuls of water, unable to understand why it wouldn't stop running through her fingers.

'Gabriel,' she began, but he had already been pulled into a conversation with her father and Sir Hurst; they were gathering the men around them, shouting instructions, and the queen pulled gently at Gwen's arm to stop her from getting in the way.

'They can't just do this,' Gwen said, expecting her mother to agree, but she didn't – because of course they could.

Her father strode over to kiss her mother, his eyes squeezing tightly shut; he pressed his forehead against Gwen's for one quick moment, and all she could think was that when he walked away, his beard would still be wet with her tears.

Gabriel didn't say goodbye. He tried – Gwen saw him take a step towards her with a hand half raised – but then there were shouts from the courtyard and her father clapped his hands together.

'Move out,' he shouted.

And they did.

33

Up until the moment all the shouting started, Arthur had been relatively convinced that his father was just being miscellaneously unhinged; he had been both baffled and furious, but not surprised. It didn't seem out of the realms of possibility that his father might just be in the mood for tying Sidney up and holding his own son at swordpoint, after all. Unlikely, but not impossible.

When he heard the distinctive sounds of panic – the deep, brassy command of a guard shouting '*Protect the king!*' – he finally realised that this was no aimless midlife crisis.

'What's happening?' Arthur shouted, struggling against the guards that held him, craning his neck as he tried to catch a glimpse of the tournament grounds behind them. 'For Christ's sake, what the *hell* have you done?'

'Shut up,' his father said, striding along beside him. It had started to rain, light but steady, the drops pattering loudly on helms and armour. 'For once in your life, shut up and *listen.*'

'Not until you tell me—'

'Not until you quiet down.'

'*Fine,*' Arthur said bitterly, wincing as his leg dragged.

'I have formed a very advantageous alliance,' his father said, practically spitting with excitement, his face ruddy and flushed behind his beard. 'An alliance that will restore glory to our house, and our name.'

'I was about to be married,' Arthur said through gritted teeth. 'To the *princess*.'

'You should be pleased then, that I've found a better way forwards,' his father said dismissively. 'The king obviously thinks little of me, and *you* certainly weren't going to argue my case or show me preference despite the fact that we are blood, something you made very clear in that delightful hate mail of yours – and I see no reason why I should wait around for the scraps of whatever the king was willing to spare. No, no – we're being offered *real* power, Arthur. As befits us. When Lord Willard takes the throne—'

'Oh fuck,' said Arthur, his eyes widening. 'Jesus. You haven't.'

'Think he has,' Sidney wheezed; he'd been punched quite hard in the solar plexus after they tied his hands, and Arthur was glad to hear him perking up.

'This isn't funny,' hissed Lord Delacey, rounding on him.

'Actually – I agree,' Arthur said disjointedly, as a guard pulled painfully at his arm to keep him moving. 'It's *far* from funny. So, just to get me up to speed, we've joined . . . This is an *ousting*? You've signed me up to a *coup*?'

'If everybody cooperates,' his father said, wringing his hands as he spoke, 'it will be a – a relatively peaceful transfer of power.'

'Right, because that's *definitely* going to happen,' said Arthur. His mind was racing; was the king still alive? Was

Gwen? *Gabriel?* The further they got from the tournament, walking through the eerily deserted campgrounds, the less he could guess at what was happening behind them. 'Do you know how embarrassing it is to stage a failed coup? You have to go all-out, and then, when you lose, everybody knows you completely and utterly shat the bed.'

'Shut *up*,' his father shouted, and Arthur flinched away from him, unable to go particularly far. 'You're in this now whether you like it or not, Arthur. The king should be dead by now.' *Dead?* Arthur's supposedly healed ribs ached. 'We are to rally the second wave and lead them in to claim the castle. Do as I say – and as Lord Willard commands – and you shall be rewarded. There might even be a place for you on the king's council one day, if you play your cards right. If only you had listened to me before, instead of throwing yet another tantrum – I thought I had sent you a very clear message about where *that* path would lead, although I admit, things may have got . . . out of hand . . .'

Arthur attempted to parse this. Somebody *had* recently told him they had a message for him, and as he tried to recall who, he felt phantom pain rack his body again – because, he realised, the next moment he'd been lying on the ground as they kicked his ribs until they cracked.

Arthur's mouth fell open. 'Jesus Christ – that was *you*? Next time you ask somebody to deliver me a message, you might want to tell them I'm supposed to be *alive to hear it*. You – you utter *bastard*, you *prick*—'

'It was never supposed to go that far,' his father snapped, as if Arthur were overreacting. He rather thought he was *under*-reacting. 'You needed a reminder of where your loyalties should lie, and you had made it obvious you wouldn't listen to reason. I regret that they were so ... enthusiastic, but the point still stands—'

'I'm going to kill you,' Arthur spat at him, straining uselessly against his captors. 'Although, hey, maybe I won't have to! Do you really think that if you win today, the people of England aren't going to mind that you've baselessly attacked the capital and bumped off their king?'

'Baselessly?' Lord Delacey said, with a humourless chuckle. 'Arthur, you've always been an idiot about these things. Willard hasn't been laying low; he's been laying *groundwork*. His claim to the throne has always been as good as the king's, and he's been slowly gathering support back to him all these years.'

'All those uprisings? In the north?' Arthur said, stumbling again and finding himself yanked up by the scruff of his neck.

'Ha! No. They were nothing. A distraction. Divert the king's attention and troops northwards, leaving Camelot undefended – that halfwit Stafford nearly lost the last of his hair ensuring that one went off properly.'

'Lord Stafford?' Arthur said, trying to recall the last time he'd seen him – their conversation in the Great Hall, Arthur drunk and melancholy and telling him ...

'Yes,' Lord Delacey said with grim satisfaction as they neared the treeline. 'Yes, you accidentally proved yourself more useful than you've ever managed to do on purpose. I did have to embellish a little, so the truth of your reluctance to be in any way useful to the rebellion didn't shame me. It certainly helped things along with certain factions to hear that the prince plans to abandon Camelot, run away to the seaside and take all the crown's gold with him to waste on *books . . .'*

'That's not what he – God, you miserable tosser, you—'

'Be quiet, Arthur, you're wasting your breath. Now that the king is dead, and his heir is next—'

Arthur inhaled sharply. 'And what about the princess?'

'I'm sure your *betrothed* is safe. She has her uses – in fact, I think Willard plans to marry her.'

'Right,' Sidney said thickly from behind Arthur. '*Fuck* this.' There was a gasp and a crunching sound, as if somebody's nose had just collided with something very hard; Arthur rather suspected it was Sidney's forehead. A scuffle followed, during which one of the guards holding Arthur upright abandoned his post to keep Sidney contained; with a sudden fifty per cent increase in freedom, Arthur finally managed to twist around to look back up towards the castle.

There were men in armour running and riding towards them, swords and faces bloodied. Sidney, having put up a good fight, was on the ground again. Seeing no reason why his father might not just order him killed this time, Arthur did the first thing that came into his head, and let his body go completely slack so that the guard only half holding him promptly dropped him. He threw himself on top of Sidney, both of them grunting at the impact.

'Arthur, will you *just*— Well met, my lord!'

Arthur's face was buried somewhere between Sidney's shoulder and his ear, but at the sound of approaching hoofs and his father's simpering reverence, he heaved himself over to look at the new arrivals.

The infamous Lord Willard was sitting astride an enormous grey horse, a dark cape billowing at his shoulders, not a spot of blood or dirt on him; the Knife was with him, absolutely drenched in gore from head to foot. Arthur watched with horror as hundreds more men poured from the copse of trees behind them, armoured and armed and clearly raring for a fight. Lord Delacey had gone to speak to Lord Willard in hushed, self-important tones, leaving his son crumpled on the ground.

'What the hell are we going to do?' Arthur said, muffled by Sidney's chest, feeling hopeless. If the king was really dead – if they'd taken Gabriel and Gwen too – then it was already over.

It was unthinkable.

'*Agnes*,' Sidney moaned. 'I didn't even – I never even slept with her, Art. I fell in *love* with her, like a pillock, so now I'm going to die when I haven't seen so much as a tit since the spring—'

'Good Lord, Sidney, shut *up*,' Arthur grunted, rolling away so that he was looking up at the greying sky, rain falling softly on his face. 'Shit. This is very, very bad.'

'Maybe . . . maybe they're not dead,' Sidney said. 'They're not stupid. And this lot have come fleeing back, so they didn't win on the first push. And – and our lot *have* got a castle.'

'They weren't ready for a battle though,' Arthur said quietly. 'They were ready for a party.'

'Well, that doesn't necessarily mean—'

'Arthur,' Lord Delacey said sharply, nudging Arthur's face with the toe of his boot. 'Get up. You too, boy.' He bent down so that only Arthur and Sidney could hear him, an extremely alarming smile fixed on his face as he hissed, '*Get on a horse, and don't make a fool of yourself.*' He straightened up again. 'The king still lives, but no matter.'

Arthur exchanged a desperate glance with Sidney. If the king still lived, it stood to reason that everybody else did too.

'We will be on the front line,' continued Arthur's father. 'Leading Lord – *King* – Willard to glory. It's an immense honour.' He strode away to meet the man who was bringing round his horse.

'They're alive,' said Sidney. Arthur gave him a weak thumbs-up. 'Although ... front lines.' Arthur flipped his hand to give the appropriate thumbs-down.

'Willard's just hoping we Delaceys die first,' he said bitterly, reaching over to untie Sidney, who, once freed, put an arm under Arthur's shoulder and heaved him up. 'So he doesn't have to invite my father to dinner parties.'

Lord Delacey glanced sharply over at them, but nobody was trying to stop them from leaving any more. It seemed pointless; who up at the castle wouldn't assume them both turncoats now, after everything Arthur's father had done? They'd likely be killed on sight.

Someone brought armour, and it was parcelled out to them in a rush. Arthur let Sidney dress him; he tried to help with the fastenings but found his hands too shaky and fatigued to do much of anything. He was cycling through their options in his head. First, and most obviously, they *could* run. They could make a break for it as soon as they were ahorse, flee and wait somewhere safe until they knew who had won the day. Either way, he'd likely be on the run for the rest of his life, labelled a traitor by whichever side claimed victory.

Second, they could stay and look out for their own necks. If Arthur *did* live, which was hilariously unlikely, he supposed he'd just have to accept whatever measly life his father and Willard offered him from that point onwards.

But that was a life in which Gabriel was dead; the king too, and perhaps Gwen with them – so neither of the first two options would do at all.

'They think I'm a traitor,' Arthur said suddenly, as Sidney led a gleaming white horse towards him and pushed the reins into his hand. 'Because of what I told Stafford. That must be why they wouldn't see me. They think I'm part of all this.'

'Had been thinking that myself,' Sidney said grimly, before going to fetch a horse of his own.

'Shit,' Arthur said to the horse; it stared balefully at him, as if willing him not to do anything that might bring about both of their demises.

'So – are we running?' Sidney said, eyeing up the messy line that was forming, newly arrived horses being brought forward into the mayhem with rolling eyes and nervous, skittering hoofs.

'Can't,' Arthur said, grimacing at him. 'You should, Sid. But I can't.'

'Sod off,' Sidney said mildly, patting his own horse on its tawny forelock. 'Fat bloody chance of that.'

'Hmmm. I suppose now would be an excellent time for me to have my very first idea.'

'Yeah, keep working away at that,' Sidney said. He cupped his hands to boost Arthur up into the saddle; Arthur almost fell back down, but with a few heaves managed to get himself up on to the horse, with no guarantee he would stay there.

Arthur was thinking, thinking, thinking. Eventually, it all seemed laughably clear.

'Do you know what the first sign of civilisation was, in people?'

'What?' Sidney said distractedly, handing Arthur a sword. He tried to give him a shield too, but Arthur couldn't bear the weight, so he kept it for himself.

'Ashworth told me when I was little,' Arthur said, shakily sheathing the sword on his third try. 'They think the first sign of civilisation was a healed femur.'

'What the hell are you talking about?' Sidney said, mounting his own horse with a grunt.

'It's a bone in your leg.'

'I know it's a *bone*—'

'Just ask me why, Sid. I'm trying to do something here. Indulge me in my final moments.'

'Fine,' Sidney said. 'Why?'

'Because,' Arthur said, as Lord Willard himself pulled ahead to the front of the line, 'it's a bad break. It doesn't heal by itself. Other people have to care about you – bring you food and protect you while you heal – when really they should just leave you behind to die. They have to make sacrifices that make absolutely no logical sense for their own survival. They have to defy all rationality, in the name of love.'

Two standard-bearers stepped forward on either side of Lord Willard holding thin scarlet banners, each emblazoned with a black tower. Close to the tournament grounds, Arthur could see the king's forces gathering, disciplined lines of men with their heads held high. He could also, he realised, just about see the king – his bannermen made him easy to spot, looking enormous astride his horse even from this distance. There was somebody next to him armoured in light, lustrous gold, leaning forward to calm his agitated horse.

Arthur thought he probably knew who that was, too.

'I feel,' Sidney said apprehensively, 'like this whole femur thing is symbolic. Because you didn't break your femur. And that – that can't be a good sign.'

'Well,' Arthur said quietly. 'If we're going to die here, I reckon we should let history remember us as reprobates for all of the questionable things we *actually* did, don't you? Not as filthy turncoats for my bastard father.'

Sidney's gaze was steady. He nodded just once.

'You don't have to follow me, Sid,' said Arthur, reaching over to put a gauntleted hand over Sidney's. 'Part of me would really rather you didn't.'

'How many times am I going to have to tell you,' Sidney said irritably, 'to *sod off*.'

'That's what I thought,' Arthur said, unable to keep himself from smiling fondly at Sidney, his stomach lurching as he wondered if it might be for the last time. 'In that case, Sidney Fitzgilbert – I have decided to make a series of poor decisions in an attempt to clear my name in the eyes of those I love, most likely culminating in our untimely deaths.'

'Well,' said Sidney, shaking out his shoulders and then settling into the saddle, chin stubbornly raised. 'Good of you to announce it this time. Usually, you just crack on.'

Gwen was standing on a parapet, waiting.

The queen had tried to convince her to stay inside; she had said that no good would come of watching, even if they could see everything quite clearly from the north battlements, and that it would be better to occupy themselves with something else until news came of the crown's victory. She had pointed out that it was, after all, raining.

Gwen had ignored her, and now the queen was standing with her back to the field and periodically asking Gwen what was happening while refusing to look herself.

Lord Willard seemed to have more men, but from what Gwen could see, they were in a state of comparative disarray; despite the fact that *they* had been the ones to organise this ambush, apparently they had been so convinced of its early success they hadn't thought they'd really need the second wave to do anything more than ride in and enjoy their victory.

Her father's men, on the other hand, had immediately fallen in line; they had marched out away from the tournament grounds and then stopped all at once, divided into clear regiments, with a few hundred feet between them and their attackers. She could see her father, clad in his dark armour and cloaked in blue, upright and steady in the saddle; next to him sat Gabriel, and even from so far away and with so much metal between them, she could tell that he was rigid with terror.

He's practised for this, Gwen thought fiercely. *He might not like to do it, but he's not a bad swordsman – he'll have an awful time, and then he'll come home to tell me all about it.*

She wasn't worried about her father. This is what he had been born to do. He was enormous, immoveable, completely unstoppable; he would cut through their line like they were butter and return with a hundred dramatic tales to tell.

'They haven't started, have they,' Gwen's mother said, in a voice that affected calm but had a tell-tale shake in the delivery. It sounded as if she were talking about a game at the tournament, not a real battle, and it made Gwen feel like she was going mad.

'No,' she said, fingers tightening against the brickwork, feeling it crumble slightly beneath her hands and hoping it wasn't an ill omen. She was feverishly hot all over, and her lungs felt shrunken and useless. There was nowhere to go; nothing to do but to watch and feel every second of this dread. The enemy troops were too far away for her to make them out individually, but she felt a sharp thrill of anger every time she imagined Arthur among their number.

No, Gwen thought, *he won't be fighting at all. Because deep down, under all that artifice and charm, he's a coward, through and through.*

'*Why* haven't they started?' said the queen, sounding as if she were being personally inconvenienced by the delay, and Gwen sighed with barely concealed frustration.

'I don't know, Mother. I don't know how it all works. I've never done this before. I don't know if they're expecting some sort of signal. Perhaps they're waiting for trumpets. Perhaps they'll all get bored of waiting and give up, and turn around and go home.'

'Don't be facetious,' her mother snapped, and Gwen closed her eyes and took a deep breath so that she wouldn't start screaming and never, ever stop.

When she was eleven, her father had gone to fight in a skirmish in the south-east. This had been no half-hearted grab for power, no tiny uprising quickly quelled with a firm hand and fresh promises of support and fealty; the boats had come from the south, and they had just kept on coming.

When her father told stories about it later, he had skipped over the most gruesome parts; he had told her only of the bravery of their men on the beaches, of the fact that by the time it was over, most of the boats that had intended to come to shore had simply turned and fled back across the Channel.

Later, a knight who'd had far too much wine at the victory feast had told her the parts she wasn't supposed to hear; they had slaughtered so many men on that beach that the sand had been stained pink for miles. Her father had stood in the shallow, gentle surf, the salt-spray tangling his hair and beard, and killed and killed until the water around him was hot and red with blood.

From that moment onwards, she'd be looking at her

father as he sat at the breakfast table, or read by the fire, or played games of chess with her on the covered balcony, and sometimes he had split in two; it was as if one of her eyes could see her kind, stern, weather-beaten father, and the other could see a man wild-eyed with murder, strong and deadly enough to change the colour of the very sea. She had never been able to reconcile the two images into one man.

Gwen knew why her mother didn't want to watch, but it was the very reason she *had* to; she had to be sure that the second man still existed. Even if her father felt human, fallible, the *king* didn't; the king would keep them all safe, and bring everybody home.

Lord Willard's men seemed restless – Gwen could see a single horseman riding along the back of their lines, presumably bringing a message. They had lost the advantage of the surprise attack, perhaps underestimated how many guards there would be at the tournament, or how many of the spectators would fight back rather than flee; many of them were her father's men, and had sworn fealty to him just the same as any knight or lord of the realm, and they had helped to beat back the intruders with whatever they had to hand.

'It's starting,' the queen said quietly. Gwen flinched. She hadn't noticed her mother coming to stand by her elbow.

'How do you know?' Gwen whispered.

'You can feel it,' her mother said. 'Look.'

A single rider from the front line of Willard's men had broken rank to do something very odd. He had removed his helm, let it drop on to the grass, and inexplicably seemed to be wrestling one of the banners away from the standard-bearers.

'What could possibly be the point of that?' Gwen said. The man had succeeded in his task just as others approached to intercede, and he immediately urged his white horse forward, breaking away from the line as he picked up speed and rode alone towards Camelot. Another horseman had tried to follow, but somebody else seemed to grab the reins to pull him back; they were tussling together as the would-be follower attempted to free himself.

'I don't know,' the queen said. 'Perhaps it's some sort of . . . trick? A distraction?'

Gwen didn't see how it could possibly be a trick, but it was certainly distracting; nobody else was moving, from her father's side or from Lord Willard's. They were all watching the solitary rider as he cantered across the field, the banner streaming through the air above him.

'He has no chance at all,' Gwen's mother said scornfully. Gwen had to agree. He was alone out there, completely unprotected; whatever he was trying to do, it was suicide.

Just as the rider reached the midpoint between the two makeshift armies, he did something even more peculiar. He raised up the banner – his arms seemed to be shaking, the flag listing in the air as he tried to hold it aloft – and then threw it dramatically to the ground in front of him, where it was immediately trampled into the black mud under the hoofs of his horse.

'Oh God,' Gwen said, as the figure drew closer, still riding with singular purpose towards the hostile front lines.

'It's all right,' her mother said, touching her arm. 'Look. The archers will have him down.'

'No,' Gwen said, leaning so far over the parapet that she was in danger of tumbling to her death. 'No, Mother, I think . . . Jesus Christ, I think that's *Arthur.*'

The rider, whose badly shorn dark hair became visible as he put his head down and made straight for Gabriel, never had a chance.

She saw her brother turn to her father, heard him shout something, but the king had already given the signal. Gwen couldn't tell which of the three arrows found their mark, but the horse startled – the reins were pulled from his grip – and Arthur fell down into the dark, unforgiving ground.

35

The horses with the very large hoofs were going to kick Arthur's skull in if he didn't move in the next few seconds. He noted this thought, and tried to get his body to do something about it; his body, having given in long before imminent trampling had been brought into the equation, didn't respond.

His ears were ringing from the impact of his fall; he could feel rather than hear that hundreds of men were running and galloping towards him on either side – that they were going to meet precisely where he was currently lying with his mouth full of mud and a stinging sensation in his arm that couldn't be anything good.

'*Get up*,' somebody yelled. Arthur was mildly irritated – couldn't they see that he was trying? It was only a mental sort of trying, of course, not manifesting itself in anything physical, but it was the thought that counted. 'Shitting *hell*,' the voice continued. Arthur's spirits rose – he knew that swearing.

Sidney grabbed him by the shoulders and hauled him out of the mud; he pushed Arthur towards his horse, but despite Arthur's attempts to be helpful amidst his terror, it must have been like trying to direct a man made out of sacks of potatoes.

'Okay,' Sidney said, clearly panicking. 'You're okay, the arrow just grazed you. If we just—'

Arthur didn't get the chance to hear what sort of plan Sidney had cobbled together in the half-second before two armies threatened to converge upon them, because suddenly the converging was very much happening in present tense. Sidney threw himself at Arthur to push him out of the way as a horse almost knocked him down; unable to do anything other than brace himself, Arthur felt Sidney heft his shield over the two of them as the world erupted.

'We have to move,' Sidney shouted; swords seemed to be clashing right above their heads, punctuated by shouts and screams and horrible wet sounds that could only be the violent disassembling of bones and organs.

'Find – Gabriel,' Arthur managed, but Sidney wasn't listening; he had put his head up over the shield only to find himself locked in combat with a stranger. *Why are they doing this?* Arthur thought hysterically, and then, *I think that man gave me his soup at dinner last month because he didn't like peas.*

Sidney managed to get a good hit in, and the man staggered away blindly, sword held aloft as if it would be able to protect him without his direction. It was raining harder now, the ground slick and unforgiving, the sky a furious, yellowish grey.

'Let's get out of here,' Sidney said. His hair was plastered to his head, his eyes constantly darting around, searching for the next threat. 'Come on – if we can just make it to the edge of the—'

'Sid,' Arthur said hoarsely, as Sidney managed to get a shoulder under his arm and start dragging. 'Bridget.'

'What?' Sidney said, preoccupied; it was only a matter of time before somebody else noticed that they were in need of a good stabbing.

'*Bridget,*' Arthur shouted insistently, and Sidney finally turned to look.

Bridget was locked in combat with Sir Marlin. Both of them were on foot, and the Knife was even bloodier than he had been before, if such a thing were possible. Bridget, incredibly, seemed unharmed.

'She's not wearing any armour,' Sidney said, sounding a little faint. It was true; she was wearing a white tunic, a necklace swinging at her throat, mud splattered halfway up her breeches. Where the Knife was wild-eyed and manic, she was moving only as much as she needed to, her expression calm and focused, and she was wielding . . .

'*Excalibur fucking Nine,*' Arthur choked out, watching as she brought the sword up to repel another enthusiastic attack.

'She's mental,' Sidney said. 'She's lost it, she's going to . . .'

Bridget's foot caught in the mud, and she stumbled; the Knife pressed his advantage and managed to knock her off her feet. She went down hard; they heard the ominous sound of bone on metal even above the madness of the battle, and Arthur saw Excalibur Nine fall from her grip.

'Damn,' Sidney said. 'Shit. Okay. Just – stay here.' He shoved the shield into Arthur's hands, and Arthur willingly collapsed to the floor, trying very hard to look already dead.

His view half obscured, he watched as Sidney threw himself between Bridget's prone form and the Knife's blade; he might not have been a tournament fighter, but Sidney completely unleashed was truly a thing to behold. Sir Marlin attempted some sort of quick, dirty parry, a move that perhaps would have unbalanced someone who was playing fair, but Sidney just dug his heels into the ground and grinned like a taunted dog.

The next time the Knife swung, Sidney ducked, and then went for his leg – as Sir Marlin tried to recover his balance, Sidney's sword found its target. The Knife staggered backwards, clutching at his side, where dark blood was bubbling up from the gap in his armour and streaking its way down the pretentious obsidian finish.

'Is she alive?' Arthur shouted, pushing himself up on to his elbows. Sidney went to check, glancing back up at Arthur with his eyes grim beneath his helm – but then his expression changed and he was barrelling towards Arthur like a bull, his eyes fixed somewhere beyond Arthur's shoulder.

Arthur turned to find that the King of England was standing not ten feet away. He was almost as drenched in blood as the Knife had been, but it didn't seem to belong to him; he was alive with purpose, radiating power as he brought his longsword down on to somebody's shoulder. He should have been surrounded by his own men, but in the chaos of battle, he seemed to have found himself fighting alone.

Arthur was confused for a moment, but then he saw what Sidney had seen: the Knife hadn't staggered off to die politely. The Knife was, in fact, standing right at the king's shoulder, helmless, his sword raised and ready to strike.

'*Your majesty*,' Sidney roared, at the same time as Arthur managed to get out a wordless shout, but it was too late; the Knife's sword slipped up under the king's armour almost casually, as if he hadn't quite made up his mind to do it until the last second.

The king didn't seem to notice, at first. He finished off the man in front of him and then faltered; he looked mildly surprised, more than anything, turning very slightly in an attempt to see who had stabbed him.

Sir Marlin removed his sword just as Sidney hit him, blade-first, in the neck; there was so much blood that he was probably dead before he hit the ground. Arthur's instinct was to faint, his vision warping – but he managed to stay conscious, his eyes fixed on Gwen's father.

The king sank to his knees; some of his men were beginning to shout to each other and fight their way to him. By the time Arthur reached him, crawling on his hands and knees to get there, the king had fallen completely to the ground with a small sigh of resignation.

'It'll be all right,' Arthur said stupidly, pulling Gwen's father into his lap with arms that barely seemed connected to his body. 'Just – hang on a minute. Okay? You're the most *stubborn* man alive, you can hold on for just one more minute, and then – and then someone will come to help.' Lightning flashed across the sky, illuminating the king's face, ashen beneath his helm. His eyes seemed to be losing focus; one of his hands jerked upwards, and Arthur grabbed it. 'Listen to me. Just – listen to me. I'm here. Gwen and

387

Gabriel will never bloody forgive me if you don't make it back, so just – just *hold on.*'

'Gwendoline,' said the king quietly, 'and Gabriel.'

Arthur could have sworn that the first clap of thunder sounded the exact moment he died.

Even if everything else was lost that day, Gwen had been given one tiny bit of solace to keep: Arthur hadn't betrayed them. At least not knowingly. Only a fool would have ridden out alone into the middle of a battlefield to make that point clear, but he always had been exactly that sort of unthinking, wonderful idiot.

Gwen had watched as the second rider – Sidney, she was sure of it – had broken away and gone galloping across the field, seconds before Lord Willard gave the command for his men to attack. The two armies had met almost exactly where Arthur had crumpled to the ground; he was immediately swallowed up, just one of hundreds of dark heads in the chaos.

Agnes appeared on the parapet. Gwen expected tears from her, but instead she just came to stand with her, white-faced and resolute.

'It wasn't Arthur,' Gwen said quietly to her.

'No,' she said simply in response.

'But you tried to tell me that,' Gwen said, 'and I wouldn't listen.'

'Yes.' Agnes should have been very angry at her – could

389

have raged at Gwen for depriving her of her last glimpse of Sidney – but instead she reached over and took Gwen's hand. 'They've sent the rest of the men out to fight, and they've been evacuating people out into the city and beyond. There's hardly anybody left in the castle, except the guard.'

Gwen nodded. It was impossible to look away from the battlefield, but it was truly grotesque to behold; where fights in the tournament had sometimes been graceful, almost beautiful, this was mindless and ugly. She tried not to focus on anybody in particular, but in looking for the people she loved her eyes would sometimes alight on a figure as they staggered gracelessly about in their heavy armour, trying to attack or to defend themselves, only to be hit and sent tumbling to the ground.

Gwen had hoped that at some point she would reach such heights of pure anxiety that she'd go numb, her body unable to take any more, but instead she felt it all. Every breath she took seemed reluctant to bring her any relief, and every shout from below plucked at her frayed nerves. She was beginning to get light-headed; she had been standing, pacing, but now she sat and put her head in her hands.

'God, when will this be over?' she said in a small voice. 'I can't stand it.'

'Soon,' Agnes said, although she wasn't quite convincing. 'Very soon. You heard what I said, they sent more men – they'll easily overpower them, and it'll be done.'

Gwen looked up at her, tears in her eyes, suddenly so grateful for Agnes she could hardly stand it. 'Thank you for staying. I know you didn't have to.'

Agnes gave her a watery smile in response, squeezing her shoulder reassuringly. 'Of course.'

A throat was cleared, and Gwen looked up to see a messenger standing in the doorway. He looked all of twelve years old. He was covered in mud and half-dead on his feet; bowing to them almost sent him toppling over.

Gwen's mother made a strangled, choked-off sort of noise, and Gwen looked at her in alarm; she had gone to stand, but sank back into her chair again, bloodless and stricken.

'What?' Gwen said, looking from her mother to the messenger and then back again. 'What, Mother? You don't know what he's going to say. You *don't*.' Her voice sounded strange to her own ears, as if she were pleading – but with whom, she didn't know.

'You're both needed,' the boy said, in a tremulous voice. 'Downstairs. Please, your highnesses.'

'No,' said the queen. 'I'll stay here.'

'*Mother*,' Gwen said crossly, getting to her feet. 'Where?' she asked the boy.

'In the – in the war room,' said the boy. 'They said – they said to bring both of you.'

'Well, I won't go,' said the queen, glaring at the boy like he'd done something to offend her. 'I won't be ordered around by – by—'

'It was the Captain of the Guard, your highness,' said the boy quickly. 'Sir Hurst. And the Wizard, Master Buchanan.'

'I won't *go*,' Gwen's mother said again, sounding near hysterics; Gwen didn't understand, but she wasn't going to waste another minute trying to make sense of it.

As she and Agnes walked quickly after the boy, she heard her mother start to cry.

The journey to the war room seemed to take an age, their footsteps echoing eerily in the near-empty castle; when they got there, Sir Hurst, Master Buchanan and a handful of their attendants were standing around the table. They looked grim; Sir Hurst was filthy, freshly returned from the fight.

'But – where's everybody else?' Gwen said, thinking they made for a pretty poor attempt at a war council.

'Fighting,' said the Captain of the Guard gruffly. 'Where's the queen?'

'She wouldn't come,' Gwen said. 'I don't understand why, she just started shouting, so if you just let me know what this is about then I can go back and—'

'Your highness, I'm afraid the king is dead,' said the Wizard. He had spoken slowly, kindly, and yet somehow nothing he'd said made sense. He was studying her closely, his eyes apologetic; Gwen just stared at him. 'Your father,' he said, as if to remove any room for doubt. 'He fell, at Sir Marlin's hand. This boy witnessed it.'

She had barely spoken to Master Buchanan before. It seemed absurd that he would be the one to say such a thing to her now.

'That's not . . .' Gwen started, but she had no idea what to say next. Her heart was beating very, very fast. There was a strange sound in the room, coupled with the sensation that she was looking at it from very far away.

The numbness she had longed for finally came as she felt herself stagger sideways, caught by the hands of her father's men. She realised in a detached sort of way that she hated them for making her come here; for making her listen to this. They helped her into a chair. It didn't feel real, even as she gripped the armrests.

'Just because he fell,' Gwen said, wondering if anybody could hear her over all that odd, muffled buzzing, 'doesn't mean he's dead.'

'I'm sorry, your highness,' said Sir Hurst, 'but it's true. And we need to make a decision now. The prince is unaccounted for. Nobody has seen him since the fighting first began. We have to assume ... Usually there would be a clearer order of command, but we were taken by surprise, so we have to make do. The queen has the authority, but if she won't come ...'

Gwen looked down at her hands. They seemed very stupid. Short, ragged nails, with smooth palms; hands that had never done anything of real worth in her entire life. 'What decision?'

'We were winning,' said Master Buchanan. 'But word must have already spread that the king is dead. And without your brother – our men are losing, your highness. The fight has gone out of them, because they think it's over. They're afraid.'

'We could send out the castle guard,' said Sir Hurst. 'Our last fifty or so men. It won't necessarily change the tide, but it might boost their spirits. That's what they need. If we do so, though, we leave the castle – and the city beyond – entirely undefended if they make it through the last of our lines. We don't know what they plan to do if they succeed.'

'Who decides?' Gwen said simply. The two men

exchanged a look, and then the Captain of the Guard turned away, clearly frustrated.

'You,' said Master Buchanan. 'In the absence of anybody else – *you* must decide.'

Gwen looked at him. She looked past him at the family sigil on the wall, so familiar that she never really saw it any more – a lion, a hawk and a cup. And then she looked down at the map in front of them; at the ancient shapes and lines of England, at all the paths and roads that eventually made their way to Camelot. She wanted to go back to her chambers and lock the door, climb into bed and wake up in a world in which her father was alive; Gabriel exhausted but waving to her on their way to breakfast; Bridget waiting for her in the stables; and Arthur knocking on her door to trade jibes and stories at the end of the day.

It was all gone, that life – and yet there was still more to be lost, if she faltered now.

'Send out the guard,' she said, standing up.

'You're sure?' said Master Buchanan; Gwen nodded once.

'You must fetch the queen and leave at once,' Sir Hurst said. 'In case the castle falls.'

Gwen shook her head. 'She won't go,' she said. 'And nor shall I.'

'Your highness, with all due respect—'

'Send out the guard,' Gwen said heavily, trying to quell her shaking as she squared her shoulders and faced him head-on. 'But first – I need you to do something for me.'

37

The atmosphere on the battlefield had begun to change the moment the king had fallen to his knees; Arthur heard consternation all around him, battle cries turning into shouts of genuine fear. He hadn't been particularly fond of the king – he hadn't really *known* him – but it felt as if England had died in his arms somehow, the country as he knew it extinguished.

'Let go,' Sidney was saying, and Arthur didn't quite understand what he meant – let go emotionally? Did Sidney want him to cry? – but then he realised that he was still holding on to the king's hand as three of his knights tried to claim his body.

'*Gabriel*,' Arthur said suddenly, as he watched the men lift the king's prone form and then put their heads down to barrel through the fray. Sidney wasn't paying attention; somebody had just tried to stab him, and he was retaliating in kind. A spray of mud and blood hit Arthur full in the face as the man toppled heavily down beside him; Arthur retched, heaving up absolutely nothing, and Sidney grabbed him and hauled him to his feet. 'Gabriel,' Arthur tried again. 'Where's Gabriel? He's – he's *king*.'

'No idea,' grunted Sidney as they began to move. 'We really have to go. It's a bloody miracle we've lasted this long with you so useless.'

Some of the king's men seemed to be attempting to flee back up towards the castle; Arthur watched as one scrambled to his feet, only to be sent back down into the mud with a hand-axe to the back of the head. It was like looking at a particularly violent painting, he thought, or watching a play; his mind couldn't comprehend that any of it was real.

'Not good,' Sidney said, looking around at the open panic on the faces of the crown's men. '*Shit*. This is going to go south pretty soon, Art. Time to run.'

'No,' Arthur said, dazed, feeling as if he were dreaming. '*Look*.'

A fresh wave of men was riding across the drawbridge and down the hill from the castle, unbloodied, unscathed, sure and resolute as they cantered towards the chaos. The rain eased; the clouds seemed to part. Leading them in gleaming gold armour, his helm flashing in the sun, was the scarlet-haired King of England.

A cheer went up from those fighting for Camelot, and it was as if they had suddenly been imbued with new strength; where they had been staggering, they were suddenly upright. Fleeing men stopped in their tracks and turned back towards the battle. Arthur saw a man who had been knocked to the ground, and appeared for all intents and purposes *very* dead, use his foot to hook his attacker's ankle and then drive his sword up through the man's neck when he fell.

'It's all right,' Arthur said, his eyes wide. 'It's going to be *all right*. And Gabriel is . . . Wait.' He kept staring as the castle guard – for he could see that's who they were now – reached the battle and began fighting in earnest.

'Yeah,' Sidney said grimly. 'That's what I was just thinking.' The purported King of England was under extremely heavy guard and wasn't particularly good at holding his sword – not that anybody seemed to notice, as they started to beat Lord Willard's men back.

'What the *hell* is she doing?' Arthur breathed. He was trying not to think about the implications of this act – trying not to assume the worst. It was becoming more difficult by the second.

'Look, she's turning around,' Sidney said, 'I think—'

Something enormous slammed into the back of both of them; it sent them sprawling into the mud. Arthur felt blinding pain jolt up his bad wrist as it tried valiantly to break his fall. *Don't be broken, you piece-of-shit arm*, he thought furiously, flexing his fingers and finding that they still seemed to work. The horse that had hit them seemed to have coped surprisingly well with the ordeal; it scrambled to its feet and took off across the battlefield, heading for the safety of the trees.

Lying in the mud once again, Arthur wondered why bards and warriors always seemed to leave this part out of their war stories; fighting was just blood, and mud, and falling down and down again until somebody put a sword in your back to keep you down forever. He felt something in his mouth, and spat it out in horror – but it was just the pendant on his necklace.

'Sid,' Arthur said indistinctly. 'I should be dead by now.'

'Yes,' Sidney groaned, rolling towards him.

'Right. Thought so. And didn't you say this necklace was—'

'It's not the bloody necklace,' Sidney said through gritted teeth. 'I'm not doing all this for you to give the credit to a piece of sodding jewellery. It's *me*. I'm protecting you. Get up.'

Arthur wasn't listening to him; he was squinting at a dark shape that had appeared suddenly next to his head. 'Does this ... does this bird look agitated to you?'

'Birds can't look agitated.'

The crow in question was standing right next to Arthur, doing a strange little dance – it kept turning its head from side to side, skipping away a few steps and then returning.

'Oh,' said Sidney. 'That bird looks *extremely* agitated.'

As soon as he'd said it, the crow took flight, swooping low over the piles of discarded swords and broken bodies; watching it go, Arthur saw something glinting in amongst the mud beneath its path.

'Oh, shit,' he said.

'Oh, *shit*,' Sidney said, with much more feeling; somebody had just attempted to kill Arthur again, which was becoming a bit of a hazard, and he had staggered to his feet to repel them. 'Just *go*, Art.'

Arthur knew, deep down, that Sidney meant for him to get as far away from the fighting as possible. He knew that he was being a hindrance rather than a help; that with him out of the way, Sidney might actually survive – nay, *thrive* – in this battle. Arthur should have been doing everything in his power to make it to the edge of the field, and away.

He decided to wilfully misunderstand Sidney's instructions.

Arthur had always known that he wasn't a good person, even without his father constantly telling him so. Recent acts of theoretical bravery, he reasoned, had been the last resort of a desperate man. It wasn't bravery that was on his mind as he crawled – really crawled, up to his shoulders in mud, more swamp creature than man – towards the thing he was sure he had seen in the middle of the field. He wasn't doing it because he was *brave* – he was doing it for purely selfish reasons.

If Gabriel were to die – and if Gwen were to follow, having inexplicably decided to throw herself into the heat of battle in borrowed armour – then he'd never get to berate them for thinking so little of him. And he really, *really* couldn't have that.

When he reached Gabriel's body, it was almost entirely obscured by someone recently deceased; Arthur used the very last ounce of his strength to push the corpse away, bracing himself for what he was about to see.

One of Gabriel's arms was so mangled beneath his crumpled armour that it barely looked like a limb at all. The other was theoretically still clutching his sword, but his grip had gone slack around the pommel. His skin was waxen, making the copper of his hair look impossibly bright where it was stuck in matted whorls to his damp forehead. His eyes were mostly closed, a thin crescent of white visible beneath his lashes.

'Gabriel,' Arthur croaked; somebody staggered past them, and Arthur instinctively threw himself down on top of the king's broken body, to shield him from view. '*Gabriel.*'

Gabriel didn't say anything. He didn't move. Arthur couldn't tell if he was breathing, or if it was just wishful thinking.

Someone fell next to them; Arthur watched as blood came cascading out of a man's open mouth, soaking his beard, and then turned away, finally feeling hot tears stinging his eyes.

'Fuck, Gabriel,' he choked, looking desperately around for Sidney and seeing nobody he knew. 'I've already done this once today, I'm not bloody doing it again. Seriously. Just – you can be dead later. Sid can't drag both of us out of here, and he's going to be a prick about it, but I know he'll do the right thing, even if it kills him. He's a stubborn arsehole, a complete pillock, but he's – well, I love him. Just don't be dead, and it'll be worth it when he rescues you instead of me, and I promise I'll just lie down here in the – in the mud, and the shit, and the blood – and I'll die quietly, I swear.'

Arthur dragged himself up on to his elbows, staring down at Gabriel's lifeless face. It was such a nice face. It really was a shame he was never going to see it again.

'Gabriel,' Arthur said, giving him a little shake, his own tears creating tracks in the mud on Gabriel's cheeks. 'You're *king*, Gabriel. Your father is dead, and I just – everybody needs you to get up, and be alive, and be king. I know you don't fancy it, but listen – it's too late for that now.'

'Excellent,' said a strangely calm voice from somewhere above Arthur's head. 'I was just about ready to give up hope, but – I see you found him for me.'

Lord Willard was standing there, his sword raised. Arthur didn't even bother acknowledging him. He looked again for Sidney – Sidney was *always* there, even when it seemed impossible – but his heart sank when he saw his best friend's face ten feet away, frowning in concentration, still locked in battle with somebody else. He was much too far away to be of any use now.

'Sorry,' Arthur said faintly, more to Sidney than to anybody else; he stole one more second of staring at him, wishing that they could lock eyes one last time, that Arthur could somehow impart everything he wanted to say with a look. But Sidney didn't turn.

Arthur pressed his forehead to Gabriel's, and closed his eyes, and waited for the killing blow.

It didn't come.

Arthur heard Lord Willard make a strange sound – a ridiculous sound really, halfway between amusement and surprise – and when Arthur turned over to see what had inspired it, he saw something he knew he'd remember for the rest of his life: Lady Bridget Leclair, caked in mud from head to toe, launching herself at Lord Willard, with Excalibur Nine raised high above her head. Arthur didn't even see where she hit him; he was staring at her face, wondering if he were already dead and Bridget had come to drag them all into the next life.

Arthur expected Lord Willard to get back up. He would get back up, and they would start this charade all over again, the pain and the tears and the death and the falling over – it felt like it would never end, that they would just keep on doing it forever, trapped in a purgatory made of churned and cloying mud.

But it really *was* over. Because Lord Willard wasn't getting up. Lord Willard, unless Arthur was very much mistaken, was dead.

Bridget stood, her chest heaving, staring down at him as if she couldn't believe it either. Arthur could hear Sidney shouting something, but it seemed inconsequential; *everything* seemed inconsequential, with the last remains of the crown and the coup lying broken on the ground in front of him.

Sidney did sound quite insistent though, and as he got closer, Arthur realised what he was shouting.

'Bridget – *shit*, Bridget – *on your left!*'

'Oh God,' Gwen said, ripping off Gabriel's helm and bending over the side of her borrowed horse. 'I think I'm going to be sick.'

'Do it,' said Agnes. 'You've earned it.' Guards were reaching up to help Gwen down; they had ridden back as far as the tournament grounds, slipping away unnoticed in the chaos as quickly as they had arrived. She could barely wrap her head around what had just happened; it existed only in quick flashes, horrifying glimpses of weapons and blood and cheers and terrified horses, and she had been exceedingly glad to put it behind her.

The guards rode back towards the battle, leaving Agnes and Gwen standing in the entrance to the arena, flags, banners and flowers abandoned and trampled into the ground all around them from when the spectators had either fled for safety or leaped into the fight. There were bodies too, further afield; Gwen tried her best not to look.

'It worked,' Agnes said, her fingers fumbling as she helped to remove the armour. 'I was watching from here. It *worked.*'

'I know,' Gwen said, pulling off the ill-fitting breastplate. She was wearing a page's clothes underneath, the first thing they'd been able to grab at short notice. 'I can only hope – I can only hope that it holds.'

If not, they would either be murdered or taken prisoner imminently; there was nobody left to protect them, nothing between them and Lord Willard's forces. Master Buchanan had stayed up at the castle sitting with the queen, waiting to find out who was coming to relieve him; their makeshift captain, with a fifty-fifty chance that he was about to go down with his ship.

'Did you see—' Agnes started hopefully, but Gwen cut her off with a shake of her head.

'I didn't see anyone,' she said bitterly. 'I could hardly see out of Gabriel's helm. I wish I *had,* but – no. Nothing.'

'Right,' Agnes said. 'Do you want to go back up?'

'No,' Gwen said. 'I'm staying here. I want to see how this ends.' She held out a hand, and Agnes took it.

A horn sounded, making Gwen jump, and a great, weary cheer followed it. Hope and fear squeezed her chest so tightly that she could barely breathe.

She exchanged a look with Agnes.

'It's – it's over?' Agnes said in a small voice, as if she too couldn't quite believe it.

'Come on,' Gwen said with obviously false bravado, her grip tightening on her friend's hand. 'Let's go and see.'

Gwen tried to walk slowly, as if seeming too eager might scare any good news away, but Agnes was going so fast she was almost dragging Gwen along in her wake. It was hard to tell at first, emerging out on to the top of the slope, who had claimed victory; everybody looked the same, armoured and bloodied and caked in muck.

Someone was shouting orders from a horse, and Gwen's spirits soared when she saw who it was; Sir Hurst, riding slowly across the field, directing others to corral prisoners and help the wounded.

'We won,' Gwen said quietly. 'Agnes – we won.'

A group of very dejected men was sitting on the ground, swords pointing at them from all directions. Gwen noticed that both Lord Stafford and Lord Delacey were among them, looking oddly clean and extremely perturbed; she imagined they had opted for a healthy distance from the action and an early surrender.

'I can't see them,' Agnes said, her grip on Gwen's hand slipping. 'Maybe we should go out ourselves and start checking for – you know, they might be lying somewhere injured, or—'

'Agnes,' Gwen said gently, but Agnes couldn't be stopped.

'I can't just go back up to the castle and wait – I'm sorry, but I really can't, I need to know—'

'No, *Agnes*,' Gwen said, her voice like a shout of laughter, raising her hand and pointing as tears began to stream down her face. '*Look.*'

Four figures were making very slow progress up the hill towards them. They were all absolutely filthy, barely discernible through the mud, but Gwen knew them at once.

Sidney was holding up Arthur, who seemed barely conscious; Arthur was using one of his arms to pretend to help Bridget, who was somehow half carrying Gabriel. They looked ridiculous. They looked completely and utterly miserable.

She had never been so happy to see anybody in all her life.

Sir Hurst had seen them too; immediately there were men sprinting towards Gabriel, shouts of shock and triumph travelling across the field.

None of them could match Agnes and Gwen for speed; they had run for the foursome so quickly that they almost knocked them over.

'Gabe,' Gwen said, sobbing freely as she reached for Gabriel's face, 'Is he . . . ?'

'He's alive,' Bridget said quickly, as two of the king's guard reached them and gently extracted Gabriel from her arms. 'I think he's going to be okay.' Sidney had let go of Arthur so that he could grab Agnes with both hands, and Arthur listed sideways into Bridget, who just about managed to keep him upright.

'Oh, thank God,' Gwen sobbed; torn between throwing her arms around Bridget and Arthur, she decided instead to launch herself at both of them. It was clumsy, and messy, and she immediately had a mouthful of mud and hair, but she felt Bridget press a kiss into the side of her head and heard Arthur make a strange, choked-up sound into her neck, and laughed with sheer relief.

'Arthur,' she said, muffled against him. 'Are you crying? Are you crying because you love me, and you're so pleased to see me?'

'Jesus,' Arthur said thickly. 'I'm crying because I was just in a bloody battle. It was awful, I hated every second of it and I would *not* recommend it to a friend. And, yes, I suppose – I suppose I'm also crying because I love you and I'm so pleased to see you. *Idiot.*'

Gwen released her grip on both of them and wiped her

muddy, tear-streaked face on her sleeve as Arthur stumbled away after Sidney.

It was suddenly just Gwen and Bridget, sweaty and filthy and silent, each warily awaiting the other. There were a lot of things Gwen wanted to say. She didn't know where to start.

'You wielded Excalibur.'

Bridget looked guiltily down at the sword in her hand. 'Not on purpose. Just had to – borrow it.'

'You know, that's the number-one reason people pull swords out of stones,' Gwen said, laughing through her tears. She was still feeling light with relief. She decided to use it to her advantage. 'Bridget . . . I feel like a complete fool. The things I thought mattered, they're just – I'm sorry I was so selfish. I *really* wanted you in my life, more than I've ever wanted anything, and—'

'Please stop talking,' Bridget said, stunning her into silence. 'I don't mean to be rude. But I'd prefer it if we . . . kissed now, talked later.'

Gwen gaped at her for a moment and then glanced around. Everybody who wasn't unconscious was gathering around Gabriel; nobody was paying them the slightest bit of notice. She barely had time to nod before Bridget's arms were around her, lifting Gwen off the ground as she kissed her hard and fast and then set her back down on her feet.

Arthur cleared his throat from somewhere behind them. 'Eyes left, Gwendoline.'

When she turned around, she saw that a knight was walking towards her, trying to get her attention.

He gestured to where Gabriel had been laid out on some sort of makeshift litter. Somebody was tying a tourniquet around his bloodied arm, not looking particularly hopeful about the outcome.

His eyes were open.

'*Gabe*,' Gwen said, rushing over and dropping to her knees in the mud next to him. 'Oh, God. Gabe, I'm so sorry, but Father – Father's dead.' He was barely there, but her words seemed to get through to him; he looked completely lost as she broke into fresh sobs. 'Gabe, it's going to be all right, *you're* going to be all right, but I just thought you should know that – that you're king.'

Gabriel held her gaze, tears spilling over and down his cheeks – and then very suddenly turned his head to the side and vomited.

The Captain of the Guard, who had been standing quite close to Gabriel's head and had stepped neatly out of the vomit's trajectory, cupped both hands around his mouth so that his voice would carry.

'The king is dead,' he shouted. 'Long live the king.'

Gwen hadn't even noticed others approaching them, but suddenly the shout was being taken up all around her; when she turned, she saw that everyone was sinking down on to one knee. Even some of the injured were making a very wobbly attempt at it, leaning on each other as they manoeuvred themselves down into the dirt. Arthur dropped to the ground immediately, seemingly glad of an excuse to be there; Bridget drove Excalibur Nine into the mud in front of her before following him. Sidney had been kissing Agnes quite enthusiastically, both of them in tears, but he gamely relocated them both southwards to pay their respects.

Gabriel let out a very pained sigh, and Gwen reached for his good hand.

'I really wish,' he said in a small, exhausted voice, 'that everybody hadn't just watched me vomit.'

Written in excellent black calligraphy on the finest parchment, carefully folded and still pristine upon delivery:

Bridget,

I'd say it's quiet at Camelot without you, but of course Arthur is here, so I barely know a moment's peace. We're all still clinging to each other like we expect somebody to knock the door down any second. I've moved back into my own room now that Gabriel is out of bed; I'm sure Arthur's thrilled, as I was thwarting his attempts to make midnight visits.

The mood here is still very strange. People have been coming from all over to swear fealty to Gabriel, which would usually feel like overkill, but is actually quite reassuring in the circumstances. He looks embarrassed half to death when they insist on doing all the customary kneeling and the ring-kissing. Plenty of cultists have come, I suppose the ones Willard couldn't turn against Father; they seem horrified by what happened here, and determined to make it very clear that they had no part in it. They think he was hardly a cultist at all, and was simply impersonating one to rally people to his cause. It reassures me, I suppose, that we won't see a repeat.

I hope they didn't mind too much that you were late to arrive at the tournament. It feels as if they should make allowances, considering.

I miss you. I hope you win.

Gwen

Scrawled on what looked like half a 'Wanted' notice, in two different colours of ink:

Gwen,

Start of the tournament was postponed for decency. Lost my first tilt, feel like a bit of an idiot, but Ned says it's the altitude. I told him it's just a hill, but he insists it tampers with the brain. I think his brain is the one that's the problem.

Somebody (Ned) let on about the battle and Willard and Excalibur to all his little squire friends and everyone keeps looking at me like they've expecting me to fly or spit fire. Actually really annoying because nobody will have a normal conversation with me or tell me where the blacksmith is.

I can already feel the weather turning. Never been so happy to see frost on the ground.

Keep holding on to each other. I'll be back soon.

Bridget

40

St Martin's Day dawned surprisingly crisp and sunny that year, and Arthur woke up in a good mood.

He knew Gabriel hadn't, despite Arthur's best efforts to cheer him the night before; in fact, when Arthur had last seen him, Gabriel had looked terrified almost to the point of vomiting. It wasn't a new expression – he'd been wearing it quite a lot over the past three months – and it was, Arthur supposed, an unfortunate and necessary by-product of trying to change the world for the better.

After the battle, Gabriel had been whisked away to the royal quarters with Gwen at his side, and nobody had been around to explain that Arthur should be allowed to visit. He had spent days going slowly mad until, one evening, Gwen had knocked on his door, given him a painful hug and told him that his presence had been requested.

When he walked in, Arthur had been greeted by the sight of Gabriel propped up in bed, bruised and shattered, surrounded by an assortment of potions and draughts and very thoroughly bandaged. Logically, he wasn't surprised to see that Gabriel's left arm had been amputated to the elbow, the wound wrapped and packed with herbs – but it was still a bit of a shock.

'Hello,' Gabriel said, his voice slightly strained. 'Can you please pass me the papers on the table? Be careful. They're very delicate.'

Arthur obliged, placing them gently in Gabriel's lap and then sitting down in the chair next to the bed.

'After you found those letters,' Gabriel said, looking down at the parchment rather than at Arthur, 'I sent them to Tintagel, and asked that the scholars there search for more. It was a lot easier, I think, once they knew what they were looking for. Most were burned long ago, but I discovered yesterday that they've already turned up these. This one –' he pulled one from the pile – 'is from Arthur Pendragon. Telling Sir Lancelot du Lac in no uncertain terms that he's in love with him.'

'Good for him,' said Arthur, not entirely sure where this was going.

'I haven't slept properly for days,' Gabriel said. 'And I might feel differently when I'm not quite so ... delirious. But my father worked his entire life to try to keep this country happy by never taking any particular stance on anything, and they still ... they still killed him for it.' He stopped to take a breath. 'If I'm going to die doing this job, Arthur, then I want to die knowing I did the best I could. I can't do that by trying to emulate my father, because I'm *not* my father. I want to be true to myself, and true to England, and ... well, like you said – shouted – back when you first gave me those letters, it turns out we've been living up to the ideals of Arthur Pendragon all along. I think it's time people knew that. I think ... it's time to do things differently.'

413

Arthur was speechless for a moment before he recovered himself. 'How long do you think you could go without sleep, long term? Because frankly, I've never heard you make so much sense.'

Gabriel put down Arthur Pendragon's letter, wincing, as if pain had rushed back to claim him. 'I'm not telling you this because I . . . expect anything from you, Arthur. I just wanted you to know.'

Arthur reached over to pat him on his unbandaged arm, slightly overcome with pride. 'Get some sleep. I'll come back tomorrow, and we can talk some more.' He went to leave as Gabriel eased himself back against the pillows, and then paused at the door. 'Because . . . I wouldn't mind, you know. If you did harbour expectations. In fact, I'd do my very best to exceed them.'

He had come back the next day, and there had been a little talking. As Gabriel got stronger there had been more of it, and on a late September afternoon when Arthur was reading to Gabriel from one of the Arthurian tomes Mrs Ashworth had sent from home, Gabriel had closed the book for him and they had graduated from talking to kissing.

Still, they took things very slowly. The shock of the coup had left both Gwen and Gabriel brittle, unfocused, and very, very sad.

He didn't blame either of them, of course – in fact, he thought they were doing remarkably well, for two people who had lost their father in the sudden violence of battle. Gabriel, especially, had started to take his new position in his stride.

He assembled a new council – some new faces, some old. He spoke his mind; he listened. Every time he didn't understand something, he asked for it to be repeated in terms that made sense to him – everything was carefully debated and voted on, pride left at the door. Arthur imagined that some of his new staff probably thought him addled from his injuries and his grief, confused by this new way of doing things. They didn't know that this was how Gabriel always would have taken to the office of king.

His quieter, gentler way of governing had certainly been called into question when it came to the matter of the prisoners from the battle; tradition dictated that they should be executed. Gabriel had scattered them across England, putting them in the care of some of his father's most trusted bannermen, indebted and indentured, but for shockingly lenient periods that had caused Sir Hurst to storm out of a meeting in disgust.

Arthur had argued that the former Lord Delacey deserved a longer sentence, and Gabriel had just given him a very stern look. He had inherited that look, Arthur noted, from his father.

Arthur was a very slow walker these days; he had never quite recovered from the attack outside the inn, or from being so ill for so long, and some days just getting out of bed made him feel like he was still crawling through thick, unforgiving mud. Today, luckily, wasn't one of them. The castle was busy, everybody swept up in preparations for the St Martin's Day feast and the address Gabriel was to give to the populace at its close. None of them knew what he planned to say.

When Arthur reached the walled rose garden, he nudged the door open with his foot and almost fell over when Lucifer shot past him; the cat bounded off into the bushes, immediately distracted by a bee.

'Lucifer,' Arthur said sternly. 'That one's spicy.'

'He'll never catch it,' Gabriel said, lifting his hand to shield his eyes from the low November sun. He had his speech on his lap, and it was very well-thumbed despite the fact that he had only finished this latest version yesterday afternoon.

'O ye of little faith,' Arthur said, stooping to kiss Gabriel's curls. He looked, as Arthur had suspected he would, absolutely ill with nerves. 'Hi, Sid – Agnes. I'm here, by the way. Don't get up.'

Sidney was sitting on the bench opposite muttering something in Agnes's ear, while she turned steadily pinker; he gave Arthur the finger without missing a beat.

'I'm still paying your salary,' Arthur said darkly, throwing himself down on to the seat next to Gabriel.

'I saved your life about eight thousand times,' Sidney said, raising an eyebrow. 'You're so indebted to me. You're so indebted to me it's *embarrassing*.'

Arthur threw up his hands, exasperated, and looked to Gabriel for support. Gabriel, predictably, was frowning back down at his speech again.

The door smacked against the wall on its hinges; Sidney and Agnes didn't bother looking up, but Arthur waved to Bridget as she stalked across the courtyard with a dour expression on her face.

'That's a very nice dress,' Arthur said, knowing he was pushing his luck.

'You're pushing your luck,' Bridget said, looking murderous as she sat down. 'I'd have stayed out on the road if anybody had warned me I'd have to wear a dress. Where's Gwen?'

'With our mother,' Gabriel said, still looking down at his speech. 'They've started playing chess together in the mornings. I don't think either of them particularly enjoys it, but you know – they're trying.'

'So let me guess,' Arthur said slowly. 'The dress, while of course an enduring symbol of your endless subjugation, is a necessary evil to make you look feminine and proper today in light of all the extremely improper things you plan to do from this day forth.'

'Don't say words like "subjugation" to me right now,' Bridget said, pressing a hand to her forehead. 'I promised Gwen I'd be on my best behaviour.'

'Luckily,' Arthur said lightly, 'I made no such promises.' Gabriel looked up sharply from his speech.

'Arthur,' he said. 'You're not serious? You know how important today is, I really can't think about anything else on top of—'

'Gabe,' Arthur said, putting a hand on his knee. 'I'm messing with you.'

'Oh,' Gabriel said, looking pained. 'Well. Don't.'

'Fair enough,' said Arthur, as the door opened again. 'Shouldn't be too much of a strain on my self-control – your sister is here to be tortured instead.'

'No more torture,' Gwen said, immediately crossing to Bridget, who pulled her down on to her lap and let Gwen bury her head in her neck. '*God*. I'm so glad you came back early.'

'So . . . it's not going well with your mother then?'

'No,' Gwen said. 'But I suppose it's not her fault. She's had a shock. You would imagine that something like . . . something like *Father* might have put everything in perspective, but apparently it hasn't. She did ask after you today, though, Bridget, so she must be trying to acclimatise.'

'You need to be gentle with her,' Gabriel said, and Gwen snorted.

'I *am* gentle with her. It's all right for you, she still acts like you're the second coming of Arthur Pendragon, even now. You can do no wrong.'

'That's stupid,' Arthur said. 'When we all know that *Bridget* is the second coming of Arthur Pendragon.'

'Stop making that joke,' Bridget said, scowling at him. 'The more you talk about it, the more people look at me sideways. I get enough of that around here without people wondering if I'm about to seize the sword again and challenge the king for the throne.'

'Oh, don't tease me,' Gabriel said drily. 'Not if you're not actually going to do it.'

'You're a good king,' said Arthur. 'You are. Bloody great king. Best one. Well . . .' he amended, seeing Gwen look at him with a rather pinched expression. 'You're up there with the greats.'

'Father would be proud of you, Gabe,' Gwen said quietly. Gabriel closed his eyes, and then threw his speech down on to the bench next to him.

'Not after today, he wouldn't.'

'You don't know that,' said Gwen. 'Neither of us do.'

'Mother,' Gabriel said with trepidation, 'is going to faint.'

'I've already told her to stay sitting down,' Gwen said.

Gabriel just sighed.

'Which quote did you decide on, in the end? From the letters?'

'Um ...' Gabriel shuffled through the pages. '*To be truly brave, first you must be afraid – and to be afraid, you must have something you cannot bear to lose.*'

'That's nice,' said Arthur. 'I still think you should have chosen the part about Lancelot's *strong, deft hands.*'

'It's not too late to cut you out of this speech.'

'You wouldn't,' Arthur said dismissively, putting an arm around Gabriel's waist and then grinning when he didn't remove it. 'You think I'm far too charming.'

'When they come for my kingdom, I'll tell you if it was all worth it.'

'Please stop flirting,' said Gwen. 'You're giving me a headache.'

'You are sitting in Bridget's lap,' Arthur pointed out. 'And I can very clearly see that she's got her hand on your thigh.'

'Right,' Gabriel said suddenly, standing up. 'I can't sit here and listen to this any more. I'm going to the south court-yard to practise, before they start letting people in. Are you coming?'

'Yes,' said Gwen, getting to her feet.

'Sid?' Arthur said.

'Yeah, yeah,' Sidney said, standing and giving Agnes an entirely unnecessary hand up. 'Obviously. We're all coming. We wouldn't miss this.'

'I think I'm going to pass out,' Gabriel said. Arthur gave him a bracing shake, and then glanced back at Gwen's nervous smile, Bridget's face blazing with determination. Gabriel was white as a sheet, his hand shaking where it held the speech, but Arthur wasn't worried.

'No you're not,' he said. 'You're going to be brilliant. You're going to be a brilliant, brave idiot. You're going to shock the entire country, but they'll come around when they realise that aside from your penchant for roguish, dark-haired gentlemen, you're the most righteous, level-headed monarch that's ever worn a crown. And just think: we'll be in Tintagel in a week – that'll give them all some time to get used to it here, where we don't have to watch them doing it.' Gabriel gave him a weak, forced sort of smile. 'That's the spirit. Now, come on. Chin up, shoulders back; let's go and show them a new England.'

Gwen disentangled herself from Bridget for long enough to give Arthur a quick squeeze of a hug as they walked. 'That was actually really nice, you know. Next time, perhaps don't call him an idiot.'

Arthur squeezed her back and then put a palm to her forehead to shove her away. 'Oh, it's always something, isn't it. Don't do this, don't do that . . . Agnes, I don't know how you expect to get through this door *while* kissing Sidney, you have to let go at some point. I think we should make *this* particular union illegal, while we're making speeches. Has anybody got Lucifer? He has to come, he *loves* feasts . . . Don't look at me like that, Gwendoline, he's a highly valued member of the royal family . . .'

From the stone crown atop the statue of Arthur Pendragon, a strangely familiar crow blinked once, shook out her dark wings, and then set off into the bright morning sky.

Acknowledgements

This book came to life in 2020, the year we spent inside. I wrote it sitting in my London flat with the balcony door cracked open to let in some air, typing in bursts between piss-yourself-funny conversations with new friends and evenings spent watching strings of satellites pass overhead like they were shooting stars (they were actually the experiments of villainous tech billionaires, but if you squinted: celestial bodies!). It's kind of a weird book. I had so much fun writing it. I'm endlessly, almost frighteningly grateful to the people who gave it a chance.

Thank you to Chloe Seager, my agent, who kicks arse for a living and looks good doing it; to Sylvan Creekmore, who made grabby hands first, and Vicki Lame, who took us to the finish line at Wednesday Books; and to Hannah Sandford, for giving Gwen and Art their wonderful UK home.

Thank you also to Fliss Stevens, Katie Ager, Jadene Squires, Nick de Somogyi, Anna Swan, Nina Douglas, Beatrice Cross, Mattea Barnes, Alesha Bonser, Laura Bird and Michael Young on this side of the ocean and Vanessa Aguirre, Rivka Holler, Brant Janeway, Soleil Paz,

Michelle McMillian, Meghan Harrington, Eric Meyer, Adriana Coada, Melanie Sanders, Kim Ludlam, Tom Thompson, Dylan Helstien, Britt Saghi, Emma Paige West, Michelle Altman and Amber Cortes on the other.

I am so grateful to Olga Grlic, Natalie Shaw and Thy Bui for my beautiful covers, and to Alice Oseman, Rainbow Rowell, Becky Albertalli, C.S. Pacat, Freya Marske, Ava Reid, Arvin Ahmadi and Lauren Nicolle Taylor for early reads and kind words.

Thank you to Nick and Hannah, who have to live with me, and my parents, who *also* had to live with me at one point but have since escaped. Thank you to Photine, Gwen and Art's first and biggest fan. Thank you to friends and readers Rosianna, El, Maggie, Dervla, Alice and Ava. Thank you to my fandom comrades, who got me through the worst of that year. A bouquet of rats for my writing group. A little kiss on the nose for my cat, and for anybody else who fancies one, especially if I forgot to thank you with words.

About the Author

Lex Croucher grew up in Surrey, reading a lot of books and making friends with strangers on the internet, and now lives in London with an elderly cat. With a background in social media for NGOs, Lex now writes historical-ish romcoms for adults (*Reputation*, *Infamous*) and historical fantasy romcoms for teenagers. *Gwen and Art Are Not in Love* is their YA debut.

@lexcanroar